To Music

London 5/12-09
Dear Lionel Carley –
Best wishes –
and thank you for
a nice meeting –

Ketil Bjørnstad

and Deborah Dawkins

ALSO BY KETIL BJØRNSTAD

The Story of Edvard Munch

To Music

a novel by
KETIL BJØRNSTAD

Translated from the Norwegian by
Deborah Dawkin & Erik Skuggevik

MAIA

Arcadia Books Ltd
15–16 Nassau Street
London W1W 7AB
www.arcadiabooks.co.uk

Published by The Maia Press
an imprint of Arcadia Books 2009

First published as *Til Musikken* by Aschehoug in 2004
Copyright © 2004 H. Aschehoug & Co, Oslo, Norway
English-language translation by Deborah Dawkin & Erik Skuggevik

Lyrics from 'Fra først av', from the album *Garman*, courtesy of Ole Paus
Quotation from Haruki Murakami, *Norwegian Wood*, translated by Jay Rubin

A catalogue record of this book is available from the British Library

ISBN 978-1-904559-35-1

Typeset in Sabon and Zapfino
Printed in Finland by WS Bookwell

Arcadia Books gratefully acknowledges the financial support of
NORLA (Norwegian Literature Abroad) and Arts Council England

Arcadia Books distributors are as follows:

in the UK and elsewhere in Europe: Turnaround Publishers Services
Unit 3, Olympia Trading Estate, Coburg Road, London N22 6TZ

in the US and Canada: Independent Publishers Group
814 N, Franklin Street, Chicago, IL 60610

in Australia: Tower Books
PO Box 213, Brookvale, NSW 2100

in New Zealand: Addenda
PO Box 78224, Grey Lynn, Auckland

In South Africa: Quartet Sales and Marketing
PO Box 1218, Northcliffe, Johannesburg 2115

Arcadia Books is the Sunday Times Small Publisher of the Year

'In the beginning, in a time before the time we measure,
    there was a sound; a note that wove itself into everything.
And ever since, all that is born or dies is music.
That same note rings now as in the beginning.'
                    Ole Paus, 'In the beginning', from *Garman*

'I feel I can reach out and touch them with a fingertip'
                    Haruki Murakami, *Norwegian Wood*

Part 1

The waterfall

THE RIVER RUNS through the bottom of the valley. Coming from the lake up by the sawmill, it curls its way down towards the bridge, over rounded boulders and smooth polished skerries that jut out of the water mid-stream, frozen rigid and immoveable, in a peculiar, cold silence. Mother likes sitting on top of the largest, Tinker's Rock, her hair wet, wearing her blue and white polka-dot swimsuit. She perches there with her legs posed self-consciously in imitation of the Little Mermaid in the Langelinie Quay, Copenhagen, where she and Father took us to celebrate their fifteenth wedding anniversary. We wave from the riverbank. Father shouts that she is the most beautiful woman in the world.

Below the bridges the river broadens into a basin. Next to the furniture factory on the west bank is a dam. I like this redbrick building; the deckchairs of teak and mahogany left in the sun to dry, the armchairs and sofas like those my mother and father have at home, in light birch and chequered upholstery. This factory made the sofa Mother always sleeps on in the afternoon, and on the nights she won't sleep with Father. Directly below the factory windows is the waterfall. It comes suddenly. A hundred metres higher, everything seems tranquil, with calm flowing water. But Father warns us about the currents. Catherine and I are never allowed to swim south of Tinker's Rock. I can vaguely remember resting on the boulders close to the riverbank one summer's day, when the current took me. Catherine saw what had happened and yelled, screaming as only a girl can scream. Father threw himself in and caught me in just a few strokes. I didn't realise the gravity of the situation, but I understood that something was very wrong. He got me into land, bundled me up in a towel, held me in both arms and began shaking. I remember the sound of his wheezing, and of my mother pounding him on the back with bare fists. Then he cried, with his hands before his face. A painful sight.

A lot has happened since then, but the area north of Tinker's Rock continues to be our bathing spot. This morning I know Mother and Father have been quarrelling in their bedroom, and I feel wretched. I'm frightened that one of them might disappear, move out, decide to live elsewhere, or even take their own life. Things are serious between Mother and Father. In the old days I lay awake listening to every word they screeched at each other in the living room, when they thought Catherine and I lay asleep. Occasionally, Catherine would start to cry. I would never cry. That much I'd promised myself. I hardly dared breathe, for fear of losing control. Somebody had taught me how to keep swallowing. That way I could stifle the tears before they began. But later in the night I'd feel sick and have to go to the bathroom. That was when the vomiting began.

Mother and Father will never find peace, and I am exhausted by all the words I've heard through that wall. But then the reconciliation comes. At ten o'clock Mother comes in to wake me, with a cigarette already, and that cheerful, slightly hysterical laugh that I can never quite believe. I know now that we're going to Tinker's Rock for a swim. Old rituals. The grown-ups will take some wine, and I am old enough to taste. I rarely protest at going. There's a joy in these reconciliations, a cautious hope. I am fifteen and I love spending time with them, in contrast to Catherine. I still want to spend my Saturday evenings with them. When Catherine, two years my senior, goes out with her gang, I sit between Mother and Father relishing their not arguing; they generally avoid arguing on Saturday evenings. They find it strange that I never go out with my mates, but that's how things are and I can't explain it. I don't feel at home on the football pitch in summer, and I don't like bandy in winter. I'm scared witless of all the fighting the other boys do. I prefer to sit playing the piano whenever possible.

I was barely out of my cradle when Mother began teaching me music. She sings all the time. Children's songs, violin concertos, whole symphonies. And then she 'travels' by radio, as she says. On the cold, dark winter evenings, when the reception is best, it feels as though she could capture the entire world: in Vienna a violinist plays Tchaikovsky, from Moscow we hear a piano sonata. Throughout the evening she tunes the radio, back and forth. 'Listen Aksel! Ravel! The G major piano concerto! Just wait until the second movement starts!' I'm certain she must know all the music in the world, and can't understand why she isn't a musician herself, as her parents were.

Father stood on the sidelines all through my childhood. He never objected to my being so attached to Mother. He sings like a crow, but appreciates the music with which my mother, and later I, fill the house. Over the last few years I have become like a mascot for them. I go to the Bechstein and play their requests. 'Play Schumann!' says Mother. 'Play Bach!' shouts Father. Then they applaud enthusiastically, as though I were a fully fledged pianist already. Catherine can't stand these ecstatic events, that I mistook for so long as genuine happiness. She gallivants with her friends from Bjørnsletta, arriving home late and making a hell for us all. But when Sunday comes, and we are all exhausted by the night's goings-on, the waiting, the drinking, by Mother's tears and Catherine's wild shrieks as she launches into each of us by turn, nobody can bear to argue more. The Vinding family rises late, and everybody in our street, Melumveien, knows it. Mother's first up, wanting to catch the morning concert on the radio. Today it's Brahms, the fourth symphony, so full of sorrow and atonement, after the evening's quarrels. There's a joy they try to recover, that they lost along the way, in these long years of cohabitation. We are still at breakfast when they inform us of what we already know: we're going to Tinker's Rock for a swim, a picnic and to 'have a nice time together', as Father puts it, in his usual helpless tone. Catherine groans, she stinks of stale beer and can't even be bothered to start her egg. But there is no way she's going to wriggle out of this. She may have reached the age of consent, but she is still a minor, and Sunday is the Vindings' family day, whatever it costs. A hopeless day of reconciliation, that makes me feel older than them, because they don't realise I've seen through them, that I know more than them, that it's no longer any use.

Yet I still want to be compliant, to please them. I give Mother a cautious smile. Brahms still rings out from the little radio in the kitchen. Brahms is our shared secret, along with Schumann and Debussy. But nothing compares to Brahms. Ti taaa ta tiii, ti taaa ta tiii. Mother and I sing for one other and wave our arms, to Catherine's intense irritation, as though we shall never be ready to leave this beautiful, solemn symphony and go out into the heartless and imperfect world. Meanwhile, Father takes a couple of bottles of wine down from the kitchen shelf. He is preparing the picnic; that joyous luncheon, which should be infinite, when people lift their glasses and make toasts, or look lovingly into each other's eyes, as according to Father they did on their Normandy honeymoon. 'I've got some cheese too,' he mutters, as Mother starts to prepare the salad we'll eat in a few hours. Why do I watch my mother so closely today? I have started comparing her to other women, to all the film stars I admire when I peek at Catherine's teenage magazines. Kim Novak. Audrey Hepburn. Natalie Wood. Mother stands by the kitchen bench and is far too beautiful for this place, for this life. She looks like Maria Callas in her blue dress. And like the Greek diva she could pass off any role. She chops onions, prepares a dressing of oil and vinegar and, to Catherine's consternation, boils more eggs. 'Nobody else round here does this sort of thing,' says my sister indignantly. 'Only you two.' She is referring to the luncheon, to our mother's extravagance, to the nonchalance that Father has cultivated in her over the years, since he, if possible, is even kinder than her. Two kind, desperate people who believed they would find love in marriage, but who find themselves unable even to share the same house. And what is more, two nervous children who lack any capacity for enjoyment, even when they're happy. This is the Vinding family. My childhood has been one eternal anxiety, an unease lodged in my nerves, a pain at the thought of our brief, intense lives; and our frailty in the midst of them, because we have no aptitude for life, because something awful might happen at any turn.

It is the end of August. The evenings are dark and star-filled. The days bathed in sunlight. An Indian summer. The wild roses give off their fragrance, lawnmowers clatter in the small well-tended gardens of which there are so many on this side of town. People have returned from their summer holidays long ago. It is far too hot. Mother and Father rarely have enough money to take time off, and for years Catherine and I have made do with trips to the swimming pool or by tram to the Student Union Café to buy ice-cream at the corner of Universitetsgata. Mother works full-time too, which is unusual round here. We don't really have the money to live as well as we do. It's Father's notion that we should live beyond our means, eat beyond our means and dress beyond our means. It makes Mother furious, because money, the solid cash that she would like to have in her hands and make choices with, is never there. Mother has taken shifts at the cinema, because the Opera closes over the summer, and Father sits in his little office in Dronningens Street, mulling over all the wretched apartment blocks he has purchased over the years, for which he does not have the funds either to improve or to maintain.

The sun is high, the sky blue, and the grass near the ski-jump lies flattened after the torrential rainfall of the previous week. I immediately notice the wind. It's too strong, too hot. We walk where the villas line the lake and dam, Mother and Father go hand-in-hand as they do every Sunday, while Catherine walks ten metres ahead in furious zigzag steps, grinding her teeth and hissing: 'I'm too old for this!'

But I am not too old. This suits me fine. I stay close to Mother, so she can have a man on either side; I'm as tall as Father now. That fills me with pleasure.

'Goodness, how you've grown,' says Mother, as if reading my thoughts. I don't answer. We walk on, staring ahead, at Catherine. She has my mother's characteristic curves suddenly.

'That's one stunning lady ahead of us!' I say, blushing instantly, since it's a bit on the edge.

Mother just laughs. 'And what would you know about that sort of thing, you rascal?'

I shrug, blushing even more. It's impossible to grow up with Mother keeping tabs on me all the time.

'I know a bit,' I say lamely.

'I don't believe it,' Mother says, giving my hand a quick, firm squeeze. I give hers a squeeze too. Moments pass. Then we both burst into laughter.

A picnic. A subdued luncheon, as though all of us were sleepy. We are the only family who comes down to this place, among the alders, the birch tree and tall spruces. Everybody else will have gone off to Bogstad or Østern Lake. But this is the Vindings' spot, where we can be undisturbed, where we can drink wine in the middle of the day, without anybody bothering. The wind speaks for us; the rush of the river too. I've never seen the river so rough. But when I point this out to Mother, she nods, but doesn't turn to look at it, as anyone else might. Instead she fixes me with those dark eyes she always gets when she's drinking wine. It's a troubling glance. As though she were thinking about something, seeing something in me I can't see myself. A tram crosses the lower bridge, on its way into the city. Mother has always yearned for the city. As have I. A little apartment even in the dreariest area around Østbanen would do. Within walking distance of most things; of the Opera, the cinema and Aula, of everything that means anything. Father and Catherine, who never talk to one another except to argue, are the ones who like it here. Catherine lies stretched out on a large, flat rock, reading John Steinbeck's *Grapes of Wrath*. She's always reading these famous, great tomes, but then refuses to talk about them afterwards. 'Was it good?' I ask. 'What do you mean, good?' she answers scornfully. 'Is Brahms good? Is your piano good?' I no longer dare to ask.

Father sits some way off from Mother, reading yesterday's paper. The property section. Or at least pretending to read. He'd rather talk to Mother, but Mother is busy sitting there staring at me, as I sit staring at the river that's so rough.

'So, will you enter the competition?' says Mother at last.

'Of course,' I answer, since I know that's what she wants to hear.

'And what will you play?'

I hesitate. Not answering. She fixes me with her huge eyes. I look up at the sky, where the small clouds are scuttling towards Nordmarka. An enormous hawk has caught sight of us. It hovers high in the air above, with complete overview of our least movement. Later I will think this was our only witness, the only being that saw all four of us from the outside. A shiver goes through me, but I hide it from Mother.

'I think you should play what you want,' she says at last.

I am wary now. Mother always has an opinion.

'What I want?'

'Yes. What do you want, my dear?'

I don't know. I don't really know what I want. Or what I want to play.

'I'll have to think about it,' I say. 'Debussy perhaps, or maybe Prokofiev.'

She nods, almost to herself. 'Debussy is lovely,' she says.

I notice that the second bottle is practically empty too. Mother has had the most.

Father is listening to our conversation. He looks up. I remember it clearly now, staring at Father. He seems so tired, as though there were nothing left of him, no hope, no joy, and I suddenly feel sorry for him, more sorry than I have felt for my mother in all these years, and it bewilders me.

'I so want both of you to be happy,' I say, looking at the cheese, the eggs, the ham and the salad that lie almost untouched in the sun.

'Don't think about us,' says Mother, almost sharply. 'You're the one that matters now.'

'Catherine and me,' I correct.

'Of course.' Mother glances in the direction of her daughter who lies too far off to hear our exchange.

'You and Catherine,' Mother says, and reaches a hand out towards the bottle. 'We'll always be with you, whether you like it or not.' She sighs. She puts the bottle to her lips. Drains it to the bottom.

Then Mother and Father talk. For the last time. In all the years that followed I have tried to remember what their conversation was about. But I can't, and neither can Father, despite my asking him so many times. The trams have passed, both in to the city and out towards Lijordet. I feel the hawk still spying on us, but no longer see it in the sky. Mother and Father have begun talking. It can't be about anything important, since I don't prick up my ears. Maybe they're discussing the decoration of the bathroom that needs doing but that we can't afford. Or perhaps they're discussing how best to organise the coming week, with Mother's evening shifts and all. But the words aren't kindly. And soon, most dangerous of all, they're talking figures. Mother has got up. From this point I remember everything.

'I can't take any more of this. I'm going for a swim,' she says.

Father glares at her in terror. 'Are you crazy? Åse. You mustn't go in that strong current! The water's freezing, even if the air's warm!'

I feel the wind again. Nothing is as it should be. Mother removes her dress, letting it fall on 'stony ground', as she calls it, not that Father laughs at her joke. We can see now that she's wearing her blue and white polka-dot swimsuit as underwear. So she's been planning to take a swim. But she has forgotten her bathing shoes. She trips and falls to her knees, coming immediately back to her feet. I remember her naked legs. The white skin. The blue varicose veins. I see she's bleeding. But she still wants to go into the water.

Father comes after her, but she wants to escape him now. A flash of irritation. One word can be enough.

'No, Åse! The current's too strong!'

'Leave me alone! Do you hear me, Hjalmar! I need to think!'

Mother's voice has a shrill tone I've never heard before. She swims towards Tinker's Rock with rapid breaststrokes, Father following her in front crawl, revealing muscles he's never had before. Even Catherine peers up from her Steinbeck. But that's the way things have always been: Father swimming after Mother, running after Mother, as she flees, slamming doors, sobbing, dashing out on to the street, a cigarette in her mouth and no winter clothes, only to let herself be caught in the end. But something's awry. Catherine's noticed it too, and she's listening to the words Father shouts as Mother finally grabs Tinker's Rock, like a stone nose sticking out in the middle of the river. But the waves are high, and the water crashes over her face. She gasps for air as Father yells something about an apartment block; he shan't buy it after all, even if he's still obsessed with these apartment blocks.

'I'll drop it, Åse!' he yells. 'Forgive me! I'll never mention it again!'

But Mother is raging, clinging hard to Tinker's Rock with both hands, and that's when I see the danger. The current is too strong, she can't hold on much longer.

'I'll drop it, Åse!'

'It's too late!' she yells, and at that moment she lets go, with a gasp, like the gasps we're used to when she wants to play-act, to dramatise, as only she knows how. But Father's strong arm is too far away. Mother slips away with the current. We see her heading down towards the dam, at lightning speed. Father manages to get to his feet in the water and starts running after her, over the boulders. I have got up and begin to run along the riverbank; there are some branches at the turn before the first of the three bridges, and as long as she isn't forced too far out into the river, Mother will be able to grab them. Father has the same idea. He has spotted a tree, a branch, she'll be able to hold on to. 'Åse, Åse!' he yells, 'The tree, Åse!' She looks to see what he's pointing at. It's nearly too late, but she's understood, she manoeuvres towards the branch that overhangs the riverbank. I run in the same direction and Father comes crashing over the boulders. She grabs the branch and clings to it. Father has lived through all this once before, with me. Now he's reliving it. As always: Father is never done with things. But it's Mother this time. She grasps the branch with both hands, her face white, her eyes like two saucers, her mouth gaping, but no sound issuing. 'I've got you, Åse! Thank God! I've got you, my love!' Father has caught hold of her. But then the branch snaps, and the water is suddenly deeper here, and the undercurrent stronger. He is forced to his knees in the water, and is about to follow her down towards the second bridge. I step forwards, grab him by the arm, and hold him back. The current is stronger than any of us could imagine. In that instant, he lets her go. She looks at me, disbelief in her face, realising before we have realised it ourselves that we're not going to save her. Father wants to plunge back in after her, but I grab him tightly with the youthful muscles of a fifteen-year-old. I don't know what makes me do it, but he mustn't swim after Mother, or they'll both vanish. Catherine comes from behind, tugs at my hair: 'Let him go! Let him go!' But I don't let go. I hold on to my father, almost strangling him, with my arm around his neck, pulling him back on to land, where we tumble over Catherine who screams: 'Run! Run!' But what are we going to run after? It's a tremendous current, and down at the dam all the water is forced through a narrow gap. But I run with Father and Catherine panting after, and it's then that I realise what I've done. My knees start to quake. We come below the third bridge. Mother's head is a dot in the middle of the water, where the river widens. Everything looks calmer here. Yet the reverse is true. The waterfall takes every living thing down with it; tadpoles, little fishes, Mother. Mother's head is just like the head of a pin in the water, and she is barely fifty metres from the waterfall. I know she can see us. She knows I held Father back. She knows she's going to die. Father collapses among the rushes, howling, as Catherine runs up on to the road shouting, 'Help! Help!'

'What shall I do?' I groan to myself. I have only moments left before she slips into the waterfall. A Brahms symphony howls in my head, and with it the sound of the river, of the wind, of the rumbling of the tram as it passes overhead, obliterating all else. Then I lift my hand. I wave to my mother. And to this day I'm not certain if it really happened. But I think I remember it. I see it as though it were yesterday: she lifts her left hand. She waves back. Yes. That is the final image I have of my mother alive, before she slips into the waterfall, before her head is dashed against the sharp rocks, before the mortuary, and all the ghastliness. She waves to me. Dying. She waves to me, to Aksel Vinding, because I am her son, and because it was only ever me and her. And even now as I write, after all these years, it is as though I stand in the same place, under the bridge, among the rushes, and see Mother wave, wave to me, for all eternity.

The alder thicket

I AM DRAWN BACK to the river. Day after day I walk between the trees down here in the depths, at the bottom of the waterfall, where there is nothing but bracken and slippery rocks, and where for two days and nights Mother lay in a deep pool before they found her, because they assumed the current would have swept her much further. She'd been trapped instead, directly below the waterfall, caught in the eddies of a pothole. The whirl of the currents had flung her body from side to side. They said a bird might have pecked at her. Then I remembered the hawk that had watched us that calamitous Sunday.

I don't feel unhappy when I sit here in the dark, just empty. I don't make any noise. The pool lies close to the other bank, where the heavy spruce trees stand. I have found myself a place, under the alder thicket on our side of the river. From here I can gaze downstream, looking for a way to cross to the other side. There are rocks that could serve as stepping stones, but the river is too rough. For now it suits me to sit amongst the black alder, listening to the rain pouring, without getting wet.

This dismal rain has been going on for days; autumn is coming. Catherine and I are scarcely on speaking terms any more. We comfort Father, each in our different ways, but never each other. Catherine takes Father on long walks at the weekends, but I'm the one who has most to do with him during the week. And since Catherine gets home from school after me, and Father is always late, I generally make dinner for us all, following Mother's simple recipes. But whenever Catherine decides to stay at home and watch television with Father, I head for the front door and pace the streets for hours, with not a thought in my head.

It is during this autumn that I first notice Anja Skoog. She lives in Elvefaret. I usually meet her when I've just escaped the washing-up, and she's on her way to the tram. I know she goes to public school, but we go the same way for part of the journey. We've been on nodding terms for years, but it's only lately that my eyes have been drawn to her as she passes by with hurried steps. I know she's in the year below. When November comes, she wears a green, worn-out duffel-coat that hangs loosely about her. She says hello politely every time we meet under the streetlights; I suspect she knows about what happened to Mother. Her glance seems somehow sad, and her smile so reserved. In this part of town, people don't always know much about each other. Families stay inside their own four walls. Perhaps that's what impresses me; that she seems to know, and that she takes the trouble to say hello. She always seems busy – I presume she must be going to handball practice or ballet, or whatever it is that slender, pretty girls like her do. Her hair is shoulder length and sleek. She never bothers to have an umbrella. When it rains, her hair is straggly long before she reaches the station. She's even prettier then.

I begin to carry her in my thoughts when I go down to the river to sit in the alder thicket. I take her with me on my escapes, when I fanta-size about the unattainable, about open horizons that might exist some place in the future, even for me. I have started to dream about non-exis-tent things, impossible things, and that Mother is still alive. She never speaks, she simply stands there, with her back to me. I'm terrified that she might turn around; I'm frightened to see her face, that look of disdain. 'My life,' she would often tell me, 'is futile, but your life mustn't be. Promise me that, Aksel.' But what can I promise her? She always said she would do everything she could to help me.

I spend far too much time in the alder thicket, brooding. I go down to the river every day and sit there under the branches, and none of my thoughts are of any use, since I only ever dream of things I feel sure I shall never live to see. I fail to participate in the big piano competition, because I know I'm not good enough. But I vow to myself that I will come back stronger next year, and with winter approaching, the time for waiting is over. Snow falls. I go skiing across the Grini Fields. The days are cold and crisp, a blue light above a pink horizon. I begin dreaming of more tangible things. I start practising the piano again. I have turned sixteen. I try thinking as little as possible about Anja Skoog.

In the bleak mid-winter

CHRISTMAS IS COMING. Father still hasn't managed to sort out Mother's things, and Catherine doesn't want to. It was always difficult between Mother and her. Mother felt she was too young when she had Catherine. She was only twenty-two. Åse Bang was a young woman from Moss who would have liked to follow in her parents' footsteps; becoming a musician, playing on cruise ships or for silent movies. But the silent movies were already on their way out, and nobody had enough money for Mother to learn to play an instrument. She had learned her love of music from going to the late-night picture showings when her mother played. She would watch as her mother's fingers flitted across the black and white keys. She was looking at a bygone era.

I clear out my mother's cupboards. My thoughts turn to the old, to the dead. They seem suddenly significant to me. Åse Bang from Moss. Her mother, old Asta, who earned a daily crust for years by playing the piano. Her husband, Rasmus Bang, my grandfather, who had been a violinist on the American steamships that sailed between Oslo and New York, until a homosexual millionaire from Egypt offered him a luxurious life-style as musical director on his cruise ship sailing between Alexandria, Beirut, Athens, Dubrovnic and Venice. How Mother loved to tell those old stories! Grandfather, who knew how to live it up: the violinist in his white jacket, with slick, greased hair, who probably played Fritz Kreisler and sentimental romances in the ship's lounge each night, before ending up in the bar or some wealthy American widow's cabin. He started to drink Cuban rum. 'It loosens the emotions, but wrecks the technique,' Mother would say. Anyway, my grandfather put on thirty kilos, and watched his musicianship slip into steady decline. Sitting at the bar, night after night, grandfather set to thinking what had lead to this appalling state of affairs. Surely somebody must be to blame for the wretchedness of his life. 'Alcohol is a creative force,' my mother would say. 'It paints enemies in the mind.' Which would lead her to the next grim chapter of her tale. After ten years of absence, my grandfather went back to Moss, to beat my grandmother senseless. Why hadn't she tracked him down when he'd taken flight because his daughter, my mother Åse, was going to be born? Hadn't she realised he was being stupid, that in truth he was the perfect father? If he'd stayed in Moss, and not run away to sea, he might have been a respectable musician today, had a permanent contract with the Philharmonic or played at all the funerals across Østfold County; of that my mother was still certain, years later. This time it was my grandmother's turn to take flight. Mother usually took a dramatic pause here. Then she would launch into the final, bitterest chapter of her tale: Grandmother took the children with her to stay with a friend in Råde, but just two weeks later, grandfather was found drowned, near Missingene, close to a fourteen foot dinghy. It was a suspected suicide. Even my mother thought so, although the police continued their investigations for some time, thinking that grandfather's demise might be linked to the smuggling of spirits and internal gang rivalry. Rasmus Bang was a multifaceted gentleman. But the men in uniform found nothing, and my grandmother moved back to Moss and ended her days selling sweets and chocolates at the Park Cinema, where the talkies had long since taken over.

Mother didn't talk much about what followed. She couldn't get a living in Moss, so she moved to Oslo. And over the years we wheedled it out of Mother, that Grandmother had known an actor-cum-musician with the National Theatre; a stout fellow who loved the sound of his own baritone, and who preferred to sing the role of ladies' man in gay operettas to the pathetic minor roles offered him in humourless Ibsen dramas. Which was why he applied for a transfer to the Norwegian Opera immediately it was founded at the Folketeater at the end of the fifties. Waldemar Schwacht was his name: a sweat-reeking monster, who bleated his base notes so coarsely that Pauline Hall, Dagbladet's infamous critic, compared his vocal skills to a goat's mating call in spring. And, what was more, according to Father, who would generally join in at this part of the story, Schwacht's war-time activities had been rather shady. Schwacht, however, managed to secure a job for the young and beautiful Åse in the bar of the Norwegian Opera. And there she stood, my mother, selling luke-warm champagne and cheap white wine to the audience every interval. Whether this was a pure act of generosity on Schwacht's part, or the result of a distasteful assault on her person that might equally as well have ended up in a courtroom is something I have often wondered. Mother never discussed it.

It was at the Opera that my mother and father met. The Utopia-believer and opera lover from Hedmark, who dreamed of transforming small-town Hamar into a great city. Norway's answer to Chicago, not by the Great Lakes perhaps, but none the less by the great lake of Mjøsa, already an agrarian-success story and prime for urbanisation. Skyscrapers! A major airport! Something to scare away the small-holders who were such a fashionable notion in Norway at the time. The sickly-sweet romanticising of poverty and all he despised. Father used to bring his business associates to the opera to give them a lesson in culture. During the intervals he would order a bottle of champagne from the charming, young lady from Moss. Father liked to think big – he also thought fast. So Mother was pregnant before she was married. It was a dreadful birth; she almost died. She often talked about that time, of how she drowned herself in opera, of how she virtually spent all those months of breastfeeding intoxicated on any music she could find on the radio, since there was scant money for anything else to get drunk on. Father played at being the big shot then, of course; everything was possible as long as the banks were willing to lend him money. For a while they believed in his Hamar project. His love for Mother was so enormous, there were no limits to what he wanted to do for her. But what could he do in 1950, when Hamar was still Hamar, and Hjalmar Vinding owned no more than a couple of useless apartment blocks he had bought for too high a price and couldn't extract the necessary rents from? Catherine was born and Mother's fate was sealed.

I followed.

The resentment Åse felt towards her daughter continued through life. As far back as I can remember I felt a negative tension between them. Catherine was in perpetual opposition to Mother, displaying it with frequent outbursts of fury of such intensity it wasn't rare for them to end in a fainting fit. I still associate Catherine's lying unconscious on the floor with family get-togethers: Christmas, Easter, Constitution Day. Things bubbled over when mutual expectations were highest.

When Catherine found her love for Mother unreciprocated, she sought it from Father, who had no time for her. Then, for a short time, she sought it from me, but I was already terrified by her explosive temper. Besides which, I had long since become a mummy's boy. Perhaps it was my mother's bad conscience towards Catherine that had led to her outpourings of love towards me. It was too late to make things up to Catherine, but I was ready to accept this love, unreservedly and uncritically, child that I was.

But Mother is dead. Catherine has no plans to slip into a caring role, as a young woman in her situation would quickly have done if the Vindings had been a more normal family. It is as if she were saying indirectly: 'You were always the mummy's boy, so it's up to you to take over from her.'

I clear out my Mother's cupboards. My thoughts turn to the old, the dead. The people who are the reason for my being here. I have started truanting from school, and I have gone into the bedroom my mother once shared with Father. Despite his taking on a local woman to clean for us once a week, there's an awful smell in here; the odour of sick, old man. But her cleaning fluids can do nothing for the bed, the cursed bed, where so many quarrels began. The odour of sweat and sleeplessness. Yet I feel no pity for Father. Mother's version of their story holds sway over me: he forced her into a corner, made all her choices for her, because he lied about his financial situation. I'm clearing out the cupboards of a woman who never lived the life she wanted. I spend an entire morning here in the bedroom, emptying drawers, peering into the backs of cupboards, searching for letters I thought must exist, but can't find. Neither, confusingly, are there any photographs. Her clothes are all that's left. Clothes and shoes. And the records that Father plays each evening, as though to summon her back. Summon Mother back? It should be so simple.

But Mother feels no closer to me even with her dresses in my hands. None the less, it feels as though she wants to say something to me through her absence. I fold all her clothes neatly together, making a large parcel for the Salvation Army. I can remember which clothes she wore when. The green dress she wore to my first afternoon student recital. The red dress she wore when she came back from dining at the

Hotel Continental, on the night she began a particularly dreadful quarrel with Father. The black dress she wore for funerals and extra-exciting parties. And as I do all this, I start to think about music; it is music, and nothing else, that offers me some possibility in life. Music, it seems, is my Mother's great gift to me. I promise myself that I shall play Debussy for Mother, wherever she might be, in next year's competition. From now on I shall inhabit a room where my dearest pictures have been taken down, leaving pale patches on the wallpaper where they once hung. But I vow to myself that I shall hang more pictures up, new pictures, better painted than all the preceding ones. The room will be unrecognisable. Yet it will still be Mother's room.

The piano

OVER THE NEW YEAR I start truanting from school more regularly. It is a dark January day. The others have already got up and left. I've listened to them: lying here in bed, I've heard the muffled noises from the kitchen, footsteps, somebody opening the fridge, bread being cut. Father and Catherine never talk much. Yet they seem to understand each other. They share a coded language, quite incomprehensible to me. I lie in bed, thinking that it'll be another overcast day, and how much I'm dreading it. It is as though I live on the fringes of a reality that doesn't exist, or that I can't comprehend. Going to school, I often look out for Anja. She has her own friends, who tend to gather round her. She goes to the public school on the way up towards Holmenkollen. So long as we go to different schools, there'll never be a natural excuse to get closer, to get talking to her, to ask her if I can walk her home. The private school is for the elite, the chosen few. I know nothing about her except that her name is Anja Skoog, and that she lives in Elvefaret. Her existence is not sufficient to prevent me from playing truant, or from succumbing to the sinful inertia of lying here, as the front door slams and I'm left alone in this house, where I've heard so much screaming and yelling, but which now stands silent, as only a snowy January morning can be.

But what am I to do with this silence? I am sixteen and scared of everything to come. In the night I dream far too many dreams.

The worst thing about dreams is that everybody has them. They are commonplace. I dream that life might be magical, that there are still possibilities. I dream of a life that might give me a sense of meaning, but I don't know where to look. I walk restlessly around this big house. I browse through my mother's record collection, but can't bear to listen to music. Leastways not to Mother's favourite recordings; the ones Father still listens to every evening with tears in his eyes. Then, I'd rather play the piano. When I practise, the practice alone gives me meaning. I can isolate myself in the music, bury myself in details, hammer out my anger, or play Chopin to unleash my tears. From one day to the next, school becomes utterly meaningless, that precious school that Father has always impressed on me to take seriously, because taking the Examen Artium could not be taken for granted in his generation. How often has he described the cruelty of the choice his parents made. His sister could be counted out anyway. And, of the four brothers, they only had money enough to support two through education. Our father and Uncle Wilhelm were chosen. So Hjalmar and Wilhelm sat the Artium, while Edgar and Arnt were condemned to taking over their grandfather's garage, and Aunty Borghild had to clean at the hospital. Father was given a great opportunity, but what did he use it for? To dream up grandiose schemes, to invest in hopeless projects, and to marry my mother. Nothing was as he had dreamed.

It's now that I start to practise in earnest, many hours each day. I practise as though I were some crazed avenger. But what shall I avenge? I let my thoughts fly as I hammer away at my practice pieces, over and over. Bach's preludes and fugues. Self-inflicted tortures. I think how Catherine went on loving Mother, and that's the tragedy of it: Mother had never loved her, she'd never even liked her – her daughter reminded her too much of herself and her own weaknesses. Catherine had never had her mother's love, perhaps that was why her desire to rescue her had been greater than mine. I, the beloved, had been the one to let our mother slip into the waterfall.

I sit at my grandmother's piano, the black Bechstein, a stubborn, old monster restored at huge expense, that I force to bend to my least whim, and that tolerates my hammering. I long to distance myself from my own fate. I want to focus on the competition. Bach and Debussy.

Father knows nothing, nor does Catherine, but I spend day after day sitting in my room now, the dead room of my childhood, feeling that the only truth I have to cling to is the one I can create for myself. Nobody can make my choices for me, certainly not Father. My childhood has been like some sorry fairytale. Both Mother and Father would bring people home from work at the weekends. Mother brought singers, musicians and stagehands. Father brought master carpenters, builders and decorators, investors and speculators. And everybody would mingle, and Mother and Father would be drunk and everything would seem possible. The doors of our house would be flung open to the world. It filled with partying and music, and at the centre of this commotion, the great piano would stand, surrounded by singing, humming people, by glasses and bottles. Yes, it was a pitiful fairytale, since it invariably ended in hangovers, and in Mother and Father quarrelling. And yet, it was no less a fairytale for that, despite Catherine and I being anxious about what would follow when the laughter fell silent, when the Bechstein stood black and untuned the next morning, ash on its ivory keys, red wine stains on its lid, now closed to the world. I want to breathe life back into that instrument. I want to learn its secrets, so it bends to my music. For wherever music is present, there will be life. More than any place else. This is the lesson Mother has left me with. And I long to rediscover that place. To make it my own. I tell myself I have nothing to lose.

Conversation at night

IT IS FEBRUARY. One Friday Father and I stay up, staring into the television. Some awful detective series; we must have dropped off. We are both so tired. With all the things that remain unspoken between us. The finances that I know are strangling him. The decision I've made, and told him nothing about. When we wake up, it is already night time. We can see Catherine has come home from her party and gone to bed; her shoes are in the hall.

'She might have woken us,' says Father, with reproach in his voice. He looks old, much older than he is, grey-haired, slack-skinned, stooped, thin. Besides which he's drinking more. Red wine, constantly now. But we've taken some nice ski trips up to Brunkollen, and a thought that I first entertained long ago in the midst of that eternal childhood has returned to me, that perhaps I am as close to Father as I ever was to Mother, since he and I have no need to create a commotion; we don't share Mother's and Catherine's habit of hammering on walls with clenched fists. Despite it being obvious to all the world that I was a mummy's boy and Catherine was a daddy's girl, I suddenly think, as I gaze at Father: this is somebody I understand. His choices could all have been mine. The arrogance, the risk-taking, his unique capacity for adulation, his boundless love for Mother that made him squander his own prospects. For a while he would send her enormous bouquets of red roses. She was livid; she didn't want them. She begged him to use the money on something sensible. But he never did. He wanted to see her dance. He wanted to take her to Covent Garden and to the Metropolitan. He's still in shock now. He sits drinking red wine, unable to piece his life together. Mother's old records will never supply any answers. And meanwhile irate envelopes from debt collectors arrive, which he hides behind the breadbin in the kitchen, unopened.

Father is glaring at me. I know I should talk to him. I think how I'm deceiving him, how my days are turned upside-down, how I share my time between the shade of the alder thicket with the rushing of the river, and the Bechstein in the upstairs living room. It is as though he's read my thoughts.

'Aksel, you must complete your schooling,' he says. 'You're all I've got left. Catherine's not going to manage.'

'Catherine?' I look at him, astonished.

'Yes. Her head teacher has called me in for a meeting this morning. Catherine's not been to school since before Christmas, it seems.'

I am truly shocked. 'Not since before Christmas?' I say, my eyes widening as though I've just uncovered a crime. 'But where has she been?'

'I have no idea, and I don't dare to ask her.' Father fixes me with a helpless gaze. The same look he used to give Mother when he had run out of arguments, gifts or bottles of wine to offer.

'But that's terrible!' I hear my voice crack into a falsetto. The tail end of the hateful process of my voice breaking.

'Yes. Dreadful isn't it?' Father shakes his head.

We fall silent. Father can't cope with the quiet. He goes to the stereo and puts on the last record Mother bought before she died. Strangely it's Stravinsky's 'Rights of Spring'. Earlier that day, when the sun stood high in the sky, it had occurred to me that spring was on its way, and that there was something cruel in the returning light, the new life that forged itself a path, steam-rollering over the old.

'I don't understand how she could do it to you,' I say. 'Wasn't it thanks to you that she got a place at the Cathedral School?'

Father shrugs. He has never been good at taking compliments.

'I did what I could, used some contacts. But one has to complete things, Aksel. Otherwise one never gets anywhere. You're at a difficult age. Your thoughts are pulling you in all directions, and your dreams even further. I know how hasty you are. You're as hasty as me. That's why I beg you to finish what you've started. That was your mother's downfall, she never finished anything. She was victim to her impulses. That's why she was so unhappy.'

I nod. I have never heard him talk about Mother like this before. There is so much I want to ask him, but now isn't the time. And what would I say? He wants to consider me a friend. He has grown so isolated over recent years. But I am too young to be a friend. Besides, I've proved myself stronger than him. It was my will that triumphed that Sunday in August. I was the one who held him back by force. Does he ever think about it?

'All I ask is that you complete your studies,' he mumbles.

I do not answer. I pretend to be listening to the music. It is growing increasingly forceful. I stare at the record sleeve. I wonder what Mother saw in this piece, so insanely beautiful, so furious, wild and brutal.

The truth

I BEGIN SPYING on my own sister. I have to find out what she's doing when she's not at school; when neither of us is at school. And I had been so sure that she at least was tied to her school desk, with all those other clever kids. Cathedral School pupils are destined for success. Only the crème de la crème go there. The kids who will influence society in the years to come. Tomorrow's high court judges, doctors, philosophers, politicians. And artists? No, I think to myself. They will come, as ever, from all corners; from rural Norway, from high-rise estates, industrial towns and fishing outposts, but rarely from the establishment. The best painters, musicians and writers we have come from the working classes. Mother reminded me of that once, when we listened to a tenor at the Opera singing Rudolpho in La Bohème. 'He suits this role,' Mother had whispered to me, 'because he hasn't got a penny to his name.' I knew she was saying it to encourage me, the upstart, since we were all upstarts in the house in Melumveien. Yes, I think, the problem with Catherine was that she never showed any interest in the music that filled our house every hour of the day. Mother craved music desperately; she couldn't abide silence. Even I found it exhausting sometimes. It was as though life had to be lived in top gear to the last drop, a ceaseless consumption of symphonies, cigarettes and alcohol. And the minute she had a free moment at work at the Opera House, she would stand in the wings drinking everything in that happened on that stage. Catherine shares her intensity, I just never thought of it as Mother's intensity until now; her eternal restlessness, her insatiable need to be out with friends, or to whiz along ski tracks hundreds of metres ahead of the rest of us. She has done all the things most kids do, except learn an instrument. In sheer protest. Instead, she went to ballet classes, gymnastics, skiing and skating. As the music boomed from the living room, Catherine sat in her room painting or drawing pictures nobody was allowed to see. If I so much as tried to take a peek at any, hysteria would ensue.

But right now, I am determined to take a peek at her activities. And the only hope I have of spying on her, and finding out where she goes each morning, is to work out which tram she takes to town. I know she always gets on at the front carriage and sits as far forward as she can. So I need to get to Ekraveien, the stop before Røa, then get a seat at the very back of the second carriage, and keep a look-out for who gets off at the stops on the way to the Nationaltheatret.

I am no longer skiving off school. I have now left. Not long after our peculiar conversation, a letter arrived for Father. It came from Roestad, my kindly headmaster: a man who wears a tweed jacket all year, smokes like a chimney, just as Mother did, looks like an Italian movie star, and whose nickname is Professor Brainbox, since he knows the answers to everything. He teaches French, Norwegian and history, and always had an eye for Mother, even though I'm sure he's homosexual. In his letter he explained that he and his staff were extremely concerned about my constant absence from school. This, the letter continued, could not go on, and my father was being summoned to a meeting the following Thursday. But catching the letter before my father saw it, and recognising its source, I opened it. I'd been forging numerous absence notes, and now I immediately rattled a final letter off on Father's typewriter. In it I regretted that 'my son Aksel Vinding has sadly decided not to complete college and to sit his Examen Artium. I would like to thank all the teachers for their considerable effort in making things as easy as possible for Aksel following the tragic event that struck our family last year. Aksel is fundamentally kind, good and hardworking, but he has decided to focus all his attention on his music from now on. He has, of course, considerable musical talent . . .' etc., etc. I rounded my letter off with further thanks and a 'yours sincerely', followed by my father's signature, copied with a precision only *I* could manage.

Father knows nothing about what I've done. Right now I have no friends in the neighbourhood, nobody who cares – a wistful time. During the course of a winter I withdraw from the world, little by little. There's nobody to miss me. But I miss Anja Skoog. And I even bump into her sometimes when she's dashing for the tram. Then my heart pounds and my blood rushes.

I have become a lone wolf. And it is as a lone wolf that I walk one slushy March morning to Ekraveien station, to spy on my sister. I am not worried about her, as my father is. Despite her having stopped communicating with us, I see a vitality behind that mask: something is going on, something has her in its grip, something that makes her eyes big and scary now and then. She doesn't want us to know anything about it. And I have a feeling that I'm unlikely to give her secret away. There's no guarantee that I shall tell Father about anything I discover today. I get on the tram at just past nine, having said goodbye to Catherine half an hour earlier, so she'll be certain I'm sitting behind my school desk by now, swotting up on French verbs. Father left for town at the crack of dawn as usual. Every morning brings new hope, every afternoon new disappointment. I don't know where he gets his strength from; this man who always seems so weak. It's as though his melancholy, or grief, were a stimulus. I know him enough to be sure he will never give up. He is working in the middle of town now on a property he hopes to sell to the Oslo Cinematography Group.

Catherine gets on the tram at Røa, as expected. I watch as she gets on at the very front. Perhaps this is the most intimate insight I'll ever have of my sister, I muse. The knowledge that she likes to sit at the front of the tram. Not everybody has such a close relationship with their sister. On these old trams it's possible to keep an eye on her through the windows between carriages. I am expecting her to get off at Majorstuen, Valkyrieplass or Nationaltheatret. But she already gets up as the tram comes into Sørbyhaugen, the small station where the lines divide. So she must, I reason, be taking the Kolsås line. She will have to wait here at Sørbyhaugen for five minutes, before the tram for Kolsås arrives from town heading westwards.

I am in a dilemma. Sørbyhaugen is far too small a station for me to get off with her and wait on the opposite platform without being seen. I stay seated and watch her from inside the tram window. I suddenly see her just as I saw her that ill-fated Sunday. For years I have lived so close to her, never really seeing her at all. To me she has only ever been Catherine, a constant, my sister, and I have always felt sure of who my sister was. Suddenly I no longer know. She seems so grown-up as she walks along the platform towards the crossing. There's something in the way she is dressed. She wears a dress and a smart coat. She has, I reflect, become a woman. And I feel hurt, because I sense I'm about to lose her.

I can't bear the thought that she too might be on her way out of my life. What will be left of the Vinding family then? I squash my nose up against the window, staring at her, forgetting that she could discover me at any moment as the tram passes her on its way to Smedstad.

But she is clearly deep in thought. She has a strange, trance-like expression that reminds me of Mother when she was drunk. But Catherine is not drunk. She is an eighteen-year-old girl, who is about to give up school, eight weeks before being due to sit her Examen Artium. Father hasn't managed to talk to her and I haven't dared ask a single question. Irritable people have an authority of their own, however small or weak or cowardly they may be. Anyway, Catherine isn't exactly irritable, I think to myself. Nor is she small, weak or cowardly. There is something that preoccupies her, more than Father and me, more than the Cathedral School, more than Mother's death. Will she notice me after all?

The tram rolls past. Catherine stands waiting at the crossing, squinting up, surrounded by dirt and slush, shrouded in the morning mist. Tears well up in my eyes. It is a habit I have, seeing the sadness in everything, Mother's sad life, Father's sad life. Catherine's sad life. It's a disaster for her to leave school. I'm doing it because I have nothing to lose. Besides, I have a plan. But has that eighteen-year-old, waiting there for the tram to pass, any plans? She reminds me of the consumptive girls in expressionist paintings. She looks so pale, as she stands there. Where in the world is she going? Has she spotted me? No. The tram rolls on towards Smedstad. At which point the Kolsås tram rolls into the station in the opposite direction. It is running late. I can catch it! I think. It'll be a near thing, since I'm at the back of the tram going townwards. Instantly I am through the door, shoving an old lady aside so she almost falls. I race alongside the tram, despite its already having moved off. I gain some metres on it, and try to cross the lines just in front of the driver, who hoots as loud as he can. At the same time the Kolsås tram has set off in the opposite direction. They'll flatten me between them if neither of them stops. I wave and take eye contact with the tram driver. He brakes and realises I want to get on. It is as though my life depended on it. I come up on to the opposite platform. The doors open and with a sigh of relief I run on; the conductor gazes at me in surprise. Just then I realise I have got into the first carriage, at the first door, where Catherine will board in just two minutes. The carriage is practically empty. Only an elderly man and a mysterious woman sit on either side of the aisle, right at the front. I look for a place to hide, while simultaneously having to pay. I fumble with my wallet, dropping it on the floor.

'Where to?' asks the conductor. 'I've no idea.' The most ridiculous answer possible. 'To the end of the line,' I stutter. 'But quickly!' 'And what's your hurry?' the conductor asks. 'I've got my reasons,' I answer desperately, managing to pay just as the tram rolls into Sørbyhaugen Station. Like a madman I make a dash for the back of the carriage. My behaviour is drawing attention, and when I see that Catherine is boarding and that she's coming my way, I fling myself down on to a seat, as though intending to sleep. The conductor instantly walks up to me: 'Sorry, that's not allowed!' he says, 'Sleeping on the tram is prohibited!' Prohibited to sleep? But people are always dropping off on the tram. I sit up straight, trying to hide my face in my scarf. Catherine has sat in the seat right in front of me. I can smell her hair. But she doesn't turn around to find out what's going on. Which is typical. She isn't curious; she has enough on her mind. So here we sit, like two strangers, in an almost empty carriage. She has no idea I'm here, and that it's her own brother's aftershave tickling her nose. She sneezes. I sit frozen, ready to make a dive for it if she turns. I contemplate what she might be up to, and where she plans to get off. And what shall I do then, I wonder, my head empty of ideas. We pass Montebello, Ullernåsen, Åsjordet, Bjørnsletta, Lysakerelven, Jar, Tjernsrud and Ringstabekk. Egne Hjem. It's Bekkestua next. She gets up. I breath a sigh of relief. Bekkestua is the biggest station, but what help is that with only four passengers in the carriage? Then a miracle: the two passengers at the front get up too. Everybody is getting off at Bekkestua! But I do not get up immediately. I wait until Catherine is on the platform. I have learned this much from music. Some pauses can never be too long. I hear the sound of the doors about to close, but I have chosen my tempo, I slip past just as they slam shut. Then I turn my back on the unsuspecting Catherine and wait. I wait until she is up at the crossing. Then I begin following her. I am following my own sister. I want to know what she is doing. Why she has given up school. Why she hasn't said a word to either Father or me.

She walks over the crossing, back towards Egne Hjem. I begin to relax, since it's clear she's in her own world. She is unlikely to turn around.

What can she be doing out here in Bærum, I wonder. Where rich men and property owners live. It comes as a surprise that she didn't take the tram into town, where life pulsates. Everything seems so sedate and boring, out here amongst the villas. The fog lies thick on the ground. The snow is melting. The asphalt is wet and black. A few solitary pensioners walk past. A dog barks. A group of children in waterproofs trundle slowly behind their nursery nurse. Everything appears so gloomy and miserable. And here I am, following my sister. Her spoilt kid brother, walking a few hundred metres behind her. I've often wondered whether perhaps she hates me. She would have every reason to hate me for stealing so much attention. A child's verse buzzes around in my head: 'Only little brother can, nobody else, you see. Only little brother can, and only, only he . . .' I was no age when it dawned on me that they were nicer to me than to Catherine. Little giveaways: my Christmas presents were larger, the meat I got on my plate nicer. I got more attention. I walk behind my sister, contemplating our upbringing to date, the things we never shared, except briefly; the play-fights on the sofa on unusually jolly days; my pride when I was allowed to go with her to the ice rink. The slender legs. The soft arched back. The rippling curls. The pirouettes that made people clap, her kid brother most of all. But it was all a waste. Mother and Father were never there. They never witnessed her pride. They were back at home yelling at each other. And Catherine and I knew that better than anybody. Even if it was quiet on our return, we could hear the echoes of their screams between the muffled sobs from the bedroom: Mother's inconsolable crying.

Catherine has walked a considerable way up Bjerkelundsveien. Suddenly she gives a little skip, a girlish curtsey. I can barely believe my eyes. Then she promptly swings through a gate. It is a yellow house with small square windows. A family villa, as they call it, although it is divided into flats. I stop behind a car fifty metres downhill. She throws a quick look in my direction, but can't see me. I'm hidden behind the back window. Perhaps she thinks I'm a child wanting to play hide and seek.

She rings at the door.

She doesn't wait to be let in. Instead, she enters without anybody answering the door. There's a familiarity in the way she disappears into the house.

What more can I do?

My sister has disappeared into a stranger's home. She should have been at the Cathedral School now. The girl who always got top marks. I am standing outside a yellow and mysterious villa. What happens inside those walls? Who is waiting for her in there? I shudder, not daring to follow the thought to its logical conclusion. Then I feel the nausea, the interminable nausea.

I throw up.

Then I walk slowly back to the tram station.

What's going to become of me, I think.

I feel strangely cheated. I think about that unexpected little skip. The girlish curtsey. The joy she must have been feeling. Would Father want to know about this? The Yellow House? No. I decide, I can't tell Father about this under any circumstances.

No man's land

SPRING COMES. I am in the living room one afternoon, struggling with a Bach Fugue – the complex C sharp major from the first book of *The Well-Tempered Clavier* – when the telephone rings.

I jump out of my skin. The telephone never goes at this time of day; there's nobody to ring, nobody at home. But the telephone has a grip on me. I rise from the piano and stand glaring down at the black apparatus, as it rings and rings. Perhaps it's a sales person. Or the police. Or somebody ringing to tell me a nuclear bomb has been dropped over Lake Mjøsa, and we have to seek refuge in the nearest bomb shelter. Or it might be Anja Skoog. I grab the receiver. It is Father.

'Right, there you are,' he says, with a weary laugh.

'I didn't feel quite well today,' I answer.

'Spare me, please, Aksel. I've talked with your headmaster. I know everything.'

He falls silent. I can't bear it. My scalp crawls. But I'm not frightened of him, and he knows it. Which is why he's phoned, because he's frightened of me. He could never look Mother in the eye when he wanted to say something important. He is more frightened of Catherine than me. But he is also frightened of me.

'What do you want me to say?' I say finally.

I can hear him considering his answer. He takes a deep breath. 'What you've done is unforgivable, Aksel. All that time, and not one word! You owe me an apology.'

'I'm sorry, Dad.'

'Please, spare me. But are you really sure you're doing the right thing?'

'I have to put everything into my music. I can't explain. You'll have to trust me. I'll enter myself for the competition in the autumn. I've got a good chance of winning.'

'So you've been sitting at home all these weeks, practising, while I thought you were swatting up on those French verbs?'

'I'm sorry,' I say.

He starts laughing again. But it's over now. I laugh too. Then I suddenly want to vomit. That's Father's way. He can never be angry. Mother was the one that got angry.

'You're a strange lad, Aksel. But you have my respect. Whatever happens, you've made a brave decision. I presume you'll let me hear what you practise from now on. It'll be quite a concert, I expect.'

We chat for a few minutes. It is easy to talk to Father over the phone. We should always talk over the phone.

But he doesn't dare ask me about Catherine and her life, any more than he dares broach the subject with her. Catherine is a stranger to us both now. We all eat dinner together, we talk about the assassinations of Martin Luther King and Robert Kennedy, we talk about any films that are worth seeing and which flowers to plant in the garden. But her voice is always monotone, and her eyes are glazed. Occasionally she loses her temper, as only Mother knew how, and flings herself out of the door announcing, in no uncertain terms, that neither of us understands her.

Summer arrives. My last summer without friends, and without a girl-friend. I have built a wall around me, separating me off from everybody else. Nothing exists for me now except my piano, the alder thicket and Anja Skoog. In our world of deceitful silence, neither Father nor I have said a word to Catherine. She still thinks I go to school. And I somehow prefer it that way. She might have got strange ideas in her head, if she'd known what I really do, just as I have strange ideas about the life she leads. What, I wonder, lurks in The Yellow House? Does she still go there? I certainly don't believe she goes there to paint pictures. She goes there to sleep with a man. My sister is living a debauched and wild existence. She lets this man do unutterable things to her body. What if this was Anja Skoog, I think, vexed. Perhaps when Anja rushes past me in the street, she's also going to some bourgeois district to sleep with a man in a Yellow House. The thought makes me ill. I go to the cinema and watch a French movie. A woman is filled with desire. I see her desire being satiated by a man, see how a climax might look. It seems unbelievable, and leaves me troubled.

In the alder thicket I stare into the river, wrestling with difficult thoughts. Perhaps Catherine is doing the right thing. She has chosen to live, before it is too late. I hear that a boy from school has leukaemia and is dying. At sixteen. I sit and play the piano until late every afternoon, and visit Synnestvedt each Wednesday, who tells me I'm making huge progress. Synnestvedt, in his grimy little flat in Sorgenfrigata, filled with grease everywhere. The grease of old *rakfisk* and *sylte* from countless Christmas Eves spent alone with his sister. Doesn't anybody ever come to do his cleaning? The ivory keys on the worn-out Blüthner are sticky and black from the grubby fingers of his pupils. Synnestvedt, the friendly, loveable loser, who never dared to make a debut, who is stupid enough to believe that I still go to school. A mediocre piano teacher and appalling pianist, a fact he reveals each time he tries to demonstrate something technical. I've overtaken him by light-years already. He tries to offer me guidance: inept interpretations, an overly sentimental voice. A man with too many photographs of himself on his grand piano, with virtually nothing to teach, afflicted with dandruff, dry airways and appalling breath, he none the less has a surprisingly stimulating effect on me: he gives me space, allows me to take on the biggest challenges, and to set myself impossible goals, such as playing Brahms's B Major Concerto with the Philharmonic before I reach twenty.

It is all Mother's fault, the money she gave me, little tokens of encouragement, because my first piano teacher was so dreadful. Fru Holtemann at Heggeli, near the cemetery, with bogeys up her nose. Grimy hands, always suffering with a cold, and with a cloying smell that came from the thick, worn-out woollies she wore even in summer. I shiver each time I remember her, how she stood behind me, sneezing into my hair, as she forced me to hammer out those ghastly Czerny études. The odour of death, perspiration and meringues. After three awful years with Fru Holtemann, Mother found Synnestvedt. The best that can be said of Synnestvedt is that he is kind, has a liking for Schumann, drinks port in secret and worships the Latin American pianist Claudio Arrau as much as I do. There's something he'd like to emulate in that imposing masculinity, the thin, black moustache, the aroma of cigars. Unattainable dreams.

Synnestvedt is pale, skinny and narrow-shouldered. Synnestvedt is a stopgap in my life, a piano teacher who can teach me nothing, with not one secret of how to improve my technique or strengthen my interpretative powers. A disconcerting fact, since I'm not *that* good. Even I need guidance; everybody needs guidance. But I'm also severely in need of courage. And Synnestvedt cheers me on every Wednesday, for the big competition in November: the Young People's Piano Competition. Since he has no idea I've dropped out of school, he doesn't know how vital this is for me. The competition could even be a major breakthrough. That snooty sixteen-year-old, Georg Fredrik Salvesen from Rykkinn, won last year. The guy who always has a drip coming from his snub nose when he plays. A chap with barely a modicum of talent, but who slipped through the eye of the needle, and ended up playing Mozart on the TV. All thanks to the competition. The Young People's Piano Competition is the great autumn event. Held every year in the Aula, the Great University Hall, with Edvard Munch's *The Sun* as a backdrop. The Aula is known to us all, since we've all visited it so often; not least when international pianists have made guest appearances here. This is the hall where the Nobel Peace Prize is presented every tenth of December. Rubinstein, Richter, Gilels and Arrau have all played here. Ashkenazy has pronounced the Steinway that stands in the Aula one of the world's best. Georg Fredrik Salvesen was ecstatic when he won. I sat in the hall clapping, even though I wanted to leave. I knew I could play better than him. Salvesen was a flash in the pan. He would soon realise it himself, give the piano up and study engineering. Winning would be easy, I thought, if the standards were that low. It made me more certain that I could succeed the next year.

It is already a year on. It is summer and time is standing still. I see nothing of Anja Skoog, despite walking through Elvefaret several times a day. Catherine has taken a summer job in Sarahs Telt. I know it's true since I see her serving foaming beers to weary customers as I walk through Studenterlunden towards Grøndahl's or Norsk Musikforlag to browse or buy sheet music and records. She should have been celebrating the end of her exams now, joining friends in their traditional Russe celebrations. Instead she took us both off guard one morning by announcing: 'I'm cancelling this whole Russe business. It's just stupid. I'm taking a summer job instead.' Father let it pass, without taking the opportunity to expose her lies. That was when I realised that we'd all gone too far. It was something in Catherine's smile: she knew that we knew that she was lying. And at the same time, she knew that I was lying too. Perhaps that was why things had grown almost comic. We no longer had the words. Everything stopped. There were too many lies, and it had become absurd. Catherine smiled; I smiled back. Then Father had to smile too. We could have laughed, but didn't dare. We no longer knew each other. When Mother was swept away, our family disappeared too, because it had been her, her dreams, her unruliness, which had held us together.

I sit indoors and practise, thinking about Catherine who sleeps with men, and Anja Skoog who may do the same. Catherine says she'll move out in the autumn, find herself a bedsit, begin studying, but I sense she'll stick around, that she's in a kind of rut, just as I'm in a rut, even though I have a goal. I am sixteen, I have freed myself from my father's expectations. I have chosen to disappoint him and to follow my own dreams. He helps me with money. I accept his help, feeling like a miserable fraud. And yet: don't I have a calling? Wasn't this what Mother wanted? Mother's will was always Father's will. So be it.

The Lectors' House

THE MUSIC STUDENTS' SHOWCASE is being held in the Lectors' House. This is where the Music Teachers' Association parade their specimens, like cat owners at a cat show. Gifted little girls are prettied up with powder and frilly skirts. Young boys, pale-faced geniuses, wear stiff-collared shirts and Brylcreem in their hair. There is no escaping these student showcases. This is where the wheat is separated from the chaff. The music teachers update themselves on the pupils of their colleagues, each dreaming of discovering the next Rubinstein. And to be sure, some of us believe we are gifted, as we gather this September afternoon, each with a music teacher in tow, to play our party piece. I've not breathed a word to Catherine or Father, since I didn't want them here. I need to succeed at this alone. They will find out soon enough whether I have talent or not.

I arrive at the Lectors' House with Synnestvedt. The smell of his breath is, just for the occasion, unlike anything I have ever encountered before. What is it with this man? He breathes over me, anaesthetising me, murdering me, with his dry mucous membranes, the onion he has devoured as well as Lord knows what. He always gets so tense before events like this. He's been drinking; he's most definitely been drinking, I think, as he whispers into my ear that I will be a sensation. Nobody has heard me play, of course, since last year, since I began truanting. Synnestvedt has no idea that I have had the entire day at my disposal for months, that I have been playing those wretched Bach fugues and Chopin études ceaselessly. My technique holds no fear any more, but the turmoil that's going on inside me, where in my music will that find expression?

Synnestvedt is expecting me to play Brahms, Opus 118. But I have different plans. I intend to give them Chopin. The 'Revolutionary Étude'. I shall demonstrate the impressiveness of my left hand, and the octave stretch I have acquired in my right. I look at these prissied four-teen-year-old girls, with their nail varnish and sequins, and think how I'll crush them to a pulp. They won't be able to look at themselves in the mirror after tonight, and they'll wish they were cheerleaders instead.

But when my eye falls on Rebecca Frost, I moderate my thoughts. She is not, at least, glammed up like the other girls, perhaps because she's so hugely rich, because she lives in Bygdøy and because her father is a shipping tycoon. Rebecca has a weird habit of hugging me every time she sees me, which I don't really like. But since her affection seems so genuine, I make allowances.

'Aksel, sweetie! How are you?' Her tone is motherly, despite her only being a few months my senior.

'I'm fine,' I say. Rebecca, a sunshine girl, a girl nobody takes any real interest in, a sweet young thing with dark blonde hair, so rich and successful she seems boring before one has even spoken to her, in spite of the ice-blue eyes and the tiny little freckles that are the surprise of her pale face. The rest of us know nothing about her other friends. Rumour has it she mixes in royal circles, but what good is royalty to us? Besides, there wouldn't be anybody our age.

Rebecca takes my hand, 'This is going to be so exciting,' she says. 'I've not heard you play for ages!'

We each deliver our showpieces, to the delight of our teachers and parents. Rebecca's wealthy father is out in the hall too. The stout ship-owner, of whom a statue is already erected in Stavanger, claps and cheers at the finish of his daughter's rather mediocre rendition of a Schubert impromptu. Under no great illusions herself, she shrugs and sends me a meaningful glance, as if to say: 'I'm sorry, Aksel, but that was the best I could do. I don't practise enough. That's how things are when you're too rich.'

Yes, I think. Mother's axiom: it is the poor who become the truly great artists. And surely I am poor? Surely I live at my father's mercy? Without a penny to my name? In some strange way the 'Revolutionary Étude' seems appropriate. Chopin's fierce solidarity with his fellow Poles! When my turn comes I mount the platform and clear my throat. There is a deafening silence in the hall. I know, they know. This is the first time I shall perform since my mother's death. Everybody knows about her death. I speak: 'My dear mentor in both life and in music, my piano teacher Oscar Synnestvedt, who is here tonight, has asked me to play Brahms. But on the tram from Røa I felt the overwhelming urge to play you Chopin's "Revolutionary Étude". I hope that neither Synnest-vedt or anybody else here tonight will object.'

Then I let loose.

This is my big night. My triumph. Adult as I feel, child as I am, I am almost embarrassed by the strength of applause, but have to admit that I relish it. I stand in the wings, refusing to go on again, even though the applause persists. This, I think to myself, will be my style: never to make myself too available. There is nothing worse than a musician who plays an encore before the audience have really asked for it. Rebecca Frost would, I think to myself, be the type for that.

And it is Rebecca who awaits me as I come backstage, turquoise flashes in her already deep blue eyes.

'You are so fabulous, Aksel! In case you didn't know! You are the absolute best!'

And then she gives me an ecstatic kiss on the lips.

I feel a revulsion. I've never kissed a girl before, even though I've been longing to for ages.

I wipe my mouth with a tissue the instant I feel unobserved.

The Torchlight Man

IT IS AUTUMN. Chilly, star-studded nights. The artificial light of the city has still not outshone the glow of Venus. As the sun sets, I take the Lovers' Path and wonder what will become of me. I long for somebody who is still unknown to me: her name is Anja Skoog. Why do I dream so much about her? Because her eyes are green? Because she has a tiny, little nose? Because she always smiles at me with such warmth, but also pity?

I go on practising. Like a demon possessed. Seven hours a day. My back aches.

Catherine has not moved out, as she has threatened to do so often. None of us knows how she spends her days. And we are as ignorant about her evenings. She is rarely home. But then she can suddenly turn up, on a Saturday afternoon, with a bag of pastries. Then all three of us can sit chatting about the world in general, as though nothing has happened.

I am down among the alders one day when something unexpected happens. I fall on the slippery rocks, and reaching out to catch myself with my left hand I immediately realise my mistake. A sprain perhaps. Carefully I test the mobility in my hand and feel a shooting pain. Something has happened.

I sense an icy thrill in me somewhere. I shall take control of this. This will, in the end, be my triumph! Never again will coincidence rule my life. I walk home and immediately phone our family doctor, the old, alcoholic Schwartz, a Swiss man who was lost to love and found himself stranded in Norway in the fifties, and to whom Mother always turned for comfort. He knows who I am and lets me come immediately to his consulting room in a basement in Kristian Auberts Vei. Getting myself an appointment with Schwartz poses no problem. He adored my mother and gave her any medication she requested in the last ten years of her life. Now he is sitting in front of me, in tears.

'She was irreplaceable, my boy!'

'Yes, we all feel that,' I say, trying to be grown-up.

He surveys me with sentimental gaze: 'You do know your mother was an alcoholic?'

'I know a lot about Mother,' I reply.

'If she hadn't drunk so much, she'd have managed to stay out of the waterfall,' says Schwartz.

'You know nothing about it, Dr Schwartz. She was completely sober when it happened.'

'Why do you say that, my boy? Your mother, Åse Vinding, drank all the time.'

'In that case this consultation is a waste of time.'

I get up and leave, without giving the doctor so much as a glance, without saying goodbye. Where does this rage come from? It terrifies me, because it makes me lose control. I have to return to the alder thicket now. My feelings are inexplicable. Minutes later I am sitting by the river, trying to puzzle out the reason for this fury. The doctor is right, of course. Mother was drunk when she was swept away by the waterfall. And she had probably been drinking heavily through the night as well. I am angry because I want to preserve a lie, and now I have spoiled my chances of getting the medical certificate I needed. I shake my head at my lack of control: not the makings of a maestro. I have a sense of disquiet. I must be careful. There are always two paths, the light and the dark. Mother and Father chose the dark. Catherine too. A destructive path, characterised by helplessness, hyper-sensitivity. I refuse to be like them! I do not want to be a destructive person! A bitter person! I am a grown-up now, I tell myself. I am extremely annoyed at my behaviour in Dr Schwartz's office. It does nobody any favours. In particular not an ambitious pianist with just one thing to cling to, if he is to succeed: total control.

I am still sitting, wrapped in self-loathing, when I suddenly realise I have not moved for hours. I struggle between dream and reality. Moon-light. I am thirsty and disorientated. The spruce trees stand in black silhouette on the other side of the river. The moon shines with icy silver. Then I hear a noise. It comes from the little lovers' path just beyond the alder thicket, where hardly anybody goes. I've not seen a single person on that path in all the months I've sat in the middle of the thicket, trying to take control of the world. Perhaps it's a doe or a fox I can hear. I sit stock-still.

Then I make out a figure on the path, going towards Lysejordet. At first I assume it must be some unsavoury character, a burglar perhaps, taking cover after his crime, but as the person passes the alder thicket, to within metres of me, I see it's a young girl.

Anja Skoog.

It is not how I would have wanted it to be, but I'm so surprised that I let out an exclamation.

Anja Skoog. One late autumn evening. Is this how our relationship will begin? Down by the river? Where only I dare venture at this time of day? I rustle some leaves. Anja must be deep in thought, since she starts violently. She gives a little squeal. And now everything is awry. She's frightened and starts running.

'No!' I yell, bursting out of the thicket.

She panics, turns and runs back towards Elvefaret, passing within a few centimetres of me. I feel a chill rising inside that urges me to act. The two of us. Alone. What chance has she got? Everything is in a spin, for a moment. But I hold back. She can't have seen me, or who I was. Only the vague outline of a shadow. It's steep up to the villas. She slips, falls, but stumbles back up. I can't hold back any longer.

'Stop!' I shout. 'Stop!'

Then she screams, at the top of her lungs. 'Help! Help!'

I could throw myself over her, I think to myself, force her to her knees so she knows who she's dealing with. That hysterical voice is intolerable. But it would lead to nothing. She runs, crawls, scrambles up the path, probably injured already. I stop, relieved that she has not recognised me. I have the taste of iron in my mouth. Blood. I am excited. But what is it that's exciting me? I have dreamed so often of our first meeting. But it was never meant to be like this. It was meant to be filled with sweetness, as only a first encounter can be. But this was the opposite. Anja Skoog is a terrified fifteen-year-old girl racing towards Elvefaret. Nobody in their right mind comes down here. Not on a late autumn evening.

I watch her vanish.

I spit, blow my nose. It is blood after all. A nose-bleed. I've stopped shouting. I stand quite still, wondering what in the world brought her down here, to this eerie valley with its tall spruce trees, where there have already been too many corpses, a woman raped in the fifties, a boy drowned five years ago, Mother's head smashed at the bottom of the waterfall last year.

I can't believe that this has happened, that Anja Skoog has run away from me, helter skelter, gripped with such fear. I'd wanted things to be so different.

Suddenly, I hear noises again. Coming from Elvefaret. I see three stars at first, but they are three torches. Men! They're coming for me! It is Skoog, Professor Bror Skoog, the surgeon, the specialist in unhealthy brains. I have seen him in the neighbourhood, circled him in these past months, a handsome, square-set, slightly dishevelled man in his forties, with hair in all directions. I feel nauseous each time I see him. Both because he is Anja Skoog's father, and also because there is something aggressive about him. I feel even more nauseous now: they are heading in my direction. They are coming to get me. The deadly attacker of Melumveien. The sixteen-year-old who dreams of Anja. They're coming to teach me a lesson! But I have one advantage: I know this valley, the path, the forest, the rocks, the alder thicket. So long as they do not have a dog. If they do, I am done for. I slink in between the trees. The men are still thirty metres away. My left hand aches. It is too late to make a run for it. I must get back to my patch, among the branches. But I am off-track. The bracken is dense. I thrash about, realising I am on the wrong path. I have come too far down; now I have to go all the way down to the river, to come up again. I slip on the shiny rocks, meet ice-old water, my shoes are wet through. Then finally I come back up, finding my lair. Do they hold competitions in fear? Am I more frightened than Anja Skoog was half an hour ago? No, I think to myself, I am not in fear for my life. But I am frightened they might have a dog.

They do not, at least not tonight. There are three of them, grown men with torches. Now and then they shine a light at me, but fail to see me through all the branches.

'Damn this dark,' one of them starts. 'It's impossible to find him.'

'If we found him,' another continues, 'we'd give him a thrashing.'

'I think I'd kill him,' says a third. Anja's father. 'No decent, honest person comes down here at night.'

'What about your daughter then, eh?'

'Anja? She lives in a world of her own. It's her music, you see. She's obsessed with it. It makes her rather strange.'

Eventually, they are gone. Leaving only the moon and the black silhouettes of the spruces, the whoosh of the river.

They may not have found me here, but they have done all they could to break me. They have tried to rob me of my hiding place. The alder thicket will never be the same for me again.

But the most important thing they said concerned Anja Skoog.

What is it with her and music?

I sit for hours, mulling this incident over. I think about her, the warmth of her skin, the weight of her body. All around it is cold. My limbs are soon stiff. I am oblivious of everything, until the sun touches the tops of the spruces on the other side. My God . . . is it morning already? I can barely get to my feet. It's time to go home and sleep.

Nausea

I MUST CHANGE my repertoire. If I had I been smarter at Schwartz's I could have had a medical certificate giving me a few extra days. I've heard that in some cases the jury can postpone auditions. That was what I'd hoped for, but that's no use now, and I can thank my unruly temper for that. I'll have to turn up with everybody else now, on this coming Thursday. The 'Revolutionary Étude' is out of the question now. I no longer have enough strength in my left hand. I'll have to find something poetic, something seductive, something I can master with musicality and refinement. But what? Debussy, without a doubt. My promise to Mother. I go through his entire piano repertoire, but fall upon the most clichéd, because it will impress the public, because I know I can interpret it to perfection. 'Clair de Lune' from the 'Suite Bergamasque', wrecked by so many, but with such a hypnotic, trembling tone. They have robbed me of my alder thicket. My pure, undefiled secret. So it seems even more meaningful now to play Debussy, even if 'Clair de Lune' holds no prestige amongst the intelligentsia. I'd have liked to try something from Ravel's 'Gaspard de la Nuit', but know I'm too young. My technique is good, but too unsure. And it never looks good when young players overstretch themselves to impress. I mustn't be like that. 'Clair de Lune' is a good, honest choice, circumstances being what they are. It may be a cliché, but it's a *refined* cliché. Besides, this modest little piece brims with sadness, and more than anything this autumn, aged sixteen and in my self-imposed purdah, I feel a deep sadness. Sadness at being on the outside; at being in love with a girl I barely know; at hiding in an alder thicket. I want to make 'Clair de Lune' translucent and modern. Give it a voice so special, so contemplative that comparisons with Lipatti will be in order: Dinu Lipatti, the man who died so young, who played so differently, so restrainedly, with a ghostliness, and utter control over each stroke. This is what I shall achieve.

And having thought the thought, everything seems immediately possible. I shall manage even the Bach, the obligatory C Major Prelude and Fugue from Book II of *The Well-Tempered Clavier*.

The qualifying round is to take place in the Lectors' House. Rebecca Frost rings me the day before to wish me luck. I picture her before me, sitting in her luxury villa, with the enormous Steinway grand, Model D, gazing out over the fjord. None of this is that important to her; she already has her millions. She may love music, but it will never be more than a hobby. Even though she does have the very best teacher, the mythical Selma Lynge, a woman who must be nearing fifty now, but who is still a rare beauty.

'What's your chosen piece?' asks Rebecca.

'Debussy, "Clair de Lune".'

I can hear the surprise in her voice. 'But isn't that too easy?'

'I've sprained my hand. I can't manage anything more demanding. What are you playing?'

'I'm playing Debussy, too. But the Toccata from "Pour le Piano".'

'Great,' I say. 'That'll be nice.'

'I'm not counting on winning. You should win this year, Aksel. Everybody thinks so. You're the favourite.'

'Thanks. But that doesn't exactly help with the nerves.'

'Oh, you're in control.'

Am I? Really? This conversation with Rebecca puts me into a strange mood. There are people out there expecting something of me. Not Father, not Catherine, but members of the musical community, that strange fraternity that consists of experts, grafters, snobs and enthusiasts. All those who gravitate to music for such a diversity of reasons. I'm aware of them, but too young to really know them. It was my mother who dragged me along to the young people's concerts at the Aula from such an early age. It was exciting at first, because Jon Medbøe, that truly remarkable man, would talk. This philosophy lecturer, who was said to have already tried his own coffin, and whose students loved him for his formidable powers of oratory, would give animated descriptions of the music we were about to hear, for us fidgety rascals. Thus far we were entertained. Thereafter it was intolerable. Being only twelve I sat for the most part and farted, understanding little or nothing of what I heard. But then I'd occasionally recognise something Mother had tuned into on the radio: Tchaikovsky's violin concerto perhaps, extraordinarily difficult and yet heart-rendingly melodious. This was how I grew up. I spent many a time during my childhood staring up into Munch's sun, at his powerful motifs 'History' and 'Alma Mata', at the naked figures by the waterfall. I listened to music I neither understood nor even liked. Whining violins, howling woodwind, bombastic percussion. And I also saw the people who wielded power in this little country's music community: the professors, the soloists, the critics, the teachers. Every week there is a subscribers' concert. Every Thursday these people are flung together to share the same music, to appreciate or revile it, as the international stars come to play for them: Isaac Stern, Wilhelm Kempff, Alfred Brendel, David Oistrakh. We are all so different, all of those who come to the Aula, and yet there is one thing that binds us: this so-called classical music. We are somewhat strange, almost like a little sect. We barely know the Beatles or the Rolling Stones. We are busy with something quite different.

Thursday comes. I wake up with a knot in my stomach. A nagging nausea. Even if I feel confident, a part of me is still insecure. What if I fail? A single wrong note, and I will ruin everything. Which is what makes 'Clair de Lune' so demanding. Because everybody knows the theme, and because when one plays something like that there is no room for mistakes. I sit all afternoon on my own, playing slowly through the short repertoire that has been set for tonight's elimination round. It will take place without an audience. The three elderly gentlemen of the jury will sit alone and listen to us one by one. These two retired piano teachers and NRK's Head of Music have decided for years who the musicians of the future will be. It is virtually unthinkable that a bright solo career could lie ahead of anybody who doesn't succeed in the Young Person's Piano Competition.

Catherine and Father both notice my nervousness at dinner. Catherine is in an unusually good mood, and asks if she should come and keep me company through the evening. I shake my head and explain that I prefer to be alone. She shrugs.

'You're so clever, Aksel, you never need help.'

I'm not sure if this is what I want to hear. I try to be witty: 'I don't think your help would be much use in the circumstances.'

Father laughs. Catherine laughs too. But the words are left hanging in the air. I rise from the table abruptly.

'It's time. I have to go.'

Melumveien on an autumn evening. I walk out of our gate. There is a fine drizzle. No snow as yet. I hear the sound of footsteps. I don't like to stare at people when I'm walking in the dark like this, but the person coming from behind is walking faster than me. The footsteps have almost caught up with me. I turn around, notice I'm afraid, yes, afraid of the dark, even though I've never feared the dark before.

It is Anja Skoog.

She nods, more fleetingly than usual. I nod back and look at my watch. Then realise why she's in a rush. The tram leaves in one minute, and there's a two minutes' walk to the station. She has overtaken me now by five metres and breaks into a run. I know I should run too. But how can I? She might start screaming again, and perhaps her nod was so fleeting because she's frightened, not of me exactly, but of a shadow that lurks among the alders at the bottom of the valley, whose identity she still doesn't know. How much easier everything might be if I'd run after her, yelling – Don't be scared! I'm the shadow from that night when you were afraid! But it's only me! Aksel Vinding! I'm not dangerous! I want to shout. But I can't, because she'll panic. She's fifty metres ahead of me. What can she be in such a rush for? But I am equally in a rush. The elimination rounds will start soon. Seven o'clock promptly. Nobody knows who will play first. I can't imagine why Anja Skoog is in such haste, but my need must be greater than hers. Am I really going to lose the competition, which I've already delayed by a year, just because some delicate fifteen-year-old public schoolgirl panics at the sound of a breaking twig? No way – I think to myself – I'm not that altruistic! The tram is there. Anja Skoog is halfway up the hill. I finally break into a run too. She hears my footsteps, turns apprehensively towards me, but doesn't scream. Thankfully she understands my reason for running. She has twenty metres left to the platform. The tram has already closed its doors and started to move, but Anja waves and yells out, a quite different Anja from the one I have built such a vivid picture of. Not a timorous, anaemic, polite girl, but strong and brave. 'Wait! Wait!' she yells, as though the tram driver could hear her fragile voice. He can't of course, but he sees her. I hear the brakes screech. Anja Skoog will be all right now, since half the tram is still in the platform. But what about me? I still have more than fifty metres to go. I am still far down the hill, and the tram driver can't possibly see me. But I go on running. As though a miracle might happen. And at the same time I can see myself from the outside: I'm one of those people who are hopelessly late, but who refuse to give up. One of those pathetic people who go on running for the tram, long after it's gone. I don't want to be like them. I don't want do anything as inadequate and laughable, especially with Anja Skoog watching me from inside the carriage. But the tram is still there; I only have twenty metres to go. It is waiting for me. Anja has placed herself in the doorway. She's told the conductor that another passenger is coming. I run so I can barely catch breath. Inside the windows the passengers stare out on to the platform, impatient, as I would have been. Then I fall. I put my hands out, but just as I do so, realise I mustn't. These hands are precious. In under an hour I will need them to play the piano. I twist my body awkwardly. My knee comes down first. I fall on to the wet asphalt, and realise I've grazed myself. But worst of all, Anja Skoog is there watching me. She can see I've fallen and that I've delayed the tram even more. In seconds I am stripped of all confidence. I rise to my knees, signalling to those on board that they should just drive on. But the tram doesn't shift. Anja Skoog is standing next to the conductor. Despite my needing another minute to regain my balance, and to run limping on, they wait for me. Anja Skoog has chosen to wait for me.

She stands at the door with the conductor and gives a little roll of the eyes and a shy smile, as the conductor waves me on.

'About time too,' he says. 'We're not always this generous, you know.'

Anja Skoog moves further down the carriage. I take that as a signal that she has helped me enough. That she doesn't want any further contact with me. She doesn't know that I've grazed myself, that my smart trousers have a hole and that one of my knees is bleeding. She has turned her back. I notice that she's smartly dressed. She has a long, crimson skirt peeping out from under her long sheepskin coat. There's always been something exclusive about her. Her hair's specially done up too, with clips and curls, as though she were going to a ball.

I don't know what to do with myself. I pay the conductor, and then move towards the back, avoiding Anja Skoog to signal to her that I've got the message.

Then the nerves begin.

It hits me; the thought of what I've embarked on, of everything I've invested, of the competition itself.

I have no other path open to me. Suddenly it all seems a madness – the fifteen months that have passed since Mother died. As though we were all mad, Father, Catherine and I; as if we'd lost the reins of our lives, as if she'd taken them with her into the waterfall. I miss her in that moment, in that half-empty tram, carrying its passengers from the suburbs into town, for their rendezvous, their evening shifts, concerts, plays and movies. The middle classes. To which Anja Skoog does not belong. She belongs to the upper classes, that much is clear from all her mannerisms. I sit on one of the old leather seats, and agonise over the demands of the evening ahead, the pathetic impression I'll make, the rip in my trousers, the wrist injury. It all borders on the ridiculous. And sympathy won't get me anywhere in this milieu.

The tram approaches Nationaltheatret. The final stop. Several passengers have got off at Majorstuen and Valkyrieplass. Anja Skoog has stayed on to the last stop. I sit behind her somewhere. A streetcar named desire; the words flash through my mind. My father had thought it an odd title. But Mother had been obsessed with the play. She'd taken Catherine and me to see it when I was only ten. Catherine sat stony-faced, but I wept, because Mother wept. There was something about the central character, about her sister, and their hopeless dependency on one another, the disastrous lies that had grown between them. And then this dreadful Polack, and his influence on these sisters' lives. A work accident. And suddenly it was too late. Mentally he succeeded in killing them both.

What brings this play to my mind now? Why do I remember crying? Anja Skoog gets up from her seat. We've arrived at the Nationaltheatret. I stay in my seat. Most of the passengers are already standing in the aisle. She casts a quick glance in my direction, too brief to reveal either sympathy or disdain.

My mind travels to 'Clair de Lune', and I think how she's a Debussy-type person: slightly transparent, although not so that one can see through her, since if one could see beneath the surface at all, it would be like looking into a mist, or into the silvery shimmer of the night, which only Debussy can describe.

We take the stairs up to street level. She walks twenty metres ahead. I wonder where she's going. She turns left, towards the Aula and the University. In the same direction as me. I enjoy following her. She has a soothing effect on my nerves. What difference does it make if I lose? Anja Skoog exists in the universe. Her presence has been like a miracle today; she's been my guardian angel, and yes, if I win the Young People's Piano Competition, which I surely *must*, I will send her some flowers.

I assume she'll turn into Karl Johan Street, but she takes another left towards the palace instead. In the same direction as me – up through the park. She must be visiting a friend in Homansbyen, to spend the evening drinking tea. She's probably one of the clever ones at school. It's not everybody who goes to public school. Perhaps she'll be a brain surgeon like her father.

We walk up the hill towards the Palace. An evening mist has settled over Oslo. I'm reminded of one of those opera movies Mother used to take me to, a Russian film, *Eugene Onegin* perhaps? Tall trees. Night. Fog. A sense of foreboding. A lover destined to die in a duel, like Pushkin, the author of this drama. But why do my thoughts go to death? I have a young girl walking through the Palace Gardens ahead of me. Reaching the guard's lodgings to the right of the Palace, she immediately takes a sharp right.

I feel my scalp creep. We are going in the same direction. We are contestants in the same competition.

That's where the Lectors' House is. Like a place of execution, standing before us.

The elimination round

COMPETITIONS ARE NOT for everybody. They are for the few, for the winners who can grab the medals and bask in the glitter of the photographers' flash bulbs. The others, the losers, the majority, will be forgotten, and will want to forget they ever took part. But they will not be able to lie themselves out of having taken part, out of the humiliation. They will have to live with it, like a scar, for the rest of their lives. Mother always said it was an absurdity to turn music into a competition. Yet I know she'd have wanted this: for me to cross Wergelandsveien tonight and, as it turns out, to realise that Anja Skoog and I are to be competitors in the same competition.

I have kept my distance all the way. I am still twenty metres behind her, when she pushes the heavy door of the Funkis-building open. Then she turns, as though she has known all along that I was behind her, as though she has known that we were going to the same place.

But this time she doesn't wait. She doesn't hold the door open. That would be too conspicuous. But she has seen me. Her look feels like a stamp. As though, from now on, the words Anja Skoog were written across my whole face.

She turns, walks into the light, and descends into the basement.

I follow slowly after.

The room is packed with smartly dressed little monsters and their parents. The kids competing in the youngest category wander aimlessly about, in their frilly dresses and patent leather shoes. Their parents are in even more of a panic than they are, since this is no mere student showcase. Meanwhile, those competing in the two older categories generally turn up for the preliminary round without their parents – there are limits, after all. But even in my age category, there are exceptions: Ferdinand Fjord's mother and father, for example, are both waiting out in the foyer. Not that the would-be-Wunderkind shows any sign of appreciating their presence. None the less, Ferdinand is in control, just as Rebecca Frost reassures me she is, as she puts her arms about my neck and whispers in my ear: 'This is just child's play for you. You'll go through, whatever happens.' Her words fail to cheer. My attention is taken up with Anja Skoog, who is still in the cloakroom, taking an eternity to remove her sheepskin coat.

'Aksel! What on earth do you look like?!' exclaims Rebecca, catching sight of my trousers.

'It was slippery,' I say. 'I fell on my way to the tram.'

'Slippery?' says Rebecca, her face like one big question mark. 'It's not even icy out!'

I don't want to pursue this dialogue. 'We'll just have to see,' I say, staring vacantly in the direction of the younger kids. Their performances are already over, and some have puked down their frocks. No, this is no ordinary pupils' showcase, I think to myself. This is a competition, and these nine-year-old kids are not prepared for what's coming. The sifting of the wheat from the chaff, the bright from the stupid. A little girl from Vikersund stands on the stairs, vomiting. I hear her mother's angry voice: 'Pull yourself together, Astrid! You came fourth at least!'

But there are no fourth places in this competition, I know that better than anybody. We reach the finals or nothing. Little Astrid from Vikersund is out of the running; she will go no further. So she sobs and vomits, alternately. The older ones among us turn away, uneasy. There is little we can do. We are about to enter the flames ourselves.

My nausea rises.

I go to the toilets.

I puke. In silence.

Only the stench gives me away.

But I flush as I leave.

Soon it hardly smells at all.

As I come out, Anja Skoog is standing there, combing her hair. She glimpses me in the mirror. Now we will have to talk.

'I didn't know you played the piano,' I say.

'That's not surprising,' she returns, continuing to comb her hair, as only girls know how. 'I've always kept myself to myself.'

'Hmm, that's pretty clear,' I say, trying not to open my mouth too wide, since it seems that the mouthwash I always carry in my pocket must have fallen out when I fell.

'But I knew all about you.' Her voice is mellower, warmer than I'd imagined. As though she could sing Brahms or Richard Strauss, like Kathleen Ferrier. I am utterly defenceless, bereft of critical faculties or sense; I worship that voice, as I worship her entire being, her neatly chiselled face, her slim waist, her proud manner. In my universe Anja Skoog has no competitors.

'How did you know about me?'

'Through my piano teacher, Selma Lynge.'

'Do you go to Selma Lynge?'

'It's been a secret until now. But not any more.'

'Why was it secret?'

'Because I wasn't too sure if this was what I wanted,'

'What, playing the piano?'

'Yes. Of course. One doesn't do this kind of thing if one isn't serious about it. Aren't you serious?'

'Sure.'

'And yet you almost managed to miss the tram.'

'I was going to thank you. You were very kind.'

'Oh, it was nothing. It would have looked pretty bad if I hadn't tried to rescue a fellow competitor.'

'So you knew I was getting on the tram?'

'Of course I knew.'

'And you knew we'd be competitors every time we passed in the street?'

'Yes. Fru Lynge had all the names. And of course I recognised yours. We do both live in Røa, after all.'

'And what else has Fru Lynge said about me?'

'That you're talented, but not as talented as you think.'

Anja Skoog laughs. So audacious. An insult. But I adore the way she laughs. I wish she'd never stop insulting me.

'Thanks,' I say.'

'Any time!' She smiles playfully.

'Aren't you nervous?' I say.

'Why should I be nervous? I know what I can do. And if I hadn't known, I would never have entered the competition.'

Then she turns. Walks on stage. I'd forgotten she was next.

I am left feeling dizzy and faintly unwell. Rebecca walks over to me, inquisitive:

'What are you doing there swaying?'

'I'm not really swaying, am I?'

'For a moment you looked like the Leaning Tower of Pisa. She has a real hold over you, that one.'

'Hmm? But I don't even know her!'

'Who is she?'

'I've no idea,' I say, 'although I've known about her for ages. She lives near me, in Elvefaret. She goes to some private school. She's the daughter of Skoog, Bror Skoog, the famous brain surgeon.'

'But who's her teacher?'

'Selma Lynge.'

'Selma Lynge? But that's impossible. I'd have known!'

'It's been a secret apparently.'

'Why should it be a secret?'

'Because Anja Skoog wanted it that way. She told me she didn't want to reveal what she was doing until she'd made up her mind.'

'Made up her mind about what?'

'About being a concert pianist of course.'

'Is she at that level already?'

'Apparently.'

'And yet none of us has ever heard her?'

'Nope. But we will soon enough.'

'I'll have to discuss this with Fru Lynge.'

Rebecca is livid. I can see why. Such secrecy is rare among music teachers. And Rebecca Frost has been going to Selma Lynge for years.

I suddenly feel foolish, without knowing quite why. It's more a feeling that there was something I'd missed. All our teachers are sitting in the auditorium now, ready to listen to us one by one. Selma Lynge is out there. And one of the Rieflings too. As well as Amalie Christie, Eline Nygaard, Karen Aars Bugge, Fru Alm, Fru Løken, Fru Stugu, Hanna-

Marie Weydahl, Maud Webster, Erling Wester, and the others. They're all sitting there in hushed silence, each nursing ambitions and hopes for their pupils. 'And there was I, not even knowing that Anja Skoog played the piano,' I mumble to myself. I notice an indignation in my voice. She could have told me.

We are not allowed to hear each other's performances. Not until the grand final are we allowed to judge each other's performances. And we are not under Munch's 'Sunrise' in the Aula yet. A battle of technique, of mind, of feelings lies ahead of us, before we come there.

Anja is the first in the older category to play for the jury.

'To think she takes classes with Fru Lynge!' says Rebecca Frost, still shaken.

'Shouldn't we have known a bit about her at least?' says Ferdinand Fjord tentatively. 'I don't remember ever seeing her before.'

'Nope, isn't it strange,' I say. 'Really weird. The rest of us have been turning up at concerts for years now. In the Aula, and everywhere else. But can anyone remember seeing her anywhere?'

'Not me,' says Rebecca Frost, emphatically.

'Nor me,' I say, a ghastly feeling stirring in me.

She emerges after a few minutes. Her face flushed, feverish, as though she has just done something sinful.

'Did it go all right?' asks Rebecca. She's always so curious; absolutely uninhibited.

Anja Skoog shrugs, a gesture that contrasts sharply with the expression of excitement on her face.

'Reasonably,' she says.

'Which means?'

'That I could have done better, if I'd bothered.'

'But you didn't bother?'

'Not at this stage. It's only the elimination round after all. It'll be different in the final.'

'So you're counting on getting to the final?'

'Of course I'll get into the final.'

'How can you be so sure?'

She shrugs again. 'Surely one knows these things? One doesn't invest that much of one's youth for nothing, does one?'

It sounds terrifying to me. What should I say to that?

I've invested every moment of my time for months. What if I don't make it? Will each one of those days stay with me like something abortive and purposeless? Or will I drag these miserable, meaningless days after me, like some enormous weight, for the rest of my life?

Suddenly I am overwhelmed by nervousness as never before. I begin to tremble and sweat all at once. I feel certain that everybody must be able to see it.

But nobody says anything. Only Rebecca stares. As though she understands. She seems rather sorry for me.

Suddenly I'm on.

I sit at the grand piano. I have lost all confidence. There's a dark wall to my side. The hall. In this hall, in this dark wall, sits an audience that terrifies me. The jury, with its three serious men, terrifies me. Synnestvedt, with his bad breath, terrifies me, as do the other piano teachers. But the one who terrifies me the most is Selma Lynge, the beautiful legend, who came originally from Germany, but who fell for the philosopher Torfinn Lynge when she made a concert tour of Scandinavia during the late fifties. Now they live together in an old house in Sandbunnveien, on the other side of the river. Yes, I think to myself suddenly, as I try to focus on Bach and Debussy, from their house, their grand Swiss villa, perhaps they can see down to the alder thicket and the pool where Mother was found. And while I've been sitting there on the slippery rocks at the bottom of the valley, listening to the rush of the river and the music in my head, Anja Skoog has, unbeknown to me, sat at Selma Lynge's piano, playing, learning, far more perhaps than I have learned, headstrong as I have always been. After all, it's a well-known fact that Selma Lynge is gifted. There are still stories about her last Aula concert in 1960, before she married Torfinn Lynge, before she abandoned her solo career, despite apparently being offered a contract with Deutsche Grammophon to play Brahms's Concertos with Rafael Kubelik and the Bayerische Rundfunk Orchestra. She was from Munich, she'd lived in Schwabing and had known great men like Paul Hindemith. She had played in the greatest concert halls all over the world, had been fêted by prime ministers and presidents. But she chose to give it all up to have children with the philosopher Torfinn Lynge, also a world name in his way, thanks to his ambitious work *On the*

Ridiculous. A work by a man capable only of sneering, according to rumour. At least, that was what Mother said, and it was Mother who was so obsessed with Selma Lynge. I'd asked her several times why I couldn't go to her for lessons, but she would get a distant look in her eyes, and say, 'She's too expensive.' But that wasn't the truth, I could tell. Mother admired Selma Lynge hugely, because she had heard her grand farewell concert in the Aula, and there had never been another concert to match it under Munch's 'Sun'. Selma Lynge's beauty and accomplishment had made her a legend, and Mother had a fear of such legends. Mother wanted, I concluded, to dominate me alone. She did not want any competition. And Selma Lynge was, without doubt, too powerful for her. And as I sit here before the piano in the Lectors' House, I sense that Fru Lynge might be too powerful for me too. I can't reconcile myself with what she told Anja Skoog: that I'm talented, but not as talented as I think. And 'Clair de Lune', of all things! The most clichéed of pieces! How can I possibly infuse it with talent, with freshness, originality and sensitivity, whilst maintaining any intellectual authority as a pianist? From where I sit, it feels impossible. In less than four minutes, all the effort of the last few months may turn out to have been in vain.

I'm off. The first D major thirds fill the hall. I have always battled with doubt, that profoundest doubt: am I good enough? Can I really succeed in this precocious undertaking, which it now appears I share with Anja Skoog: that of carving out a career as a concert pianist? How did things turn out this way? How did it become so important to me? I feel sure it had something to do with Mother, a hold she had, an influence over my life, of course, but beyond that it was as if she knew me better than I knew myself; as if she guided me, despite my having a will of my own. But Mother was always the one who could tell me if I played well or not, who could detect any affectation, and I needed her to tell me those things. Now I have nobody to ask. I sit here on the stage, in the middle of Debussy, overwhelmed by self-doubt. My teacher, Synnestvedt, sits out in the hall praying that I'll go through to the final, since if I do his professional reputation will soar. Of course I'll go through, I tell myself as I make sure my left-hand arpeggios are neither rushed nor shabby, a frequent fault in the performances of pianists far better than me.

I am, I think to myself, playing for three women: for Anja Skoog, who *cannot* hear me; for Mother, who *may* be able to hear me; and for Selma Lynge who most certainly *can* hear me.

My forehead is sweating. Droplets land on the white ivory.

When I am finished, I have a sinking feeling. Can this really go well? My interpretation has relied so heavily on pianists that have gone before. The moonlight I have offered the jury has less than an original glow. They clap limply. The chairman, the thin musical director, Lange, thanks me politely. Some of the other piano teachers also clap. I register Amelia Christie's and Eline Nygaard's more generous applause. And the sound of the heavy palms of my own, hopeless Synnestvedt.

But from Selma Lynge there is silence.

I go out into the foyer. Rebecca comes rushing towards me, as does the hopelessly gawky Margrethe Irene Floed, who wears a brace and insists that we all call her by both first names: Margrethe Irene. I often wonder how many friends she's likely to have in the future. But here they all are. Even Ferdinand comes over, despite the fact he's about to enter the flames himself. They want to be friendly. They want to ask how it went. But all I want is to find Anja.

'Where did she go?' I ask.

'Who? Anja Skoog?' teases Rebecca in a singsong voice. 'How obvious can a man make it that he's in love?'

'Spare me,' I say, grumpily. 'She said something interesting, that's all. Something I wanted to discuss with her.'

'Well, she left,' Margrethe Irene says.

'She left?' I stare disbelievingly at those awful front teeth. And when she doesn't answer, I try to coax more information from her: 'Margrethe Irene?'

'Yes. She left,' she repeats laconically, almost tetchily. I know how hard it is for girls of that age to accept that a boy is attracted to somebody else, no matter what a hopeless option the *boy* is.

'But what about the jury's decision? Didn't she want to wait for the decision? Whether she's made it to the final?'

'Nope, she didn't,' Rebecca interrupts, meaningfully. 'She was totally sure she'd go through.'

The finalists

So the finalists are selected, we have come through to the final; Rebecca, Ferdinand, even Margrethe Irene, besides a couple of other boring specimens, and myself.

And Anja Skoog.

She is already a legend. Selma Lynge is circulating among the other piano teachers, smiling and accepting their congratulations. Anja must have out-performed us all. I have a sinking feeling in the pit of my stomach.

We go back to Margrethe Irene's house. The Floed family own an enormous apartment near the Bislet Stadium. We drink hot chocolate and tea in the large living room, with the exclusive Bowers & Wilkins speakers, and the collection of Beethoven records that belongs to old Floed, chief engineer. Rebecca talks the most. She can't understand why Fru Lynge would keep it under wraps that Anja Skoog was such a talent. Why, she wonders, has Anja never appeared at Selma Lynge's showcases?

'I think it's got something to do with her father,' I say. 'The brain surgeon. He's not quite right.'

'How d'you mean?'

Margrethe Irene pouts. Her brace seems to disappear into the roof of her mouth. She suddenly looks like a corkscrew.

'He goes around with a torch at night, watching over his daughter.'

I could have bitten my tongue off. What am I saying? If Anja gets to know who was hiding in the alder thicket that night, I'm done for.

'A torch?' Rebecca's curiosity is aroused.

'It's only a rumour,' I mutter.

'Oh, but tell us more!' she insists.

'I don't really know anything,' I say. 'The Skoog family have always been stand-offish. But if this is the strategy, it's pretty shabby, isn't it?'

It's a sentiment that releases something in us all. Everybody nods. We've all been aware of each other for years. We've almost become friends. But we have no overview of Anja Skoog at all, and it's scary.

My admiration for Selma Lynge mutates into hostility.

'Who is Fru Lynge really,' I say, 'if she can be that manipulative? Can you ever trust her. *Do* you trust her, Rebecca?'

'Me?' Rebecca seems reluctant to answer.

'Well, yes, you're her pupil. She has as much obligation to take care of your career as Anja Skoog's.'

Rebecca reflects. She doesn't like my question.

'Of course I trust her.' She sighs. 'But she's kind of weird too. And her house is like a world in a world. She decides not only how you play the piano, but how you should talk and dress.'

'That says it all!'

'Hey, let's put a record on,' says Margrethe Irene, in a conciliatory tone. More than anybody, she likes things to be pleasant.

'Yes, let's!'

'It's not helpful to bad-mouth our teachers.'

I back down, with my hands in the air.

The Floed family's huge record collection lines the white shelves behind the loudspeakers.

'Let's all listen to the pieces we've just played,' Rebecca suggests.

'Oh no,' I moan.

'Yes, why not!' the others agree.

I stare at them all. There's a growing sense of solidarity among us, but right now I'd rather be with Anja Skoog.

We listen to the music. I am obliged to listen to José Iturbi's highly personal rendition of 'Clair de Lune'. 'You play better than him,' says Rebecca. 'Thanks,' I say with relief, waving my injured hand in the air. Later we each play our favourite pieces in turn.

We are sixteen years old. Music shapes our very thoughts. It speaks for us. We are the finalists. And it is still fun.

In the shadow of Anja Skoog

ANJA SKOOG. I know so little about who she is. We've never even been to the same school. The world seems unfair. How often does somebody have the person they've worshipped, mythologised from afar, suddenly step into their own arena to become their archest rival?

The problem is I'm not angry with her. I'm just filled with even more admiration.

Margrethe Irene is more persistent than usual, and wants to play records into the early hours. But we're all exhausted, and I need to catch the last tram home.

At home Catherine and Father are waiting up for me. I can see from Catherine's expression that it was Father's idea.

'You're back at last,' says Catherine. I notice she's completely out of it. I'm surprised that Father hasn't noticed too.

'How did it go?' he asks, slapping me on the back, in his clumsy way.

I notice his face is more drawn than usual. If my life is hard, then his life is harder. But true to form he's unlikely to tell me anything. Sometimes I've asked myself why I held him back that day. Why I didn't let him slip over the waterfall with Mother, doomed as they both were, in their relationship.

But right now, as he stands in front of me, I am happy he's alive. He cares. He means well. He wants what's best for me.

'It went fine,' I say. 'But it was pretty close.'

'Why was it close?' Catherine is sullen.

'Because a young she-devil from Elvefaret suddenly appeared, and out-played us all.'

'A young she-devil?' she says, suddenly showing interest.

'Yes, Anja Skoog. The daughter of the brain surgeon.'

Father nods. He knows her. Catherine's eyes grow wide.

'How could you call her a she-devil?'

'Why not?'

'But she's a jewel, Aksel.'

'And what would you know about her?' I ask, curious.

Catherine swiftly moderates her tone. 'Oh, nothing really. Besides, she's three years younger than me. But you can see, straight off, that she's one exceptional young lady.'

'You can say that again.' I say. 'And tonight she proved herself to be an exceptional musician too.'

'Did you hear her play?'

'No, but I saw her aura.'

'Her aura?' Catherine glowers at me sceptically.

'Yes, or whatever you call it. I know, without even hearing, that she out-played us all.'

I wake up very early the next morning but pretend to be asleep, since I can't face either Catherine or Father this morning. I'll wait for them to leave. I'm looking forward to being alone in this big house. I'm in a state of confusion. I dreamt of a path. I felt safe and sure of where I was going. I continued walking deeper into the forest. But then suddenly the path stopped and there were no more tracks. Nobody had ever walked further than this; neither human being nor animal. But I had to walk on. I pushed the first branches aside. This was no alder thicket. This time I was surrounded by a forest of bracken, dense and green. I couldn't see a metre ahead. Yet I wanted to walk on. I had to find my way out of the darkness; to find the world; to find the light. Somewhere, there was a living human being, with a beating heart and ungovernable will. And I had to find this person. Because it was me.

But isn't it the real me when I ring Anja Skoog later that afternoon? Perhaps not, since it's unusual for me to be *so* impulsive. What in the world do I want from her? Perhaps just to make the unsafe a little safer? Now, on the day after, as the snow suddenly starts falling, I realise that I am not only hopelessly and helplessly in love with her, but that I have to see her: just to stay in balance, just to be able to endure the hours at the piano that await me now, day after day, until the final in two weeks.

And suddenly I'm there, the receiver in my hand, because I am a man of action. I haven't, it occurs to me, actually *thought* much at all.

It's all intuition, feelings, moods. None the less, I feel so adult. Sixteen. Is it the music that makes me so adult? I picture us all on the previous evening: a bunch of deadly serious sixteen-year-olds who sit and listen to one of Beethoven's last piano sonatas. Perhaps we aren't so adult. Perhaps we're just weird.

In which case I like our weirdness. I call Anja Skoog. I'm looking forward to hearing her voice.

But it's not Anja Skoog who lifts the receiver, it's the Torchlight Man. 'Yes?' he barks.

'Good afternoon,' I say to the surgeon.

I could have bitten my tongue. I should have hung up. I get the feeling that I've made a fatal blunder.

'Who am I speaking to?' says the Torchlight Man, his voice nasal, yet sharp.

'This is Aksel Vinding, sir,' I say, feeling a little proud at my own formality. 'And who am I speaking to?'

In just one sentence he has made me angry; indeed, not just angry, but almost incensed. It's his inviting, and simultaneously sceptical, manner.

'Skoog,' says Bror Skoog. 'Wasn't it Skoog you were phoning?'

'Yes, absolutely,' I say, weighing every word, since I mustn't make things difficult in relationship to Anja. I fumble for the words but the Torchlight Man gets in before me.

'Was it Anja you wanted to talk to? She's not speaking to anybody before the competition.'

I can barely believe what I'm hearing.

'You know who I am?'

'Of course I know. You're one of the finalists.' He laughs. 'Lots of clever people among you youngsters these days. I'll be coming to listen to you.'

But I cling to my formality. It is my weapon.

'So you couldn't help me contact your daughter?' I say.

'No, that's out of the question,' answers the Torchlight Man. 'She needs all the concentration she can get.' He laughs briefly again. Then says: 'Perhaps we should consider this conversation at an end now?'

And without even waiting for any response, he hangs up.

I sit in shock by the telephone table in Melumveien. Who is this man? Who does he think he is? My cheeks are burning as though I've been slapped. I'm blushing, not so much from shame as fury. He has paralysed me. But am I really paralysed? Would *Mother* have been paralysed?

I have a little inheritance from Mother. A few kroner she wanted me to spend on my education.

I phone the florists.

'Yes?'

'I'd like some flowers for Anja Skoog,' I say.

'Right? A bookay?'

'No, a *bouquet* of red roses,' I say.

'Very well,' says the lady. 'And what size d'you want?'

'The biggest you do,' I say. 'Don't skimp on anything.'

'Oh, that's what they all say,' says the lady.

'But I mean it,' I say. 'Take twelve. That's a nice number, don't you think?'

She's not interested in entering into any deeper conversation with me.

'And what do you want on the card?' she asks.

'For Anja, with deepest respect and with thanks from Aksel in Melumveien.'

'Is that it?' The voice sounds sceptical. 'Aksel in Melumveien?'

'That'll have to do,' I say.

'Youngsters these days,' she mumbles.

What drives me? Years later I will wonder what it was that triggered this obsession in me, this preoccupation with Anja Skoog. Had I somehow always known she was my rival? It seemed beyond belief that she'd stayed outside our little community for so many years, and that she too had been sitting at her piano practising without any of us knowing. There were not many of us, after all. It seems almost eerie that I've known her for so long without knowing the most important thing of all: that she wants to be a fabulous pianist. But where has she taken her inspiration from? While the rest of us bought standing tickets for the Aula, and made a dash for any empty seats after the opening orchestral piece, as we sat staring at Munch's monumental paintings, listening to the finest soloists, Anja has been at home in Elvefaret or together with the mysterious Selma Lynge, preparing herself in her own way.

I have sent her flowers. I want to feel close, to gain some admittance into her life, no doubt further prompted by her father's outright rejection of me. This competition is no longer as simple or as fun as I'd thought. And I miss Mother's strength. She could have advised me now. Yes, even if she'd been drunk and weak, she would have been able to tell me what best to do.

I long to return to the alder thicket. It is a mild, foggy November, with scarcely any daylight. I have no idea how the others are coping in Melumveien, except that Father is hoping to sell a block of flats, and Catherine has taken a temporary job at the reception of the National Gallery. She has also taken up handball. This means she isn't at home any more in the evenings. Father and I sit together watching television, pretending everything is normal, when we're not playing Mother's records and listening our way through a Brahms symphony. But it's still too upsetting. We eventually try to avoid it.

Which is perhaps why my longing for the alder thicket strengthens. Mother is down there. Her soul floated among those trees and over the pool. I can't free myself from these thoughts. Am I going to let the Torchlight Man hinder me? Days pass. I hear nothing from Anja Skoog. Not that I've expected to. But surely the brain surgeon can't be crazy enough to wander about the valley during the day, hunting down some possible attacker, instead of operating on his patients?

I have to return. Perhaps I've inherited it from Mother, this tenacity.

I visit the alder thicket again. One afternoon a few days before the final. I'm still having trouble with my left hand. Chopin feels difficult. I'm still betting on Debussy's moonlight.

There's nobody down here. Apart from myself, a couple of magpies and a few blackbirds. And the crash of the waterfall. I sit here among the trees, hoping that Anja Skoog might step out from the mist. Why shouldn't she?

I wait. With the blind hope that only somebody in love can feel. I wonder if she's perhaps guessed that it was me here that night.

She does not appear. I sit here. I am cold. I have Bartók chiming in my head: 'Concerto for Orchestra'. Exuberant, humorous even, and yet simultaneously heartless. Mother had a feeling for Bartók. But what use is that to me now? I sit with these orchestral sounds filling my head, and have no use for them. Some hours later, I make my way dejectedly back up towards the villas. I have just turned into Melumveien when I bump into her. She is on her way home off the tram.

'Hi there,' I say, as casually as I can.

'Hi,' she answers, without the least sign of shyness at meeting me. I suddenly realise she hasn't received my flowers. I stand there somewhat perplexed. She must notice my unease.

'How's it going?' she asks.

'OK, I suppose. I'm having problems with my left hand. And you?'

'Oh, I'm looking forward to it. You don't play the piano if you don't think it's fun, do you?'

She says it so directly, so naively, so earnestly. I don't know where to fix my gaze. It's now or never.

'Did you get my flowers?' I ask.

'What flowers?'

She stares at me with an almost fearful expression. I notice how pale she is.

'I sent some roses. I wanted to thank you for what happened with the tram.'

She rolls her eyes. So sweetly. As if she's unaware that anybody else can see it.

'You mustn't worry your head about stuff like that,' she says, almost in a tone of rebuke. 'Naturally I had to help you.' Then she seems suddenly filled with uncertainty again. She must be thinking of the roses.

I say nothing.

We stand there staring at each other, both of us filled with indecision.

'Thank you very much for the roses,' she says eventually.

I know she's lying. She hasn't had them.

'It was nothing,' I say.

She strokes my cheek quickly. 'Things like that are really touching,' she says.

Then she turns and walks on.

I let her go. There is nothing more to say. I stare after her, as she heads towards Elvefaret. In her slightly washed-out yet elegant clothes. Her green duffel-coat, her brown corduroy trousers, her long, freshly washed hair. She makes beauty seem like a matter of course.

I wonder what happened to the flowers. Are they standing on the table? Has that crazy man thrown them in the rubbish? I begin thinking about Anja's mother. What do I know about her? Only that she is also a doctor, a gynaecologist in town somewhere, and that she looks like her daughter.

The nausea rises. It never fails. I walk calmly uphill towards Melumveien. Then I can hold it back no longer. I find a ditch close to the courtyard of the old cottages where the elderly ladies live.

It feels liberating, as though it's been too long since last time.

Finals fever

THE NOVEMBER FOG still hangs over the city. Father comes home increasingly late from the office, and Catherine is hardly to be seen, apart from late in the night when I go into the loo, and find her hunched over the toilet bowl. Then we blink at each other in the glare of the fluorescent light, disorientated, each with our own agenda, before making our way back to our rooms.

But I have set about my task almost fearlessly. Haven't I experienced enough tragedy in my short life? What more is there to fear?

My mother used to say; 'What is the absolutely worst thing that can happen? Keep that in mind, my boy, and you'll feel calm.'

But this has the opposite effect. I start to imagine the worst that can happen: that I shan't win. Everybody expects me to win. Added to which, the spectre of my dead mother hangs over me. It will be impossible to shoulder the burden of everybody's pity if I lose the title of Young Pianist of 1968.

I must defeat Anja Skoog.

I couldn't bear to lose.

I sit at the piano and practise like never before. I decide not to mull over the consequences too much. Deep inside I know that I have no choice. I must win this competition.

But I would have loved Mother to come back and talk to me from the dead. I would have loved her to sit with me, cross her legs, light the cigarette that had to be lit no matter the hour, and offer me some home truths about my choice of repertoire, and about my relationship, or non-relationship, with Anja Skoog. But Mother no longer speaks to me, she no longer comes in my dreams. She lies like a blanket of mist somewhere over the pool by the alder thicket. And nothing is more silent than mist.

The day arrives, a Sunday. I will suffer this many times throughout my life: the cramp in my belly, after a nervous sleep, which is no sleep at all, but a bath of sweat in which I encounter my worst fears. Am I a loser or a winner? It's that simple, that banal. What will the day bring? What will I be thinking tonight, in twelve hours, when all this is over? My uncertainty turns to undiluted panic. I pretend to be sleeping when Catherine and Father leave the house together for once, at about nine, despite it being Sunday. It is late for Father, and early for Catherine. But Catherine has a lot to do nowadays. The National Gallery awaits. As does the Njård Sports Hall for her handball practice. And the Yellow House, where her activities are still a mystery. Their leaving for town together underlines the fact that the day is special, which makes me even more nervous of course. Last night they both made extra effort. Catherine made hot chocolate and Father turned up with some special cookies; where he got hold of them was a mystery. Earlier I begged them to stay at home and not use the tickets that he'd already bought, but my pleas fell on deaf ears. They both seemed determined to come and hear me deliver my apprentice piece. 'I shall come and cheer you on,' Catherine promised. It's a remark the full implication of which I will not understand until later. Father went on in more sentimental vein. 'You know how much your mother would have wanted to sit in that hall,' he said. 'I shall be there in her place, my boy, although of course . . . well . . . I'd have wanted to be there anyway . . . and . . . well . . .' Father was tangled in one of his meaningless ramblings that had always caused Mother such infinite irritation: 'Hjalmar, why do you always have to dither!' 'I don't!' Father would protest. 'I didn't dither when I chose you!' But there was nobody to protest to now, and he was obliged to let his sentence fizzle into inanity. Cathrine and I listened politely to the mumbling silence that ensued.

But they are both intent on coming. I shall have my father and sister in the audience. They shall finally see for themselves how I have spent all my afternoons in our upstairs living room.

The final hours before I have to take the tram down into town are intolerable. I run through the compulsory études, the preludes and the fugues. I try a little of Beethoven's 'Waldstein Sonata', to take a rest from the evening's programme and to soothe my nerves in the seemingly open and optimistic key of C major, which, in truth, I find incomparably melancholic, thanks to Schubert. It's a clever tactic, but proves fruitless: a tingling sensation in my back warns me I am tired. It is time for a walk.

It is still mild. I walk along the river; a self-inflicted penance. I stare towards the dam, looking to find Mother's waving hand. How pathetic, I think, that we expect the dead to continue helping us in our lives. As if they wouldn't have enough in dealing with their own demise. Why call on them? The wall between life and death can never be torn down. And what do I want with Mother right now? Am I so incapable of standing on my own feet? Must I cry 'Mummy' at the first hurdle? When I have already enjoyed so much help, all the way, and from so many?

Then, as I walk through the grey November mists, I suddenly think about the tram. The finalists are all scheduled to arrive at the same time. Anja Skoog is bound to be on the same tram as me! Suddenly gripped with nerves, I reel to the side of the path. An old couple walking right behind me burst out in alarm, 'What's the matter with him?' I stand motionless in the ditch. The metaphor is clear: my life driven into a ditch. This very afternoon perhaps. What if I lose? I shall have nothing left to build on. I can't imagine taking on a multitude of different jobs like Mother, just to ensure a minimum income. I am far too like my father, I want something big; perhaps not to make Hamar town into a Chicago, but to accomplish something, to dare something, before I grow up. Although, in my own eyes, I already am grown-up – nearly seventeen. And my main problem is: which tram will Anja Skoog take to town? But then, as I ask myself this question, it dawns on me that Anja is unlikely to take the tram at all. She will almost certainly go by car. In the Torchlight Man's Volvo Amazon GT. I stare at my watch. It's already eleven. I'm running late.

A sensation

SHE SEEMS DISTANT as she sits there, her legs neatly drawn together and studying the score for Chopin's neck-breaking Étude in C Minor, which she will be performing for the jury in just a few minutes. It seems impossible that she has the fingers to attempt those incredible arpeggios, I think to myself; surely she's too young. There's something so fragile about her, despite her height. And surely girls like her never practise; they have far too many other things to do.

Anja Skoog in the Aula. She came by car, as I thought. Nobody dares to say a word to her. She's due to go on straight before me.

She is standing in my path, and I love her.

The toilets are engaged, and the huge urinal is out of the question. I rush out to the back of the university building and vomit in the hedge that runs along Christian IV Street. Rebecca has seen me. She's a spy and a gossip, yet she has the infuriating ability to seem irreproachable, and thereby cash in on any praise that's going.

She waits for me at the door as I come back in.

'With nerves like that you can just forget it!' she says.

'Forget what?' I ask, stuffing a liquorice pastille into my mouth to remove the smell.

'Winning, of course. You have come here to win, haven't you? Everybody thinks you're going to.' Rebecca touches my cheek lightly, by way of comfort.

She seems nonplussed at being unable to draw me into conversation. She loves going around and disturbing us all just as we're about to enter the flames. She approaches Anja Skoog, but Anja is deep in concentration and brushes her off, before climbing the steep steps up to the stage. There is a round of applause. It is for Ferdinand Fjord who studies with Riefling, and who has just finished playing Schumann. A quite unique talent. He descends the stairs, his face pale.

'Everything went wrong,' he says, to any one who wants to listen.

He cuts a comical figure in his oversized suit, playing air-piano and explaining how he lost his place three times. This must be a pianist's worst nightmare: losing one's place, not knowing where one is in the music, the mark of an amateur. This damned insistence on playing without the music. But my attention turns to Anja. I can't escape having to listen to her, since I am going on after her. I'd have preferred not to listen to the others, then I could be the best, at least in my own mind. I stand in the doorway, observing how calm Anja seems as she walks on to the stage. She even gives me a smile, a smile that's shy, yet sure of victory. My stomach turns, as though she were twisting it. I'm intent on hearing every note. Ferdinand and Rebecca also seem keen to know what she can do. Some of the girls from the youngest category gather round in their frilly dresses, and stand there with pompous little faces, listening through the door to this new apparition.

'She's going to win!' whispers one, making a face.

Anja is taking a fearless tempo. This is a marathon for both hands, with octave reaches the whole way. Parallel shifts across the entire keyboard. Her tone is portentous, as Chopin no doubt intended, with heavy bass notes moving into each new swathe of sound. I hated this piece, giving up on it before even trying. She's unbeatable, I think, swallowing frantically. She's even better than I thought. Has she really sat there in Elvefaret acquiring this technical prowess, these emotions, which belong to an adult, to somebody with experience? She's like a bird fluffing her feathers. She is larger than a moment ago. After days, weeks and months of toil, and with Selma Lynge's strong will for guidance, she is growing in stature before our very eyes. I listen, and the thought returns: she is in my path, and I love her.

Behind me, Rebecca snarls: 'Girls like that are shameless!'

'Shameless? What do you mean?' I ask puzzled.

She shrugs. 'Springing up like popcorn. Missing out on the long, tortuous path.'

I don't answer. Mediocrity, is that what Rebecca would prefer? The mediocrity that governs this world. All the hideous mothers, fathers and piano teachers who cheer it on? All the same, Rebecca Frost is among the best.

And in a way, I understand. Anja Skoog hasn't been on the scene before. And the rest of us? We know each other, our various ambitions and, not least, how much talent each has. Our artistic struggles have been there for all to hear, at pupil showcases, events and competitions. We've learned a mutual tolerance. We smile, we wish each other luck and dish out compliments we should be paid for. And then this beautiful, completely unknown, gangly girl, this hothouse plant from Elvefaret turns up, and plays Chopin with an authority and quality few have ever equalled, irrespective of age. Anja Skoog's technique is terrifying, there is nothing more to say. She's like a crazy alpine skier, yes, like Jean-Claude Killy himself, the triple gold medallist from Grenoble. She is utterly fearless, hurling herself into each fresh turn, without fear of what awaits. Down the slope at breathtaking speed, sometimes skirting the limits of her own balance. Everything goes so fast. Whoosh, and she's crossed the finishing line, without slip, without hesitation, to thunderous applause and cries of bravo. An ovation that seems to have no end.

I stand by the door, after pushing an elderly, black-suited gentleman aside. I've taken over as the door-opener. The energy in the Aula is stupendous. Who has the courage to demand the audience's attention now? But I have no choice.

It is my turn after Anja Skoog.

I hold the door open for her politely as she leaves the stage. She is quite a different person from the girl who walked out on to the stage a moment ago. Flushed cheeks, shining eyes, the scent of fever and calendula. I congratulate her, stammering and stuttering, but the most crushing thing is that she doesn't hear me. All Anja Skoog can hear are the shouts of bravo from the packed hall. She goes back on stage to take the applause a second time. Totally unheard of, I think to myself, but what is she meant to do when they go on clapping? I watch her from behind, she gives a deep, old-fashioned curtsey, she's clearly been to ballet classes. Then she gives a childish wave to somebody in the hall, probably the Torchlight Man and his family. And as if that were not enough, she sits back at the piano!

A gasp goes around the hall.

I exchange glances with Rebecca. Does she really intend to give an encore? This is unheard of, completely contrary to the regulations! We have been given our instructions long ago. We should be judged, like with like. Our obligatory and chosen pieces have all been carefully timed. Our obligatory pieces are already behind us. We played them for the semi-final. And now, in the final, we will play the pieces we have chosen for ourselves; this handful of bewildered teenagers, who barely know what they want in life, will step out on to the platform, and our sweaty little fingers will work furiously to satisfy the expectations of our parents.

Anja Skoog plays Grieg's 'Wedding Day at Troldhaugen', and the jury allow her to do it, the atmosphere in the hall demands it. Not the most difficult piece in the world, far from it, but the perfect showpiece nevertheless, because it sounds so impressive. She launches into the long crescendo, pushing the tempo to a maximum, before delivering the middle section, lyrical and mournful, so perfectly that Rebecca and I find ourselves exchanging glances again. Is it possible? Is she so audacious? Can she contain her feelings with such elegance, to heighten the contrasts? This is just how the rest of us, who are standing here listening, dream of playing. But can one really play like that at such a young age? Surely it's unnatural? We have been coming to the Aula for years already, we have listened to Rubenstein, Richter, Gilels, Ashkenazy. Oslo attracts pianists from the world over, but this time it's Anja Skoog's turn. It is as though a terrifying side to her personality has unveiled itself, something almost speculatively controlling. She plays Grieg so everybody is moved to tears and, when she's finished, the audience wants to tear the house down. The stamping of feet and cries of bravo, such as are reserved for the greatest. I stand swaying at the door, thinking again that an encore is counter to regulations. It is enough to disqualify her. But who'd dare to find fault with her now? Anja Skoog leaves the platform through the door that I hold open for her a second time. She giggles, fixing us with an uncertain gaze and mumbling, 'That wasn't quite according to regulations.'

I don't know what to say. I am the next one up on the platform. She seems to realise the situation. There is something almost sympathetic in her gaze.

'That was totally magnificent,' I say at last.

She squeezes my hot, sweaty hand.

'Goodness me,' she says, 'There's no reason to be that nervous. Relax. They're receptive. They'll like you. Can't you hear that fantastic atmosphere? Play them into a trance, Aksel.'

The master of ceremonies has already begun introducing me. I nod, confused yet thankful that she took my hand, that she said my name, that in the midst of her own ear-splitting triumph she observed my fear and tried to comfort me.

Clair de Lune

As I finally go on to the stage I feel how the excitement in the hall deflates. As though a magical trip in hot air balloon had been brought to a sudden end, because there was no more gas left to keep the balloon aloft. The Aula is transformed into a mournful field, where yard upon yard of silk spills out over the grass, where reality is fastened once more by ropes, and where everybody realises the adventure is over.

And now, there's another finalist at the piano.

It is me. Aksel Vinding.

Play them into a trance, Aksel.

I cling to these words. The words of the girl I love. The words she said almost in passing, but which will bind us from now on.

I note the reluctance of this huge beast, the audience. A sensational event has just taken place beneath Munch's grand 'Sun', his 'History' and 'Alma Mater'. The audience have had all they could want. And there is nothing more terrifying than a tired, sated audience. They want to go home now. Their stomachs are filled with gas, which they pass as soundlessly as possible. They have begun to think about what they might have for dinner. Some cough, without meaning harm. The majority are 'close family', an expression I associate with accidents, illness and death. But then, the Young People's Piano Competition is a matter of accidents, illness and death. And triumph. For the one person who will win.

I sit quietly at the grand piano, and think I can hear the sound of all those gases making their way through the audience's orifices. A woman belches in the second row. A man coughs in the fourth. Rotten bodies, I think, assembled in this hall, just because somebody has to win a competition. The odour of rancid vinegar, of spoiled wine. *Play them into a trance, Aksel.* This is my chance. With Debussy's moonlight. I have selected the only right piece to follow Anja's star turn. And I still haven't given up hope. Anja might be a virtuoso, but where was the soul in her performance? She has offered cascading notes, furious passages, sparkling technique. But I shall touch the audience with a gravelly melancholy, soothe their bloated bellies and fearful hearts with exquisite tones, with restraint and dignity. I take my place at the piano. My hands are trembling; this isn't going well. They need to be steady, these hands. 'Clair de Lune' is dangerously clichéd, shameless in its reliance on mood, technically undemanding, but completely transparent. I'm gambling on it, because I know I can create an unusual softness of touch – a trick I learned from Rubinstein. On the television he'd said how indispensable the damper pedal was to playing lyrically. Eliminating a number of strings, he gave the piano a transparent quality, reminiscent of Lipatti. I begin. Delicate thirds in D flat major. One of my favourite keys, filled with an inner tension that makes audiences prick up their ears. Debussy knew what he was doing. I feel my emotions come; that I am finely tuned and alert. I am, after all, playing to win. I mustn't forget that. Everybody in the group expects it. Anything else would be a disgrace. I've practised more hours a day than any sixteen-year-old I know. Music has become an obsession, something all-engulfing and, even as I am playing to win, I notice the sound's effect, how the harmonies and notes possess me, and with a new intensity brought about by my meeting with Anja Skoog. Can I impress her with Debussy? Is she standing behind the door to the stage, listening, as I listened to her? I doubt it. She's in her own world. She seems almost untouched by anything that happens.

I have begun. But my head is still crammed with distracting thoughts. For instance, that Father and Catherine are here in the hall, sitting in the fifth row. I'd caught a glimpse of them, like two shadows, as I took my bow. Their presence makes me uneasy.

But then the music grabs me. Finally I am in the flow. Just as Mother had wanted. As Synnestvedt wished for, so desperately, for his own reputation's sake, and of course because he's fond of me. For a few seconds I'm in control; my hands have stopped trembling, I manage to make the swelling arpeggios in the left hand neither fussy nor turgid. Behind Debussy's music lies a cool intellect, a composer who couldn't stand sentimentality. Mother always saw through sentimentality. 'Listen to him!' she'd yell sometimes, when there was a concert on the radio, 'Just listen to the way he plays to the gallery! Such pretentious pauses. Even he doesn't believe in his own silence!'

I have arrived at the most transparent section of all, the trance-like conclusion, in which the main theme returns but with a decisive seventh chord in place of the original. A compositional masterstroke, stolen cheekily from Edward Grieg – but then all composers stole from one another. I know that I've touched on something special, but success is still eluding me. I can feel it by the concentration in the hall, a silence that lacks, a space that refuses to open up, or a colour I can't see, when I close my eyes. Every musician's nightmare. My allotted minutes will soon be over, and my faith in Debussy's music is suddenly shaken, as is my faith in my interpretation of it. I play the seventh chord, allowing it to reverberate so that the music almost halts, since all music can tolerate being played slowly, but not all music tolerates being played fast: it's one of Synnestvedt's pedagogical pronouncements. And yet there's truth to it. Which was why I often chose to play slower than everybody else, like my hero Glenn Gould, who took Brahms's first piano concerto so slowly with the New York Philharmonic that Leonard Bernstein warned his audience in advance. Pure terror. A world-famous conductor stood on the podium and announced that the evening's soloist would make an interpretation the conductor himself couldn't stand by. Now I must stand by my interpretation of Debussy's 'Clair de Lune'. But that fabulous dominant seventh has made no effect. Until, that is, I almost allow the theme to dissolve – yes, I suddenly play so slowly that there's time for an after-dinner nap between each chord. Then it works. Something happens. The electricity I have been waiting for fills the room at last. I feel the three jury members like shadows to my right. At last the old fools will see who they're dealing with. If I can sustain this to the end, I will have gone deeper than Anja Skoog. And it will have been my own mastery that created this quality of tone. Success will be mine.

I am only a minute from my goal. I am concentrating on the final, restrained, heartfelt sigh from Debussy. This, I say to myself, is for Anja Skoog, whether she can hear me or not. But at that moment a noise comes from the hall. A loud, sharp noise. It startles me so that I nearly swerve and make a mistake. Did I hear correctly? For a moment I think my nerves have played a trick, but then I hear it again. There's somebody shouting. Somebody on the fifth row has risen to their feet. The sound of a woman's voice rings out, loud and shrill. 'Bravo!' Yes, 'Bravo!' she shouts. I sit there at the piano not knowing what to do. I want to look out into the hall, but if I do I'll break the spell I've created. And I'm not yet finished. I'm in the midst of the closing section. Somebody has broken the spell for me, ruined everything, and in the most insidious way possible, by shouting, by yelling, but at the wrong time. How cruel and mocking the sound of these misplaced 'bravos' is, compared to the ecstatic cries that showered Anja Skoog just minutes ago. And it strikes me that only a specially evil or disturbed person could do such a thing. I can hear the tension rising in the auditorium; people begin to laugh, others gasp in shock, or in fear-tinged excitement. Shouts of bravo in mid-performance? Nothing like this has ever happened before, not in this venue at least. The Aula is not known for scandal. More shrieks through the last thirds. A parting mockery. The moonlight has gone. My fingers tremble. I'm not prepared to stop now, having come so close to conquering them. Lobster-faced, I play on. The keys go into a mist. Only my motoric memory finds the right chords. The shouts persist. There is a loud scuffle below. Somebody has finally grabbed whoever is mocking me. She starts screaming. I bow my head, pretending to have noticed nothing. Tears fill my eyes. As the last D flat major chord rings out somebody is finally carried from the hall. I rise to my feet, unsteady, just in time to see that the person vanishing between the red curtains at the back of the hall is my own sister, Catherine Vinding. Father is left on the fifth row, staring beseechingly up at me.

The applause that breaks out is genuine enough, since I have succeeded in getting to the end. But there is no thrill at the top of the wave of sound. Only pity. Everybody wants the episode over with as quickly as possible. I give a quick bow and go to the door.

The choice

ANJA, REBECCA, Margrethe Irene and Ferdinand are all waiting for me inside the door. Their eyes are almost popping out of their heads.

'What happened, Aksel?'

'A crazy woman?'

'She deserves shooting! Skinning alive!'

'You just don't do that!'

'How cowardly!'

'But who was it?'

'It was Catherine,' I say. 'My sister.'

We are all in the artists' foyer. The conversation is animated. They mean well, everybody insists I should be allowed to play again, with Anja being the most vociferous, since she doesn't want any kind of doubt or speculation over her own victory. But I do not want to give her that pleasure. I know that I shall lose now, I shall lose whether I play 'Clair de Lune' twice or not.

'Wild horses wouldn't get me back on that stage again,' I say.

The chairman of the jury comes in.

'The jury have decided unanimously that you must be allowed to play again,' he says seriously. He stares solemnly and sympathetically into my eyes. Now all the world knows that madness runs in my family.

'I really can't,' I say. 'Besides, it was my own sister who sabotaged me. I shall have to take responsibility for the deranged actions of my own family.'

I think this sounds rather grand. I suddenly feel a kind of perverse control over events, a few minutes of influence. I have become the centre of attention, although only until Anja wins, which she will, in less than half an hour, since there are only a few more pieces to be played before the jury retire.

'For the last time,' the chairman of the jury says, 'you may play again.'

'No thanks,' I say quickly, before any headstrong impulse has the chance to scupper my plan. I don't want to be the man who lost the Young People's Piano Competition; I'd rather be the one who *might* have won, but whose hopes were dashed due to a family tragedy. That seems somehow fitting. Besides, everybody knows my mother drowned in the river.

'Think about it,' says Anja, almost pleading with me.

But I know her concern is not for me. She has an eye on her own indisputable victory. I feel wretched. What on earth possessed Catherine? Does she hate me that much?

'I've thought about it,' I say. 'It's a kind offer, but no. It really doesn't matter. I'd almost finished, anyway.'

The chairman of the jury nods, as though in agreement. I feel wounded. Was I still hoping for something unattainable? To win the competition despite everything?

Anja looks nervously at me. Her cheeks flushed. This is a matter of life and death for us both. And she's lovelier than ever.

Half an hour later Anja Skoog is announced winner of the Young People's Piano Competition, 1968. Rebecca Frost receives second prize. Third goes to Margrethe Irene Floed. A gasp goes around in the hall as her name is announced. The audience must have expected that I'd at least be guaranteed a prize. Out of sympathy, if nothing else.

For the first time in my life I find myself infected by bitterness. Destructive, and almost incurable; once bitterness has sunk its talons into you, it can never be banished. I don't want this feeling!

I know I haven't played as well as Anja Skoog. But I also know that I was better than both Rebecca and Margrethe Irene. Everybody in the hall knows it. Even they seem embarrassed, as they sit there with their diplomas. Two stiffly got-up girls, I think to myself, with Christmas presents they don't deserve.

Anja Skoog gets to give yet another encore. She surprises us all with Prokofiev. The demanding third movement of his Piano Sonata no. 7.

The sound of machine guns. Or festive fireworks. Octave stretches one can scarcely imagine a slender, almost frail, fifteen-year-old mastering.

'She surpasses Martha Argerich herself,' whispers Rebecca, her face pale.

I nod back in silence.

The applause is endless.

The party

WE ARE TO CELEBRATE at the Hotel Astoria. I would have preferred
to escape the formal festivities, but that would seem cowardly and petty,
and besides Anja will be there. The participants' parents are not invited
to the dinner, but I have watched Anja being congratulated by the
Torchlight Man and his wife. The brain surgeon Bror Skoog lifted up
his daughter as though she were a doll. There was a fearsome authority
in that masculine figure. I watched how, like a little girl, she grew soft
and passive in his arms. She smiled with abandon, and let him kiss her
on both cheeks, as though acting the child she no longer was. At
the same time I noticed Anja's mother. I knew now that her name was
Marianne, since I'd looked her up in the telephone directory. But I'd not
realised she was so young, as the mother of such a grown-up daughter,
nor that Anja was her spitting image.

Father comes over to me before I leave the Aula. The despair in his
face reminds me of Mother's funeral.

'She didn't mean it,' he stutters. 'You mustn't be angry with her.'

Not angry? Should I be pleased perhaps? I say nothing.

'She's having a hard time,' Father continues. 'And I'm frightened for
her.'

'So she's the one who deserves the attention tonight?'

Father stares sadly at me. 'Don't judge her too harshly, Aksel.
Perhaps she was drunk. She listened to you play and couldn't hold back
– she was so enthralled.'

'I'm sorry, Father. If she has that little control, she shouldn't be
allowed out.'

Hjalmar Vinding doesn't answer. He shrugs his shoulders and leaves
the hall, his back stooped.

And I stare after him, feeling angrier than I've ever felt before. But why do I want to subject him to my wrath? Because he was party to conceiving this monster? I want to rip her apart, to wound her.

Suddenly the Yellow House comes to mind.

Later. Dinner. Further humiliation. Sitting there with the nobodies who made up the jury, and who showed such utter lack of judgement that one might expect even the prize-winners to feel awkward.

We sit at the long table, eating lukewarm veal steaks, potatoes and peas. The adults, the jury members and competition organisers drink red wine. The young people drink alcohol-free champagne. The intermediate and youngest categories are represented here too. Their parents are waiting downstairs at the reception. Besides Anja, a nine-year-old and a twelve-year-old are competition winners today.

But tonight Anja Skoog is at the centre. Her victory is even more absolute than I imagined it could be, since I'm not even a prize-winner. Had they granted me second place, I might have created some uncertainty: shouldn't that poor Aksel Vinding have won perhaps? But as long as I'm only a finalist, with no other honour, the strength of her win is undeniable

'You should have won,' whispers Margrethe Irene, with the steel in her teeth glinting, a helpless look in her eyes.

I can't answer. I feel miserable. As self-absorbed and gloomy as can be. I stare across the table at Anja Skoog who sits in serious conversation with the chairman of the jury. Perhaps they are discussing the decision, the injustice they did me.

Suddenly, Rebecca's lips are at my ear. 'You're too young to sit here moping,' she whispers. 'Stupid things happen. Don't be stupid and let it upset you. Pull yourself together. Besides, you didn't play that well.'

Shock waves

REBECCA GETS ME THROUGH the evening. She ribs me, suddenly witty and cheerful. 'You'll have to watch yourself, Aksel,' she says a couple of hours later. 'You want to sit in judgement on all of us. But I won this second prize, and you always said yourself that you can't compete in music. Or was it your mother who said it? No matter. Somebody must have liked me. This is my evening, Aksel, more than it's yours. Have you even congratulated me on coming second?' she glares at me with her innocent ice-blue eyes and her tiny freckles. 'Behave like a man now.'

I listen and nod shamefully.

'Congratulations,' I mumble.

But inside I am in turmoil. Right opposite me sits Anja Skoog. Is it really possible to love someone who has beaten you, who has crushed you in the biggest contest of your young life? Yes, I think to myself. How can I not love her, as she sits with her cheeks flushed, sipping the wine one of the jury members offers her. I can hear them discuss Emile Gilels. Goodness, I think, where did she get her knowledge? This girl who has never shown her face before. The girl who captured Selma Lynge in complete secrecy.

Yet Selma Lynge was sending me strange looks earlier, as I stood talking with Father. As though she was trying to tell me something. She stood there in the auditorium, a dark-haired and slightly over-made-up beauty. But at this point in my life, I think almost every woman is beautiful. She was smiling triumphantly. It was *her* pupil who had taken the prize.

Synnestvedt was feeling less good. He could barely talk to me afterwards. His breath smelled like rusty, steamed-up steel.

'You didn't deserve that, my lad,' was all he said, shaking his head before taking his hat and heading for the door.

My eyes sting, and my heart aches. It occurs to me that Anja might take the tram home, sooner or later. Then I shall have her to myself. She has sent me the occasional quick glance tonight, but I notice I'm less interesting to her now, less dangerous, now that I've not even won a prize. She prefers instead to gossip with Rebecca and Margrethe Irene. The three of them are in the toilets constantly, sharing girlie secrets in front of the mirror. I sit alongside Ferdinand Fjord and drink lemonade. We talk about pianists we admire, about Arrau, Gilels and Barenboim. We talk about the teachers we'd like to study under in the future, the conservatories we will apply to. Tonight, the two of us are losers.

I keep an eye on Anja.

When will she leave? I want to have her to myself, for the whole long journey home. When she looks at her watch and gets up to go, I also take leave of this honourable company, making sure to shake hands with all the jury members. The eldest among these tired old men casts an inscrutable look at me and says: 'Your biggest problem is that you think you're so good, better than you actually are. But keep working, steadily and carefully, young man. Sooner or later you're bound to succeed.'

I stare at his nasal hairs, and nod. Some of them are grey. What could he possibly know of my future? I mumble some reply.

The party is breaking up. Anja is not the only person leaving. We spill out on to the pavement, Anja first, the rest of us following. It's snowing – huge, wet snowflakes. As though we were all walking inside a child's snow globe.

Then I spot the Torchlight Man. He is waiting for his daughter. The Volvo Amazon stands there, its engine running and an open door. His wife, the gynaecologist, is standing beside him. They are both completely absorbed in Anja. I catch snippets of their conversation: *Has she enjoyed herself? Where is her diploma?* I feel dejected. They'll drive her home, of course. But then I notice there's space in the car.

'Excuse me, but could I have a lift?' I say.

Bror Skoog surveys me from behind small spectacles. He has stared at me before, through the dark, but without seeing me. Now, it's as if he recognises me: the local boy, the one whose mother went in the waterfall. And now there's a crazy sister too. People are bound to have been talking as we sat eating our veal steaks. I shudder, recognising some of Anja's features in his face. I don't like it. The intense eyes scrutinise me.

'Do you live locally?' he asks, sceptically, as though he'd like to shield himself from an affirmative answer.

'Yes,' I say, 'In Melumveien.'

'What a shame,' he answers, glancing swiftly at his wife and daughter, 'that we haven't any space.'

But there is space. Two whole seats. I say nothing. I nod politely and make my way to the tram.

Home again

FATHER IS WAITING UP FOR ME. The house stands in silence. I know that Catherine's in, but that she's gone to bed. Father sits with some wine, staring at the wall. He has some property details lying open on the table in front of him. He is hoping to convert some flats in Gamlebyen into offices.

'Where is she?' I say.

'She's sleeping off the effects,' he answers.

'The effects of what?' I glower at him. At that cowardly, despairing face. Have I ever really respected this man? He's always so slow, turning up after the event. If he'd been quicker on the draw that Sunday, Mother would still have been alive.

He squirms. He talks in a whisper, not wanting to wake Catherine.

'She's not herself, Aksel. She's on something.'

'Yeah, right. And you've only just discovered that?'

'I didn't know it was that serious.'

'And what did you do after?'

'I brought her home. She wanted to go straight to bed.'

'Do you think she can get off that easily? Do you realise how much she's wrecked for me?'

'Yes, of course I do. And she knows it too. Don't judge her too harshly.'

But I can't stand more of this bullshit. I go into her room. She thinks she's so much stronger than me. Her room is always out of bounds. Even when I'm alone in the house, I don't dare to go in. Besides, she has locks on all her cupboards and drawers.

She is lying in bed, awake. She's been expecting me. As she sits up, with large, dark eyes, I notice her nightdress. It's her old one, with Snow White, the one she wore when Mother was alive. I perch on the edge of her bed, noticing the smell of alcohol. And something else.

'Why did you do it?'

She stares at me, imploring, saying nothing. I do not intend to push her. It can wait.

'I just wanted to cheer you on, Aksel.'

She slumps back on the bed, drunker than I thought.

'Cheer me on?'

'Yes, like in handball. When somebody scores. You know. When people cheer.'

'My God. This was a concert! You know what concerts are about, don't you?'

She starts to cry.

'I was so proud of you,' she says. 'You played so, so beautifully. I was touched. Overwhelmed. Besides, Anja Skoog had everybody cheering for her. I wanted the same for you. You're just as good as her.'

'But she won, Catherine! I didn't even get a bloody prize!'

I'm almost on the point of tears myself now.

'I didn't mean any harm,' she whimpers.

'No, you just didn't think.'

'How can I make things better?'

'You can't.'

I leave the room, shut the door. She cries like a child.

Father is sitting on the sofa. 'You can't leave her like that.'

'It'll pass,' I say, completely drained, so tired my whole body aches. 'Everything passes.'

The Yellow House

BUT IT DIDN'T PASS.

I'd lost the 1968 Young People's Piano Competition. Admittedly, I was a finalist, but then who wasn't? Some lightweight from Veitvedt, who was only ever destined to study medicine, and a gormless girl from Asker who wanted to be an architect. What did losing mean to them? Nothing at all. But for Ferdinand and I, it mattered. There they'd sat, three girls on the podium, with prizes and diplomas, while Ferdinand and I sat there with nothing but diplomas. Those of us who actually *had* to be musicians had lost.

Catherine stands before me in the kitchen, her face swollen.

'Can't we talk about it?' she says.

'There's nothing more to say,' I answer.

Does she want to have her cake and eat it? This all reminds me of Mother, somehow. Her craving for attention. Come what may, she's always at the centre of things.

'You're not that interesting,' I add. And then in an attempt to be crushing: 'What happened really wasn't very interesting. You just told the entire world that you're completely out of your mind. Well done!'

She starts to cry again.

But it doesn't last. She's off to work. She fixes me with an icy stare.

'We'll never mention this again, then,' she says.

Who is she to decide that, I wonder. Is it her place to determine when a conflict is over? I want her to know how much damage she has caused.

But when Father and she are both gone, and the house is empty, when I'm left alone with my thoughts, my mind drifts to Anja Skoog. She would have won anyway.

And if I'd been given the second prize, instead of Rebecca? Would that really have been better? Second place in the Young People's Piano

Competition 1968? Would the conservatory have flung its doors open to me? Would those famous teachers, Dr Leygraf in Germany, Dr Seidl-hofer in Austria, Mme Lefebure in France, Ilona Kabos in London, Rudolf Serkin in Philadelphia, have bowed before me?

Unlikely, I think to myself. Hardly. Perhaps I am just as well off with my diploma. A finalist. An unremarkable start to a career. Better than a humiliating second place. He who laughs last, laughs best.

Yes, he who laughs last, laughs best, I think to myself that afternoon as I board the tram from Røa to Sørbyhaugen, and change platforms for the Kolsåsbanen tram out to Bekkestua.

Catherine isn't here today. She is at the National Gallery. That much I know.

But here it is again. The Yellow House. In Bjerkelundsveien. Just as before.

Why am I *here*? What kind of crime scene is it that draws me back, what is the object of my vengeance? One thing is for certain, my venom is directed at this house, the Yellow House, to which Catherine has been such a frequent visitor in these past few months. What kind of life does she have inside these four walls? What is it that brings her here? That causes her to be so unpredictable?

A thought nags at me that I barely dare formulate: that there's another person inside, that I can wound one and destroy a second. A November afternoon; the smell of cabbage and coal, birch wood and bacon. A Monday afternoon. It is Advent soon. The first candles have been placed in windows. I am walking on snow; more than a metre must have fallen in the night. Shovelled snow lies in piles everywhere.

The snow has been cleared in front of the Yellow House; a neat path up to the front door, and a wider one to the garage. A wheat sheaf hangs in the apple tree near the kitchen window that stands open. Smoke from frying. The smell of meatballs.

My heart pounds faster. I have no plan, no idea what I want. Or perhaps I do, clearer than I think. I stop at the gate, watching the silhou-ette of a woman through the kitchen window. There's no turning back now – she's spotted me. I can't run away. She'd think I was a thief.

I open the gate and walk in, feel the snow creak, realise suddenly how cold it is, that I am frozen, that I am trembling. I should have worn another scarf.

But I don't hesitate. I ring at the door.

Seconds pass. A woman opens the door.

I can see she's in her fifties. Beautiful. Like Marianne Skoog. As though her face still remembers its youth and refuses to let it go. She must have been every boy's dream. Now she stands, staring inquisitively at me.

'Yes?'

'I want to speak to Catherine Vinding, please.'

'Vinding? Catherine? There's nobody by that name living in this house.'

'Oh, really?' I take a chance. 'But she comes here to visit. Daily. Almost every morning. I've seen her here myself.'

The woman falls silent. Anxiety clouds her pale face. Her lip trembles. I almost feel regret. She stares at me.

'Vinding? Catherine?' she repeats, as though to acquaint herself with the name, as though she already knows it is a name she will never forget. 'She doesn't live here. What do you want with her?'

'I'd hoped to get some help. There was something important I wanted to ask her.'

A man comes up behind the woman I am talking to. She turns to him, angry and frightened, almost imploring.

'This young man is asking for a Catherine Vinding?'

The man emerges from the shadows of the hallway. The outdoor lamp's pallid light hits his face mercilessly. Each detail is illuminated: a man of the world, drunk with sleep, somehow nervous, off guard.

'Vinding?' he says, abruptly.

'Catherine,' I say. I notice that this female name hangs on the air between us.

He hesitates. So, I think to myself, he knows who she is. From here on, each word will be fateful. I study him closely. The beginnings of a paunch, contrasting with his thin, sinewy legs. Despite his smoking a cigarette, it is clear that he is determined to fight his age.

'What do you want with her?' he says finally.

Smart, I think to myself. But not that smart.

'Well, she's been going in and out of this house for months. So I thought I might find her here. I had something important to ask her.'

I notice, to my satisfaction, that the woman is looking at the man in horror and disbelief, as though he were turning into a stranger before her eyes.

'Who are you?' asks the man, more brusquely now.

'And who are you?' I ask in return. 'Since you take up so much of my sister's time?'

His eyes widen. 'Are you her brother?'

I nod. He looks at his wife in bewilderment. Searches for the words to rescue the situation, but there are none.

'Well, you know where she lives. You can speak to her there.'

'I need to speak to her now. As I said, it's important.'

The silence is far too long. None of us can take another second.

'Well, say something!' the woman screams at him, panic in her eyes.

His gaze seems suddenly veiled. Nobody can reach him now. Although he can still talk.

'She's no longer my pupil.'

'Your pupil?'

'Yes. In Art History.'

'Art History?' I say, taking a longer dramatic pause than necessary.

'Yes?' he says, questioningly.

'But she hasn't even got her Artium!'

He looks at me in confusion. Then at his wife. This is all so dreadful, I think. How could I do such an abominable thing?

There's an impotence in his face. A realisation that there's something on the horizon significantly more dangerous than me.

'Well, she's not here,' he says calmly.

'No, she isn't here,' the woman repeats, dully, as though she doesn't know what she is saying herself.

'It's time you went now,' says the man.

He slams the door.

I remain standing there outside. As though I don't want to leave.

There is a heartrending scream.

I turn and walk back to the tram station.

My mission is accomplished.

Part 2

The road to Brunkollen

I AM TAKING A WALK with Anja Skoog. It is summer, early June. I am seventeen years old. Anja has turned sixteen. The other residents of this well-to-do neighbourhood will soon leave for their holiday cabins in Fetsund, Hallangspollen, Randsfjorden, Bamble, Onsøy. Summer cabins that are even more unassuming than the houses they live in, and much less comfortable, and without running water. But that is the way we like it here in Norway.

'We've got a cabin in Skjebergkilen,' says Anja, smiling.

'And – why are you smiling?'

'Because we never use it. Mummy loathes it. The brackish water, and muddy shoreline. But Daddy goes occasionally, in the autumn, to think and look at the stars.'

So, Anja calls her parents Mummy and Daddy. Not Mother and Father. I watch her, listen to the minutiae of her life. It must be very different to have a mummy and daddy, instead of a mother and father. I am trying to work her out. I still know so little, which is what's so strange – that after my painful defeat in the piano competition, absolutely nothing changed. Everything continued as before: the same empty days. The music I sought refuge in. The alder thicket I sat in. Catherine's sour looks. Too much had happened, and we could talk about none of it.

But then one day I met Anja on the street. The lilacs were already flowering. She seemed happy and purposeful, as she stood there in her white blouse and jeans and inhaled the summer in deep breaths.

'We've got a fair bit to talk about, haven't we?' I said. 'Couldn't we take a walk together to Brunkollen, for example?'

My heart leaped when she agreed. 'Tomorrow, Sunday?'

'Yes, why not? I can bring some wine.'

'I don't like wine.'

'I'll bring a bottle anyway.'

Which is why I'm here now, walking alongside Anja Skoog. Because she said yes. Because her parents are away and won't be back until late. We walk past the dam and up towards the slopes of Fossum. It's a hot day. Small, white clouds in a blue sky. She has a jumper tied around her waist, and she wears a washed-out pink t-shirt and the same jeans she was wearing when I dared to invite her out.

Each detail she shares with me is like a gift. I worship her to such an extent that I sometimes forget she can talk. It seems her parents have been in Poland all week. Either she's not entirely sure herself, or she doesn't want to tell me. Eventually I manage to coax it from her that they've been attending a conference in Warsaw. I picture brain surgeons from all over the world, drinking and raising their glasses to each other and their wives. But is Bror Skoog ever capable of being sociable? Of clinking glasses and laughing? I can't imagine it. She says Mummy and Daddy. There is a colossal gap between Mother and Mummy, I think to myself. And Father and Daddy. She is closer to her parents than I am to mine. It's too late for me to call my mother Mummy. Not to mention Father.

I walk at her side, wondering if I might dare to touch her, to brush her arm, to hold her hand. It would be nice to walk to Brunkollen hand in hand with a girl. I have never done that before.

But I don't dare.

We have been walking for some time when we finally start on the slopes from Østern Lake. I can see she is soaked with sweat. Her breasts are very prominent, her nipples small and hard, but my passing glance seems not to trouble her. She walks with a lightness that surprises me. I'd assumed she spent most of her time at the piano.

'Crumbs,' I say. 'Do you do a lot of sports?'

She stares at me, uncomprehending. 'What do you mean?'

'You move like a runner, or a gymnast.'

She laughs, visibly pleased that I've noticed.

'In that case, I must have got it from Daddy,' she says. 'He's an old sprinter. He won bronze in the National Championships, hundred metres.'

It's clear from the way she talks about him that she's proud of her father. She tells me that she trains at the sports ground near the cinema sometimes, early in the morning, when nobody's around to see, when only she and the birds are up. My heart beats faster. Could I dare to be there, then? To lie hidden at the edge of the forest, observing her, fixing her every movement on to my retina? I wonder what kind of tracksuit she wears. An old-fashioned one, or the type that's more revealing? And where is the Torchlight Man then? Is he asleep? Or is he the one that trains her, passing on his technique?

'And do you do any sports?' she asks suddenly, as though trying to shift the focus from herself. 'Do you get out into the forest much?'

'Pianists aren't into forest walks . . .' I say, stuttering.

I want to tell Anja about the alder thicket, this place which is so important to me, and which she inhabits, unbeknown to herself. But I don't dare. I am too shy. I have an uncomfortable feeling, from all she's said, that she is very close to this daddy of hers. He must never find out who frightened her that night.

Occasionally we fall silent as we walk. Yet we seem to be trying to tell each other about our lives. She asks me about Catherine. She tells me she knows about Catherine, because she went to handball for a while, before realising how risky it was for her hands and fingers. She thinks for a while, then tells me she likes Catherine, but that she can't understand what got into her when I was playing in the Aula.

I try to seem upbeat and indifferent. 'All the bravos and hurrahs you got were echoing around in her head, I think.'

Anja laughs. Her laughter is carefree and studied, as though she's learned it somewhere. 'But even then!' she says. She rolls her eyes again. It suddenly strikes me that she does this a bit too often; it seems nervous.

I don't know what else to say. I don't want to discuss it any more.

Anja is suddenly serious. 'Do you think Catherine tried to ruin things for you on purpose?'

I turn it over in my mind; it all seems so distant suddenly.

'I don't know,' I say finally. 'Even though we're brother and sister I don't know her that well. And things have always been awkward between Catherine and me.'

I want to change the subject. She yields. We talk on, since we must talk about something as we walk here side by side. I tell her about the

Sunday Mother died, because I can see she's curious about what happened. I explain how incomprehensible it is that Mother, a grown woman, couldn't get herself back to the shore. Anja listens attentively and stares at the ground. I say nothing about how drunk Mother was, but I describe how strong the current was that day, and how I held Father back, to Catherine's despair. I notice Anja become suddenly guarded. Who is this person, telling this dramatic tale? Perhaps I've been too frank? Perhaps I've made myself look too responsible for Mother's death? I regret what I've told her now.

But then my story peters out. I don't want her to know how I began bunking school, without telling Father. She is still at school preparing for her Artium. She thinks I left school with Father's approval, and finds it strange: 'There's so much for us to learn still,' she says. And as she says it, everything seems suddenly so unattainable: my mission, my desiree to be a concert pianist. I'll need money from now on; the money Mother left me is almost spent, and I don't want to go on living at home like Catherine. I must find something for myself, rather than scrounging off Father. Perhaps I'll work in a music or record shop. Where am I going to live? Where can I practise the piano? All these practical problems seem suddenly insurmountable. I am walking beside Anja, who seems to have done everything right in her life so far, and who hasn't burned any bridges, and who has also come a good deal further in her artistic career. No, I don't want to tell her any more about myself. I want to hear her story, her secrets.

We have come some way up the hill. We can see out towards Holmenkollen now and further in towards town. A feeling of being watched makes me turn my face to the sky. I shudder. There it is again, just as it was two years ago.

The hawk.

Anja follows my gaze. 'Look,' she bursts out excitedly. 'A hawk!'

I am glad I haven't mentioned it. A feeling of gloom descends on me. A taste of blood in my mouth. The hawk hovers steadily in the air, a hundred metres above us.

'It's lucky we're humans and not chickens or cats or mice,' says Anja.

I nod, but can say nothing. 'Are you ill?' she asks alarmed.

'No,' I say, realising we have come to a halt. I start walking again. 'Can't you tell me more about yourself?'

I want her to tell me everything: about her life as an only child in Elvefaret, about how she started playing the piano. I want to know why she goes to a private school.

Then she talks about her daddy, although it was her mummy's idea, she tells me, for them to buy her a piano. She tells me she liked sports, acrobatics and running, and that she was quite good at hockey. She talks simply and directly, but falters and hesitates now and then, as if she doesn't quite trust me. I learn that the Torchlight Man is also a hi-fi man. Anja knows all the proper terminology. She describes the huge Tannoy loudspeakers in their living room. The fabulous AR loudspeakers that came later. She tells me about the famous electrostat loudspeakers from Quad, the ones that are in the basement. Not to mention the valve amplifiers from McIntosh that still stand on the window ledge. I picture them, standing there, like neon-lit skyscrapers in a great American city at night. I remember Ferdinand's family have something similar. Anja is walking at my side. Her thoughts have transported her to the rooms of her house. She must love her home, I think. She talks about the Garrard record player with the SME tone arm and the priceless Shure diamond-headed pickups. She tells me they were specially built by a Japanese doctor-colleague who made pick-ups as a hobby, who sold them to brain surgeons all over the world for thousands of kroner apiece.

'And so that's how music came into your house?'

She nods. I can see him before me, the Torchlight Man, prowling about in his living room, improving his sound system, testing out new amplifiers or speakers, searching for perfection. She tells me about the music he played for her as a child. Tchaikovsky's symphonies. The last three. Over and over. Particularly the scherzo movement of the 'Pathétique'. But it feels to me as though there's something else she's trying to tell me. Not only that she grew up with lots of drama and emotions.

'Doesn't your mother ever play music?'

'Of course. She plays *music*, and she gives a damn about the sound, if you know what I mean? The Schubert Romances with Fischer-Dieskau and chamber music. All of Beethoven, Schubert, Schumann and

Brahms. And some jazz and rock, but Daddy doesn't understand any of that.'

I walk at Anja Skoog's side, listening to her story. The hawk above us has vanished. We walk peacefully between tall spruces. The occasional runner or cyclist hurries past. But we have all the time in the world.

'Why didn't we ever see you at concerts?'

'There's a perfectly natural explanation. Daddy wasn't interested in concerts, so long as we could have a concert hall right in our living room.'

She explains that they didn't dare to let her go into town alone. Her father was terrified that something might happen to her. Added to which they often worked overtime.

'But even then!' I say.

Anja Skoog looks at me, thinks it over, shakes her head. 'You know, I didn't miss the rest of you. We had everything at home in Elvefaret. Daddy built an entire world for me. My concert hall was there all the time. Why would I need Munch's "Sun"? That painting's far too concrete for me. Why should I have to concern myself with Kragerø's skerries, when I listen to Honegger? I'd rather stare into the old tube amplifiers and their mysterious light.'

I laugh. It surprises me that she's so articulate, so sure of her words. I try to brush her arm with my own, but it's as though she was fore-warned and moves away. I pretend not to have noticed.

'Remember Mummy and Daddy wanted what was best for me,' she says thoughtfully, in her slightly self-important way, as though she was linguistically stuck in the fifties. 'Being an only child can feel lonely, but I was never lonely, because they opened a world for me.'

The Torchlight Man had wanted her to go to private school because he wanted to give her the very best of culture and education. Anja describes the concert evenings at home in Elvefaret. 'Every Thursday, it was Daddy, Mummy and me. Daddy would often dig out the same repertoire as the Philharmonic were playing that evening. Then he'd say with a triumphant grin: 'Would you prefer the Berlin Philharmonic with Karajan or the Philharmonic Company Orchestra with that vegetarian Swede? He meant Herbert Blomstedt. He never knew how good Blom-stedt was. But I never said anything. Daddy had a network of colleagues who tipped him off about the newest and best recordings. But it was

Kjell Hillveg, that amazing chap down at Karl Johan, that he listened to most.'

'In the Norsk Musikforlag, you mean? Yes, he's indispensable to us all!'

'Yes,' continues Anja, spurred by my enthusiasm. 'Isn't it amazing how one man can have such influence on an entire milieu? A record store in a little city, in a little country. Daddy's been to New York and London, and never found anything better. I wouldn't have found out about Martha Argerich if it hadn't been for him . . .'

'And now you play almost as well as she does,' I say, flattering her shamelessly, and simultaneously cursing myself, since I should have said that Anja played better than her. But Anja seems unaffected.

'Anyway, Hillveg recommended all these records to Daddy. I was the first to hear everything new, the first to get to know Jacqueline du Pré . . . My God, have you heard that woman?'

It's the first time Anja Skoog has interrupted herself: this girl who is always so composed is suddenly showing her feelings. Her face is flushed, just as when I stood at the door to the Aula stage and she was carried on a wave of cheers.

'No,' I say.

'Then I shall introduce you to her! Daddy's tube amplifiers will take care of that.'

'But who is she?'

'Barenboim's wife. Don't you know?'

'Oh,' I say, 'The *cellist*?' I think of the photographs I've seen of that intense young woman who apparently gives her all on stage.

'Yes,' says Anja decisively.

'There's something about women and cellos,' I say. 'Like women and horses.'

'Perhaps we shouldn't talk about that right now,' Anja retorts.

We walk in silence. I must have said something wrong.

'Anyhow, we were discussing Daddy's concerts in Elvefaret every Thursday,' she says at last, as though she can't bear too long a silence between us. 'I'm not as unfussy as Mummy. I admit sound does matter. Daddy's stereo system can transport me to the Avery Fischer Hall, Concertgebouw, Musikverein, and to the Berlin Concert Hall whenever I want. No, I don't particularly miss the Aula or Munch's "Sun".'

I walk along listening to her; she seems so certain of her reality: she can describe it, at least, without a trace of doubt. I see no shadows, even if I do sense an undercurrent. She is just sixteen, I think to myself. If only I could appear as outwardly confident and self-assured, whatever the real truth. It's as though she can never be surprised or frightened again, so long as she's out in the daylight and doesn't stray into the thicket at night.

She has explained a great deal, but not everything. It's hard to imagine how she could have lived so hidden within the safe walls of her family. And yet, I muse, we have both listened to exactly the same things: to the same symphonies, quartets, romances. But in Melumveien we've not had AR and Quad loudspeakers to bring us the orchestras and soloists from all those concert halls. We've only ever had the medium wave on Mother's cranky radio. And Mother and I have stood, waving wildly to Tchaikovsky's 'Symphony Pathétique', as the signal has come and gone, as though we were in outer space. As Anja sat listening, with her knees neatly drawn together, Mother and I performed a war-dance before our radio, thrilled by each new discovery, each new destination. I don't know if I want to share this with Anja.

We have arrived where the road swings to the left. A narrow path comes down from a cabin up in the forest. We are walking more slowly now. As though our talking dictates it.

'You must tell me about Selma Lynge,' I say.

She stares in surprise. She's reluctant. What do I want to know?

'Why did you keep it a secret that you were taking classes with her?'

She hesitates, thinks about it, sighs.

'Is it so strange?' she asks, evasively.

'Yes.'

She sighs again. 'It was Daddy who heard about her. They had a chat. She wasn't sure if she wanted to take me on at first. She only takes the best, like Rebecca.'

'Rebecca's not the best,' I say.

'No, but anyway,' Anja hesitates again. 'Selma heard me play, and it was decided. Daddy had a plan, he thought I needed calm. All those student showcases and mock competitions would just be unsettling. He had this idea that I should wait with presenting myself in public until the really big competition.'

'Well, he was right about that.'

Anja nods. 'There wasn't to be any pressure on me, you see.'

I say nothing.

Not receiving any response, she continues. 'But it was a bit weird, of course – always going to Selma when I was sure I wouldn't meet her other pupils.'

'You call her Selma?'

'Yes, why not?'

'Rebecca calls her Fru Lynge.'

'She's Selma to some and Fru Lynge to others. That's not so odd, is it?'

'Perhaps not. It means you're close to her.'

'As close as you can get to someone like that.'

'What do you mean?'

Anja looks at me with surprise. 'Haven't you noticed her aura? Don't you realise she's a living legend? She was one of the leading pianists of our time. An international name. She was on the verge of her great breakthrough, a contract with Deutsche Gram– '

'I know all about . . .'

'. . . and then she falls in love with Torfinn, the Norwegian philosopher, and settles down with him . . .'

'In Sandbunnveien, yes, I know.'

'. . . and has all those children with him . . .'

'But is she really that extraordinary?'

Anja nods slowly. 'She's taught me everything.'

'Everything? What's everything? What's the most important thing? There must be one thing that's more important than anything else?'

'You mean, you don't know?' Anja looks genuinely surprised at me. 'No,' I admit.

'Well, the most important thing is never to be indifferent. Even when you're practising, you must play as though each phrase, each touch of the keys, is the last thing you will ever do on this earth.'

'That sounds tough.'

Anja gives me a sidelong look.

'But then life itself is tough too,' she says quickly.

We walk in silence for some time. Anja's thoughts seem suddenly gloomy. She doesn't want to share them with me, and I sense I mustn't ask. But I'm curious none the less. What she says is contradictory. When she qualified for the finals last year, she didn't play as though every touch of the key might be the last. She'd even said she couldn't be bothered to play better. I want to challenge her, but don't dare.

At last, we reach the top of Brunkollen. We take the path towards the cafeteria. A bunch of students are sitting outside the cabin; I hear their voices before I see them. Their presence makes me uneasy. I look furtively up at the sky, but see nothing but a lonely crow flapping from a spruce to a pine.

There are seven young men in their early twenties. I recognise two of them as coming from Røa. But we don't nod, since there's too great an age gap between us.

More than ever, I want to put my arm round Anja's shoulder, but I don't dare. The students are sitting on the grass drinking beer. I see rucksacks and sleeping bags. They clearly plan to stay the night. I catch sight of vodka bottles in among the beers. There's a massive party in the offing.

They're eyeing Anja. Perhaps some of them recognise her. Their gazes are appreciative, travelling from top to toe. I can see she doesn't like it.

'Let's go a bit further on,' she says.

There are plenty of places to sit. A middle-aged couple are sitting at the edge of the forest. We choose another path, walking between two shady trees and emerging in the sunlight again. One of the students yells something after us.

'Oh, heavens,' she mumbles, uncomfortable. 'I'm hardly a pin-up.'

I don't know how to reply, so I choose not to comment. 'Let's sit here.' I say and point at a bench. But it still doesn't feel far enough away. The students are sitting behind us making a racket. I turn around; they stare back. The talk stills. They whisper something. I can see that Anja is tense.

'Are they bothering you?' I ask.

'Why would they bother me?' she answers with a little smile, turning her face to the sun. She tilts her head back and closes her eyes, so as to sun herself. She stays like this for a long time.

'What are you thinking about?' I ask, after a while.

With her eyes still closed, she answers:

'I'm thinking how nice this is. How warm the sun is. And how we have our whole lives ahead of us.'

I like her saying that. It excites me. Anja Skoog is happy. And she is with me.

I have eyes burning in my back. The students are staring at us, because Anja is such an exceptionally beautiful girl. Although that's not the entire truth. They are also staring at us because we're such a pair of oddballs. We're not like everybody around us. We've escaped our music, and taken a welcome little break from our practice. But it's the piano that will drive us on through life, and music is the language through which we understand each other. We're sitting here on this bench, I think to myself, like representatives of a sect. The students are shouting to us now. Won't we join the party? Seven boys are hoping that this young woman will bring some sparkle to their evening. But they don't know Anja Skoog, I think to myself. We pretend not to hear. Anja still has her eyes closed. I open my bag. I have brought a few things. Some chocolate, red wine and blueberry cordial. I open both bottles.

'You don't have to open the wine on my account,' she says quickly, as though she has had her eyes half-open. 'I don't drink alcohol.'

But I have already opened the bottle. The perfume of red wine. Prokupac. Wine from Yugoslavia.

'Some blueberry cordial for you, then?' I say.

She must have registered the disappointment in my voice.

'Yes please, but I'd love a bit of chocolate too.'

She could have reassured me that it was all right for me to go ahead and drink the wine I've opened. But she doesn't. It makes drinking it awkward. But I drink it, all the same. I've been picturing the two of us lying on the grass, drinking wine together. Chocolate and wine, I'd thought. A hopeless combination. But girls seem to like it.

Now it's impossible. Seven students sit behind us making a racket, raising beer bottles and shouting toasts. I lift my wine bottle, to toast them back. Anja doesn't like it. She sits with her face turned to the sun and pretends they don't exist.

Everything has turned out differently from the way I'd imagined. I sip my wine while Anja suns herself. We don't speak. She nibbles at the chocolate, while I take enormous swigs of Yugoslavian red wine. Rich and anaesthetising. It feels sad sitting here, drinking wine on my own.

A sudden shiver of cold.

Anja looks as though she's almost asleep.

I look up to the sky.

The hawk is back.

It hangs there in the sky, above us. Following my every movement.

I drink.

The shouts from the students are coming from far away. 'I think I'm getting rather drunk,' I mumble. But Anja doesn't hear.

The viewpoint

I WAKE UP SUDDENLY. The sky cloudless. Judging by the light it's getting late. The sun has already moved far into the north-west. I sit up, confused that I've fallen asleep, and that I'm lying in the grass. I hear noises coming from the cabin. The students have gone inside. Screams and shouts are coming from in there.

I panic. Where's Anja? Is she in there with them?

I stumble around the area. The middle-aged couple have gone. Then I spot her. She's standing at the viewpoint, staring out over Asker and Drøbak and on towards the sea. She's told me how much she dislikes Munch, yet, standing there, she reminds me of one of Munch's motifs: that proud, womanly back, with the face turned to the horizon. I am the dark man at her side.

'Anja,' I shout, guilt-ridden and disorientated.

She turns and smiles as I come running towards her. Her face is welcoming. As though she might fling her arms open for me, and I might finally embrace her. But she doesn't – and I don't dare. I stop abruptly, two metres from her.

'I must have dropped off,' I say.

She laughs. 'You needed to sleep. After all that wine.'

I look at the empty bottle, understanding nothing. 'How long was I gone?'

'Not long,' she says, amicably. 'You must have been tired. You should look after yourself.'

She says it so directly. Without reproval. Without threat. The wine makes me daring; I walk right up to her. She looks at me with her clear, blue eyes. Something inside me bursts.

'I love you,' I say.

She doesn't answer. She just goes on staring at me as though I hadn't said it. As though she hadn't heard.

Everything's unreal.

I pull her close to me, feeling the warmth of her skin. I don't dare more. I am dizzy with happiness. I kiss her forehead.

'Don't,' she says seriously.

Shooters Hill

THE EVENING IS APPROACHING. But being June it's not dark; not at these latitudes. All the same I feel a sense of urgency. There's a sudden cool breeze from the north. I clear up the bottles and chocolate wrapper. I have drunk the entire bottle of wine on my own; she's only drunk a little bit of the blueberry cordial. I go to pour the rest out.

'No, don't do that,' she says, replacing the cork.

I put the bottle and rubbish in my rucksack. From inside the hut, we hear singing. Swedish student songs: 'Sjung om studentens lyckliga da'r.'

'Let's walk quickly past,' she says quietly.

We are on our way home.

'I know a short cut,' I say. 'So we won't have to go all the way back to Røa. We can take the tram from Lijordet.'

She glances at her watch. 'That would be good. Mummy and Daddy might be back soon, and they'll worry if I'm not home.'

'Are they always worried about you?'

'Daddy mostly.'

'I'll get you home soon. We'll take this path – it leads straight down to Østern Lake. And from there we can walk along the edge of the shooting range.'

She halts the moment I say it. Then we both hear the sound of shots.

'Why did they have to put a shooting range here?' she says.

'It was probably the most natural choice. Years ago the Germans shot their enemies down here.'

She walks ahead of me on the path. I can see she's shivering.

'I always forget there's a prison amongst all the trees down there.'

'Grini,' I say. 'It's called Ila now. The whole forest was littered with corpses during the war.'

I don't know why I say it. It's utterly untrue anyway. Anja Skoog slips on a smoothly worn root sticking out of the earth. She doesn't fall. She has the balance of a gymnast.

'Let's get back to Lijordet quickly,' she says.

I've walked here before. I think I remember the way. But I walk behind Anja Skoog, staring at her. She's so thin and lithe; capable of surviving anything.

When we come down to the lake, I grow confused. The path splits to the left and the right. 'Which way?' asks Anja.

I hesitate. 'Right,' I say.

The path seems almost overgrown. We walk in among the tall spruces. The sun can no longer reach us.

'There can't be many people walking here,' she says.

'Only moose,' I answer, 'and a few berry pickers in the autumn.'

She unties the jumper that she's had round her waist and pulls it over her head. It looks warm and home-knitted, in soft mohair.

'Nice jumper,' I say.

She turns and smiles. 'I got it from Selma.'

'Golly, can that woman do *everything*?'

'Yes,' says Anja. 'That's the funny thing. She can do everything, and has time for everything. She's the kind of woman I want to be when I'm fifty. Strong. Fearless . . .'

'And a bit mysterious. And a bit vain too, perhaps.'

'I suppose so, yes,' she smiles.

I am so engrossed in watching Anja that I forget where I'm going. A root catches my foot. I fall forwards, my hands going deep in the moss. Something sharp meets my fingers. A barbed wire fence that has come down.

'You're drunk,' she observes.

I feel hurt; she's so matter of fact. But I'm not drunk. Does she really think I was drunk when I said those grand words to her up at the view-point?

I regret having said them. I feel so foolish. Whilst she's in control – and not just that – I think to myself, brushing the moss and pine needles off my trousers as she watches on: Anja has dignity. When did I ever have dignity?

'I'm not drunk,' I mumble.

She shrugs. 'It's not important,' she says amiably.

We are very deep in the forest. The path has vanished under our feet. It was only a moose track, and suddenly the moose have gone in separate directions. I am walking ahead of her. The sound of shooting is getting louder. I must have got confused between the paths and tracks as we left the road.

'Aren't we going the wrong way?' she says, letting out a squeal each time we hear a bang.

'No,' I say. 'We're doing just fine. We're walking the length of the shooting range. The path's a bit rough, but we'll soon be in Griniveien Road.'

'But aren't those shots getting louder?' I see fear in her face for the first time. I begin to get frightened myself. Has the wine really played a trick on me? No. I recognise the hillock in front of us. We must be close to the main road now. The forest is thinning. The sun is shining again.

'Just walk up to the top,' I say, as calmly as I can. 'You'll see the Lijordet sports track on the other side of the road.'

She looks questioningly at me for a moment, as if to see if she can trust me. Then she takes her decision and leaps quickly to the top of the mound. I come panting after. Suddenly she freezes. There's a thunderous shot. She shrieks before falling straight in front of me.

In the next second I see the same thing as Anja saw before she fainted. A line of shooting booths. The mouths of pistols. We have strayed into the middle of the shooting range.

We are live targets, and we are standing on the wall behind the practice targets.

Back to Elvefaret

'LIE STILL!' I SHOUT to her. I can see she's coming round. Five men come leaping towards us, but without pistols. The biggest of them, a strangely effeminate man with leather trousers, looks furiously at me and yells:

'What the hell are you doing?'

I stare in confusion at these shocked men. They are all wearing heavy boots, and look like sheriffs, apart from the one who's addressing me.

'We lost our way,' I stutter. 'We were trying to take a short cut to the road. We've come too far into the forest.'

Anja is helped up by the two strongest men. I haven't felt as helpless as this since Catherine yelled 'Bravo!' in the Aula.

'You had too much wine,' she remarks.

I stare at her, pleading. Does she have to humiliate me in front of everybody? But she doesn't seem angry, just irritated.

'I'm sorry,' I say.

She nods. 'It's OK. But I really hate fainting.'

'I'll take you home now,' I say.

The man in the leather trousers views me sceptically. 'I think we'd better take charge of her from now on,' he says.

Then she comes to my rescue. She glares authoritatively at the pistol shooter. 'No, thank you, we'll be fine. Now that we know where we are, Aksel can walk me home as planned.'

I could hug her.

We walk side by side towards Lijordet Station.

'I'm so sorry,' I say.

'Don't say another word,' she says warmly. She gives me a quick squeeze with her hand. I can't believe it is true.

Then we walk on in silence.

Suddenly she says: 'You don't know how much I hate fainting.'

'I can't imagine anybody enjoys fainting,' I say, grateful that she still even wants to talk to me.

'No, but I hate it so much.'

'It can be quite pleasant sometimes,' I say, carefully.

'About as pleasant as dying,' she says.

'Do you think a lot about death?'

She nods. 'Yes, all the time,' she says. 'Don't you?'

It is my turn to touch her hand. But I don't dare. She wouldn't like it.

When we are on the tram at last, I finally pluck up the courage to ask:

'What do you think your parents will say about it?'

She reads the despair in my face. She might have intended to say something else, but she says: 'They don't really need to know, do they?'

I can't thank her. That would sound too daft. And I get the feeling that she'll probably tell the truth anyway. To Daddy.

We get off the tram at Røa.

'Can I walk you home?'

'If you really want to,' she says warmly. 'But maybe you can stop before the last turn? I expect Mummy and Daddy will be home by now.'

I do as she says. It is evening now, a blue and crimson June evening. The fragrance of lilac is heavy and intense. We walk past my house in Melumveien. I can't see any lights on inside. Catherine is probably out, and Father's probably sitting in the living room reading a book, listening to music, and has forgotten to switch the lights on. I feel sad, sadder than when Mother died, but I don't know why.

As we pass by the lilac bush that tumbles over our garden fence, I tear off a sprig and offer it to her.

'Do you want it?'

'Yes. Thank you.'

Then we walk on in silence.

As we come closer to Elvefaret, I feel a rising panic. When will I see her again?

'Do you remember you said you'd introduce me to Jacqueline du Pré?'

She nods.

I feel as submissive as a little boy. 'Will you do that? One day?

'Yes, one day,' she says. 'But you can't come any further, now.'

I stop. She walks on without a word of farewell. But before she turns at the last bend and disappears, she turns and waves.

Catherine's world

I WALK BACK to Melumveien, dejected; anxious and yet filled with hope. It hadn't occurred to me that a trip to Brunkollen could be so eventful. As I wander up the hill towards Melum, where the old cottages are, I think over what has happened, and what I've said.

I told her I loved her.

I feel ashamed now. Was that necessary? I had been drinking. Perhaps I *was* drunk, as she'd said. But I could have said it again.

So much has happened today.

I stop halfway I up the hill. Thinking. Pondering. There's a fairytale world all around me. Purple and white lilacs everywhere, and blossoming fruit trees. It is almost eleven o'clock, but the air is filled with insects. A young couple, in love, walks towards me. Perhaps they've been to the Røa Grill to share their first beers. The boy looks dependable, handsome, decent. She is more scruffy, but even happier. She has a sprig of lilac in her hand, just as Anja had a moment ago. She smiles at me, at the world. She seems ready for anything. I feel a pang deep inside of me. Tonight is filled with possibilities for him.

I have come to the house. Our home. It feels so strange now. In the bewitching light of this late June evening, it is as though Mother never lived here. This is Father's little palace: a neat wooden villa on the west side of town. He always dreamed of owning something grander, a brick house at Fagerborg, perhaps, with frescoes, wooden panels and stained-glass windows. But he could never afford it. He never had the money.

This house is almost cartoon-like. Small, flimsy. As though the walls are made of card. A fake innocence.

Everything's dark inside.

But Catherine is standing in the window. I get a glimpse of her pale face, before she withdraws. Has she been waiting for me? Was she watching us as we walked past? She is also obsessed with Anja Skoog.

I let myself in.

She is waiting for me in the living room. I see only her dark silhouette, against the light from outside the window, the white blossoms on the apple trees. The lilacs. I suddenly want to hug her, to let everything be forgotten, to cry it all out with her, to get a sister back. But I just stand there, completely silent.

'You haven't gone to bed?' I say finally.

She turns towards me. I can barely make her out.

'At eleven o'clock?' She smiles, with that tough, boyish smile I like so much.

I forget that I've been drinking. I see the wine bottle standing on the living room table.

'Have you got a glass for me too?'

She nods and seems friendly. It's so rare. I'm happy. A nightcap with my sister. I can scarcely believe it. She pours me a glass.

'Father's at the office,' she says.

'He works too much.'

'Perhaps. But maybe he likes it. What else would he do?'

'Be together with us.'

'But we're never together.'

Both of us laugh. She must have drunk rather a lot too. She sits in the sofa, flinging her legs over the armrest. She lights a cigarette, draws the smoke deep into her lungs, as though it could never go deep enough. She exhales with relish: a lust for life, a lust for everything. How magnificent she is, I think to myself. The thick, glossy hair. The broad shoulders. She's long-legged and strong. A handball girl. Nineteen years old already. I have always liked her, no matter the feuds and distance between us. But I haven't yet seen her with a boyfriend. I have only seen the Yellow House. She holds out the packet of cigarettes.

'Want one?'

'No, thank you. I haven't started yet.'

'Weird us sitting here,' she says.

'About time.'

'Perhaps. Where have you been? Where did you take her?'

I take a gulp of wine. It is better than the wine I drank alone on Brunkollen. Richer. At the same time softer.

'To Brunkollen,' I say. 'How did you know I was with Anja?'

'I saw you walking back,' she smiles, and lights a candle, a sign that the evening might go on late. 'I saw you give her a sprig of lilac. That was sweet.'

'And there was I thinking it was dark at all the windows.'

'There's always life in my room. You should know that.'

'Should I?'

She leans towards the wall, observing me, measuring her little brother, as though wondering: 'How much can I be bothered to confide in him?'

And there she sits, leaning back. Cigarette glowing.

'You know I lost my job at the National Gallery?'

'I don't know anything.'

'Really?'

'Well, how would I?'

'No, I suppose that's true.'

None the less, she looks at me with surprise. 'So you really didn't know? You mean, you didn't find out?'

I shake my head.

'How would I find out?'

'No, you've never had much idea about your big sister, have you, Aksel. Despite me thinking you kept track of my every move – even going as far as to follow me on the tram.'

It's as though the blood stops in my body. I don't know what to say.

'Relax, little brother. Drink some more wine.' Catherine shakes her head and laughs, as she pours my glass. 'Just how stupid is it possible to be?'

The moment the words are out, it is as though everything looks different, she seems somehow different, although it's probably just a figment of my imagination. Something hard, a look of desolation has entered her face, like a chronic hangover. It doesn't help that she's drinking so fast. Another bottle of red wine stands, already opened, on the coffee table.

'Does Father know about all this,' I ask, feeling instantly stupid.

'No, why should he? He's always the last to see anything. We stopped being a family when Mother died. Christ, Aksel, at least we had *conflicts* then. We're nothing but three pathetic destinies now, that mope around, side by side, incapable of helping each other.'

'You could have said something!'

'I wanted to spare you. I still do. Spare you from myself.'

'And the handball?'

'I quit that six months ago. Didn't you even know that?'

She stares sadly at me.

'I don't know anything,' I say.

It's obvious that we're both desperate to discuss Anja Skoog. But we're not ready. Not yet. Our experiences are still too fresh, our stories too incomplete. Catherine finds it easier to talk about the Yellow House. About the man who lives there. He has a name.

'Walther's to blame,' she begins. 'He's like most men, and I pity all of them. But even when you pity somebody, that doesn't stop them being to blame for stuff.'

'So what's he to blame for?'

She lights another cigarette. Pauses. Drinks more. Takes a pill. I don't dare to ask what it is.

'He's to blame for me going off-track. He tempted me down into his basement. Oh, he liked it so much down there.' Catherine stares at me with the saddest eyes I have ever seen. She stops herself. Shakes her head. 'I shouldn't tell you any more.'

'Why shouldn't you?'

'Because you're too young.'

'Oh my God, Catherine. I'm eighteen in a few months.'

'All right.' She has made up her mind. She takes a deep breath and begins her story.

'You remember,' she says, 'because you used to see me serving beers down at Sarahs Telt. I was so desperate to grow up after Mother died – to take responsibility, to earn money. I thought I could do just fine without school. We're all so reckless at that age. Weren't you? But I soon started to feel trapped, standing there with all those beer glasses on a tray, and gazing out over all those customers, the occasional confused tourist, but mostly a hard core of Norwegian afternoon drinkers who have enough self-respect left not to have to hide themselves away in some shady corner of Postkafeen. You can't imagine how often my bum was pinched. But one man who didn't pinch my bum was Walther Askelund. He was a professor from the University. He'd often sit with colleagues, but just as often he'd be there alone writing a book – as it turned out, it was a book about Caravaggio. Whenever I brought his beer over, he'd manage to keep me there, making small talk. He was thirty years older than me, but I never gave that a thought, I was too impressionable and curious. He said I reminded him of one of the models in one of Caravaggio's lesser-known paintings. I can never remember its name, but I came across it in a book once and saw what he meant. He used to say to me: "I'm always serious, even at my most frivolous."'

Catherine stops, recalling something she doesn't want to tell.

'So you took the bait?' I ask after a while.

'Not the bait . . . the champagne.' She laughs, joylessly. 'He was waiting for me one evening, asked if he could buy me a nightcap. It was July. You know, the town never slept. He knew a place down by the sea. A strange little inn. He mixed some powder in with my gin and tonic. It just made me more awake. His wife was away, near Holmsbu. She was a secretary for some government department. They didn't have any children. It's all so pathetic. We took the last Kolsås tram to his place. Do you want to know more?'

'Yes, why not?'

She shrugs. Perhaps she's never told anyone this before. 'I suppose I was curious,' she says, 'I wanted to come out of my childhood, out of the stagnant, rotting backwaters. I wanted to escape Mother's death, if you know what I mean. Get away from this sad house, away from you, from Father. You were both just faffing about with your own stuff. Life had to be something more! And the professor was something more. He was old and knowledgeable, and he opened a door on to a different world; the one Mother came from perhaps even, where rules for how to behave weren't written in big letters on the wall.'

She comes to a halt again.

'So, what happened?' I ask gently.

Catherine stares at me, as surprised as I am, that this conversation is even taking place. My head is still filled with Anja Skoog. But Anja will have gone to bed now. There is nothing more I can do for her right now. Instead, I am sitting in the living room with my sister, happy that she's here, and that there's somebody to talk to tonight. This is the Catherine I recognise, and yet not. The glazed look in her eyes makes her so different, but I've started to get used to it. Then I think of a comment

Margrethe Irene, of all people, made to me. It was one of the last times we'd met. The girl with a head stuffed with astrology fixed me with a mysterious gaze, and said that people were attracted to each other according to the existential places they were in.

'So that losers seek losers, and winners seek winners?' I had asked.

'If you like,' she'd answered. 'But more than that, people with an urge for life will always find each other, and people who want to be in love will find each other and *fall* in love.'

Was it true? I think about Anja Skoog, and how life will prove us winners or losers. That the stories we write now will bind or separate us. It occurs to me, now that Catherine is so far into *her* story, that she and I can only have this conversation because we are both desperate. We both have our antennae out, turned towards each other, perhaps because we're both drawn to the same thing at this moment, something we are both terrified of losing.

I daren't follow this thought to its conclusion.

Catherine notices that my mind has wandered.

'Aren't you following?' she asks.

I quickly straighten up in my chair. 'Absolutely, I want to hear everything!'

She nods, almost to herself. Then she looks at me, quizzically, with big-sister eyes. 'You don't know much about girls, do you?'

I have no idea how to reply.

She sees me waver and goes on. 'I wanted him, because he could give me something, and because I knew that what I could give him was even greater. I liked the fact that he was crazy for me, that he was risking his security, that he talked to me about his wife, that we slept in the same double bed in the afternoons that they would sleep in that night. I didn't know her, and it felt bad, because I betrayed her so brutally. But that didn't overshadow the joy of what I actually did, or of being valued as the most important thing in Walther's life. He was besotted; he'd do anything for me. You can't imagine the effect that had on me, just that, after all these years at home. At last I felt noticed, understood, valued. I'd have given him everything, except children. But you don't know anything about that, do you? How, in a flash, sex becomes the only thing left in your head; how, in a fit of love or madness, you start living for these short, wild moments that belong to only you and him; those sinful moments that make you feel stronger than the world, yes, that make you feel invincible. The pleasure is so enormous. Nothing can threaten you, nobody can make you feel small. Because somebody desires you, and because you can return those feelings, even if you don't think this is the love of your life, and all that. The most important thing is that you feel young and alive, that you're experiencing everything for the first time.'

'Did you visit him in the Yellow House every afternoon?'

'Almost. At least, when Dorthe was at work. I still can't bear to think about her, and I didn't then either; Walther managed to talk his whole marriage away, if you know what I mean. He lived the life he had to live, got enough money from the University to be able to stay at home, whiling away his time on Caravaggio. But I was the one he was really whiling away his time on. And I was happy. I had a happy few months. All the things he showed me, everything we'd do together. It didn't get out of control – at least not for me. I always came out on the other side a happy person. But the power of my senses terrified me; a colour could occupy the whole of me; I had no control over the sounds I heard or the images I saw; I had no sense of time. He tempted me with plans, the book we'd write together, an art history for teenagers. At first he hated the thought that I didn't have my Artium. Later he saw he could use it against me, the silly academic that he was. He loved phrases like paradigmatic shift, aesthetic values, spirit of the époque. He was a spoilt oddball, who I knew it was possible to love. That was when you followed me, my poor little brother. I knew all along that you were on the tram. That you'd got on at Ekraveien station, and that you changed at Smestad, while I changed at Sørbyhaugen. I didn't think you'd manage to get the other tram. When I realised you were on it, I had to laugh. I had such fun sitting down right in front of you. And you hid between the seats, with that stupid aftershave of yours filling the whole tram. I got off at Bekkestua without giving you a second glance, because I knew you were there. I relished the fact you were there, that I was important for you at last – that you didn't just think about your music the whole time, even if it seemed like it.'

'Was that why you gave a curtsey just before you went in to Professor Askelund?'

'Yup, exactly. Out of pure joy that I was being watched. Not just by some old professor, but my own little brother. That I had my secret life, a life that was just mine, full of freedom and enjoyment. Until things began going downhill.'

We sit looking at each other. The night has turned. The sun will rise soon and light up the forest on the other side of the river. I think about the alder thicket, and how nice it would be to sit there with Catherine right now. But then, we're here in our living room in Melumveien, and that's not so bad either. It doesn't really come as any surprise that she's so open and direct, since she gets it from Mother. Father and I are the ones who beat about the bush, never saying what we mean. Catherine has told me a lot now, but as she's talked I've had to ask myself why she's telling me all this, and I feel a creeping sense of foreboding. I feel sure she's trying to tell me something else, as she pours yet more wine into our glasses and Father still doesn't return from the office. What a family. But what is she trying to tell me? Could it be something to do with Anja Skoog? Is she trying to warn me against the life I'm longing for? She goes into every little detail about the sex with Professor Walther Askelund. I don't want to hear it, but she persists, and a lot of what she says makes me shiver, since there's so much contempt in everything she says, not just for him, but for all men.

'Things were still going on when you came and finished it all,' Catherine continues. 'We had some stolen moments, but it was already fading. But I was still angry when he phoned me, and said that you'd been at the door. You've destroyed a marriage, did you know that? Dorthe's filed for divorce, and since it's her house the Professor lives on the goodwill of friends. It's weird, he has his salary and grants, but he needs his wine, his champagne, his women. Lots of art historians are used to the good life. They can't quite work out where the limits are. I know now that I wasn't the first of his Caravaggio girls. I've met three of them already. We've all talked quite openly. It seems we've all choked on him, to put it that way.'

'Are you still angry?'

'No, not any more. You just carried out some necessary sewage works. You were the plumber, Aksel!' Catherine laughs, but seems still angry. 'You washed away all the crap, so we could see what was left. And there was nothing.'

We are still here talking. Daylight has come. Why don't we want to go to bed? And where is Father? Outside the window the birds are singing. Blackbirds, great tits, starlings. The window is open. We hear the sound of insects. The fruit trees are glistening in the morning light. A new day has begun.

'So, what you're trying to tell me is that you're finished with men,' I say finally. There. It's been said. The boil is lanced.

Catherine is suddenly alert. She hadn't expected this.

'What do you mean?' a hint of hostility in her voice.

'That from now on we're rivals.'

She thinks it over, staring across at me. Who did she think I was? Just a piano-playing little brother? That I spend all my time thinking about Debussy, Brahms and Bach, and nothing else?

'What do you mean?' she repeats, in a more tempered tone.

'Once it was Mother. Now it's Anja Skoog.'

She puts her head in her hands. I sit in my chair calmly, letting it happen. She has been so far away. I have no responsibility for her, I think. Not for her, not for Father, not for anybody. I feel a kind of strength, and a liberation.

She can see that I don't intend to say more, that the rest is up to her. She looks up, red-eyed and tear-stained.

'Put some music on,' she says. 'Play something Mother would have liked.'

I go over to the bookshelf, where the records are kept. I sift calmly through the collection. I know all this music inside out. Mother's world will never let us go. I pull out Ravel. The Piano Concerto in G major. I have the second movement in mind.

'I don't know why,' I say. 'But perhaps this music might speak to both of us; I've always felt it told two stories in parallel.'

I put the record on. It's well-played. Crackles. Scratches. Before the piano begins. Quietly, almost hesitantly. An unknown Frenchman at the piano. The Orchestre de Paris. Catherine listens.

'I don't remember this music,' she says, bewildered.

'From now on it'll be our music,' I say. 'It will bind us.'

I have no idea why I say it. A ridiculous and banal sentiment. Yet it seems to have a certain ring, as I sit here in my armchair, at the end of this long June night. And just then, Father comes into the room.

Catherine still hasn't noticed him, but I have, and he puts his finger to his lips, not wanting to disturb us in this moment. He stands quietly at the door, looking at us as we sit there. And he smiles because he thinks we're both happy; that we are honouring Mother's memory, and that things will turn for the better now. The thought overwhelms him, and I watch a tear run down the length of his nose. A large, shiny tear belonging to a middle-aged man. And he still has a finger to his lips. And I sit here, thinking how I would give anything to stop time right now. There is no need for it to move on. Not for my sake. Nor for Catherine's.

W. Gude's visions

AUGUST AGAIN. Two years have passed since Mother died. I haven't seen Anja all summer. I've wanted to call, but haven't dared. I've been pacing the streets, morning and night. Goodness, I know them off by heart! Elvefaret, Fådveien, Ove Kristiansens vei, Nøtteveien, Melumveien, Kristian Auberts vei, Finnhaugveien, Vækerøveien. June's white blossoms have transformed into the first hard fruits. All the families who live in the villas have been away and come back. Catherine, Father and I have lived our separate lives in Melumveien. Now and again, Catherine has asked me if I've seen Anja at all. But I don't know where she is. Anja's house is hidden behind tall trees, like so many of the houses here in Røa. If it had been winter, it would have been possible to see if anyone was home, from the lights inside. But in summer it's impossible. I stand there sometimes, in the hope of hearing the great AR speakers she described, but I only hear the birds' delicate song, and soon even *they* will stop singing. Besides I can't stand here for too long, it would seem suspicious. And the garage, in which the Volvo Amazon stands, is closed. Which is why I wander the streets so much, becoming a dreamer, and sitting in the alder thicket for hours, thinking only of her.

Rebecca Frost calls me one day. I know that she likes me, for one reason or another. She has kissed me on the mouth. But I'm only one of many. She could equally well have kissed Ferdinand.

'Aksel, you're not disappearing out of my life, are you?'

'Me?' I say, befuddled, 'Not at all!'

'So how was your summer then?'

'Practising. The 'Waldstein Sonata', 'Gaspard'. But I've not cracked it. And then Opus 109 too.'

'The best of them all, I reckon.'

We talk about Beethoven's last sonatas. The masterpieces, which feature death so strongly. Why are they so attractive to us youngsters? I forget to ask her how *she* has been. Or am I just avoiding it? Because she's so rich; because she'll have been sailing with her posh friends, and practising on the Bösendorfer they have at the cabin, which she likes even more than their Steinway at home in Bygdøy. Her father, the mega-wealthy ship owner Fabian Frost, who earned so much on his oil tankers thanks to the unrest in the Middle East, has probably been sailing with the royal family again. There's so much sunshine in Rebecca's life, I think grudgingly. Bright sun, smooth oceans, flowery wallpaper, and paintings of ships in gilded frames.

But that is not the reason for her call. She has called to talk about W. Gude.

'He wants to meet us,' she says.

'Who? The impresario?'

'Of course. W. Gude himself. He wants to meet us, all the finalists from last year. He's invited us for lunch at Blom in a fortnight.'

'What does he want?'

'To discuss our futures. You can't turn this down, Aksel, you've got to be there,' she says.

'All right, I'll go.'

Of course I'll go to meet W. Gude. The great impresario, whose office walls are probably covered with signed photographs of Rubenstein, Heifetz and Kempff; pictures that are doubtless not only signed but inscribed: 'For my dearest friend W. Gude . . .' and other extravagances. W. Gude organises Oslo's entire music scene single-handedly. There are a few other names, including entertainment impresarios who keep to Frank Sinatra, motocross and boxing events. But there is only one W. Gude; and as young pianists we all know very well that his interest should not be scorned. It can be important to us all. Rebecca calls me some days before the lunch, to tell me who has accepted the invitation. Besides herself, they include Ferdinand, Margrethe Irene, Anja and myself. So Anja will be there, I think, relieved. At last, I shall see her again.

September in Oslo. A melancholy hangs in the air. Sharp gusts of wind from the west bring clear weather and announce the coming autumn.

University fresher week. Oslo's town centre is filled with first-year students wandering about wearing absurd hats and solemn expressions. The anticipation of new experiences, new relationships, a new life. I myself am sick with desire for something to happen, as I walk up the steps of the station at the Nationaltheatret, disappointed at failing to get the same tram as Anja. Losing the competition has diminished my status, but my friends, it seems, have not deserted me. I'm grateful to Rebecca for inviting me to come to this meeting with W. Gude. Something is bound to come of it. I have set myself a deadline to sign up for more competitions by next year. The most obvious one is the New Talents Award, held by the Philharmonic every January. And some international competitions maybe. The ultimate goals are the Tchaikovsky Competition in Moscow, the Queen Elizabeth Competition in London, and the major US competitions. I don't have any doubts; I'll make it, but it might take time. Recently I've had to practise with the damper pedal down, because Father has been forced to rent out a couple of the upstairs rooms to lodgers: Skaar is a peculiar chap from the west country, a devout Christian who runs cross-country in the summer, skis in the winter, and studies the natural sciences in between; Bendixen, a dour young man from Toten, stinks of old sweat and chewing tobacco and studies philosophy. But the two of them are often home until late afternoon, so I can no longer practise at full volume for three hours non-stop. Once, when I did try, Skaar stood in the doorway, pasty-faced and whinging: 'There are limits! There are limits!'

Not being able to practise as I want has made me angrier with the world. Anja's absence has too. Nevertheless, I'm filled with optimism as I stride towards Blom in Karl Johan, a restaurant I associate with Mother. Wasn't it here that she celebrated her fortieth? With half the Opera? I hurts me to think of her. What would she have said, what would she have done, if she were alive? There are things about my mother's fate that frighten me: her failure to break the pattern, the way she stayed in a hopeless marriage, never realising her dreams. Yet what were those dreams? Nothing more perhaps than vague excuses to complain about the life she lived. I walk towards Blom, thinking of Mother, looking at the latest intake of young, happy students as they stream towards the university, and high-school kids who have flocked together to hang around the ice-cream bar, Musikk-Huset and Tanum-Cammermeyer. They have such a clear sense of purpose, while I seem stuck in memories and emotions. Perhaps W. Gude will be my salvation. He has a magic wand. He can point us to orchestras and concert halls. He can show us the way to the Carnegie Hall.

I thought I'd be among the first to arrive at Blom, but I'm the last. Everybody is already sitting around the table. Anja is furthest away, her hair in a ponytail. It makes her face seem slimmer, her gaze more intense. She looks at me with a friendly gaze. I nod back, unable to take my eyes from her. Then I say hello to the others; they're the same as ever, then finally I greet W. Gude himself, in a white shirt and bow-tie. He rises politely and greets me with such a hearty handshake it nearly pulls me over.

'There you are, our last great talent!'

I have observed this man so many times in the Aula. For years he has emerged from the door to the left of the stage, from where I listened to Anja, before taking his accustomed seat in the front row. W. Gude has been the face I have associated with all these great experiences. Always, two minutes before the house lights sank, no matter whether Arrau, Barenboim or Bishop were performing, he would be there, coming out of the door beneath Munch's mural of naked figures. I'd always watch him with the greatest curiosity. What, I wondered, had he been doing back stage? Had he been talking to the great artists in the greenroom? Had he stood by that door, on his toes, ready to respond to the least signal? Each time he walked through that door, he looked both confident and expectant, as though he had been in deep, lengthy conversation with these stars. As though they had been planning huge concerts all over Europe, or discussing Schopenhauer and his grim view of women. Right now, he is doing his utmost to put me at my ease as I take my place. He flings his arms open and nodding, as though to himself, he declares: 'The whole world awaits.'

Rebecca giggles. I try to catch Anja's eye, but she is concentrating on her prawn canapé. She is not alone. An identical sandwich sits on each plate. Lunch at Blom with W. Gude as host. He claps his hands enthusiastically, welcoming us all. Sitting here with his shiny pate, protruding ears and professorial gaze from behind round spectacles, he looks, more than anything, like an ostrich, a bespectacled ostrich, jovial but powerful. Nobody would think, looking at him, that he could outrun us all, but that is exactly what he does. He's running ahead of us all, shouting: 'Stand aside! Stand aside! Here they come: Anja Skoog, and Rebecca Frost, and Aksel Vinding, and, and . . .' He has gathered us together now, this band of hermits, incapable of running their own careers, or even starting them up. Margrethe Irene sends me a meaningful look. I don't like it. It's as though we have something intimate going. As though she knows best. But she knows nothing, I think irritably, and when I glimpse her braces again, they seem bigger than ever. Do they make corkscrews for magnum bottles? I feel sorry for her. I haven't got space for her in my life. I wish she'd keep away from me.

W. Gude taps a teaspoon against his water glass.

'Welcome, my young, forward-marching children!' he chortles delightedly, looking at us all one by one. 'Of course, none of you are children, I know that. Seventeen-year-olds, eighteen-year-olds, nineteen-year-olds – yes, I felt extremely grown-up at your age.' He mumbles something to himself. Then he raises his glass in a toast. The rest of us all toast with sparkling Farris, apart from Anja who stares ahead of her stiffly.

'We are gathered here,' he continues, 'because your formidable abilities have come to my attention.' He sneezes violently, pulls a crisply ironed handkerchief out from his jacket pocket, blows his nose, gazes contentedly around, stealing an extra glance at Anja, but without getting her attention, and then continues. 'My own talents are humble. I am here on this earth to make others shine. I devote my life to the ancient Egyptians, and to you youngsters. In between, I organise the concerts you all know about. But the big stars are old and tired. And so I have been asking myself for some time now: when will the new generation come to kick up the dust? When I heard you all in the finals of the Young People's Piano Competition, I thought: here at last is something new, fresh and daring. Anja's virtuosity. Rebecca's charm. Margrethe Irene's precision. Ferdinand's contemplative disposition. And Aksel's lyrical talent. Yes, I thought, this is irresistible: a young generation of new, independent voices. This is what we want! You are tomorrow's stars. You will all taste the sublime experience of being allowed to play with a large orchestra. I've invited you here today for canapés and a little sparkling water, not to bombard you with offers, but to tell you that I am right here *with* you, that I am always in my office in Prinsens gate, for you, and that I shall follow your progress with a magnifying glass. And who knows? One day you might want to work with a bumbling old fool like me. Perhaps you'll want to play at the Palace for the Parliament dinner, or with the Philharmonic in Bergen, or Stavanger, or . . .? The possibilities are endless. All I want to say is: I can help you in many ways.'

Anja has got up. She stands and looks calmly at W. Gude. I suddenly notice how pale she is, as though the summer has passed her by completely, as though all she's had are hours at the piano.

'And is that everything?' she says.

W. Gude dabs his mouth with a serviette and stares in astonishment at the young woman who was probably his main reason for organising this lunch.

'Well . . . in a way,' he says, disorientated. 'But . . .'

Anja interrupts him and grabs her handbag. 'Then I'll say thank you.' It is clear she intends to leave. W. Gude seems disconcerted.

'It was nothing.'

'My days are very full,' says Anja. 'Unfortunately I have somewhere else to go. But thank you for the prawn canapé and the mineral water.'

She curtsies, like the well brought-up girl that she is. Then she sends me a helpless glance and rolls her eyes. As though I will understand. I also rise, but not to leave.

'Excuse me a moment,' I say, following her out, between the columns, between all the artists' coats of arms, the purple noses, the Ravensburger paintings. The others watch us open-mouthed.

'What was that all about?' I ask, when we reach the cloakroom.

Anja shakes her head vigorously, as though she's not ready to hear any argument but her own: 'I can't bear him,' she says, 'not now. I'm sure he is very kind, but I have my own plans to keep to.'

'And what are they?'

She stares at me joylessly. 'I've been selected for the "New Talents" concert with the Philharmonic. I'm going to play Ravel with them in January.'

'The G Major?'

She laughs, 'But of course. I shan't play the "Left Hand Concerto" until I've lost my right arm.'

'So W. Gude isn't of any interest to you?'

'No. We have our own plans.'

I can see she wants to turn her back on me and disappear as fast as possible.

'Please, wait,' I say. 'Where have you been? What have you been up to? And what about Jacqueline du Pré?'

She brushes most of my questions off, but the last one makes her pause.

'You can come,' she says solemnly, as though discussing a funeral. 'One afternoon in the autumn some time. Is that O K? I'll phone you.'

I nod.

'Perfect,' I say. 'But don't feel under pressure.'

'I never do,' she says.

I stand and watch her disappear through the glass doors. She is young and agile, and has a terrifying power. If only I had her strength, I muse.

I go back to the others. It seems that everybody is relieved that Anja has left, apart from me.

'She seems to want to go her own way, that one,' says Rebecca pragmatically, licking mayonnaise from her lips. I notice that W. Gude is watching us closely now, to discover the balance of power, to see who takes the lead. To have a career as a pianist one needs to be strong. So far we have only shown a fraction of what we can do.

'Anja Skoog is a great talent,' says W. Gude, allowing his face to take on fatherly folds. 'Let's hope she knows what she is doing.'

I turn to Rebecca: 'Do you talk to Selma Lynge about her?'

Rebecca shakes her head. 'Nope. I can talk to Fru Lynge about anything, but not about Anja. They're in league together.'

'She's going to play Ravel with the Philharmonic in February.'

'Yes, I know,' says Rebecca. 'That's one of the reasons we're all here.' She glances quickly at W. Gude, who signals with a little nod that she can go on. 'I thought: why are we all so slow? Why don't we do the same thing as her, and put ourselves up for "New Talents" or start planning our debuts?'

'That's easy for you to say,' says Ferdinand. 'You're doing all right at school. The rest of us are struggling; music's just too demanding.'

'That's right,' I say, laughing. 'I'm not at school at all.'

W. Gude looks at me with interest. 'You're not taking your Artium, are you, Aksel?'

'No, I've left,' I say and blush, to my own consternation, since it probably looks as though I am blushing out of shame.

W. Gude tries to be sensitive. 'Has it anything to do with . . . the tragedy?'

I shake my head energetically. 'No, it was solely for my music. I wanted to give all my concentration to the piano.'

'But why haven't you changed teacher?' says Rebecca, sounding like a big sister. 'Synnestvedt's going positively mouldy. What on earth can you learn from him?'

'He gives me freedom,' I say angrily.

'Freedom is important,' Margrethe Irene nods. She's always quick to back me up.

'Maybe we should all think about changing piano teachers soon,' says Ferdinand. 'Reifling's fantastic. But he's definitely holding me back. I wanted to make my debut next autumn, but he says that's too early.'

'You should have gone to Fru Lynge,' says Rebecca emphatically. 'It's a mystery to me that you can't see we have a genius, a figure of international rank, living in our midst in this crappy little town. I can't speak about myself, of course. But how do you think Anja got to be so bloody brilliant? Do you think she got there on her own?'

'These things are all individual,' Margrethe Irene says emphatically. 'I still feel Fru Föhn has tons to teach me, even though she isn't exactly a Fru Lynge. All of us know our failings and what we need to improve on. I think the significance of teachers is overrated.'

W. Gude is listening attentively. I'm warming to him. He seems sincere in his interest.

'Yes, everything is individual,' he says, 'but that is precisely the reason a teacher can be so important. I talked to Rubinstein on this subject when he visited our little country last. It worried him that the latest comets – Barenboim, Ashkenazy, Bishop and Lupu – all practise so hard. In his opinion, their teachers had done them a dreadful disservice, since to communicate anything worthwhile as a pianist one needs many more experiences than just an exploration of an instrument.' Gude waves his arms wildly and screws up his eyes. 'The experiences of life itself, my children!'

Margrethe Irene nods vigorously and peers over at me.

'And that,' W. Gude continues, 'means that we must also open our eyes to all the other things life has to offer. Rubinstein confessed to me that he never practises more than three hours a day. 'There are books to be read,' he said, 'women to meet, pictures to see, wine to be drunk.'

'I adore Rubinstein,' says Margrethe Irene with stars in her eyes and sending a meaningful glance in my direction.

'He's right, of course,' Rebecca nods. 'We really shouldn't take this peculiar activity of ours too seriously. We must take more chances, throw ourselves into it. Worship pleasure.' She looks hesitantly towards W. Gude. They clearly have an agreement in place. Can she make her announcement? He nods gently. Yes, she can. 'I am going to make my debut,' she bursts out, raising both hands in the air, like a sports star, 'this autumn!'

We all clap and cheer. W. Gude smiles contentedly.

'That is so brave of you,' says Ferdinand earnestly.

'It was Fru Lynge's idea,' Rebecca continues. 'She suddenly asked me one day: "What are you waiting for?" She'd been listening to me play Schubert's A major, the posthumous one. She was pleased. She reminded me how young Schubert was when he died. Reminded me about Mozart and Dinu Lipatti. She said: "You can go to W. Gude now. Say hello from me. He'll take care of you."'

'And so that's what you did?' I ask surprised.

Rebecca and her impresario nod in unison.

'I felt extremely honoured,' W. Gude says genuinely, 'that one of Selma's pupils should come to me, on Selma's recommendation. You have to remember that Selma and I are old friends. I was the one who arranged her farewell concert.' His eyes go dreamy as he reminisces. 'You can't imagine what an event it was. She'd decorated the place with flowers, and with carpets. She put a painting by her favourite artist, Emile Nolde, on an easel close to the piano, and she read poems by Hölderlin. But more important than anything, she played. Oh heavens, how she played!' Tears well up in W. Gude's eyes. Suddenly I see an ageing man before me. A man who lives on old memories; there's nothing he can experience today that he hasn't experienced before. Which is why he looks to us, as if our youth will give him a new spark of life and help him to forget that death awaits, around the next corner.

'What was it she played, again?' asks Ferdinand politely. He knows, of course. We all know. Because despite none of us having been there, we've discussed this concert countless times. But W. Gude is eager to oblige: 'She played Busoni's piano transcription of Bach's Toccata, Adagio and Fugue (– what a prelude!), before following on with Schubert's C Minor sonata, the least known, but perhaps the most brilliant among the posthumously published works. Then there was an interval, during which the audience were treated to a glass of German sack and a piece of German raisin cake, which she followed by a rendition of her old friend Paul Hindemith's "Ludus Tonalis" and then Schumann's symphonic études, no less. It felt as though the cheering would never end. First, she played three or four encores, all by Grieg, as a tribute to her new homeland, but when her audience still refused to let her go, she went back to Bach. She played all the French suites, just like that! After almost four hours the audience staggered contentedly out of the Aula, knowing they had had the experience of a lifetime. And Selma withdrew to her private life, to her husband and children . . .'

'And to her house in Kvikksandveien,' I interject.

Rebecca scowls at me: 'In *Quick-sand*-veien?' She repeats what I've said. Everybody is gawping at me, confused.

'Yes,' I continue, as confused as they are, 'I live nearby, on the other side of the river.'

'Selma Lynge doesn't live in *Quick-sand*-veien, you nutter,' she whispers, giggling. 'She lives in Sand-bunn-veien.'

'You do say daft things sometimes,' Margrethe Irene mumbles.

I pull a face, and everybody laughs.

'I'd better sharpen up,' I say.

But the most important thing has been said. The super-rich eighteen-year-old Rebecca is making her debut. The date has been set for 11 November.

'Well, that doesn't leave much time,' says Ferdinand.

She nods. Shudders. 'Don't remind me!'

'What will you play?' asks Margrethe Irene, gazing at Rebecca admiringly.

'I shall take them all by storm,' says Rebecca firmly. 'They all think I'm nothing but a superficial, rich kid from Bygdøy, but I'll show them. First with "Le Tombeau de Couperin" by Ravel. Then Beethoven's Opus 109 – put *that* in your pipe, Aksel!' she pokes her tongue out at me before going on. 'And to round off, I've simply got to play Chopin's four ballads.'

We all gasp. It's an ambitious programme, but not more than necessary. The time is long gone since the critics could be palmed off with a rousing version of 'Frühlingsrauschen'.

'Congratulations,' I say.

Rebecca lifts a hand to silence me. 'Don't congratulate me yet. Wait for 11 November.'

I see W. Gude looking urgently about the room in search of a waiter. He finally spots one. 'Waiter, champagne! Yes, and sparkling drinks for my children! This calls for celebration! A toast to youth, to courage, to the future, and everything yet to be done!'

The Young Pianists' Society

W. GUDE HAS LEFT US. With handshakes and even embraces he's reassured us that he's our friend for life, that all we have to do is to come to him, and he will arrange whatever concerts we need. But we have drunk champagne. The party's not over. We are on the way to the Floeds' apartment in Bislet. Margrethe Irene insists that we can't go our separate ways after such a fabulous lunch. W. Gude has set the wind in our sails, with his canapés and champagne.

'I feel like making my debut now!' she says. 'W. Gude makes me feel so safe. Imagine having the same impresario as Rubinstein.'

'Oh, come on,' mumbles Ferdinand, 'he's only Rubinstein's impresario in Norway.'

'That's typical you,' Margrethe Irene replies. 'But then, you won't make your debut for another fifteen years, being with Riefling, ha-ha!'

Ferdinand ignores the jibe. 'Riefling knows what he's talking about. W. Gude is only after the money.'

'That's stuff and nonsense, but we should discuss all these things,' says Margrethe Irene, her arm confidently locked in mine, as we stroll up Pilestredet. 'This turning point must be marked. Tonight we'll found "The Young Pianists' Society"!'

'Together into the future,' Rebecca laughs.

'One for all and all for one . . . until the first wrong note!' Ferdinand jokes.

'It's all your fault, you know,' I say to Rebecca. 'You've set us against each other now. If we don't make our debuts before we're nineteen, we might as well go on the dole.'

She shakes her head. 'W. Gude is a wise man. He can see we're all growing up and that we need challenges. I have to thank Fru Lynge for all this. She's so generous. She had flowers and pictures at her concert; I shall invite everybody back for a brilliant party afterwards at home at Bygdøy. We shan't skimp on a thing.'

I wriggle out of Margrethe Irene's grip, and stare at Rebecca in awe. She has made an important decision. I can see she's relieved. But the thought of what she's embarked on makes me nauseous: Ravel, Beethoven, Chopin. Why haven't I thought along these lines? Why have I got yet another year before me, in which nothing will happen, apart from the daily routine, the endless strolls around my neighbourhood, the hours spent in the alder thicket, or at the piano, the Wednesdays with Synnestvedt, with his ghastly breath and well-meaning platitudes. It occurs to me that I despise him, that I keep expecting him to say: 'I can't give you more, my friend. I think you need to find another teacher now.' But he never does. Instead he sits listening to me, in the same slumped position. He doesn't suggest I make my debut. He never asks me to sign up for 'New Talents'. All he wants is to be my teacher. And I conclude, in this state of lightheadedness, induced by champagne and Rebecca's show of courage, that Synnestvedt is spineless. If it was up to him he'd be my teacher for all time and I'd never make my debut. Yes, I decide, Synnestvedt is a dead end. I have to get away from him. But whose door should I knock on? Selma Lynge's?

Rebecca catches me brooding. 'No gloomy thoughts tonight,' she says. 'We're going to celebrate each other. We're going celebrate W. Gude and his generosity. We're going to celebrate the Young Pianists' Society!'

We are in the Floeds' apartment now. Home to the chief engineer and his family: a mother with a homely, sympathetic face, and a brother whom I've never seen before, and who, it transpires, does ballroom dancing. We sit in the living room, with the Bowers & Wilkins loud-speakers, the Beethoven records and everything else. Margrethe Irene's parents are admirable in their discreet absence. They have arranged a bedroom and TV room in the old servants' quarters of the apartment. Their son spends most of his time in Manglerud, living with a friend. So luckily we youngsters can be alone. We celebrate with the red wine that Margrethe Irene opens. Rebecca's forthcoming debut must be marked. She sits in her chair, in command as ever, and yet not. The girl who has always been there to cheer the rest of us on has taken a giant step herself. There's no ill-will between us. The fact is, we like each other. We want the best for each other. We talk about the future. The future that holds such terror, with the yellow platform that awaits us, the black grand piano, the critics and the public. And all in the name of music.

'You all have to follow my lead now,' says Rebecca, 'or it'll be no fun. We have to show them!'

'I don't even have anywhere to practise,' I say.

I tell them about the two students: the Christian cross-country runner and skier, and the sweat-reeking philosopher from Toten.

'Well, I suppose they have far greater missions in life, young Aksel,' says Rebecca in mock seriousness.

Then Ferdinand comes to: 'That's a bit rich, Rebecca! We know nothing about them. How do we know how great our contribution to this world will be?'

'Aksel's contribution is the most important,' says Rebecca, raising her glass. 'Let's toast Aksel!'

I protest loudly, but they raise their glasses. We toast each other one by one. And we listen to Schubert's C Minor, performed by Gieseking.

'I shall play it better than that,' says Rebecca.

It's getting late. We all want to go, but Margrethe Irene wants me to stay. She whispers gently in my ear: 'Can't you stay, just for two more trams? That's all I ask. I've got your horoscope here.'

I look at her. She is prettier, after all that red wine. An expression darts across her face. A look of seriousness, of pleading, that makes me hesitate.

'That's settled then,' she says. 'You shan't regret it.'

The others leave. We are now a society: the Young Pianists' Society. We shall meet regularly, talk openly, share our joys, our plans, our frustrations. I stand hugging Rebecca in the hallway. Suddenly she takes my face in her hands. 'Be careful with Margrethe Irene,' she says. 'But I suppose you know.'

I nod. I take her face in my hands too. She's suddenly a different person, and it's frightening. Just the knowledge that she has decided to make her debut makes her different. Stronger. Bolder. More attractive. These thoughts are unsettling.

'Are you looking for somewhere to practise?' she says quietly into my ear. 'That's no problem. Go to the Norwegian Broadcasting House, the reception desk. Ask for the studio guard. Say hi from me. He's called Geir. There's a gorgeous Steinway in Studio 18. You can sit there in the evenings. And you like the evenings for practising, don't you?'

All Rebecca's contacts, I think. The privileges of the rich.

She gives me a peck on the cheek and disappears together with Ferdinand, who gives a parting smile, polite and amiable as ever. I wonder what he could possibly have got from the day.

So, here I am. Alone with Margrethe Irene.

She stands in the living room looking at me.

This is what I had always hoped to avoid. Being left alone with Margrethe Irene.

She smiles shyly, trying to hide her braces behind her lips. I feel a pang of guilt. She is not completely without charm. A well-heeled young woman, asking me to stay. I am not used to such things.

'Let's go to my room,' she says. 'I've got some more wine in there, and your horoscope.'

'OK,' I say, following her. A large bedroom. A bed. A picture of Rita Streich. I stare at the poster. There at the bottom is the logo for Deutsche Grammophon. Every musician's ultimate dream.

'She's my favourite singer,' says Margrethe Irene. 'You must have heard her?'

I nod. 'Mother worshipped her. She's a coloratura. For example in *The Magic Flute* – the Queen of the Night.'

'Yes, she really was a queen of the night,' says Margrethe Irene.

She signals me to come over. I'm to sit on her bed.

I sit down, noticing that she has a little stereo system in the corner. A few records lean against the wall.

'This is my most sacred space,' she says earnestly.

'I feel honoured,' I say.

'Now, I shall draw up your horoscope.'

'Don't we need some music?'

She puts a finger to her lips. 'Later.'

She sits next to me and unfolds an enormous sheet of paper. I see a circle. Lines in all directions. Triangles. A jumble of paths.

'This is your life,' she says.

I do not want to hear it. But she points.

'There's your ascendant. It's in Taurus fortunately. You're Scorpio. Poor you.'

'Is that tantamount to death?'

She is sitting beside me. She stares at the sheet with utter concentration. At the top, in capitals, it says 'Aksel'. This jumble of lines is my life.

'No, not death,' she answers. 'More like life. But far too many lines.' She looks at me gravely, holding my hand. I don't like it, yet her sincerity touches me. The fact that she's taken on these investigations, all on her own. That she's so interested in me.

'You let yourself get distracted, Aksel. There's so much you want. But you should focus your energies on one thing.'

'And what should that be?'

She stares bewilderedly at me. 'I don't know,' she says. 'Only you can know that.'

I nod and listen. She is making an impression. Of course she is right. I allow myself to be distracted. To think she can see me so precisely. And she is right! I'm not in a good state, I'm incapable of concentration.

'But you have a chance now,' she points at a line that runs between two planets. 'Your energy will dominate from now on.'

I nod again.

'That's nice,' I say.

'But you'll have to make choices.'

She gets up to go over to the record player. She pulls a record out of its sleeve. I can see what it is. Samuel Barber. The 'Adagio'.

I hear it crackle. The music begins.

'Right now, it's just you and me,' she says.

'Maybe,' I say.

She comes back to the bed. This is not what I want. Yet I obey her slightest signal.

'Lie down,' she says.

'Why have you chosen such mournful music?'

'Because that's what suits us.'

I've longed to lie like this. Together with Anja. The perfect music. Her mouth. Those green eyes. Almost everything is right. Apart from the most important thing. This is Margrethe Irene. We lie next to each other, on her bed. I don't know how she's managed it. 'Adagio for Strings' and all.

'Now you have to kiss me,' she says.

I don't want this. I look at her huge eyes. Like saucers. She can see I am fighting it, that I really don't *want* it. Then she puts her hand calmly on my trousers, over my crotch.

'Are you fighting it? This too?' she says.

I have no idea what to say. I have never experienced this before.

She looks at me again. I have to kiss her now.

She has always aroused disgust in me. Now I am lying next to her, letting this happen.

'Rubinstein,' she says, ' I love Rubinstein.'

I close my eyes. It's Anja I love.

'Look at me,' she says. I obey. She unbuttons my trousers. Her eyes are wide. I kiss her carefully. She grasps me tight. It feels good.

'You mustn't be scared,' she says. 'You can't make babies like this.'

She guides my hand gently inside her trousers.

I lie motionless.

'Now you have to do the same to me as I do to you,' she says encouragingly.

Minutes pass. I have no idea what she expects of me.

'Haven't you learnt how?' she whispers in my ear. I feel her hand. Firm. No other girl has known this about me. I am incapable of resisting.

'Do you like it? I can feel you like it. You're my boy. Can you do the same to me?'

She places her hand over mine. Guiding me. So simple, I think, surprised. I had never dreamed it was like this.

She starts to groan. Not many seconds pass. Then she comes, with a gasp. She kisses my neck, clinging herself to me. I listen to her breathing. Not knowing what to do.

'Thank you, Aksel. That was so good.'

I lie calmly at her side. Giving her time. She is gasping for air. But she does not let me give up. We are listening to Barber, but everything is going faster.

'I'm not sure I want to.'

'Yes, you do!' Her voice commands me.

But I can only think of Anja, of her hands, her mouth. I think of the Yellow House. The smell of the alder thicket. Of the forbidden. I think of Catherine, of her breasts, of her legs. And yet only of Anja.

But Margrethe Irene knows she has me now. In that eager hand of hers. We kiss, my lips touching her brace. She laughs triumphantly.

'This had to happen. It should have happened long ago.'

She has a firm hold now and does not let go. I come in her hand. So violently it goes on her trousers. How shameful. Immediately I search for a handkerchief.

'There's no hurry,' Margrethe Irene laughs, kissing me on the mouth. 'We've got all the time in the world. Don't worry. Enjoy this now. Thanks to Rubenstein. Thanks to you. You're not to practise more than three hours per day. Remember? Long live the Young Pianists' Society!'

Conversation with Father

I RETURN HOME after midnight, my hair mussed up, ashamed and confused. Margrethe Irene Floed. Who'd want her as a girlfriend? It's just something that happened, I think to myself. And it will never happen again.

Father is in the living room, he has dozed off in front of the loudspeakers. His back slumped, hands down at his side. I go over to the player, look at the record cover, the face of Rita Streich. How strange. It surely can't be coincidental. She has been singing Mozart.

'Father,' I say, putting a gentle hand on his shoulder. 'Can you hear me, Father?'

He wakes with a start, confused. Then he sees me.

'I must have dropped off.'

He shakes his head, and shudders.

I go out into the kitchen. Fetch two glasses of milk, put them on the table. Catherine is not home. I can sense it – a certain peace. She is out in town somewhere. Father stares at me. His eyes are flickering, in a way that always meant things were serious when Mother was alive.

I sit down on the sofa and run my fingers through my hair. A sudden feeling of grown-upness. A strange mix of pride and shame. Maybe Anja is the one who has something to lose now.

Anja is the only one filling my thoughts. Yes, the day's events are merely a step towards her, I reflect.

But Father sits dejectedly in front of me.

'What's the matter, Father?'

He stares at me helplessly, as though I might know the answer, as though I should be able to say the words for him.

'I've sold the house,' he says.

I nod. It hardly comes as a surprise. We drink our milk.

'So there's no money left?'

'Not a dime, my boy.'

He looks into my face, almost in bewilderment. His expression scares me. It reminds me of Mother when she was swept away with the current. When she realised she had gone too far. I must, I note, never go too far.

I pat him on the shoulder. My own father. I've never done that before. I pull my hand back.

'So Father, what's the situation?'

He takes stock of me, as though unsure if this is the right moment.

'I'm giving up.'

'Why?'

He looks piercingly at me.

'Everything has gone wrong, my son.'

He takes a large gulp of milk.

'What do you mean, wrong?'

He shrugs.

'Nothing more than it's all an absolute failure.'

'Are you so sure about that?'

'Yes, son. That's one thing I can be reasonably sure of. Not a single one of my projects has succeeded in these last years. '

'But surely that happens sometimes?'

'Not as often as with me.' His gaze falls on Rita Streich. That lovely face. That perfect coloratura.

'It was your mother who saw it first,' he says. 'And now I'm terrified that it might hang over this family like a curse.'

'What, Father?

'The way we aim too high,' he grabs me by the shoulder. 'I've aimed too high. And your mother was the first to see it.'

'But she was an adventurer too, wasn't she?' I say comfortingly.

'Not in the same way. She never took things this far. She always knew when things were out of reach. That's an important talent, Aksel, recognising that.'

I nod. This evening began as mine, it's fast becoming Father's. I let him have it. He's clearly had more to drink than me.

'I've been managing these properties for years now. It can't go on.'

I sit, listening, wanting to be the perfect son. 'What can't go on, Father?'

He stares gloomily at me. 'The business,' he says. 'The busy-ness won't be busy for much longer!' He laughs at the banality of his own joke. He's drunk as a newt. 'This market's dominated by one man, Herr Throndsen, the devil incarnate: he does everything right, and I do everything wrong. That's how it goes. Next autumn we'll have to move.'

I sigh with relief.

'Not before?' I say.

'You simply don't understand a thing,' says Father.

I lie in bed, unable to sleep. What was Father trying to say? That I thought too much of myself?

Father has gone to bed too. His snores come through the wall.

I think about Margrethe Irene, her hand in my trousers, my hand in her knickers. I think about what happened. Her brace, her lips, her hands. My burning shame. I think about Anja who will play Ravel with the Philharmonic. I think about Rebecca, who will have her debut so soon. I feel a distaste, a mix of restlessness and desire.

Then I hear a noise.

Catherine. She tiptoes in. Goes to bed in her room.

One more year, I think to myself. Before we are cast out into the world.

We still have time. Everything is still possible.

Studio 18

I MAKE MY WAY up the hill to the radio broadcasting building, NRK, one evening in late September. I am carrying a pile of sheet music. The working day is finished for most. Only the radio announcer and the guards are still here.

I think of everything that has been broadcast from here, all the music that Mother and I have stood in front of the radio listening to, while the radio's green eye blinked hypnotically: the morning concerts, the afternoon concerts and evening concerts. The operas, symphonies and chamber music. The lady at reception smiles warmly. I ask for Geir. Geir emerges from behind some brown panelling. He smells of tobacco and keys. He knows who I am.

'She's a lovely girl, that Rebecca. She's told me all about you. So you've chosen the artist's path too, have you? Remember it's a thorny one!'

'I know,' I say. 'But that doesn't frighten me.'

We go down a corridor, walking on green felt which makes us both electric. It gives off sparks, a veritable fireworks display.

'Don't worry about that,' says Geir. 'When you're sitting at the piano, you won't notice. So what are you practising these days?'

I show him my music. Brahms. Beethoven. Prokofiev. He nods appreciatively.

'Very nice, too,' he says.

The piano stands in the big room, waiting for me. 'You can sit here until midnight if you like.'

I thank him. Geir leaves. His keys jangling as he moves.

I am alone in Studio 18. I try the instrument, an old Steinway C. Not the best, but perfectly usable. I glance through the music I'm planning to play. But other thoughts distract me – the thought of Margrethe Irene and the things she has shown me. I don't want to think about it. I go over to the door. Switch out the light.

Things seem different in the pitch back. I can play what I want now.

I want to invoke Anja.

I play Schubert.

Elgar in Elvefaret

ANJA CALLS, one Tuesday. The house is empty. I am sitting here alone, playing Brahms, Opus 119. 'Can you come now?' she asks.

'Now? But aren't you at school?'

'It's half-term,' she says.

There are yellow leaves falling from the trees as I cross Melumveien minutes later. The clouds are hanging low, and there is a sharp October wind. I have been avoiding the world, spending my evenings at NRK in utter darkness, and my afternoons sitting at home in the daylight, practising with the damper pedal on. I generally don't answer the phone when it rings, since it's often Margrethe Irene. She's after a steady relationship, and wants to talk it over. I don't know what to say, even though I long to repeat our experience. She calls it our dirty little secret. I don't know what's dirty or what's clean. But I don't want to be tied down. Anja fills all my thoughts. I know more now about what she hides. That makes her more desirable than ever.

I walk down the slope towards Elvefaret. All the houses seem empty and deserted. Only inside *me* is there any life. It's hard not to break into a run, but I don't want to be out of breath when I see her. Afternoon in Røa. A solitary man and a dog. An old lady with her trolley. Ordinary lives. Ordinary days, each identical to the next. That is not what I want. Anja fills my life with magic; the thought of her sustains me. And it is to her that I'm going now: she has decided to let me in at last. But is this what she wants, or is she doing it because she feels obliged? I hesitate at the gate. The house lies dark and gloomy behind the tall trees. They can't like the light, I muse. The sun never comes in here. But, I like it. I like everything that belongs to Anja's world.

My heart pounds as I open the gate and walk up the paved path that leads to the steps and the brown front door with its small leaded window. An old brass sign says 'Skoog'. I take a deep breath, and I ring the bell.

Seconds pass. I hear her steps. She opens up. I hardly dare to look at her. Will she give me a hug? No. But she opens the door wide and says: 'Come in.' I can never get used to the deep, warmth of her voice. Finally our eyes meet. I had forgotten that her eyes are green and that she is so blonde. She is wearing a lilac cotton top, black trousers and thick felt slippers. Her hair looks newly washed. She doesn't have a scrap of make-up. Everything she does seems so right. She rolls her eyes in her sweet, quirky way, and asks me into the living room. I think of all the things I could do with her, and where we'd lie to do them. Yet I daren't even touch her. She goes ahead of me into the room. There are huge abstract paintings on the walls; I recognise Jens Johannessen and Gunnar S. Gundersen. On either side of the large window looking over the valley and river, stand the AR loudspeakers, like two temples. The exclusive McIntosh amplifiers and the huge Garrard player fill almost the entire window ledge. Positioned for ideal listening stand two Barcelona chairs. The other seating consists, she informs me, of two Le Corbusier sofas and two Wassily chairs. All in black leather. The coffee table is glass and looks expensive. On the other side of the room stands the grand piano with its lid open. A Steinway A-model. Anja observes me carefully, as though every object were her responsibility. She expects me to say something.

'It's like walking into a design magazine,' I say, impressed.

'The living room's Daddy's pride and joy,' she says. 'That table there for example, that is Eero Saarinen.'

'Gosh,' I say.

I look at the glass cabinet where all the records are kept. I look at the large window with the trees outside.

'There's something timeless about everything here. I can understand why you don't miss Munch's "Sun".'

She nods. 'This is my world,' she says.

She has put some fruit out, and asks if I'd like some. But I am not hungry. 'No, thank you,' I say. She looks at her watch. Then she walks over to the cabinet with the records. 'It was good you could make it today,' she says. 'This is the perfect weather for Jacqueline du Pré, and for Elgar too, of course.'

'How do you mean?'

She smiles. 'The heavy rain clouds. So low in the sky. All that wind.'

'So you like that too, do you?'

She nods. 'I couldn't live without it. I get fed up when the sunny days go on for too long.'

She doesn't know that I've already listened to all this music; that I went down to Kjell Hillveg and I bought every single Jacqueline du Pré record in the shop, on the day after our walk to Brunkollen: Haydn, Elgar, the chamber music with Barenboim and Zukerman. I have played her daily and heard Anja in every note. Du Pré's loud breathing has been Anja's breath. The intensity of the cello's tone has been Anja's passion. Yes, I have grown used to seeing Anja to this music, to fantasising about her, as the images of what we might do together grow increasingly daring, although never as wild as du Pré's interpretations. Since there's another Anja, whom only I have the power to invoke, when I turn the light out in Studio 18 and play Schubert on those long evenings: the translucent second themes, the long horizontal lines of the expositions of those last three sonatas. How odd that Rebecca should decide to play one of them. They belong to me. When I play them, Anja is always so close.

'Are you off in a dream?'

I'm standing in the middle of the Skoog family's living room, lost in thought.

'Oh, I'm sorry . . .'

'What were you thinking about?' Anja asks inquisitively.

I'd like to share everything with her. But of course I can't. How can I tell her that I sit in pitch darkness in the NRK studio, dreaming her up? She would be as frightened as she was on the night among the alders.

'I was just thinking how lucky we are to have music in our lives,' I say.

'You're right,' she says, putting the record on the turntable.

We sit next to each other in the Barcelona chairs. As though we were at a concert. The familiar crackling begins, leading into the cello, the orchestra, and finally that rich, heavy theme. The sound of Jacqueline du Pré's breathing. The almost terrifying passion of her performance. The wind rages outside. Along the bank of the river, the tall spruce trees sway. I think of Mother, who died down there in the valley. Would she have liked this person who sits beside me, knees placed neatly together, exuding the fragrance of marigolds, of calendula? Anja Skoog, who has bewitched both Catherine and me. I am frightening myself now. My feelings are too strong; not normal. Despite sitting right next to me, and even inviting me into her house, Anja is as untouchable as ever. It would be madness to reach out for her hand. Her thoughts are somewhere else. She is ignorant of the kinds of things Margrethe Irene and I have done, which we continue to do when I can no longer hold out. She is *in* the music now. Listening to Elgar's lavish tone-painting, hearing the sea's waves and watching the restless spruce trees outside the window. Even though I daren't turn to her, I know she is crying, that she feels the music very strongly, even if the tears don't fall. It's loud, the amplifier is on full blast. Jacqueline du Pré could be sitting right in front of us, between the two AR loudspeakers, as though the whole orchestra were in the room, despite that being a physical impossibility. We are nearing the great climax of the first movement. Anja has started swaying, inhabiting the music, starting to groan almost and to breathe heavily, just like Jacqueline du Pré. Then suddenly a gust of cold air comes behind us. A door has opened. I feel the chill. There's somebody in the room. An ominous feeling. I turn around just as Anja leaps from her chair.

It's the Torchlight Man.

Bror Skoog, the brain surgeon is standing in the doorway, watching us.

For a moment Anja seems completely paralysed. Then she dashes over to the record player and lifts the needle. But her hand is unsteady. There is a ripping sound. The surgeon's face contorts with agony. Then he smiles weakly.

'You needn't have taken the music off, Anja,' he says, affably.

'But of course, Daddy. Have you got work to do?'

He nods. 'I have a report to write. It's urgent. I never seem to get enough quiet at the hospital.'

'We can be quiet.'

Bror Skoog stares at me. 'What a shame,' he says, 'perhaps you can play Elgar together some other time.'

But there will be no other time. I can see it in his face, and Anja's too. There is no space for me here. They want me to leave, but neither of them dare say so.

'I'll be going then,' I say, 'I just popped by, anyway.'

The Torchlight Man smiles, but his eyes are expressionless.

'Another time,' he says.

I go out into the hallway and put on my coat. Anja looks pale. It feels as though she wants to say something, but she is silent.

'And how's the career going?' asks the Torchlight Man.

'So so,' I answer evasively.

'And what is one practising, in Melumveien?'

'One is practising Brahms and Beethoven,' I answer.

He nods quickly, and appears to be finished with me already. 'Well, one never tires of Brahms and Beethoven.'

I try to catch Anja's eye, but she doesn't dare to look at me.

'Thank you for letting me come,' I say to her.

She mumbles something.

'You'll come and listen to her with the Philharmonic in January, won't you?'

'Of course,' I say. 'I am looking forward to it already. But Rebecca's debut is coming up first of course.'

The Torchlight Man's eyes open wide. Anja looks surprised too.

'Rebecca Frost? Is she making her debut?'

'Yes, on 11 November. I'm sure you'll be invited,' I say to Anja.

'How strange,' says Anja and looks at her father, perplexed. 'Selma hasn't mentioned anything.'

'I'll ring her,' says Bror Skoog, testily.

I understand nothing. It suddenly feels extremely close in here. My head is burning. I open the front door. And as I do, I feel the nausea rise.

'Thank you,' I say.

'A pleasure,' says the Torchlight Man, speaking for the two of them.

I make for the alder thicket. Immediately I have turned the corner and they can no longer see me, I take the turn to the right. It is still windy out, but down here, amongst the trees, it is calm. I'm as hard as rock. Minutes later I can't take any more. I throw up, retching long after there is anything left. My eyes are blind with tears. Then comes the headache. With hurried steps I walk home. I grab the telephone receiver. I ring Margrethe Irene.

'Can I come over?' I ask. I hear her breathing in my ear.

'Yes, of course you can,' she answers.

Marianne Skoog

THE NEXT DAY I sit with the telephone directory in my hands, having searched the business pages. Doctors. Gynaecologists. I still feel dirty after yesterday's visit to Bislet. Pleasure, followed by shame. I am demeaning not just myself, but Anja too, I think to myself. How shall I ever see her again now?

Marianne Skoog. Gynaecologist. Pilestredet 17.

I call the number; it is already well into the afternoon.

It rings five times. She takes the receiver. I hear the voice. Yes, it's her. I see her before me. So much like Anja. She doesn't scare me like the Torchlight Man. In the Aula when Anja won, she had looked at me for a long time. It had made me feel safer. It gave me hope. Perhaps one of the Skoog family might understand me at least.

'Marianne Skoog,' her voice is friendly.

'This is Aksel Vinding. I know your daughter, Fru Skoog. I played in the competition.'

'There's no need to call me Fru Skoog,' she says.

'All right.' I begin to stutter, trying to explain the reason for my call. But what is the reason? Because I am in love with her daughter? Because I have started to contemplate suicide? Because I have no idea what to do?

'I need to speak to somebody. It's about Anja.'

'What about Anja?'

'I love her.'

The words just tumble out of me. She laughs, a kindly laugh.

'Well, Anja's certainly worth loving.'

I tell her what happened yesterday. She listens intently. It is clearly news to her. I tell her that I feel frightened off by her father. That I'm at my wits' end. I ask if I can talk to her.

She doesn't dismiss me. She is thoughtful and, after a moment's silence, says:

'Where are you now?'

'At home in Røa, but I can jump on a tram.'

'I've got a meeting here in town tonight, but I have a couple of hours to spare now.'

'I'll come as fast as I can.'

I grab some money, and make a dash for the station. The tram has never gone so slowly. I am about to meet Marianne Skoog. It almost feels like meeting Anja. This was the woman that gave birth to her! But what should I say? What impression am I making? I'm not even eighteen. She must think I'm a child. But I'm not, I think to myself. I know as much about life as any adult now.

As I emerge from the Nationaltheatret station, it is dark. The weather is still miserable. It's been raining all day, but for now it's holding. I run across Karl Johan and up Universitetsgata. I'm running towards somebody who might help me understand what's happening to me, and help calm me.

She lets me in with a buzzer. I take the lift to the third floor. She is waiting for me at the door, still wearing her white coat. Her room is bright. She shakes my hand and looks penetratingly at me. I look back at her, almost having to take a step back. She is so much like Anja; the same green eyes. I find I have to avert my gaze.

'You look so much like her!' I exclaim.

The observation pleases her, 'Well, how lovely,' she says brightly, 'to resemble somebody that someone loves.'

I blush. How ridiculous of me to be so open. She must think I'm soft in the head. Then I notice the chair. The gynaecologist's chair. I have to support myself against the wall. I suddenly see the reality of what she does. I see the daily duties, the rubber gloves, the fingers, all the women, the pain, the worry, the splayed legs.

'Are you unwell?'

I don't know what to say. We certainly cannot stay here.

'Are you hungry?' I ask. 'Can I invite you for a meal?'

I cannot believe my own words. Have I lost all inhibition? As if Margrethe Irene had tugged on a thread and the whole weave had started to unravel. Marianne Skoog laughs at my audacity. Then looks at her watch.

'Hmm, why not?' she says. 'I could do with something to eat.'

'It's on me!' I say.

She laughs even more. She removes her white coat. Underneath she is wearing a green twin set and a pearl necklace. And to my surprise she is wearing jeans.

But she's not laughing as we walk side by side down towards Blom. It has to be Blom, because that was where Mother went, and where W. Gude goes, and he's a man of style and good taste. Marianne Skoog has nothing against going to Blom. I am nervous and excited, and can feel I want wine again. It is almost getting to be a habit. I drank at Margrethe Irene's yesterday too.

Minutes later we are at a table, in the far corner, beside the beautiful sunken aquarium with its waterfall. The red wine has been brought to the table. Chicken has been ordered.

'So, you're an unhappy young man?' says Marianne Skoog, without a hint of irony.

'I'd love to spend time with her,' I say, 'and of course I don't want to impose. But we went for a walk once, and I thought she enjoyed being together with me. Besides, it's not just me. All the pianists in our group would like to spend more time with her. But she always sneaks off.'

Marianne Skoog is thinking as I talk. I see the fine lines in her face, and it strikes me once more how young she is. She can't have been more than twenty when she had Anja, I reflect. She's not even forty.

'Do you find her abnormally distant?'

I nod. 'I think we all do. We never see her; not at concerts nor at the Young Pianists' Society. And she's always invited.'

Marianne Skoog sits quite still staring straight ahead. I feel I've said enough. It's her turn to speak. But she says nothing. She has so much of Anja in her. I suddenly like the fact she is almost forty.

A tear rolls down her cheek. She doesn't try to hide the fact that she is crying. But her tears are silent. She opens her handbag, takes out a handkerchief and blows her nose.

'There's a lot you don't know.'

She takes my hand. Her hand is warm. Anja's hand almost, I think.

We both drink our wine with our free hands.

'Should I tell you this?' she says, mostly to herself. She looks at me intently, measuring me, but it seems she has made up her mind.

'You can trust me,' I say, 'All I want is what's best for Anja. I hope you understand that. If she doesn't want anything to do with me, I'll accept that. But then I would want her to say it first. There is something about her father that . . .'

'Yes, there is something about her father,' Marianne Skoog repeats. I know now that we like each other, that we are on the same team. A silent joy rushes through me. Slowly she lets go of my hand. The food arrives at the table, but neither of us eats.

'It is strange that you should phone me,' she says. 'Since I know more about you than you think. I had your mother as a patient. There was nothing wrong with her, but it shook me when she died. When I saw you in the Aula that evening, I realised how you felt about my daughter. I was happy to see it. I think Anja is most definitely worth loving. Sometimes I can hardly believe I'm her mother, and perhaps that's not so strange. I was only eighteen when I had her . . .'

'No older than I am now!' I exclaim.

She smiles carefully. 'No, but you know yourself that one can have feelings at that age.'

I blush. Stutter. 'Then you . . . are . . . just . . .'

She is reading my thoughts. 'Yes, then I am only thirty-five,' she says.

'Almost a youngster!'

We both laugh, before she grows serious again.

'I knew you'd been for a walk,' she says. 'And I could hear from the way you played Debussy that you're a sensitive chap. There are so few people I can talk about Anja with. Everything that worries me. The strange thing is that I was considering contacting you, in the hope you might know what's going on in her head.'

'But I don't know anything.'

She nods thoughtfully. 'So I see. Then it'll be up to me to talk, in the hope we can both understand more.'

She nibbles at a bit of chicken. It will be the only thing I see her eat.

'I'll have to go back to the beginning,' she says. But nothing happens. I straighten my back and sit waiting as quietly as a mouse. 'Bror is seven years older than me,' she says at last. 'He'd almost finished his medical training when we met at a party at Dovrehallen. Anja arrived, on our first attempt, so to speak. But neither of us was ready for parenthood.'

I nod. This is what I want to hear. The story. The details. All the things Anja hasn't said. Marianne Skoog is talking to me, a little motherly at first, almost teacherly. She tells me about the Torchlight Man, who wanted her to have an abortion. She explains that she couldn't do that, and that she had Anja. The child was a gift, but she didn't intend to give up her training. 'I wanted to be a doctor, and as you might have realised, we're both from well-to-do families. There was no problem finding a nanny for Anja. We moved to Elvefaret almost straightaway. I studied for seven years. I got what I wanted. But Anja was always a source of guilt for both of us. And most of all for Bror. He could never reconcile himself with the fact that he'd tried to prevent her from being born at all.'

It is getting harder for her now. What is she going to tell me about her husband? That he was plunged into deep, existential crisis? That he adored Anja the instant he saw her, but that his love was tainted by remorse? That he could never do enough for her? That he grew obsessed with her to the point of sickness? She tells me about the Torchlight Man, about Bror who was a fine man, cultured, understanding. But then how the more difficult aspects of his nature had surfaced, the unstable personality, the limitless desire for control, for rules, for systems. He wanted to give Anja the absolute best, and to do that he had to raise her himself. It was getting too much.

'I tried saying something, but it was impossible. We just ended up yelling at each other. Love didn't flow easily between us.'

I sense another, more brutal story behind the one she is relating in such measured words. She tells me she had wanted a divorce. That the Torchlight Man had gone crazy, threatening her life and screaming that it would never happen. That it scared her. That he was frightened that Marianne would take Anja away. That he might be capable of killing them both. Yes, I think to myself. Perhaps that's why she's telling me all this! History is full of crazy men! And if I'm to believe what she is telling me, Bror Skoog must have been crazy. Perhaps he still is. I listen to Marianne Skoog and feel I can see the whole story through her eyes; that she didn't dare leave, that she could have let him have Anja, but that this would have been an even greater defeat.

She pauses, shakes her head. It is my turn to take her hand. It rests on the table, almost stretched out. I try to comfort her, young as I am.

'What a price to pay,' I say.

She nods and continues, wanting to complete this miserable confession. 'So I stayed,' she says. 'It isn't so impossible, you know. Millions of people do it all the time, remaining in relationships they don't really want. I did it for Anja's sake. I thought, I'll sacrifice a few years, but then, when Anja turns eighteen, I shall leave him. That's a year away now.'

'Does he know?'

She hesitates. 'He senses it. We never talk about it. But he knows my love is dead. I live in Elvefaret because I want to be a mother to Anja, and no more. I know I can pacify Bror when necessary, his more extreme behaviour. But there's an axis between Anja and him, a world into which I'm not allowed. Sometimes I'm really frightened that . . .'

She hides her face in her hands.

'What are you frightened of?'

She looks at me, clearly frightened at having said so much; at having said anything at all to this good-for-nothing youth. But I have never felt so grown-up.

'What are you frightened of?' I ask again.

She doesn't give any answer. A shiver goes up my spine. As though I can hear the words she cannot say.

We stay in Blom until late into the evening. Marianne has forgotten her appointment. I feel a strange seriousness, a solidarity with this woman who is so like Anja, and yet not. I tell her about my life; she is interested to hear how I spend my days. I tell her about the piano, the practice, the dreams. And as I talk I have the sensation, whether real or imagined, that something is happening between us, that the confidences we have shared now will leave their mark. She is no longer Anja's mother. She is Marianne Skoog, seventeen years older than me. I think of her differently now from before my arrival. I think she is beautiful; that she is a woman.

We rise simultaneously, as though we both suddenly realise that we risk crossing a line. She wants to pay the bill, but I have my pride. I pay with money that is barely mine to spend. She accepts.

'All right,' she says, 'But next time it's my turn.'

As if there ever could be a next time, I think to myself. We walk together up Karl Johan on our way towards Nationaltheatret station, only to discover that neither of us intends to take the tram home to Røa. She looks at her watch.

'I can still catch the end of my meeting,' she says evasively. There's a restlessness in her gaze that causes me to disbelieve her. I think there is a man.

But I keep it to myself. I too suddenly have plans for the rest of my evening.

We give each other a brief hug, too brief perhaps, at the station entrance, before going our separate ways.

'It was nice to meet you,' she says.

'Yes, thank you for taking the time.'

'You know more about me now than anyone else.'

'I won't tell.'

'No, please don't.'

She walks in the direction of the Saga Cinema. I stand there watching after her, both excited and confused. From behind I can see no difference between her and Anja.

The wind buffets me. It begins to rain again.

I set off through the Palace Gardens, towards Bislet.

Rebecca Frost's debut

EXPECTATION HANGS in the air. Tomorrow Rebecca Frost will make her debut. She will do the very thing we all dream of, but which we don't dare. Taking that step into the adult world. We're all a little envious, but also a little proud of her. I am lying in Margrethe Irene's bed. The usual things have happened. The only difference being that Margrethe Irene's dentist has finally come to his senses and removed her brace. I didn't know she had such pretty teeth.

I find it a relief that she never undresses completely, and that we never go all the way. She doesn't want to use contraception. And doesn't want me to use anything either. And doesn't want babies. It suits me better perhaps than she knows. What we have is more than enough for me. She thinks she's using me; but I'm the one using her. We'll never get married, I think to myself. Now is the time to have fun using one another.

'So when do you intend to make your debut?' she asks, as though we've never discussed it before.

'I need to get away from Synnestvedt,' I answer. 'But that might take time.'

'Are you such a pushover? Why do you make allowances for that pathetic man? It's all completely upside down.'

I know she is right. But I can't bring myself to hurt Synnestvedt, and neither am I ready for my debut. There's something still lacking. I've felt it when I let my thoughts fly, sitting in the dark of Studio 18, playing music that is almost beyond me. That's when the expressiveness comes. That's when my delivery is right. Because Anja is in my thoughts. But I could never tell Margrethe Irene this.

'There's no hurry,' I say.

She tweaks my nose. 'Because you want to be the biggest sensation. Because you think you can out-perform us all.'

She's right, of course. But I can't admit it.

'You'll make your debut before me,' I say, kissing her sweet mouth. I like her more and more.

'And I'm not even sure I want to be a musician,' she says. Margrethe Irene is still at school. Everybody is still at school apart from me. I feel like a layabout. What I do with Margrethe Irene seems so depraved. I have lost so much confidence. It troubles me that I'm no longer so sure of myself.

But it's Rebecca's moment now. It's 10 November. When Margrethe Irene and I get up from bed, it is in order to stroll up to NRK, to the great, empty broadcasting house, where Rebecca has invited our Young Pianists' Society for a dress rehearsal in Studio 19, with Geir's blessing.

Studio 19 has the best instrument: a Steinway Model D, with its heavy action, preferred at the time, and as I like it.

Anja has had an invitation too. Sent in the post. But she isn't here. Rebecca comes over to me and kisses me on the mouth, primarily to irritate Margrethe Irene. She is wearing jeans and a crumpled white blouse, as if to stress the informality of the rehearsal.

'Anja phoned, she isn't coming tonight,' Rebecca says, flashing a look at Margrethe Irene, clearly designed to tease. 'But she's coming tomorrow. And she says she'll even come for the party!'

She rolls her eyes, imitating Anja so precisely that all three of us break into giggles. Rebecca is clearly both nervous and expectant. I observe how nerves can make people so beautiful. I want to tell her how pretty she is, but I keep it to myself. Margrethe Irene has suffered enough.

A handful of us have come to hear Rebecca. Not just the hard core of the Young Pianists' Society, but some promising singers and string players too. Rebecca has always been a generous girl. She has lots of friends. She has arranged the chairs in a semi-circle around the grand piano, and has put out some fruit, sparkling water and wine. But we've come to listen. It is courageous of her to hold the dress rehearsal on the day before her debut. 'I'm doing it to tame my nerves,' she says. 'If this goes well, the most important thing will be done. Tomorrow will be a walk in the park. And you have no idea what a fabulous dress I've got!' she says, mostly to Margrethe Irene. 'In light blue satin. Straight from

Paris. Daddy insisted that I mustn't count the cost. You'll die of excitement. I promise!'

She sends a meaningful glance at the two of us. It feels so embarrassing to stand here, hand in hand with Margrethe Irene. It's as though the world knows what we do when we're alone. But Rebecca's concerns are elsewhere – she has a task ahead. She is about to sit within inches of her most demanding, but also most devoted audience. I admire her for her courage. None of her family is invited. Nor, strangely enough, Selma Lynge. Rebecca has chosen to have her dress rehearsal among trusted friends, with nothing to distract her. This concert will be her apprentice piece. She wants comments, criticism. We must, she tells us, be one hundred per cent honest.

We take our seats. The concert begins. A small slip at the start of the gauzy Ravel prelude, and then I see her concentration rally. Rebecca has made impressive progress in just a few months. She sweeps through the horrifically difficult Toccata as though it were nothing, despite its repetitive intricacy and demanding octave reaches with their chords in the middle. Our applause is enthusiastic. She gets up and curtseys; she has regained her natural poise. Next comes the Opus 109, the piece I'm so sure I can play myself. There's something magnificent about her, I think, a dignity in her straight back, her proud neck. She has no hidden agenda. And tomorrow evening she will make her debut. I close my eyes in the most emotional sections, the variation movement, listening to its pauses, its diversions, as though Beethoven mirrors my own fragmented frame of mind. I sit, holding Margrethe Irene's hand, but thinking of Anja. Tomorrow I shall see her again.

Rebecca completes the Beethoven Sonata and four Chopin ballads. As each piece opens I am impressed; not least by her technique. But each time I notice my enthusiasm wane, my interest cool. The contrasts on which she depends begin to be contrived, as though I can hear Selma Lynge's voice behind everything. Something learned that she can't hear for herself. I feel uneasy on her account.

Nevertheless we applaud loudly when she is done. Stamping our feet and shouting bravo. Rebecca gestures us to be quiet, demanding that we give her instant criticism. But we're not daft. We are her friends. Whatever we might have been tempted to say, it is too late to do anything anyway. Only Ferdinand ventures an opinion. 'Give yourself even more time in the F Major Ballad,' he says, 'in the lyrical section, because you play it so beautifully.'

She thanks him, looking inquiringly around the room at us all. Don't we have any negative comments? Really? None? We shake our heads. Suddenly I can see how nervous she really is. Tomorrow she will sit under Munch's 'Sun', before the critics and an eager public. She is expected to triumph, and to be carried on the shoulders of the crowd all the way home to a lavish reception in her beautiful Bygdøy mansion. Everybody will be there; her class from high school, our little band of pianists, her family and friends. Even Catherine is invited, although I have no idea why. 'Well, she's your sister, isn't she?' was her curt reply.

Rebecca needs to go straight home to bed now, although she assures us she will not sleep a wink. She drives her own car, having just passed her test. Her reward from her parents was a Saab Cabriolet.

'See you tomorrow!' she waves at us outside the broadcasting house. 'And afterwards we'll all get so-o drunk!'

The day arrives. 11 November 1969. Brilliant sunshine, no snow yet. There are still yellow leaves on the trees. Rebecca gets massive coverage in all the major papers. 'Shipping magnate's daughter chooses music,' *Aftenposten* declares. 'A Touch of Frost tonight', writes *VG*. 'Classical music should be more rock'n'roll,' she's told *Dagbladet*. Gorgeous photographs of her everywhere. Catherine leans across the kitchen table reading the articles with me. 'She is so stylish,' she groans. 'So funny. So wise.'

And suddenly I can see it. Rebecca is attractive. God, have I begun to lose all inhibition? Are there, I ask myself, no limits? I've even been dreaming about Marianne Skoog who, incidentally, I've not seen again. We must both have been frightened by our shared confidences.

Catherine is proud and happy to be invited to such a prestigious event. She has given her word of honour that she will not shout bravo before the end of the concert.

And I am excited at the thought of seeing Anja again. At 6.30 p.m. we take the tram into town. I notice we're both on the lookout for Anja, but she isn't there. I've decided not to tell Catherine anything about my visit to Elvefaret, or my dinner with Anja's mother. I don't want her being my big sister all over the place. She is not going to be allowed to complicate this too. I have turned eighteen. I will be taking my driving test soon. I can run my own life.

There is huge excitement outside the Aula. A queue at the ticket office. There are rumours that it's sold out. Debuts are always special, and Rebecca Frost's debut has attracted the elite. Fabian Frost has been somewhat liberal in dishing out free tickets and invitations. Not necessarily the best concert audience, I think. Elderly, rich, alcoholic gentlemen who doze off, and women who yawn or, even worse, clap between movements.

How is Rebecca likely to be feeling now? I wonder, as I walk up the steps with Catherine, knowing that one day, not too far in the future, it will be my turn. Then it'll be my turn to wait in the green room, hands sweating, as Rebecca is no doubt doing right now, as W. Gude scurries about. How is she coping? Is she trying to empty her mind of all the things she has to remember by heart, the thousands of notes she must reproduce, during the course of this one concert? She may not suffer from nausea, as I do, but she might feel faint. She will be hearing the sound of the auditorium slowly filling up, and she will constantly need to pee. As I stand in the cloakroom queue, thinking these things, Anja suddenly appears beside us.

'There you all are!' she says cheerfully, squeezing Catherine's arm, who is closest to her. She sends me a glance, as though she wants to say something, but stops herself. 'Heavens, I'm nervous!'

'You too?' I say relieved. 'And I thought you didn't know what nerves meant?'

'Don't be daft, Aksel,' she comes between us. 'I've barely slept all night.'

'But Rebecca will be fine.'

'Of course she will.'

It's so good to see her again. With her green duffel coat, her huge, mauve woollen scarf. The scent of calendula. Catherine whispers something to her – I'd so like to hear what it is. Anja's nervousness has made me feel even more nervous. And there, at the top of the stairs, by the entrance, stands Margrethe Irene, in a fake fur and with her hair in artificial curls. She is waiting for us. I have dreaded this moment. Now Anja will know that we're a couple. Idiotic, I think, feeling a pang of guilt at the sight of Margrethe Irene's pale face. We've never discussed it, but she knows how I feel about Anja. Once, just as I was on verge of coming, she stopped, loosened her grasp and asked me, almost spitefully: 'Is your mind on Anja now?'

Margrethe Irene walks towards us, kisses me demonstratively on the mouth, greets Catherine politely, and hugs Anja.

'Oh golly! I'm just so nervous!'

'How did it go yesterday?' asks Anja.

Yesterday . . . ? I think to myself, disorientated. Yesterday feels so long ago.

'She played superbly,' Margrethe Irene says emphatically.

'Then I'm sure it will go well tonight,' says Anja, with a deep sigh.

I peer at her curiously. She seems unusually uptight. But then it will be her turn next. In two months she will play Ravel's G Major with the Oslo Philharmonic. Just thinking about it makes my stomach turn.

The tension is contagious. People are standing in the cloakroom, talking boisterously. There's a party mood in the air that is far from soothing. We go into the auditorium. Rebecca has reserved seats for us on the fifth row. With a certain glee, I notice Catherine's uneasiness. People have recognised her. But I trust her tonight: her eyes aren't glazed and she doesn't smell of booze. In fact, she's put a bit more make-up on than usual, and she's wearing a smart suit she must have bought recently. She looks a bit boyish. She and Anja are nattering away, but I can't catch what they're saying, so long as Margrethe Irene insists on talking to me.

Munch's 'Sun': a permanent sunrise over the shoreline of Kragerø, painted after the artist's breakdown in Denmark. The image suddenly seems to gain symbolic value, signalling hope and bright times. I contemplate the technical minefield Rebecca will embark on for the next couple of hours, the repertoire she has chosen, filled with technical demands with scarcely a moment for breath: Ravel's octaves and repetitive notes, Beethoven's impossible trills, and the treacherous tempests of Chopin, the tortuously difficult end sections of all the ballads, the thirds, the fourths and, again, the octaves, and the firmness and clarity of touch, so crucial.

'Good luck,' whispers Anja, almost to herself.

She is sitting to my right. Margrethe Irene is on my left. Catherine sits on the other side of Anja. I so want to grab Anja's hand, but it's Margrethe Irene's that I hold. Anja seems impervious to everything. She has no such feelings for me, she doesn't love me. Neither does Margrethe Irene. But at least she wants sex with me. And Catherine over there. Who would she like to have sex with? Irrelevant, I suppose. Anja is all that matters here. Anja must be loved, nothing less.

I sense a pair of eyes behind me. I turn. A sudden chill. Who is looking at me? My eyes scan the back rows. There he is. I recognise that face. He ducks immediately he recognises me.

It is the Torchlight Man.

I say nothing to Anja. There's a buzz in the Aula as feverish as before some big event; before, for example, the presentation of the Nobel Peace Prize to a US President or to a controversial Middle Eastern politician. I have never experienced anything like it since the performances of Rubinstein or Richter or Argerich. The auditorium is heaving. Even the side benches are filled. And the standing places are completely sold out, occupied by inquisitive pupils from the music conservatory. Synnestvedt is here too. Sitting in his usual seat on the other side of the gangway. He waves at me, as always. I wave back. I am seated between 'The History' and 'Alma Mater', Munch's visual treatise on human existence, on time and creation. I can hear Anja sneering about them, telling Catherine how she's always found these paintings so banal, so shallow, so sentimental. It troubles me. Mother once said: 'People who sneer about sentimentality are generally self-important and ungenerous with themselves.' But I'd rather not think about Mother. It's not long now; there are five minutes to go. The critics are beginning to arrive: the well-respected Hans-Jørgen Hurum from *Aftenposten*, Klaus Egge, the old grouch from *Arbeiderbladet*, as well as Finn Arnestad from *Friheten* and, following close on his heals, the courteous Conrad Baden from *Morgenbladet*. But who's representing *Dagbladet* and *VG*? There they are: Magne Hegdal and Folke Strømholm. And from *Nationen*? And *Morgenposten*? So many newspapers. So many opinions. And they're all here; music's weapon bearers. Running straight from their restaurant tables to take their seats at the very last minute.

Four minutes to go. Fabian Frost arrives with his wife Desiree. He wears a dinner jacket. She wears a simple, ruby-red dress. Rebecca's choice, I feel certain. Nevertheless a mother mustn't outshine her daughter on a day like this.

Three minutes to go. Selma Lynge arrives, dressed in a tight-fitting but severe turquoise dress, which accentuates every curve of her body. All eyes are on her as she makes her way up the central aisle, and to the front. Her husband Torfinn Lynge, international philosopher and author of *On the Ridiculous,* follows her, a step behind, as though she were queen, and he a mere prince consort. She's keeping well for a fifty-year-old mother of three, I think. As she passes our row, she turns to Anja and smiles. I notice the warmth of her gaze. She flashes a look at me, followed by Catherine and Margrethe Irene; a look that says that we're all utterly transparent to her. Her black hair is elegantly fastened in a bun.

'She behaves like a queen,' I mumble, not intending anybody to hear.

'She *is* a queen,' says Anja, enthralled.

Selma Lynge takes her seat with her husband in the third row. The buzz in the hall settles; everybody knows that the moment is near. We are just waiting for W. Gude now. Soon he will emerge from the door on the left. He will have exchanged a few final words with Rebecca, before she has to come to the platform, revealing the dress she has talked so much about. And there he is! In his black suit, white shirt and bow tie, as smart as ever. He looks serious, as always on these occasions. He sits on his regular spot to the side, sweeps the audience with his gaze, squints, and nods to some aquaintances.

The lights dim.

The chatter stills.

Everything is serious.

Oh my God, Rebecca! I think to myself, with a strange sense of premonition.

But there she comes! Entering not from the usual side door, clearly visible to the audience, but from another at the back of the stage, used by few soloists. But the instant I see her, I understand her decision. By taking the longest possible route to the piano, she can display herself. She wants to create a stir. Her dress is dazzling, in the same turquoise colour as Selma Lynge's. But where Selma Lynge's dress is severe, Rebecca Frost's is sumptuous. Naked shoulders. Cunning curves.

Narrowing at the bottom, as if to impress the boys at a summer ball rather than to deliver an apprentice piece. Only now do I notice the flower arrangements on each side of the stage in a matching colour. We sit in the audience devouring her with our eyes. I start to relax. Everything has been planned and directed to the minutest detail. Of course, I think to myself. Rebecca Frost is never rash. The audience start clapping. Loudly, warmly and excitedly.

Then she trips.

It happens on the stairs that descend to the lowest platform, where the grand piano awaits. She steps on her own dress, tumbling forwards. The hall gasps; we cannot believe our eyes. Rebecca Frost is suddenly prostrate on the floor. Somebody screams. I recognise Selma Lynge's voice. Rebecca lies on the floor. I look at Anja, she grabs Catherine's arm with both hands.

'I refuse to be part of this!' Margrethe Irene whispers in my ear.

But we have no choice. Rebecca is lying there. W. Gude rushes up on to the platform – I will never forget him for that. He is immediately beside her, on his knees, talking to her. But she is refusing to move. She lies with her nose to the floor. I may not be a woman, I may never have worn a dress, but I know exactly what must be going on in her head. She must wish herself far away. Wish the ground could swallow her. Her concentration lies in tatters. She can never fulfil the task she has set herself.

The Aula stage is freshly polished, which is why she fell. From where she lies now she can see her own reflection. W. Gude keeps talking to her. Finally, she seems to be listening. She stirs, and gets slowly to her feet, with the support of her impresario. Her shoes have come off. He helps her put them back on. She brushes dust from her dress, wobbles for a second, then straightens up. W. Gude whispers a few more words in her ear. They have a deal. She smiles, kisses him on the cheek, waves him away. He returns to his seat, straightens his bow tie, squints a little and takes his seat.

Rebecca Frost is left standing on the stage, trying to look her audience in the eye. She clears her throat. I cannot recall it ever having been so quiet in this hall. I glance over at Anja. She is holding my sister's hand.

'I dreaded something like this happening,' says Rebecca, in a loud, clear voice. 'This very thing happened to somebody else once. Thirty years ago. She was so devastated that she couldn't carry on with her debut. But I will carry on! I'm sorry that all this has distracted you all. I had no idea that the stage was newly polished.'

A sigh of relief from the audience. Laughter. Thunderous applause. Everybody is routing for her to succeed.

She sits at the grand piano.

'And there was I thinking she wouldn't manage it,' whispers Margrethe Irene.

But Rebecca is off, throwing herself into Ravel. Mistakes flow thick and fast. Her concentration is, of course, ruined. It would be impossible, I think to myself, for her to gather herself so quickly. But after a catastrophic start, things start to improve. The Toccata is adequate. Still, nothing is as it was yesterday. Her playing is not as good. I feel sorry for her. There was so much magic in the air; she could have made this concert a triumph. But I can hear that she is shaking, that the shock of the fall can't be cured that fast. But she no longer has any choice. She had to cancel or complete the performance. Now she has to complete it.

The applause for the Ravel is warm-hearted, but measured. She chooses not to leave the platform before the Beethoven. She's naturally afraid of making another entrance.

The critics are making their notes. The atmosphere of the hall is flat, slightly strained. The audience's nerves are shaken.

Beethoven.

Rebecca's coping, I think to myself. But nothing more. Plenty of people could perform as well as this. Her back is no longer straight. And her movements are overly expansive. She lifts her hands too high at the end of each phrase. Is this what is known as playing to the gallery? None the less she is maintaining control.

Anja is still holding Catherine's hand.

My admiration for Rebecca is growing. There aren't many people who could handle this. My mind goes to the poor Trøndelag boy who made his debut some time last spring. He didn't have the courage to play without the music, despite its being an unspoken but absolute requirement. The newspapers were merciless: 'The debutant turned up with a page turner, which did nothing to dispel the amateurish impression.'

Rebecca is sitting there, fighting. Fighting for her life. And when she comes to those difficult trills, the almost hopeless, technical challenges towards the end of the Beethoven, I can see that she's practised. Those long, tedious days at the piano are paying off. She pulls through, determined not to give up. She gives just enough to lift the mood in the hall, just enough to allow everybody to go out for the interval without feeling too bad.

I catch myself wanting a drink – or to smash a glass. Anja is still holding Catherine's hand. They're standing in a corner, talking in lowered voices. Margrethe Irene notices that I've seen them, and puts her lips to my ear: 'Don't upset yourself about that, Aksel.'

'I like you, a lot,' I say, touched by her consideration for me, by her generosity.

There are tears in her eyes. 'We all have to help each other now,' she says. I hardly hear what she says. People are talking so loudly. Everybody has to have an opinion on what's happened.

'Extraordinary that she's keeping at it!' a voice declares shrilly. It's hard to place the dialect, but I suspect it comes from Rebecca's chic neighbourhood on Bygdøy.

I feel anger growing inside me. But I don't know why. Then it occurs to me: perhaps I should go backstage and talk to her. To this girl who's always taken the time to talk to me, to spur me on. Why not cheer her on now, when she needs it most?

'Excuse me a minute,' I say to Margrethe Irene.

She doesn't stop me – she knows where I'm going. I return to the auditorium and run along the left-hand aisle, along 'The History'. If only I was as steady and wise as the old man in the painting.

Nobody stops me. I open the door and rush down the stairs. I find Rebecca sitting in the artists' foyer between W. Gude and Selma Lynge. Finally I have a reason to look the legendary Fru Lynge straight in the eyes. She confronts me full on, her gaze dark and commanding. She is fuming.

'What do you want?' she spits.

But Rebecca calms her. She's pleased to see me.

'Aksel!' she shouts, flinging both arms about me. I can smell her sweat, feel her stress.

'You're doing magnificently!' I say, almost starting to cry, feeling a sudden fondness for her. She has always been there for me. I want to give something back.

'I never want to live those forty-five minutes again,' she says, whilst Selma Lynge strokes her hair as though she were a child. She is still sending me disapproving looks. W. Gude withdraws, leaning against the wall. He doesn't belong in this drama.

But Rebecca sees only me. Selma Lynge realises, and withdraws into the corridor. Taking the hint, W. Gude follows her out. I am suddenly alone with Rebecca in this little artists' foyer with its red walls. A room with the feel of a bygone Russia, I think suddenly. A place of passion, of revolution and intimacies.

'I mean it, Aksel,' she says. 'Never again. It's not worth it. But I shall get to the end. I promise.' She pulls me closer. 'But for now, only you and I know that this debut will also be my farewell concert.'

'You don't mean it.'

'Shh!' Her lips tickle my ear.

'In forty-five minutes it will all be over.' She whispers, 'Never again. I'll go through with it so as to guarantee the party afterwards, and to please my parents. But life is too short, Aksel. When I lay there on the floor, I was as happy as a baby.' She steals a look at the others in the hallway. They cannot hear us, since she is whispering so quietly. 'I'm doing this for Fru Lynge's sake, for W. Gude, for Mummy and for Daddy. But after that, it's over. I'm looking forward to the party. I'm looking forward to starting a completely new life. Remember Rubinstein!'

'You too!' I say.

The second half might even prove a huge success – although it will all be in vain, I muse dejectedly, since she will use her victory for nothing. Anja is still holding my sister's hand. Anja and Margrethe Irene are burning with curiosity about what Rebecca said, what she's thinking and feeling. But there's no time to say anything before the lights dim.

She delivers the four Chopin ballads dutifully. Little more. Her rendition is conscientious. First the G Minor ballad infused with feelings bordering on the trite. Followed by the F Major ballad, with its extreme contrasts, from pianissimo to fortissimo. She remembers Ferdinand's advice and slows the tempo in the pure, lyrical sections. Then the A Flat Major ballad, a fragmentary distraction, which seems like a boring reception with too many guests, before the composer finally gathers together his threads and works towards a long, intricate crescendo. I'm impressed by how she tackles the octave leaps, but then notice that she's suddenly losing power; she is losing energy before she reaches the most difficult ballad of all: the F Minor, a single long counterpoint, a dark, destructive passion, without proper drive, whose ungovernable feelings lead nowhere, but which always serves as an effective finale. In Chopin's day, I imagine, the pianist might have leapt from his seat before the final chord had rung out. But Rebecca stays seated, as rather too many pretentious performers do. But this is no moment of pretension. Rebecca is worn out. She is too young for this, I think. Far too young. Which of us is ready to compete with Dinu Lipatti?

And, in two months, it will be Anja's turn.

The reception is polite, but doesn't lift the roof. The public is an unforgiving creature. It never allows itself to be tricked, except perhaps by the occasional flamboyant showman. When something falls short, it falls short. The audience is applauding Rebecca Frost now. Selma Lynge is already on her feet. Friends and acquaintances follow suit. How embarrassing, I think, when family are the first to stand up and cheer. Besides, Rebecca has no need for their applause. She meant what she said in the interval. This career is finished, before it began.

But she looks beautiful as she takes her applause. Seen from outside she is triumphant. A winner, as one would say on the sports field. But music is not a sport. We may admire her. We may pity her. But she will never win gold.

She plays an encore, 'Wedding Day at Troldhaugen'. A little jibe at Anja, I suspect. Everybody claps politely and enthusiastically. They assume they will hear her again some time. Only *I* know that we will never see Rebecca Frost on the platform again.

The party at Bygdøy

'I DON'T KNOW what to think,' says Anja. She whispers to me as we all rise, surrounded by noise. I look around for the Torchlight Man, but he is nowhere to be seen.

'Do you have to think anything?' I say, suddenly angry at her for saying something so stupid. Nobody has asked her opinion.

She shrugs and rolls her eyes. 'I only want the best for Rebecca. That's what I mean. After all, we share the same teacher. We have to cheer each other on, if you see what I mean.'

'Rebecca knows better than anybody what she's achieved,' I say.

Catherine watches us, as though she feels momentarily excluded. This is our world, the pianists' world. Catherine is not a pianist.

The mood is subdued. Everybody goes out to the cloakroom, collecting their jackets and coats before going their separate ways, apart from those of us who are invited to the party, and who must pay a polite visit to the artists' foyer. Friends and relations. There are many well-wishers, but we hardly dare talk to each other. Where are all those high expectations now? What did we all hope to witness, a miracle? It was only Rebecca Frost up on that platform: brave, steadfast Rebecca, a young girl with exams to take in the spring, and so much else to think about. W. Gude is there to greet us as we come down. A long queue trails up the stairs. I recognise some of these insanely rich people, who occasionally appear in the papers. Fabian Frost's sparring partners. They don't know what to say, as they stand waiting; but some of their wives talk loudly, declaring how marvellous it's all been.

I spot Rebecca, down on the right, inside the foyer. I can see she's already had enough of this whole charade. She's opened a bottle of champagne, and clearly wants to get drunk. She kisses cheeks, shakes hands, dispenses hugs, thanks everybody for their congratulations and flattery, which she knows to be false, or at best ignorant. I'm behind

Anja in the queue. She stands on the step below. If I dared, I could stick my nose into her hair and smell calendula. I could whisper in her ear that I love her. But instead I stand holding Margrethe Irene's hand, while Catherine takes her place behind us; after all, she isn't part of our crowd.

I am worried about what Anja will say. She can be so unpredictable. When her turn comes, she gives Rebecca a sisterly hug.

'It went well, Rebecca, really well.'

Selma Lynge and W. Gude stand observing these two young girls. I would give a great deal to know what they're really thinking. But it is Rebecca who reigns supreme:

'Save it, Anja,' she says. 'You know as well as I do that it was mediocre.'

For some reason Anja starts crying.

'Hey, it wasn't *that* bad, was it?' Rebecca jokes. She manages to get Anja laughing before it gets too embarrassing, and extracts a promise that she'll join us all at Bygdøy. Then she flashes a smile at me, but underneath is a gallows humour, and I think I see confusion somewhere in the face of this exquisitely behaved girl.

'You are coming to the wake, aren't you, Aksel?'

We sit in a coach on the way out of town. Fabian Frost has hired a coach, which is mainly filled up by us poorer folk; the music students, high-school kids, various friends. The wealthier ones of the older generation are going in their private cars.

But Rebecca's travelling with us. She's at the front, holding the microphone, making corny jokes. In the semi-dark of the bus I sit behind Anja and Catherine, and next to Margrethe Irene, who has a hand teasingly shoved down my trouser pocket. I don't want her hand there, with Anja sitting in front of me, but it would be rude to protest. She rests her hand calmly down there, possessively. I think how fast things have gone, yes, how fast it went from the moment Mother lost her grip out there by Tinker's Rock. Up to then, life had stood still. The days were endlessly long, but then Mother drifted down with the stream, and the film rolled faster. I watch Rebecca, as she stands in the half-light at the front of the bus, and realise how grown-up she suddenly is, far more grown-up than I am, and facing the hardest thing of all:

having to disappoint other people's expectations. She's still wearing that stupid, excessive dress; yet perhaps it's not *so* stupid. For the first time, throughout the long concert, I see Rebecca as a woman. Magnificent, strong, and with her own agenda. She has made her debut. The reviews will be averagely good; neither unkind nor impolite. She's the West End girl who envisaged a fairytale ending for herself; and perhaps she'll still get it, with a handsome financier or doctor or lawyer groom at her side. And she'll wear a bourgeois white wedding dress, and have four children, a country mansion in Tjørme and, of course, lots of music. But music will never be as absorbing again, never as serious. Music will be there for the sheer pleasure of it, or as a pastime.

But will Rebecca's family ever know what she's been through? How it is to sit and play Beethoven's Opus 109 to a packed house, in the Aula? They know nothing, I think to myself.

'You were far away, just now,' says Margrethe Irene, kissing me.

'No, not so far away,' I answer. 'Just in the future somewhere.'

The party is underway. Fabian Frost has welcomed us all, and said some nice, if somewhat flowery, words to his daughter. He is proud of her; Rebecca will go far, this is only the beginning. We queue at the buffet table, filling our plates with smoked salmon, chicken pieces and something in mayonnaise. Margrethe Irene is clinging to me, and I hate it, because I still have Anja in front of me. She's constantly in front of me, at Catherine's side. I don't know what they're thinking of, what they have in common, coming as they do from such different worlds. W. Gude comes towards me, fixing me with grey, disillusioned eyes, beads of sweat on his brow: 'So, my boy, what's your opinion?'

'She did her best, circumstances considered.'

He nods and considers my answer. 'Hmm, fair comment,' he says. He ignores Margrethe Irene completely. I am the focus of his interest now. I notice it's making me stressed. Anja isn't in his stable, of course. Perhaps he's hoping *I'll* be the next to come forward? I'm not sure that I want that. I feel suddenly nauseous. It was other people's expectations that forced Rebecca into this corner, planting ideas in her head, making her go through with this insane project: a debut in the Aula, at the age of eighteen. Oh well, she'll have some pleasure from it; a scrapbook she can show the many children I'm sure she'll have. And they can be proud of their mother. She has played Beethoven's Opus 109. In the Aula. Without the music. She has played Ravel and Chopin. And perhaps that will be enough for her. Perhaps it is enough for a lifetime.

Then I notice Selma Lynge. She is standing over by the piano, attracting all the attention without saying a word. So far the party has floated on a wave of almost artificial enthusiasm. The champagne has gone straight to some people's heads, the financiers being the worst, I observe with satisfaction, although it's beginning to affect me too.

Selma Lynge claps her hands, demanding silence. The conversation stops instantly, since everybody knows this woman is extraordinary, an authority.

She has put her champagne glass to one side. Behind her stands the grand piano, its lid open. A buzz of expectation hangs in the air: will Selma Lynge play? Will she rise tonight like the star she once was, the legendary Selma Liebermann, before whom Europe's music world genuflected? The woman who could have recorded Brahms's piano concertos for Deutsche Grammophon with Kubelik, but who refused because she'd found herself a Norwegian philosopher whose mission was to write about the ridiculous? She clears her throat. Everybody listens. Rebecca is seated in front of her.

'My dearest Rebecca,' she says, in her slightly broken Norwegian. 'I want to salute you tonight.'

Everybody claps. Rebecca stands up and curtseys. Selma Lynge continues: 'Tonight, you have given us a fantastic concert. We have listened to you with enormous joy. You got off, literally, to a stumbling start. We will have to blame your vanity for that. You looked dazzling, stretched out there. But it was a magnificent feat that you got up, and completed your impeccable programme.'

Everybody laughs. I watch Selma Lynge as she speaks. Something about her reminds me of Munch's 'Madonna': the pale skin, the black hair. I think about everything she's gone through. It still mystifies me that she threw in her career for the sake of that peculiar fellow who stands behind her tittering, hair in all directions; an intellectual, I suppose, but to judge by appearances more a twit than anything. *On the Ridiculous* must surely be a veiled autobiography, I think to myself.

'You have been my enthusiastic student and good friend for many years now, Rebecca. When you decided, in such a flash, to make your debut, I had to rush to find an appropriate present for you on your big day. Luckily fate and coincidence came to my rescue. I saw that a dear friend of my youth would be here in Oslo today. I phoned my good friend W. Gude, whom you all know, and who also happens to be this man's impresario. I asked him if it was possible to give you this man as a present, because, Rebecca, you deserve the very best. And, miracle of miracles, with the help of W. Gude, this man agreed. Tomorrow he will play with the Philharmonic. He is one of the greatest pianists of our day. But tonight he is in this room. His name is Claudio Arrau!'

A gasp goes through the room. Mainly from the youngsters who know who Claudio Arrau is. The rest only have the vaguest notion that they have once heard the name.

Rebecca is, of course, absolutely delighted and runs to the dark-haired Latin American with his dapper moustache and embraces him, with a self-assured elegance that must surely have been taught her. But the strongest reaction comes from Anja. When she realises that Claudio Arrau is actually in the room, she turns to me in disbelief, finally letting Catherine go. Suddenly she's interested in talking to *me* again.

'It's unbelievable,' she gasps.

'Why? He's been to Norway a lot. While you've been sitting in front of your AR speakers, watching the spruce trees by Lysaker River, the rest of us have stared at Munch's "Sun" and listened to Gilels, Richter, Arrau and Argerich play.'

'Don't talk about Argerich,' she answers, moodily.

I don't know why, but I notice we are suddenly cross with each other, that Rebecca's debut has played havoc with our nerves.

'Shh,' I say.

'There's no need to *shh* me.'

She looks at me fiercely. She's not to be trifled with when she's in this mood. Arrau is already positioned at the piano. We stand there awestruck. Fabian Frost and his anonymous wife cast icy glances at their wealthier friends; those with so little musical know-how that they clap between movements or who think Shostakovich never wrote a fifth symphony, since that was written by Beethoven.

Arrau begins. Chopin. The Nocturne in F flat minor. Anja is completely spellbound, although it does feel strange, even to me, to have the master so close. Selma Lynge has taken a seat, right behind him. She seems relaxed and happy, her husband out of mind, listening to the friend of her youth, this international star. Arrau strikes me as the Humphrey Bogart of pianists. The *true* lover, who never lives out his passion. A passion that is restrained, but visceral, just as in Arrau's playing; always melancholy, even bordering on the dismal, but beneath all the restraint the feelings bubble.

Still mesmerised, Anja Skoog stands listening. Nobody would dare to touch her now; not Catherine, not I. Rebecca seems distracted already, too exhausted or too drunk to concentrate. And then something strange happens, as though we're all standing in a black-and-white movie, which is suddenly turning to colour – but the only colours in the room are Claudio Arrau and Anja Skoog. The rest of us are left in black-and-white. An ageing master plays for a young admirer. Tentatively I come up alongside Anja. I've never seen her face so naked, so transported. I would give years of my life to swap places with Arrau, to be the one who could cause her to open up and reveal herself as she does now. Mother adored Arrau, just as I adore Arrau. But nobody adores him more than Anja Skoog. And I'm not even jealous. Such are the laws of music.

But there is more. Arrau finishes playing, holding the silence after his last note just a little too long, as the great names often do. The applause is ecstatic. Rebecca allows her hand to be kissed, as planned. But none of this has the least effect on Anja Skoog. She is in her own world – I've never seen it before – a world which she defines, and which includes only Arrau and herself. She no longer seems to know where she is. She walks towards the piano, oblivious to the fact that Rebecca has planned a speech, because she sees only Arrau; Claudio Arrau, the Chilean master, well over sixty now, whom Selma Lynge has none the less referred to as a childhood friend. But Selma is forgotten now. All eyes are on the young, slender figure of Anja, who nears Arrau; reverential, almost in a trance. She has all his LPs at home in the cabinet, bought for her by the Torchlight Man. She has listened to his versions of Brahms, of Chopin and Beethoven, the spruce trees standing immoveable outside her window. The room falls silent. I don't like what I am seeing, and yet she is so desirable, as she stands there. I would give up my career for her, I would live in the forest, bake bread, break rocks, as long as I could live with Anja Skoog. My feelings of desire are so powerful they terrify me. I don't know how to handle them. Perhaps I am my mother's son now, I think to myself. My thoughts and feelings have such a dangerous sway over me. But I don't move, I glance at my sister, standing nearby. I feel she might be having the same thoughts as me, she seems transfixed by Anja. We both desire her. We watch on like helpless worshippers as Anja closes in on Arrau, whose eyes finally alight on this exquisite young woman of the bright north. And now, to Rebecca's horror, she stands before him. What is Anja doing? What can she want?

Then she bows down.

Anja Skoog kneels before Claudio Arrau.

Again, I'm put in mind of a film. Surely something like this can't happen in reality? And yet it is happening. Anja thanks her hero. Once again, the shy, timorous Anja has stolen the show, just as she did when she took an encore in the Young People's Piano Competition.

'My God!' says Margrethe Irene right behind me. I had almost forgotten she was there.

'My God, what?' I ask.

'How can she be so outrageous?'

'Why is that so outrageous?'

She glares at me in surprise. 'Can't you see? This is Rebecca's evening, not Anja's. And Anja's getting all the attention.'

The party is in full swing again. Ferdinand engages in deep conversation with Arrau, but most of us are eyeing the table set with bottles of wine. Margrethe Irene goes off with Ferdinand and Arrau into a side room, which suits me perfectly. I have no real desire to meet Arrau. He is just one of my many heroes. I have listened to him several times, when he sat in the piano dealer's shop, Grøndahl, beyond the large room with all the Steinways, in the long, narrow artists' room with its two grand pianos, where I hope to sit myself one day, before some important concert.

I want to concentrate on Anja and Catherine, but they're suddenly out of sight.

Then Selma Lynge appears before me.

She has a glass of champagne in each hand. She gives me one. I notice the smell of alcohol on her breath.

'Well, I think it's time we two great people finally meet,' she says with a smile, stretching her hand out.

I don't know if she intends to be ironic. I hope so, since this is what the very young pianist Nordraak said to the equally young Grieg in Tivoli in Copenhagen, but never mind. We've never actually greeted one another before; this is the first time I have spoken to her directly.

'It's a great honour,' I say.

She smiles broadens, with a certain satisfaction.

'Well, how nice,' she says. 'So, what do you say about Arrau? And what do you think of my pupil?'

'I don't have words for either of them.'

She views me sceptically. That was too glib. I regret my own words.

'I think Rebecca did very well,' I say, 'although it could have been better, of course.'

She accepts this. A more satisfactory comment. She nods.

We stand, looking at each other. Her husband is on the other side of the room, in conversation with someone. Nodding vigorously. He gives a short burst of laughter.

She continues to look at me. Lifts her glass.

'It astonishes me,' she says, 'that our paths haven't crossed earlier.'

I nod. It's simply how things have been. I'm not quite sure how to respond.

But her face contains a whole world. She smiles at me. Watches me. I am energised, thrilled by her gaze.

'It's a great honour to meet you, Fru Lynge.'

She shakes her head. 'Don't be so formal. I'm Selma, and you are Aksel.'

She has a strength that I am ill prepared for. In the space of a minute I am on more intimate terms with her than Rebecca has ever been. Since she is Selma now, and not Fru Lynge.

I've not actually planned to ask, but it's as though her presence demands it: 'Do you give classes to people like me?'

She smiles again, doubtless because she finds my question so sweet.

'But of course,' she answers. 'It would be a pleasure to give classes to someone like you.'

I give a little bow. It's essential she knows I'm polite.

'Well, maybe we have an agreement then,' I say nervously.

She observes my insecurity, and pats my cheek. 'You just give me a ring, my boy.'

Then she turns her back on me.

I feel unwell.

Immediately I am out of Selma Lynge's magnetic field, I am on the hunt for Anja Skoog again. Where can she be? There's Arrau with Margrethe Irene and Ferdinand. Bully for them. I need to talk to Anja; I want to ask her whether now really is the right time for me to take classes with Selma Lynge. She knows the answer, better than anybody.

But I can't find her. She has vanished without trace, together with Catherine. Why are they so interested in each other? They barely know each other, they live two completely different lives. Besides, they're girls.

I weave in and out amongst the guests, observing that Arrau is still keeping Margrethe Irene and Ferdinand occupied. Nothing could suit me better: it leaves me free, and I don't want to be tied down. Then I meet Rebecca's eyes. Her face lights up. She's radiant. And I understand why. She's thrown it all in. She's never been happier. Her blue eyes. Her enchanting little freckles.

'Aksel!' she says, putting her arms round me.

We hold each other. Her body is warm. I feel her skin above her strapless dress.

'You are so strong. And you're fabulous,' I say.

'Because I've made a choice,' she says. Kissing me lightly on the cheek.

'So you've really decided?'

She nods emphatically. 'It wasn't even a choice. It was obvious. It feels as though I have my life back.'

I look at her and realise she is right. She's losing a career as a pianist perhaps, but she's gaining something else: control over her own life. I feel a sudden nausea. She notices that I feel unwell.

'It came to me as I was playing,' she says, reaching for the champagne glass she put down to hug me, and resting her other hand supportively on my shoulder. 'When I lay there scrabbling on the floor, not knowing if I could go on, I suddenly saw myself from the outside. I could see what a pathetic, nervous little person it was that was so desperate to succeed. I saw all my ambitions, rushing past on a conveyor belt, or in a scrapbook. I wanted fame, I wanted to play with this particular orchestra, and that conductor. I wanted to be a superstar, like Arrau over there. I wanted to play all Beethoven's sonatas, all Bach's preludes and fugues, Prokofiev's enormous sonatas. And I lay there on that floor, and didn't want to give it up, because it all seemed so important. But when W. Gude helped me up, when he said those fantastic words, when I finally sat in front of the piano, preparing myself to go through with it, I realised it was over.'

'What did he say?'

Rebecca peers over at him. He is standing close to Claudio Arrau, in conversation with Selma Lynge. She's smiling at him. He senses Rebecca's gaze, gives her a discreet little wave of the hand, and sends her a smile.

'He told me that no situation is ever so bad that you can't find a way out. He told me everyone would understand if I didn't manage to go on. He said that life goes on, regardless.'

'Yes, I suppose it does,' I say laconically, and in that instant I see it clearly: the final image of Mother.

'He gave me a choice, Aksel. Even though he is my impresario. He gave me the chance to surrender.'

'And you surrendered?'

'Yes, but that was only afterwards.'

I nod, touched by what she is telling me.

'Because I realised it wasn't worth it. I'm not made for this, Aksel. The sacrifices, the miserable hotel rooms, the loneliness. And all just to play music that other people can play just as well as I can, and probably far better.'

I nod again. Of course what she says touches me. She won't go to Vienna, to London or Paris. Her whole life lies open before her. We are the ones who must live as though we're stuck on rails.

'Does anybody else know about this yet?'

'No,' she whispers in my ear. 'So far, you're the only one I've told.'

'What will Selma Lynge say?'

'Oh, she knows me; she's already guessed. I could never have been like her anyway, that stunning personality, that streak of originality. I'd always have had to struggle, and I'd never have got to the top.'

'But won't you miss Opus 109?'

'Opus 109 is there, Aksel, forever. That was precisely what I realised, there on the platform. I can't live without music, but it can manage perfectly well without me.'

'I wish you every happiness.' I say. 'Are you going to announce it tonight?'

'No, this is a party. The reviews will arrive soon. Father has a driver doing the rounds of all the newspapers in the centre of Oslo. And he'll bring their collective judgement out to Bygdøy, hot off the press, at about two this morning.'

'I'm sure they'll be fine.'

She pats me on the cheek again, as if I'm the one in need of comfort. I envy her. She has made her choice. She has finished her debut concert. She is free.

I leave Rebecca and walk out into the hallway to find a place to vomit, but there is a queue outside the toilet. I walk further up the stairs, in the hope of finding somewhere on the first floor. There are rich paintings on the walls, Dutch hunting scenes with dogs, deer and spilt entrails. Blood and human hands. Bulging eyes. Death throes. I can barely take more. I am looking for another toilet. Perhaps Herr and Fru Frost have an en-suite bathroom up here, next to the bedroom. The corridor leads into the darkness, with doors on either side.

I try the furthest door.

A bedroom, the master bedroom, I think.

Everything is dark. And yet I sense somebody is in here. I fumble for a switch.

A dull, inadequate light flows down from the ceiling. Lying there is Anja. Stark naked below the waist, apart from her tights, still attached to one foot.

She lies stretched out on the bedspread, her white hips half hidden among the folds. Yet it is not Anja I see. I see only Catherine, my sister, lying with her head between Anja's legs.

She turns to me, disbelief in her face. Anja lies motionless, her eyes closed. I don't know where to look, what I should do. I can contain it no longer – it's got to come. Chicken, champagne, prawns, red wine and white wine, and bile. I throw up on the Frosts' pale pink shaggy carpet.

The two girls stare at me horrified, in the semi-darkness. Anja has lifted her head from the bed. They both yell at me:

'Aksel! What are you doing?'

Part 3

Sleet

A FEW DAYS HAVE PASSED since Rebecca's debut. I stand waiting for Anja at the tram station. I know precisely when she gets back from school. She is not getting rid of me this time.

Slushy snow. Joyless weather. Gigantic snowflakes that splatter on the ground. But I'm not giving up.

There she is, her hair in a bun, with the old-fashioned duffel-coat that suits her so well. She smiles when she sees me.

'Were you waiting for me?' she asks, in that friendly tone I can never quite get used to, that always surprises me.

'In a way,' I answer, already stuttering. 'I wanted to ask you something.'

'Ask away,' she says, as we walk side by side down towards Melumveien. She doesn't seem the least fazed by what happened at Bygdøy.

'Do you think I should start classes with Selma Lynge?' I say.

'Of course I do!' she answers enthusiastically, giving my arm a quick squeeze.

We walk next to each other. My shoes are getting soaked through in the slushy snow. I have an umbrella that covers us both. And I also have a spare arm I could have wrapped round her.

Instead I go on: 'But isn't she a bit difficult?'

'Yes,' Anja says thoughtfully, 'she's demanding and eccentric, like all great musicians. But isn't that how it should be?'

'Should it?' I stare briefly at her. We walk on, past Melum, the beautiful farmstead with the old ladies. 'Rebecca's given up. Her reviews weren't that bad, she could have made a career now; but she's decided not to. Have you ever considered giving up?'

'Never,' she answers firmly.

We walk past my house. It will be ours for one more winter. I know that Father is sitting on the phone. He has found himself a lady friend, but doesn't want to tell us who, and pretends that nothing has happened. He has put a new telephone line in his bedroom. Catherine's activities are, as usual, a mystery.

I notice that Anja sneaks a look up at the house. It is probably unwise of me to ask, but I can't hold back.

'Are you seeing any more of Catherine?'

She doesn't answer. I blush, filled with shame; on her behalf, as well as Catherine's and mine. Maybe I should have kept quiet. But then I realise that she is mulling it over.

'Why do you ask?' she says finally, by which time we are already well past my house.

'Because I'm curious,' I answer.

She sends me a quick glance.

'It's not what you think,' she says.

'So what is it?'

'Surely it's not that difficult to understand. Right now my head's filled with Ravel. The G Major concerto. Playing with the Philharmonic. And then I'll have my Artium. Isn't that enough?'

'Sure.'

'Catherine is a close friend. But you're a close friend too.' She squeezes my hand.

'I'm glad about that,' I say.

So Anja thinks I should go to Selma Lynge? Yet it seems an irrelevance right now. Surely Anja is the only one that really matters now. My concentration has deserted me, returning only sporadically when I sit in the pitch darkness of Studio 18 playing Schubert in the evenings. The truth is it frightens me that Rebecca has given up. It frightens us all. Not least because her decision was so swift and brutal, as she lay on the platform, in her ball-gown, under Munch's 'Sun'.

It feels lonely to go on without her.

But Anja is here. That is the most important thing.

I will never get over what I witnessed.

I visit the alder thicket.

Nothing is as it was.

Birthday celebrations

IT IS MY BIRTHDAY. I am turning eighteen. I refuse to celebrate, despite Father's attempts at persuasion. But in the morning he and Catherine come into my room, with a candle and coffee and cakes. What more could one ask on a grey November morning, I reflect, as I smile at them feebly. They perch on my bed. They've both brought presents: records. Catherine has Horowitz. The Carnegie Hall concert, the one that begins so liberatingly with a stupendous mistake. Father has brought two Mozart concertos played by Ingrid Haebler. I thank them and give them a hug each. As I hug Catherine, I can't stop thinking how close this head has been to Anja's most private parts. I think of what Catherine has already plundered, and how Anja seems so unaffected by the whole event. I am tempted to tell her, but let it pass. Catherine has her own life. She has got her job back at the National Gallery. And right now that's the only stable thing in her life.

'Thank you,' I say. 'Thank you both.'

'Surely we can celebrate your birthday?' says Father. At last there seems to be some joy in his face again. 'I'll take us all out to the Theaterkafeen.'

'I'm sorry, Father, but you'll have to spend your money on something more useful. I have my own plans.'

They accept that. They have no choice. And as they finally disappear out of the front door, I am happy to be alone. But how shall I spend my day? I sit on the sofa. There are butterflies in my stomach, because I'm about to do something I've been thinking about for a long time

I ring Sandbunnveien. A strange name for a road, Sand-bunn-veien: the road at the sandy bottom . . . But this is the road where Selma Lynge – the beautiful, scheming, legendary international star, Selma – lives with the man whose hair grows in all directions, who looks as if he just fell out of bed, and who wrote the masterpiece *On the Ridiculous*, although all he can do himself is titter. Selma, it seems, enjoys her self-imposed retirement, just like Rebecca. She has no more concerts to practise for. No more Brahms with the Philharmonic, no more Schubert sonatas in Oslo's Aula or in Munich. She can simply be Selma Lynge, lauded for her successes, and as beautiful as Munch's Madonna. No critic can tear her down now.

'Lynge,' she says, into the phone.

'This is Aksel Vinding,' I say.

She laughs. 'And about time too.'

'Have you been waiting for me?'

'But of course.'

'It was a good thing I phoned then?'

'Absolutely.'

'When can I come?'

She hesitates. 'The day after tomorrow. Come early in the afternoon.'

I can't settle to anything afterwards. I don't know what to do with myself, mentally or physically. Unable to think of anything better, I sit at the piano and practise. The hours pass. There are times when I practise for twelve hours on end. But today I do only six or seven. At three o'clock I know school is over. I consider standing at the window to watch for Anja, but feel that I should be careful now. I ring Margrethe Irene instead.

'Oh, Aksel! I just walked in through the door! You beat me to it. Happy birthday!'

'Thanks,' I say.

'Have you got any plans for tonight? No? Excellent. Because I have a *very* special present for you. Can you come at seven? Mother's going to her sewing circle, and Father's at the Rotary Club. I'm offering you Irish stew. Can you refuse?'

No, of course not. I need Margrethe Irene just as everybody needs a vice. I always feel dejected when I come to her, and I always feel dirty when I leave, but that's hardly surprising. It isn't my imagination, but the truth.

Today, I even manage to arrive early. We have so much to talk about and, of course, there's the other matter: the stolen pleasure, the stinging joy.

She kisses me on the lips. 'Congratulations, Aksel!'

'It's no big deal.'

'Eighteen years? Yes. That's pretty old.'

I look around for my present, but there isn't one.

'Come and have some Irish stew,' says Margrethe Irene.

We eat, and drink a bottle of red wine. It is my eighteenth birthday. We talk about everything that's happened: Rebecca's brief appearance on stage, and the party afterwards. Margrethe Irene is lighthearted this evening.

'I got ever so close to him – to Arrau. He was even open to my taking classes with him. Imagine being Claudio Arrau's pupil! But you were so distant all evening, Aksel. What were you up to?'

'I wasn't well. Maybe the shock got to me. What happened to Rebecca just reminded me of what might lie ahead for me – or any of us.'

Margrethe Irene shakes her head. 'Don't paint such a bleak picture. What happened to Rebecca was a blessing. She did what she set out to achieve – and then saw the world with fresh eyes. I envy her in a way.'

'Me too.'

'But we mustn't think like that! The whole world awaits us. In a few months I'll have taken my Artium. And you've already got your freedom.'

She takes a gulp of her wine. I follow suit. Our eyes meet. There's a distance between us now, an uncertainty. She has a safety net. I have none.

'I don't know what I'll use my freedom for.'

'You'll make your debut, of course. And you'll be better than all of us. Better than Anja Skoog. Better than me. Because you are better, Aksel. You just haven't discovered it yet.'

'Stop. That's not true, and you know it. Why this myth that I'm so good? When did I ever play that well? Never. But I chose to gamble everything on it, to quit school, and that frightened you all. But what have I really achieved? Nothing.'

'Your time will come. Never fear.'

We sit in her living room, with its Bowers & Wilkins loudspeakers and dozens of records. It's more welcoming than at Anja's. I have to admit I've always liked it here, although my initial dislike for Margrethe Irene, mixed with so much lust and shame, have meant I no longer know what I feel.

'What do you fancy listening to?' she says. 'It's your birthday.'

'How about Schubert,' I say. 'The C major quintet.'

'Schubert it is.'

She goes over to the records. I watch her as she pulls out an LP and puts it on the turntable. Her movements are clumsy, yet she's so self-assured. I have never desired her. But she can do what she wants with me. Some people are like that.

'I've rung Selma Lynge,' I say. 'She'll take me on.'

Margrethe Irene turns, clearly surprised.

'That was quick!'

'She's been sending a few signals.'

'Yes, I suppose Rebecca will stop going to her now. So there'll be a spare place.'

'Am I doing something stupid?'

'It can't ever be stupid to take classes with Selma Lynge. But be careful, Aksel. She can be bit of a witch.'

I nod.

'And surely you've already got enough, with all your lady friends,' she giggles.

'What do you mean?'

She doesn't answer. The record has started crackling in the loud-speakers. The music will follow soon. Schubert. Articulating the unfathomable. The music that binds me to Anja.

Margrethe Irene and I kiss. The music has come to an end. I want to leave.

I get up to go. 'I've had a really nice time,' I say.

'You're always so polite, Aksel.'

'Politeness is a virtue, isn't it. But I really have to go.'

She stares at me, takes me in her arms. Her eyes are shining.

'But you can't go. You haven't had your present yet.'

She leads me towards the bedroom.

'Tonight we're doing it for real,' she says.

I feel a sudden sense of gloom.

'Oh, I'm very tired.'

'Not *that* tired.'

She's the one who makes the decisions here. The bed has been made, she has lit a candle.

'Perhaps it's not right?'

'Why shouldn't it be right? You don't have to worry about anything. I've taken precautions.'

There is no escape. It's sad it should be like this.

Soon we lie naked. With nothing to hold us back. The candle flutters each time I move. I look at her pale face. She is beautiful in this light. I kiss her forehead, her mouth, her breasts.

I can't go on.

'You really are tired, Aksel.'

'Yes, I'm afraid so. Some other time perhaps.'

'Let's do it the old way, eh.'

I am suddenly aroused, but it is too late to take her first offer. We do what we know best. We are almost grown-up. She lies close to me. Naked. Holding me tightly.

'I am your birthday present, Aksel. Remember that. No matter what, I'll always be your present.'

Farewell Synnestvedt

I SIT WITH SYNNESTVEDT in his little living room with its upholstered furniture, its old piano, its musty smell. He tells me he understands.

'Selma Lynge is an excellent teacher,' he says.

'It's not just that,' I say. 'But there comes a time.'

'Of course – there comes a time,' Synnestvedt repeats.

He offers me coffee and cakes and potters out into the kitchen, where he rattles the cups and fetches plastic-wrapped cakes that keep for three years. I give him a helping hand, as I always have. He seems utterly helpless as he returns to his chair. Reeking of his insides. I should have got him into a home, I think to myself.

'Things move on,' I say comfortingly.

'Rebecca Frost's debut was magnificent,' he says. 'We can expect a great deal from that young lady.'

'Undoubtedly.'

'And when will you make *your* debut, Aksel?' He fixes me with the kind, alcoholic gaze I know so well, as we sip our coffee and munch our cakes. He never drinks in my presence.

'So much has happened, Synnestvedt. I need to give myself time.'

'Of course.'

He sits, pondering. And I ponder too; over how much he's failed to teach me. I've never had a more inadequate teacher. I try to think of just one thing that he knew which proved useful, but come upon nothing. But I'm fond of him; mostly because he's never held me back, nor robbed me of my courage. It feels sad to leave him. Everything will be much harder from now on. Synnestvedt represents the safe, unchallenging standards I've been satisfied to aim for. But he has an excellent ear, none the less, and has always applauded me in the right places. He has never been negative, yet I always sensed when he was less than enthused. So what am I aiming for now? The top? Where I'm told it's so hostile and cold? I am afraid of everything that lies ahead of me. Synnestvedt had a genuine love for music, at least.

'So, what about the Brahms?' he asks suddenly.

'The Brahms B major? It will have to wait. Lots of things will have to wait.'

He nods. 'You really have nothing to fear. You're the best of them, my lad. You'll make me proud one day.'

I don't answer. I walk over to his record player. Put a record on. Schubert's C major quintet. The second movement. Tears roll down our cheeks.

'It's beautiful,' I say.

'Yes, it shouldn't be allowed,' he says.

Selma Lynge

I AM AT THE FRONT DOOR of a large, gloomy house. Selma and Torfinn Lynge's house. Within these walls live two international celebrities, a pianist and a philosopher. The two of them are already institutions, as a couple and separately, and I fear them both. They seem somehow dangerous. None the less, I feel compelled to seek her out.

It's Torfinn Lynge who opens the door to me. He blinks out into the November light from behind his spectacles, the ones that only cost half a krone in the Narvesen kiosks, and which all the Oslo intellectuals love. His hair stands out in all directions as usual, and there is an unexpected crust of sleep around his mouth and eyes, as if he'd just been released from a psychiatric unit, and hadn't yet been washed. He recognises me, and smiles somewhat sheepishly.

'Oh, so here's the wanderer, come over hill and dale in search of the Princess herself,' stutters the philosopher, sniggering to himself loudly and excitedly.

'Perhaps,' I say.

I feel queasy. Distinctly uneasy. I can't tell whether he's retarded or just joking with me. Both options seem equally plausible.

'Do come in, young man,' he says, with an exaggerated bow, as though he is my servant.

I walk past him noticing his shirt is covered in flecks from a boiled egg, and that his trousers are crumpled. It is hard to believe this is really Selma Lynge's husband.

But there she stands, at the centre of the living room, waiting for me.

I wonder if she has made a special effort? She is wearing a long red dress and turquoise shawl. Her make-up is heavy, giving her face a harder appearance. Her eyes are dark, her gaze almost coquettish.

'Welcome, Aksel,' she says, offering me a cool, slender hand. I squeeze it lightly and deferentially, as though she were a queen.

Torfinn Lynge stands mumbling to himself and squinting. Selma Lynge suddenly flashes her husband an almost evil look, whilst maintaining a smile. Going over to him she says: 'We don't have any bread, Torfinn. I forgot to buy it. Couldn't you take the tram to town and buy a seeded loaf at Merkel's? They're open until late today.'

The philosopher grunts something. Obviously in protest. Is it really necessary?

She glares at him sternly. 'Torfinn?'

He stands there with a drip hanging from his nose. Foam appears at the corners of his mouth, despite his not even opening it to talk.

She continues to glare at him, unmoved.

Finally he nods vigorously, his grey curls flopping in all directions: 'Yes. Yes, of course. I shall do that.'

I cannot believe my eyes as Torfinn Lynge goes into the hallway, puts his hat and coat on, and leaves.

'Have a good class!' he calls to me from the front door, as he wipes the drip from his nose, and the foam from the corner of his mouth with a tatty old cotton handkerchief.

Selma Lynge turns to me the instant the door is closed, with a totally different smile on her face.

'There goes a truly gifted man,' she says laconically.

We are alone.

Apart from the black-and-white cat sitting in the chair, in the corner, which fixes me with a cautionary gaze: there are certain rules in this house.

I look around. Selma Lynge has put two teacups out on the coffee table. The tea is already brewing in a porcelain pot. The living room is large, filled with heavy, Germanic furniture. There's a fireplace, and an enormous, dark, lacquered cupboard, probably inherited from the Liebermann family. Paintings line all the walls, some abstract and modern, others more traditional, including a genuine Munch print, 'Separation'.

She notices me looking at it.

'Do you like Munch?' she asks.

'Anja doesn't like Munch,' I answer.

'You'd rather talk about Anja?'

'The woman's long hair in the picture reminds me of Anja.'

Selma Lynge draws closer to me. Only now am I suddenly aware of her fragrance, the perfume she's wearing; it must be lilies, I think to myself. Lily of the Valley, the scent my mother was so fond of.

'You smell lovely,' I say, immediately struck by how idiotic I sound. Hardly the way to start a piano lesson with a world-renowned teacher.

'I'm glad you like it. It's Chanel Number 5. A classic. But, I'm sure you knew that.'

'I don't know much about perfume,' I say.

We sit at the coffee table.

'Would you like some tea?'

I nod, because she has no alternative. She fills our cups. She has put some milk and sugar out, but drinks it black. I choose to do the same, knowing nothing about tea. We're all coffee drinkers at home in Melumveien. Coffee and alcohol.

We have our tea. I look over at the grand piano. It's enormous, a Model C. She follows my gaze.

'No, it's not a Steinway,' she says, 'we have an Austrian streak in our family, a touch of the Hapsburgs almost, but that's another story. I prefer Bösendorfer.'

'Bösendorfer's perfect,' I say. 'Why does it have so many extra notes in the bass?'

She shrugs her shoulders, but takes my question seriously.

'I suppose it's because of the late Romantic period,' she says. 'They were breaking new ground. The grand pianos were constantly growing in size during the nineteenth century. You can find some real monsters in my home country. Brahms composed his piano concertos for extremely large pianos. They dreamed of pianos as long as ballrooms, in those days. But, of course, as with everything in life, there are limits.'

I notice that her Norwegian becomes more broken as she talks about Germany. I look at her, and find myself confused by the sudden tension between us. She could be my mother and yet, to me, she is a woman, in all meanings of the word. A touch of the Hapsburgs? That implies there's something Alsatian or Spanish in her blood. Yes, Spanish perhaps, I think, stealing a look at her every time she turns away, as though I daren't quite look her in the eye. Is it because of her authority, or my respect for the myth surrounding her? I know she has played for all the great conductors: Ferenc Fricsay, Raphael Kubelik, Karl Böhm.

She knows the acoustics of the Musikverein, the Concertgebouw and the Salle Pleyel. And here she is, in Sandbunnveien, bothering herself with a young man whose only achievement in life is to have turned eighteen. There are always youngsters in the classical milieu, of course, but am I really worth the bother? She doesn't have many pupils. Her days are long and free. So why is she taking me on? The young man who failed in the Young People's Piano Competition. Does she, none the less, have enough faith to enter me for the Tchaikovsky Competition or to let me make the early debut I have in mind? I think about Ferdinand Fjord, and his struggles with Riefling.

'So, what do you want from me?' asks Selma Lynge, having observed me intently for some moments.

'I want to learn,' I say. 'Synnestvedt wasn't that great a teacher, although he was a good listener.'

'And *what* do you want to learn?' she asks.

A dangerous question. I think it over.

'How to bring music up to the surface, how to find it in the depths, wherever it is.'

'Nobody knows where music is,' she says abruptly, as if I've said something stupid. 'And who can explain our dependency on it? Not to mention how we understand it? Our preferences? Why a seventh might sound better than a sixth, at a given moment. Or vice versa. Music is invisible, and when it's not being played, we still carry it inside our heads.'

I feel angry, it's as though she's being purposely dismissive and obtuse.

'And then,' she continues in the same vein, 'who can explain why it has such power over us?'

I am lost for words. I have not come to Sandbunnveien to be humiliated on my first day.

'I just want to be a better pianist,' I say, my cheeks burning.

She observes me calmly, smiling at my rage, in complete control of the conversation.

'You will be,' she says. 'You can be sure of that.'

I sit down at the grand piano. It's old and the varnish is scratched. The lid stands open. My neck is stiff, my shoulders tense. Selma Lynge sits in her chair drinking tea and watching me.

'Who do you think about when you play?' she asks.

'Who?'

'Yes, everybody thinks about someone,'

'Do they? Who do you think about?'

'I think about my mother.'

'Why do you think about her?'

'Because I want to move her. To bring her back from the dead.'

It seems strange to hear her say that. Mother is never in my thoughts when I play the piano. She's been in my mind at important moments, when I've needed her strategically, as one might pray to God before flying off the ski ramp.

'Do you know what happened in the valley here?' I ask.

She nods.

'I talk to her almost daily. There's a place where I think her soul is. And yet I don't really think she exists at all. Not like that. Mother is dead. I don't play for her.'

'Then you play for Anja Skoog,' says Selma Lynge with a smile.

I start to play. And perhaps Selma is right; perhaps Anja is the person I play for, I think to myself as I set out reluctantly on Chopin's Sonata No. 2 in B minor, with its Funeral March. The entire composition is so complex, such a technical minefield; I can't think why I've chosen it – perhaps because it has so much aggression in it. Not a moment's certainty, until the Funeral March. Everything is fleeting, ephemeral: first a tempest of passions; then the mourning; and finally, the visitations of the ghosts. A sad piece of music, unsuitable for one so young. But here I sit, at Selma Lynge's Bösendorfer, ready to work through it, to show her what I can do. But then, perhaps the Sonata isn't such a bad choice: doesn't it match my own feelings entirely? So volatile, so restless, so doom-laden.

I am finished with some of the thorniest sections. I've made some hideous mistakes in the scherzo, and I am hugely nervous. I start out on the Funeral March, taking it at an average pace, seeing no cause to make the tempo too extreme.

Then Selma Lynge rises from her chair. She walks slowly over to the piano, a signal that I mustn't stop playing. Then she stops right behind me. Suddenly I feel her hands on my shoulders, where my muscles are tense. She leans closer. The fragrance of Chanel almost anaesthetises me. Her skin is so close to mine. We are cheek to cheek.

'Go on, Aksel, don't stop,' she whispers.

I do as she tells me, and play on. She massages my shoulders. Slowly.

'Don't you feel it? Slower, Aksel, slower. Hold the tempo back. Feel the rhythm.'

The rhythm is there in her fingers. I can see what she means now. But can it be right? I wonder. To play it so slowly? I pull the tempo back, little by little, a startling ritardando. Nobody plays this slowly, apart from that strange rock band from the US who call themselves The Doors. I feel myself being sucked down into another world, a sensual, sensitised world, in which each and every note has its own value. I've always cultivated a slow tempo, but I've never dared consider playing this slowly.

'Slower, Aksel.'

Even slower? Her lips are close to my ear now. Sending shivers down my spine. What sort of power has she managed, in these few seconds, to cast over me? But I can hear now that she is right, as the rhythm settles, and passes from note to note, through the pauses, and on in one long arc through the music.

I have never heard Chopin's Funeral March played like this.

And I'm the one playing it.

'You are playing for your dead mother, now,' Selma Lynge whispers in my ear. 'Or are you playing for Anja Skoog? Think of someone. Imagine there is something you want to say, to somebody important, somebody you cannot live without. This person is always out there in the audience. And then you must think to yourself: this is the very last time I will ever play the piano. The very last time I will hear music. You must give them everything, never let your feelings slacken, always be generous, even when you're holding back.'

I continue to play, despite her whispering in my ear. I feel a new immediacy, as though each touch of the keys were a matter of life and death. I remember how Anja tried to describe this experience. It sounded so exhausting, and yet it's quite the opposite. Selma Lynge doesn't distract me. Instead, her voice rests under the music, leaving my head clear, strengthening my intuition, reinforcing the choices I make at each turn: when shall I hit the next note?

And now she begins to let me go. Loosening her grip, she gets up slowly and lets me go on alone. The Funeral March has found its shape. What enormous sorrow, I think with dismay. What loss. And I do not know what I have lost. I only know that the music will communicate it for me.

I sit exhausted at the piano.

'Good,' says Selma Lynge from her chair. 'Very good.'

I don't dare to look at her. 'You'd have been burned as a witch, if you'd lived during the Inquisition,' I say.

She laughs, flattered.

'It was Ferenc Fricsay who taught me this,' she says. 'A musician's worst enemy is routine. That is why classical music can be such a bore. Even Glenn Gould can be a bore. He is cerebral. Bursting with ideas all the time. He is so close to the music that he never allows himself the distance to communicate the things he wants. He gets manic, exaggerated and frightening. Can you imagine a woman wanting to go to bed with Glenn Gould? Horrendous. Glenn Gould is a brute. Compare him to Martha Argerich. The two are worlds apart.'

She shocks me with her directness, the speed with which she alludes to the subject of sex. This makes even more tension between us. She is older than Mother would have been, I think to myself, as I sit on my piano stool, finally daring to look straight at the woman who has bewitched me, this proud figure who sits there, teacup in hand, passing judgement on me.

'Your technique is no problem. That can be sorted. You should, by the way, strengthen your fourth finger on the right. It's too weak. Use Chopin's Etude No. 2, Opus 10. But, apart from that, everything comes down to your expressiveness. You've practised too hard, become too mechanical. You must rediscover the music, so that it engages with your own life. Forget these showy pieces for now. I want you to practise something simple for next time. Without any technical difficulties. Debussy's "Girl with the Flaxen Hair" perhaps. Who comes to mind with that title?' she says, casting me a meaningful look.

I do not answer.

She smiles teasingly, and gets up from her chair.

'Was that the first lesson?' I say.

'Yes,' she nods. 'And I shall whisper more things in your ear next time. '

As I'm leaving I bump into Torfinn Lynge at the front door who is just back from town with the bread. He titters foolishly.

'I'm not too early, am I?' he says. Eyes like two satellites floating in desolate space.

'Oh, no, we're finished,' I say, feeling awkward. What on earth must he think about us? With a wife like that. What does he think we've been up to?

Selma Lynge comes up from behind, nudging me out. 'That's enough for today,' she says. She plants an adoring kiss on her husband's lips and grabs the bread.

'Next Thursday, same time?' I ask.

'Of course,' she says.

Advent

IT's SNOWING, in large wet flakes. The Christmas decorations are up in the centre of Røa. There are lights in windows, strung between lamp-posts, and on the large spruce tree in the square. I stand on the station platform, waiting for Anja. I am practising 'The Girl with the Flaxen Hair', and think only of her. Meeting Selma Lynge has been like pouring petrol on a fire. Her life experience has kindled something in me. She demands that the senses be opened, that each moment be lived to the full. And what have I chosen? A cowardly refuge in Margrethe Irene's embrace, offering comfort and pleasure, but no future for either of us. I have dreamed, but I have failed to bring those dreams to my music, where they belong. My senses were open only when I sat in the alder thicket. Never in my music. And in life itself? This great, marvellous life? I have been mere flotsam, I conclude.

And yet at the same time, I feel uncomfortable with having to express my love for Anja so shamelessly. And there she comes, in her green duffel-coat, descending the steps of the old brown tram with its wooden panelling on the outside. It is afternoon and dark already. Seeing me, she smiles, without a trace of irritation. I breathe a sigh of relief, since I would hate to seem clingy.

'Hello there,' she says amiably.

'Can I walk with you for a while?' I say.

She nods. 'Of course you can. Were you waiting for me?'

'Yes,' I admit, beginning to stutter. She has such power over me. She can rob me of all my confidence in a flash. 'I wanted to say thank you. I had my first class with Selma Lynge last Thursday.'

'I heard,' she says with a smile. She links her arm with mine; an action so unexpected, so sweet, I barely know what to think. We head towards Melumveien.

'You've heard then?' I say, with exaggerated surprise. 'I didn't think she gossiped about her pupils.'

'Well, she talked about you at least,' says Anja, with a giggle.

'And what did she say?'

'That you're very clever, a quick learner, and that you need to forget your technique for a while, that you need to concentrate on your expressiveness.'

'She's utterly fantastic,' I say. 'She exceeds all my expectations.'

'That's good,' says Anja, giving my arm a little squeeze. 'That's exactly as it should be. But everything's more serious for you now, isn't it?'

'She can talk about one movement in a Chopin sonata, but she's talking about the whole of life.'

'That's exactly how I feel. And perhaps Rebecca did too. Perhaps that's why she was in such a rush to make her debut? As though she felt her time was limited?'

We walk past my house, both of us stealing a look up towards Catherine's bedroom window. Her room is dark. I don't want Anja to feel awkward.

'But I suppose time is always limited, in a way,' I say.

We walk on in the snow, past Melum and downhill towards Elvefaret. I cannot think of anything more to say.

'It's nice of you to walk with me,' says Anja.

I want to tell her how impossible it is to live without her. Instead I say, 'Well, you walk past my house every day.'

'I wish I could give school up,' she sighs.

'Yes, I've always wondered: how do you have the energy to practise when you get home?'

'I just have to. Just a few more months and I'll be free.'

'But you have six weeks before Ravel's G major.'

She shivers. 'Don't remind me, please. Do you know anything about him? My conductor? Miltiades Caridis? What with never going to concerts . . .' she mumbles.

'I know that the orchestra like him. That he's clever and knowledgeable, and perhaps a bit boring. You'll soon have him in your control.'

'Don't be daft. I'm only a seventeen-year-old girl. He's an experienced Greek. I was hoping for Blomstedt. I can't understand how the Philharmonic thought they could afford to get rid of him.'

'New brooms and all that. Look, don't worry. Caridis is as good as anybody.'

'So long as he knows what to do. And understands that he has to help me.'

We have reached Elvefaret now.

'You probably shouldn't walk me any further,' Anja says, hurriedly.

I think of all the things she doesn't know: that I went for dinner with her mother, that I know way too much, and that Marianne wants a divorce as soon as Anja is eighteen.

'Has your father got that much against me?'

'It's not you, Aksel,' she squeezes my arm again. 'It's all boys. He's frightened for me. He thinks anybody who walks me home is suspicious.'

'Does he know about Catherine?'

'Don't talk about Catherine, please.'

We are standing under the street lamp at the final turn in the road. Her hair is wet from the snow. Mine must be too, although I can't feel it. I look into her face, the friendly, trusting gaze that always takes me by surprise. For the first time today I notice how thin she is. Thinner even than usual. She strokes my hair, fleetingly.

'Don't be angry,' she says.

I cannot hold back. 'I love you,' I say again.

Then I plant a kiss on her forehead, just as before.

'Please, don't,' she says.

'Why do you say that?' I ask, my lips close to her ear, as I have learned from Selma Lynge.

'Because they're like blessings: your kisses, your words. And I'm not worthy of them.'

'How can you say that? Nobody is as worthy!'

She pushes me away. 'There's so much you don't know,' she says, and runs the last stretch, around the next bend, and out of my reach.

At home Catherine is expecting me. Father is in the bedroom talking on the telephone in hushed tones. What a family, I think.

But Catherine is sitting in the kitchen in a gloomy mood, drinking cocoa, eating buns, and waiting for me. Christ, in just months we will all have to leave this house, but she's been about as inefficient as me in getting her act together.

'So, you keep a lookout for her nowadays?' she mutters moodily.

'What do you mean? Were you watching from your window? Do you sit there, in your dark room, spying on me?'

'What, like you spy on Anja? Pathetic. You lie in wait for her at the station. You don't give her any choice at all.'

'And how much choice did you give her?'

Catherine is suddenly cagy. 'What do you mean? Has she said something?'

'Anja and I can talk completely openly about things.'

'Then I suppose you also know that there's something seriously wrong with that family?'

Catherine starts crying. I am lost for words. It comes so unexpectedly. I sit down next to her, and put an arm round her shoulders; it feels awkward, but I have learned it from Selma Lynge.

'What is so seriously wrong?' I ask.

'That's the question.' Catherine dries her eyes, wanting to talk.

'But I have the same feeling too. What is it that gives us that feeling?'

'Her father of course.'

'The Torchlight Man?' I want to bite my tongue off.

'What did you just say?'

'Just a slip. Bror Skoog. We are talking about the surgeon, aren't we?'

'He wields so much power over her.'

'Have you been in there, together with them both?'

'Only with Anja. At least I thought Anja was on her own at home. I was trying to get her to join the handball team. We were up in her room. Have you been in her room? She has a picture of her mother and father over the bed, and Bach and Beethoven on either side, if you know what I mean.'

'I didn't get that far,' I say.

'We'd been talking for half an hour, when her father knocked on the door.'

'What did he want?'

'Nothing. He just asked if we were all right. Then I realised how suspicious he was of me: Catherine Vinding, the sinful friend. I knew I had to get out.'

'That's exactly what happened to me!'

'The funny thing was that Anja didn't protest. She seemed to think that it was all normal.'

'Yes, exactly!'

'So I left. I was nearly chased out of the door. That was what I wanted to catch up on, at Rebecca's party.'

'Well, you succeeded all right!'

'Don't go over all that. It wasn't what you think. Remember Anja is sweet, bordering on the naive. Despite all the schools she's been to, and the other kids she meets, she's been living for so long in a world of her own that it's almost impossible to imagine.'

'What are you trying to tell me?'

'That she's hypnotised. That she lives for music.'

'And who's hypnotised her?'

'Her father, of course.'

'Catherine, are you trying to tell me something?'

She puts her head on the table, and hides her face in her arms.

'Well, if I am, it's so horrendous I can't put words to it.'

Sandbunnveien in December

IT IS JUST BEFORE Christmas. I have had two more classes with Selma Lynge. It has already become a ritual. First, I arrive at Sandbunnveien and take off my shoes, dripping wet with melting snow. Then the philosopher-genius is packed off on the tram to Oslo to buy bread. After which we drink tea, then chatter unreservedly. She wants, in particular, to hear more about my feelings for Anja Skoog. After half an hour she asks me to sit at the piano.

I play for her. Simple pieces: 'The Girl with the Flaxen Hair' and 'The Sunken Cathedral'. She stands behind me. I anticipate the touch of her hands on my shoulders, her breath in my ear, the wise things she will say, which are so obvious, but which have never before occurred to me. And always, the demand that I play more slowly. 'You must let those fifths ring out, Aksel. Can you hear what is hidden beneath the water? The echoes of a distant past, of past events, of past lives. Only you can bring them to the surface, Aksel. The sunken cathedral perhaps? Or your mother? Or Anja Skoog?'

I note that Anja Skoog is cited amongst those things lost to the sea. At the end of a class I venture to ask her, as delicately as I can: 'Anja idolises you. You know her better than anyone, Selma. Should we be worried about her?'

Selma Lynge had been about to show me to the door. Suddenly she is attentive, and asks me to sit back down.

'Haven't you noticed,' she says, 'that Anja lives in a world of her own?'

'Yes, but what is Anja's world?'

Selma Lynge shrugs. 'Only Anja can know that.'

'Don't you worry about her? Isn't she too thin?'

She shakes her head. 'Why should I worry about Anja? It's only here in Norway that you expect your great talents to behave as though they were going to business school. Becoming a great artist, Aksel, doesn't just happen. Even with a lot of talent and work, there are no guarantees of success. When I was young, in Munich, we all knew that we lived on the edge of normality – of what was acceptable. The reality we inhabited could be shattered at any moment. It was fragile. Some drowned themselves in alcohol, others sat and practised for twenty hours at a time. You have to be extreme if you want to reach extreme heights. That was why I mentioned Glenn Gould, when you first came. A man who sits with his legs crossed while he plays is, of course, very extreme. His behaviour teetered so often on the edge of what is generally acceptable that you might have thought he belonged in a mental institution. This was the man who spat on Mozart – who declared Mozart should have died sooner rather than later, whilst still interpreting his music. But Gould's Mozart is ice-cold. I met Gould in Toronto, at a symposium. Fortunately I didn't have to play for him – he tried to kill me with words, from the first moment. Gould questioned me about my repertoire and slung insults at it. Why did I choose that sonata? When another was so much better. And why play Brahms's B major when his first concerto in D minor was so much more interesting? He went on and on. A male chauvinist pig, no less. A poseur; worse than all those he mocked in his essays. At the time, in Toronto, I kept thinking about Wilhelm Kempff, his complete opposite: a humanist and philanthropist. But musicians of his kind are the exception, and are rarely the greatest. Their humanism attracts fame; all their charity concerts with second-rate orchestras and countless television appearances. I shan't say Kempff and Menuhin are bad musicians, but it's possible they will not be remembered, because ultimately cruelty wins out over humanitarianism. Cruel people reach the top in all the arts. Which brings us back to Anja. She's the greatest talent I have ever heard. She is much greater than you, Aksel. And I am sure you can stand my saying that, because you love her – that much is clear. She gives herself entirely, in every moment as she plays. As though her life depended on it. Which is why she is not cruel, although she is a little asocial perhaps. She has set herself some heady goals. So she already has to live an abnormal life, since it's hardly normal to debut with Ravel's G major when you're only seventeen, and it's certainly abnormal to take your Artium at the same time. But she is doing both. You know how sheltered she's been. My task has been to help her handle her own feelings, not just the feelings of some dead composers. We've often spent more time talking than playing. We've both sat here, with our teacups . . .'

'Why did you keep it secret from Rebecca? Don't you realise it hurt her?'

'Her father demanded it.'

'You mean Bror *Skoog*?'

Selma Lynge is taken aback by me, by my intensity.

'Well, yes, who else? He is a classic father. We have many of those in Germany. He wants the very best for his daughter. He is already her manager. I'm sure you must have seen that. W. Gude didn't stand a chance.'

'But isn't that abnormal?'

'When it comes to classical music, my dear, nothing is abnormal. This is an arena for cripples and geniuses. There is a surprisingly short way to the top if you play your cards right. If not, you can become an eternal plodder, a first-class loser. Bror Skoog has the highest ambitions for his daughter. As her teacher I must adapt to that.'

'But what if it's a threat to your health?'

Selma Lynge pauses, and shrugs her shoulders.

'Then you don't belong to this world.'

The invitation

IT IS THE FOURTH Sunday of Advent, just before Christmas. I'm still practising my simple pieces. Father spends most of his time on the telephone in his bedroom. Catherine goes in and out of the house. I still have no idea what she is up to, but I don't think it has anything to do with Anja.

The telephone is suddenly free, and somebody rings. Father picks it up immediately. It is strange that he is so shy, and that he thinks he can hide his new girlfriend from us. And why doesn't he spend more time with her? I suspect she's not yet quite free, that she has somebody else.

Father comes to my door with the receiver: 'It's for you.'

'For me?' I grab the receiver. The mellow voice. It is Anja.

'Am I disturbing you?'

'Heavens, no.'

She hesitates. 'I was thinking about last time. When you were over at my place. Things turned out so stupidly. I didn't mean things to be like that. Are you busy this evening?'

'This evening? Why?'

'Well, I've practised enough, I'm very tired, and I could do with some company. Mummy and Daddy have gone out to somebody's fiftieth at Geilo. The Holm Hotel. I'm not really used to being alone in the house. Have you eaten?'

My hair stands on end. 'No, I haven't eaten,' I say.

'I could make something for supper.'

'Shall I bring Catherine?'

'No, I was thinking just the two of us. I'd like to try some Ravel out on you.'

I nod. That's the explanation. 'Yes, sure,' I say. 'I'll be right over.'

I hang up.

'Where are you going?' asks Father.

'That's none of your concern. But, whatever, don't mention it to Catherine.'

'Where is she?'

Just then Catherine emerges from her door, eyes red and swollen.

'I know where you're going,' she says.

'Well, perhaps it's my turn now.'

She shakes her head. 'Then you don't understand anything.'

'You mean I shouldn't have accepted her invitation?'

'Do as you please. I can't say anything. But be careful with her. There's so much you don't understand.'

'Since you've been listening in, I suppose you also know that I asked if I should bring you with me.'

Catherine stands swaying. Her skin is grey. She has shadows under her eyes. Suddenly I see how enormous her pupils are. How tired she is.

'It wouldn't be too clever to take me anywhere right now.'

'She wants to play me some Ravel,' I say, by way of explanation.

Catherine nods slowly. 'I think she should do that.'

Father stands there looking at us both in confusion.

I walk down the hill towards Elvefaret. I've taken a shower, speedily. If I'm to see Anja, I want to be clean. There's a fresh layer of snow. I stare at all the houses, excited about the meeting that lies ahead. This is my home. My life is here. For just a few months more. How will things change with the summer? Anja will be finished with her exams, Father will have sold the house, we'll be scattered to the winds.

But is this the evening for sad thoughts? I don't have to grieve over anything tonight. I arrive at the junction where Elvefaret begins. It's colder now and the snow creeks underfoot, I can see the lights on the other side of the river. Up there in the forest somewhere is Selma Lynge's house. It almost feels as though I can make it out between the trees. The geography is right, I think. Mother lay, down there, in the pool. It is a long time since I've visited the alder thicket. Perhaps that's a good sign.

Yes, I muse, tonight is special. I am not prowling about the neighbourhood like some sick animal. And I don't have to stop at the last bend. The Torchlight Man isn't around. And neither is Marianne Skoog – although that's almost a little sad: I haven't seen her since we parted at the Nationaltheatret station that evening. She seems to me like a carbon copy of Anja. She knows everything, and looks almost identical.

But she's years older. It confuses me that I relate so strongly to older women. Is it because of Mother? Is it really that facile? But Anja is the one who truly fills my mind, even when I'm lying on Margrethe Irene's bed.

I turn the last bend, past the point where I have always been left behind. I can see the angular Funkis house from here. It is, I observe, blood-red. Yes, as though blood were literally running out from between the timbers, as though a victim lay inside, suffering from life-threatening wounds.

My heart pounds as I stop at her gate. I am entering a forbidden zone. But she's invited me, hasn't she? Aren't both Father and Catherine my witnesses?

I walk up to the steps, observing that the snow could have been cleared better.

Anja is in there. And she is waiting for me.

I ring the bell.

She's been waiting for me. In less than a minute she opens the door.

Always that friendly smile that takes me by surprise.

'There you are,' she says.

Anja's house

SHE EMBRACES ME. The scent of calendula. I breathe it in, without her noticing.

'It all went so stupidly wrong last time,' she repeats. 'It wasn't how I wanted things to be.'

'Don't even think about it,' I say. 'Inside these walls you decide.'

'Daddy could have been more accommodating.'

'I expect he needed space to work,' I say, trying to be friendly.

She doesn't answer. Helps me off with my coat.

'It's great you could come.'

She is wearing the same lilac pullover, the same black trousers and felt slippers as last time. She rolls her eyes, and shows me into the living room. I am touched. On the coffee table is a bottle of wine and two glasses. She follows my gaze.

'But I'm not drinking, not until afterwards, and then only a bit.'

'You're going to play for me first.'

'Yes, if you'd like to hear me. And I've got a salad for afterwards too. Are you hungry?'

'No.'

'You can drink some wine, while I play. Since you like a bit of wine, don't you? I want you to feel relaxed.'

'I do feel relaxed.'

'Pour yourself a glass then? You're cleverer at that sort of thing than me. Then you can start to drink. And I can start to play.'

'An honour.'

'But I'll only play the piano parts of course. So you'll have to imagine the rest. You know Ravel's G major?'

'Of course. It was one of Mother's favourite concertos. Particularly the second movement.'

'That's what everybody says, and that makes me so nervous.'

'I expect Selma Lynge has been standing behind you, drawing out all the right feelings.'

'Don't say that. Let me start straight away. But you must take a sip of wine first.'

I do her bidding. She sits at the grand piano. The whole living room is lit with little spotlights. The snow-covered spruce trees stand outside the picture window. The amplifiers stand, glowing, in attendance. The costly chairs and sofas form an audience. A rather stern audience, I think.

But I am also a part of this audience. Sitting in my chair, sipping my wine, I will her through the first movement, observing how she throws herself into it with a concentration I myself have never possessed. She is nothing short of brilliant.

She looks questioningly at me in the orchestral breaks: 'I'm not playing too slowly, am I? You don't think Caridis will want it faster?'

'Tell him you're Selma Lynge's student,' I answer, 'and he'll probably understand. He has to listen to what you want, even if you're only a beginner.'

She nods. 'Thanks,' she says. 'Now for the second movement. Selma and I have discussed this so much. In her opinion it's so happy. But I'm convinced it's sad.'

'Yes, it's terribly sad,' I say.

'But why?' she asks, excitedly, 'Can you explain?'

'It's the key. E major. It seems so outwardly open, it pretends to be happy, but I think it's the openness of a clown, and under the laughter lies a melancholy, and you don't get *sadder* than that.'

'You might be right. Thank you for saying that. I'll have more courage to play it the way I want now.'

Anja Skoog plays the theme for me, pure and without artifice. I watch the delicacy of her movements. Meticulous. Dutiful. The small tosses of the head. The tight shoulders, coupled with emotions that beg for release, but which she holds back, just as Selma Lynge has taught her: nothing should be described, nothing explained. The music should arrive, without imposition. For that an inner strength is required. And a magical voice can never be created if the tempo is rushed. Now it is just slow enough.

I get an urge to come up behind Anja, just like Selma Lynge does. I want to put my hands on her shoulders and whisper some encouraging words: 'It will all be fine, Anja. You are not to worry.' Because from where I sit in the Le Corbusier chair I can see the true extent of her nerves. The concert is fast approaching. It will be her turn in the New Year. She's entering the musical arena early, just as she does everything early. Her mother had talked about that, when we ate together in Blom. She talked about the difficulties of being a parent. What and when should one teach a child? She had felt that each child had different needs. Some needed to learn later, others were more impatient. But is it so certain, I wonder, that Anja wants to venture out so early? Ever since Rebecca made her decision, things seem so gloomy, so frightening to those of us she left behind. We must justify the enormous investments we have made, so early in life. I no longer feel like a child, and neither, I think, does Anja. But are we adult enough for the task we have set ourselves?

Anja is about to commence the third movement. But she comes no further. She just sits staring down at the keys.

'I'm sorry,' she says. 'I suddenly feel so tired.'

'You mustn't play more. It's enough. It was the second movement that I most wanted to hear.'

'Then I'll play that for you at the concert. You've always been so kind to me.'

'Have I? We've not seen that much of each other, really. And you've been kind to me too.'

We laugh at our clumsy exchange. 'We've both been kind, haven't we?'

'I shan't play the third movement now, then,' she says.

'No, it can wait. Besides, it's so predictable.'

She bounds up from her chair, happy as a little girl. 'Let's eat instead then!'

We stand in the kitchen, designed down to the smallest detail. No Portuguese ceramic tiles here, but shiny black granite and German aluminium.

'I'll chop some onion,' says Anja.

'I can help.'

'No, I want to do it myself.'

I stand next to her as she chops. I compliment her playing, and I mean every word.

'Selma's right; you put everything into it, as though it were a matter of life and death.'

'Yes,' Anja laughs, 'but it shouldn't sound totally desperate either.'

'It doesn't. You'll be a sensation.'

'Please, don't say that!' she holds her hands over her ears, still holding her knife.

'Who else is performing at New Talents this year?'

'There's a singer who's well into his twenties: Bruseth I think is his name. He's singing Mahler. And then there's that violinist, you know the one who tosses his hair about and poses every time anyone looks at him. He's going to play the first movement of Sibelius. And there's a pianist from Bergen, Hellevik, who I've never heard of, but who's playing the usual Franck.'

'The Symphonic Variations? Isn't that more for a fourteen-year-old?'

'Yes, and he's older than me. And the funny thing is that I'm the only one allowed to play a full concerto.'

'And where are you on the programme?'

'At the end.'

She is busy with the onion as she chatters. Then she cuts herself.

'Ouch! Hell!'

'Is it deep?'

I see the blood trickling from her index finger.

Her face is white. She looks at me hopelessly.

'Oh dear . . . I can't stand the sight of blood.'

'But it's almost nothing.'

She stares, dumbfounded, at the little drop. She tries to say something, but nothing comes out. I realise she's about to faint. But it happens so quickly I fail to catch her. She slips through my arms, drops the kitchen knife, and bangs her head on the stone floor.

'Anja!'

I bend down. I put the knife on the kitchen worktop and my hand under her head. Her head isn't bleeding, and the cut on her finger is so tiny it's already stopped bleeding. I wipe off the blood with a tissue. She can't lie here on the cold, stone floor. I need to carry her up to her bed, where she can come round again, with a pillow under her legs, so the blood flows back to her head.

It feels strange to take her in my arms. But I have no choice: I grab her under the arms and knees and lift her. A shiver goes through me. She's no weight at all; just skin and bones. I stand there, swaying, horrified that my hands seem so close to her skeleton, that there is scarcely any flesh on her body, that she's so different to the way I'd imagined. I realise now that her lilac woolly jumper hides the shape of her body. Her face has never revealed her true state. How much can she weigh? Forty-something kilos? I carry her upstairs. She whimpers, still dazed, and grips me harder around my neck. I come up on to the landing; luckily the doors to all the rooms are open. I pass her parents' bedroom first. It has an electronically adjustable double bed that can be raised and lowered into all kinds of positions. Hardly surprising perhaps, since the most important thing for the Torchlight Man is to be in control. Next I pass a bathroom, silver and austere, with huge mirrors, before recognising the room that Catherine described: Anja's bedroom, with a wide grand-lit bed, a wedding picture of Marianne and Bror Skoog over it, and Bach and Beethoven on either side. I almost start to laugh.

I put Anja gently on the bed. Her eyes are closed and she says nothing. Maybe she's still unconscious. I take a pillow and put it under her legs, as I've been taught. But after that I don't really know what to do. I watch her, as she lies there. I sit down beside her. She is a skeleton. I can't understand how she's managed to keep it so hidden. Has she been sticking little cushions to her body, under her clothes, to cheat us all? I want to wake her up, to shake the truth from her. She is as pale as a sleeping Juliet, although I am no innocent Romeo, since I already know much too much about her.

I can't resist. I lie down next to her, with a hand tucked under her neck. She needs calm, I think to myself. It might take time before she wakes. And how often have I fantasised about lying like this, completely still beside her.

The room is completely still. The only sound is of her breathing. She's not well. A chill seems to come from her body, an odour. Not of calendula this time, but of something stale, rotten.

'Aksel?' she says suddenly, her eyes still closed.

'Yes?'

'I fainted, didn't I?'

'I think so. It was your finger. There was a trickle of blood.'

'How daft.'

'Don't worry. But I hope it's not a family weakness!'

'What d'you mean?'

'Well, with both your parents being doctors.'

She giggles. 'It must just be some childhood trauma. It's ridiculous, not being able to stand the sight of blood. I'm not that much of a coward after all.'

'Don't talk too much. Try to get your strength back.'

'My head is still buzzing. I hate it so much. Fainting. Do you remember, I told you when it happened on our walk.'

'Perhaps you should eat more food.'

'Are you going to start that, too? Or were you thinking about the salad down in the kitchen?'

'Golly, no. Certainly not that.'

'We can go down and eat it now.'

'I think you should stay here for now.'

'It feels good. You've got a safe pair of arms.'

'It was nothing.'

We lie still. I feel a kind of peace. I feel suddenly much older than her. As though she's a child in my arms. I kiss her gently on the cheek, with no ulterior motive. Mostly to comfort her.

'You can sleep with me if you want,' she says.

I have my lips on her cheek.

'You don't mean that,' I whisper.

'Why not?' She turns towards me. Her eyes are far too close to me. 'I always mean what I say.'

I am silenced, lost for words.

'You could at least carry on kissing my cheek,' she says.

'Stop it.'

I kiss her, uncertain that I have heard correctly. But I am loath to think too much. Suddenly our lips meet. I kiss Anja Skoog, and sense her willingness. She was not saying it to be polite.

I close my eyes. I have a dream image of her, an image that has inhabited my nights without her. That has followed me to the alder thicket.

'I love you,' I say, kissing her on the mouth.

'Don't say that,' she answers, affably.

I don't know what I should believe. It is as though she has made a decision. Is this really going to happen? Am I really going to sleep with Anja Skoog? But this body that I have desired for years is skin and bones. It feels wrong to take off her clothes. Besides, I've never undressed a woman.

'Do whatever you want with me,' she says.

She lies perfectly still. The rest is up to me.

I cannot resist.

I sleep with Anja Skoog. I never thought it would happen. So quick, so sweet, so painful. She shows no enjoyment, but her body seems strangely knowledgeable, in a way mine is not; the short, thrusting rhythm with which she meets me. It's as though I can feel her bones through her skin.

'How long shall I hold back?' I say.

'Don't hold back. Come, my love.'

Her body seems impatient, as though she wants it to be over. I can't hold back.

It happens. I come soundlessly, terrified of harming her, almost hoping she won't notice.

But she notices.

'That was nice,' she says.

'But was it good? Really? For you?' I feel empty, uneasy.

'Good enough,' she answers. 'Don't worry.'

'I've never done it before,' I say.

'Neither have I.'

'But Catherine?'

'That was different. Please, don't mention that now.'

We lie quietly, close to one another.

'Yes, it was good,' she says suddenly.

'And it wasn't risky?'

'Babies, you mean? No, luckily I have doctor-parents.'

'Of course, your mother,' I say, feeling stupid. 'She's a gynaecologist.'

'No, Daddy.'

'Really?'

'He's obsessed that I shouldn't get pregnant too young.'

'And so . . . what's he done?'

She doesn't answer. I dare not ask. I can picture it. The cap. Or the coil. Those skilled, professional hands.

'Let's not talk about it,' she says at last. 'It was good. It's enough. For tonight. You mustn't get ideas though. We can't do this again. Not for ages, at least. There's Ravel to come first. I can't afford to lose concentration. It means everything to me. Do you understand that?'

I kiss her quickly on the cheek. 'Of course,' I say.

'Perhaps you'd like a taste of that salad now?'

But I feel my nausea rising. 'No, thanks,' I say. 'I couldn't contemplate food right now.'

'It's up to you,' she says, gazing up at the ceiling.

We lie motionless next to each other.

I have experienced more than I could have dreamed.

But still I am sad.

Back in Melumveien

IT IS WELL PAST MIDNIGHT as I wander back home through more fresh snow. Not a soul in sight. Only my own footprints.

What has happened? I feel that I've betrayed somebody. Have I betrayed Anja? Things were never meant to be this way. Everything is strangely altered now, and the country I longed to conquer, that I conquered, is a country with no future.

Gripped with fear, I turn the key in my front door and let myself in. I am hoping that everybody is asleep. But I can hear Father's muffled voice talking on the phone in his room, and I can see the light under Catherine's bedroom door. She emerges immediately she hears me, and stands before me swaying, her eyes like two shiny marbles.

'How was she?'

'She could have been better.'

'That I can believe. But she played fantastically, yes?'

'Rest assured. She'll be this year's sensation.'

'Just as she was last year's. And – what about the two of you?'

I do not know what to say. What she really wants to hear.

'She's far too thin,' I say.

'Is that all?'

'Yes. And I can't believe you haven't noticed.'

Catherine scoffs. 'Are you suddenly starting to worry? She's that sort. It's just a phase. She has an important concert.'

'Yes, exactly.'

'Anja isn't the person you think. She'll get by. She always will. You and I are the ones who will come off worst.'

Meeting Marianne Skoog

IT IS JUST BEFORE Christmas. I meet Marianne Skoog at the junction of Kristian Auberts vei. I'm walking back from the alder thicket, and I'm always in my own thoughts then. But seeing her, there in front of me, I throw my arms open in greeting. She does the same.

'Hello there. It's been a long time.'

'You could have rung,' she says, with a smile.

Does she know I have slept with Anja? Has Anja said something? Suddenly overtaken with shame, I stare at the ground.

'My dear boy.'

She hugs me close to her. I feel the weight of her body. A powerful exchange of feelings between us. She is more like the Anja I dreamed of than Anja is herself.

She looks down at her watch. 'I really must dash home. We're making the gingerbread tonight.'

I don't know what to say. I can picture it all before me. I stare at her helplessly.

'Is everything OK?' she asks, with concern. 'You look pale.'

'No, I'm just fine,' I answer.

But she can see I'm not.

'Has something happened?'

I shake my head. Nothing *she* needs to know, anyway. I feel a growing anger. Does she have no idea of what is happening to her daughter? Can she really just go home and bake Christmas biscuits, and not ask any questions?

'I think Anja's very nervous, before the big event,' I say.

She scrutinises me, cups my face in her hands. We are far closer than we ought to be.

'Is there something you're trying to tell me, Aksel?'

'Yes. She's too thin. Appallingly thin. Haven't you noticed? She's just skin and bones. She has hardly any strength left. She's seventeen years old, and you're sending her on to the platform of the biggest concert hall in Oslo, with the Philharmonic Orchestra. What are you thinking of?'

Marianne Skoog shakes her head, as if to shield herself from what I am saying.

'Anja goes her own way, together with her father,' she says.

But I can't bear her cowardice. This is her responsibility too.

'Send my best wishes, then,' I say, coldly. 'Bake some lovely biscuits tonight. Christ, Anja's way too loyal to the two of you. Can't you see that?'

Marianne Skoog is about to say something, but I have turned my back, terrified by the intensity of my anger and of my feelings for Marianne. I am already on my way up the hill to Melum.

New Year's Eve

NEW YEAR'S EVE, 1969. The dawn of a new decade.

Margrethe Irene has invited the Young Pianists' Society to a party at Bislet. She is obsessed with the moon landings, Apollo 12, and with the abolition of the death penalty in Britain. As well as the latest new plane: the giant Boeing 747 with room for more than four hundred passengers. She wants to read my horoscope again.

I haven't said a word to her about Anja. It's rotten of me. And it's too late to say anything now. We go on as before.

Anja is not here tonight. That's not surprising. She made some excuse or other to Margrethe Irene over the phone. A headache perhaps. I don't even ask, since I want her left in peace until her concert. I have sent her flowers, of course, but have no idea whether she's received them. Inside my head, it is as though nothing has happened. I haven't slept with Anja Skoog. What happened that evening was too strange, too sad. We've not seen each other since. Christmas has been. But I've watched her from my window, as she's walked back home from the tram. Under those layers of clothes, it's impossible to see how thin she really is.

But she really *is* that thin, I reflect, as the Young Pianists' Society sit down to a New Year's celebration that might be our last before we're scattered to the winds. And perhaps that's why she didn't want to come; because she knows how transitory all this is, that nobody will miss her, except me. Rebecca is here. Ferdinand too. And some strange, younger girls from Bærum who Margrethe Irene has dug up, and who spend the entire evening playing records from the Floed family's rich collection, refusing to join our conversation.

Rebecca is the most interesting person here tonight, to me at least. What does she think about everything that has happened? She has grown so stunningly beautiful. Her pale skin. Her little freckles. Her vivid blue eyes. She is drifting away from us, from our little group at least. Perhaps that's why I find myself increasingly fond of her. We sit eating Swiss fondue. Margrethe Irene's father may be well-travelled, but he's gone overboard with the kirsch. The cheese tastes of pure alcohol. We can barely force the cubes of bread down our throats.

'You don't regret it, do you, Rebecca?' I ask her.

'No, it was the most important decision of my life.'

Margrethe Irene has Rebecca's horoscope ready, and waves a sheet of paper: 'It's all so clear here, it *had* to happen.'

I exchange glances with Ferdinand, my rival, whom I've never really feared, because he always seemed rather feeble, and because he's bound to make his debut *later* than me. He may be ambitious, but he seems such a dawdler. I can't see it turning out well. I am still the favourite, the one destined to create a sensation. Not that I know why. Still, I'm keen for everybody to go on thinking it. My time will come after Anja Skoog's debut.

We sit drinking wine and forcing down pieces of cheese-dipped bread. It will soon be our turn to enter the flames. But there's still time. Margrethe Irene is not yet planning a debut. She says that she wants to go to Vienna to study with Professor Seidlhofer first. And Ferdinand wants to go to London, to Ilona Kabos.

'So, Aksel, when are you going make your debut?' says Rebecca, fixing me with a piercing, though not unkindly, gaze.

'I'll have to talk to Selma about it.'

'So you call her Selma?'

'Yes, it seems natural. Although I know you prefer Fru Lynge.'

'Perhaps I was brought up too well,' she says, smiling.

'Don't you have any contact with Selma Lynge any more?'

'Nope. She lost all interest in me when I gave up.'

'Really?' Margrethe Irene raises her eyebrows.

'Yes, why wouldn't she? She thought she was going to get this great pedagogical success. And I disappointed her. Now she only has Anja.'

'And me,' I say.

'Yes, but Anja's first up. Poor Anja.'

'Why do you say that?'

'Maybe I shouldn't tell you this,' she hesitates, 'But it might come in useful. When Fru Lynge realised that I'd decided to quit, she took me behind closed doors and told me: "Nobody has ever disappointed me as much as you."'

'Did she really say that?' Ferdinand asks, in disbelief.

'Yes. I couldn't believe my ears. But those were her exact words.'

'So she saw your giving up as a betrayal.'

'Absolutely. And it was even a betrayal, somehow, that I ruined my debut by tripping over my frock. She said she'd expected more from me. I was the first debutante she'd had for years. I'd been feeling for ages that she wanted to prove something through me. My debut was meant to be a sensation: the boring little up-town girl would demonstrate to the world what could be done with the right teacher.'

She looks round at us helplessly.

'You've never been boring,' I say quickly.

But I am lying. For years I saw Rebecca as the most boring one among us. And now, after giving up, she's suddenly become the most interesting. It's disquieting. She's blossomed. She is so composed, so self-assured, and she'll have taken her Artium in a few months. She has liberated herself from Selma Lynge, without ever having quite fallen into her grasp.

'So, Rebecca, what are you going to do this autumn?' asks Margrethe Irene. She can feel that I have a lot I want to discuss with Rebecca, but she is having none of it, to judge by her body language at least. She sits next to me at the table, with her left hand under the table, placed safely on my crotch.

'I'll do a foundation year,' says Rebecca. 'And then take medicine.'

'So you want to be a doctor?'

'Yes, why not?'

'Should I feel touched?' says Margrethe Irene, pointedly. 'The little rich girl who cares so much for others, and wants to save lives.'

I give Margrethe Irene's thigh a warning pinch. Rebecca seems unaffected.

'Who knows whether I'll be able to save lives?' she says calmly. 'But whatever, I do want to be involved *in* life, not just sitting on the outside.'

Rebecca doesn't want more attention now, she senses Margrethe Irene's ill will, like a sudden attack of jealousy, but I urge Rebecca to go on: 'Please, tell more.'

She hesitates, shrugging her shoulders. 'All of you are in the middle of it, of course. I have no good explanation for what I did. But I remember all those afternoons, as I sat practising after school. I remember the lonely hours, the aching back. I remember all the time it took up. And I thought: is this really worth it? And for what? To what purpose? At what price? Am I doing this because I am mad enough to believe I can give the world a revolutionary new version of Beethoven's Opus 109? Am I doing it because I love music more than anything, because I need to surround myself with it, to slog at it, for five or more hours a day? Or am I doing it because I want to be famous? To bathe in other people's admiration. To *be* somebody? None of it seemed to make any sense. What shocked me most was that I didn't actually have any goal, or any deeper consciousness of why I was doing what I was doing. Of course I wanted a career; but for what? That was the most painful thing about my debut. After I'd fallen over up there on the podium, I realised that I was a mediocre musician, who would never express anything unique, or play anything really worth listening to. Up until then, my confidence had all hung on my dress. We are women after all. We like to look good. But I hadn't realised how much vanity was wrapped up in it all. Fru Lynge was always stunning. Older, maybe, but still one hundred per cent woman. She always wore make-up, chose a different outfit each day, to suit each student. She radiated strength. And I thought I could capture that strength, just by putting on a bit of make-up. But as I lay there on the stage, dressed to the nines, it was as though all my make-up was gone.'

She exchanges a glance with Margrethe Irene. 'Only a woman can understand what that means. There I was on that stage, feeling as if I didn't have a scrap of make-up; I might as well have tumbled out of bed and sat at the piano in front of the audience in nothing but a nightie. The make-up, the clothes, the shoes were all meant to help me through with my debut; which was a doomed project from the outset. And now there was nothing left for me to hold on to apart from Ravel, Beethoven and Chopin. Not only was my playing mediocre but I felt certain I looked awful – and it was the latter that upset me most. That was when I realised how little the music really meant to me, how half-hearted my desire was to really communicate anything. It was when that hit home, somewhere in the middle of the concerto, that I realised the time had come to be honest with myself. I played the four Chopin ballads without any feeling. I remember almost praying to our patron saint: "Please, Saint Cecilia, help me through this concert, so I don't make things even more embarrassing for the people I love. Then I shall bow to the laws of music, continue to love and honour it, but give up any wish for personal gain." And she answered my prayers; she got me through.'

Rebecca's words make a huge impression on me. We sit eating our fondue in silence. Margrethe Irene seems rather tipsy already. She still has her hand placed strategically on my crotch. I shall have to go to bed with her tonight. There is no escape.

But before that happens, I'm determined to have a word in private with Rebecca. When I see that everybody has finished with the fondue, I get up from my seat quickly and announce: 'Rebecca and I will clear the table. The rest of you can go and find some nice music for us all to listen to.'

Ferdinand and Margrethe Irene stare at me in astonishment. What has got into me? The two Bærum girls, who have barely been at the table, offer to help.

'No, thanks,' I say firmly. 'Rebecca and I have something to discuss.'

I have got what I wanted. I am in the kitchen alone with Rebecca Frost, stacking the dishwasher, and pouring the remains of the alcoholic sludge into a bin bag, whilst continuing to drink more wine. It's a good thing, I think to myself, that Rebecca shares my liking for wine.

'I suppose you realise I want to talk about Selma Lynge?' I say.

She looks at me in surprise. 'Oh, I thought you wanted to talk about Anja.'

'Selma and Anja are two sides of the same coin, in a way at least. But why in heaven's name do you call her Fru Lynge?'

'Don't you see?' says Rebecca, smiling calmly. 'It was Selma, as you call her, who decided on it. She didn't want us to be on friendly terms. I was never to be anything but the pupil, the girl, the child. She wanted to teach me everything from scratch.'

'But Anja's even younger. And she calls her Selma.'

Rebecca takes a sip of wine, and looks at me with concern: 'You're not still besotted with Anja, are you?'

'That's not what I wanted to talk about.'

Rebecca sighs: 'You're right, of course; Anja is younger. But she's also more fragile. She needs the security, the encouragement that comes from that kind of closeness. I was stronger. More sure of what I wanted. So I needed to be cowed.'

'Is Selma really that crafty? That calculating?'

'It's more a question of power. You have to remember that Fru Lynge is hugely ambitious. Listen, Aksel, since we're alone, I can tell you what really clinched things for me. You remember in the interval, when you came to the artists' foyer?'

'Yes – you were furious.'

'Yes, that was because of Selma Lynge: she'd just whispered in my ear how ashamed she was of me; that everything we'd ever done together was in vain.'

'She really *said* that? In the interval?'

'Yes. She was deeply disappointed in me because I didn't perform as she'd expected.'

'And W. Gude?'

'He didn't hear. Which was just as well. He already looked miserable enough.'

'But what about her speech afterwards? Selma said you'd given a fabulous concert. And what about Arrau, whom she'd invited in your honour?'

'Just playing to the gallery. What else could she say or do? She had no choice. But inside she was furious, more furious than me, because a pupil so strategically important to her reputation had let her down when it mattered most.'

'Which, I suppose, is why we're standing here,' I say. 'Because I can't help wondering how much pressure she's putting on poor Anja.'

Rebecca laughs. 'Oh, I'm sure Anja will come out of this better than anyone. That girl is fearless.'

I hesitate, wondering how much I should tell her. I decide to tell her nothing.

'So what do you think Selma Lynge's strategy is?'

'To be best friends with Anja. The girl's got a mother, of course. So Fru Lynge has to find another way of getting power over her, rather than from above and down, or as an older woman speaking to a young one, if you understand what I mean. And Anja's been kept secret from us all; so she's relatively isolated. You mustn't forget what a devilishly good teacher Fru Lynge is, she can talk you into a trance, make you accept *her* terms, almost before you know it. She wants to transform herself through her pupils. They give her her dignity back. An artist who's reached those heights will never quit. Her pupils are her piano keys now. In my case, it was obvious: I had to be brought to my knees. She and I could *never* be friends. I doubt she really even believed in me to begin with, but then she saw how determined I was, and I suppose, like so many other people, she couldn't help thinking: *This girl is stinking rich* ... It's an awful thing to say, but money creates a magnetic field. And I still don't actually know how much Father paid her for all those weekly lessons, year after year.'

I listen, nodding and feeling strangely uneasy. Can it be true? Is Selma Lynge really such an evil person? This woman who, in a few weeks, has opened new vistas to me and brought me so close to the meaning of music, closer even than Mother did. Suddenly I think of Mother, of the selfless and spontaneous way in which she shared her joy in music with me. Would she have wanted this? To see a group of teenagers thrashing helplessly about, not knowing what to do, which way to turn? Would she have approved? My mother always experienced music as a gift. It is New Year's Eve; and I miss her.

Rebecca looks at me.

'Wow, you were far away then!'

I shake my head. 'No, I was just remembering my mother; her delight, even when the medium wave crackled at its worst, and all we could catch of Tchaikovsky's violin concerto, from some radio station in Poland, was the cadenza of the first movement.'

Rebecca touches my cheek.

'Go on,' she says seriously.

'It's just such a contrast to one of the first things Anja ever said to us.'

'What was that?'

'After she'd won. And she'd done so brilliantly. She said: "You don't invest that much of your life for nothing." Do you remember?'

'You talked a lot about that. I shall never forget it.'

'Well, it was terrifying.'

'Yes. Because it was an echo of Selma Lynge.'

'Has it never occurred to you how thin Anja is?'

Rebecca hesitates. 'No, not really.'

'She's like a skeleton.'

Rebecca seems not to see the gravity of the situation. 'That's not necessarily so strange, Fru Lynge has massive plans for her now.'

'You mean with Anja playing Ravel with the Philharmonic?'

'Yes, poor thing.'

Rebecca shakes her head.

'Anyway, Aksel,' she says with a mischievous look in her eye, 'what plans does Fru Lynge have lined up for *you*?'

'She's not mentioned anything yet.'

'Oh dear, that doesn't bode well,' she says, pinching my cheek.

'What do you mean?' I laugh.

'That she must have very *great* plans indeed, and that she has to keep them under wraps, because they're so shameful.'

'Shameful?'

Rebecca looks at me humorously: 'Don't you know? She has a weakness. A vice.'

'And what's that?'

'Young men.'

'What rubbish!'

'No, Aksel, it's the truth.'

Rebecca is suddenly serious. 'And Torfinn is considerably younger than her.'

'Really? That dribbling, mumbling man?'

Rebecca laughs. 'He's just your typical European intellectual! Yes, my friend, he's ten years younger than her.'

'But he looks so old!'

'Of course. Life with Selma Lynge can hardly be invigorating. Predators like her need a constant supply of fresh prey.'

'She sends the great philosopher out to buy bread every time I come.'

'Then we really are talking danger zone!' Rebecca laughs triumphantly.

'Don't say that. And where are all her children? '

'Good question. There are three of them, aren't there? Or four? I think they wander about in the forest down by that rotten river, with some emaciated German au pair.'

'Don't say that!'

'Oh God, I'm sorry!' She covers her mouth with her hand. 'I forgot . . . the river . . . your mother . . .'

'Yes, forget my mother,' I say. 'She has nothing to do with *this*.'

'Oh, don't be so sure. Fru Lynge wants a finger in every pie.'

'Even the dead?' I laugh.

'Perhaps that too.'

'But tell me more about the living. What is it with these young men?'

'Oh, there are rumours. She sleeps with guys. Didn't you know? Torfinn's a hopeless cuckold.'

'Oh, you're on first name terms with *him*?'

'It follows. But he hasn't a clue himself, poor man, that Fru Lynge's having an affair with one of the cellists in the Philharmonic.'

'A cellist?' I say. 'Anja's hooked on the cello. Jacqueline du Pré, and all that.'

'Well, perhaps there's a link. Perhaps du Pré has served as the perfect excuse for Fru Lynge to discuss the auditory delights of the cello, the instrument that her young man plays. When you're in love, you want to spend every second of every day in your lover's universe. Besides, she'd naturally go for du Pré, being such a glutton for passion. And du Pré is a woman.'

I nod. There's some logic to what she's saying. I feel nauseous; inexplicably, really, since I'm not about to go on stage or anything. The spotlight is turned on Selma and Torfinn Lynge now, not me. It's been strange to hear Rebecca talk like this. It's as if Selma is even more real for me than before.

Margrethe Irene pops her head round from the living room, clearly irritated.

'What *are* you two doing, at a quarter to midnight?'

'We're tidying up your kitchen. Besides, we were discussing Selma Lynge,' says Rebecca loyally. 'She's not the easiest person to handle, you know. I'm giving this young man a little advice.'

'Fine by me. But it's time to come out now,' says Margrethe Irene sharply. 'We're about to enter a new decade. In a few minutes it will be 1970. There are champagne and sparklers waiting out on the balcony.'

So here we are, the Young Pianists' Society, barring Anja Skoog, but including the two budding pianists who flit about, completely lost in their own world; Margrethe Irene is very sweet with them. We gaze out across Bislet, the famous skating rink. We drink champagne while the younger guests have lemonade. Fireworks shoot across the sky. Margrethe Irene and I have our arms around each other. But I'm longing to be like Rebecca; to be free of all attachment. Rebecca has travelled further than any of us. I know everybody else at the party feels sorry for her. To them she is a loser. But I know otherwise. I envy the feelings she has right now.

An explosion of rockets. It is New Year. Margrethe Irene whispers into my ear: 'I want to go to bed with you. You shan't escape. The others won't be back until tomorrow evening.'

I stand, swaying. Thinking about the future. I can't help thinking again how fast time seems to be going now. We all grab hold of each other and wish each other a Happy New Year. Then it's Rebecca's turn.

'Try to be happy, Aksel,' she says, kissing me on the lips.

It's a long time since she did that. For a moment I'm aware of feelings I've never had for her before. Then I look in her eyes.

'You too.'

She gives me a hug.

'You know what I mean?' she says, 'We can't talk more here.'

I nod. 'We'll talk another time.'

'But you've got the message?'

I nod again. 'Yes, I have to be careful of Selma Lynge.'

She smiles.

'You've got it.'

Everybody's gone. Only our hostess and I are left behind. I sleep with Margrethe Irene. And tonight, the girl who has always remained a slight mystery takes off all her clothes, and stands naked before me. She has nothing to hide. I have the feeling she suspects something, and that she doesn't want to lose her hold over me, over my strange existence. But what is it she desires? Who am I? A bumbling idiot who wants to be a somebody in this world, who hasn't yet made a single important decision in life. Neither of us knows what we really want, or what we might be good for. None the less she's laying plans for me, for *us*. I've no idea what these plans are, none at all, not the slightest. I take what she offers: short-term happiness, with no price tag. And tonight I feel no disgust for her. No resistance. No shame. She has a body I can hold. She's drunk, but not *so* drunk. We're both conscious of our actions here in the dark. If it wasn't for Anja, I could tell her that I loved her, just as she tells me. I am touched by her sweetness, by her tenderness. We enjoy each other twice more. Then she starts questioning me once more about the future, what I think, the plans I've made. But I have no plans.

'I must read your stars,' she says sleepily.

'Yes, some day,' I answer.

'No, now, immediately!' she mumbles, drifting off, tired at last.

I smile, kissing her forehead. She tries to go on, but the words don't come. Moments later she is sleeping, happy and satisfied, in my arms.

I slink homewards. It's too early for the first tram. Perhaps there's snow, but I don't notice. A new decade. It doesn't feel good: to have slipped from a girl's naked embrace, to dress in the dark, in hushed silence, without washing; and to come out on to the street without saying goodbye, and to realise you're too lightly dressed.

The long way home.

Along Sørkedalsveien, and all the way to Røa. There aren't many people in the streets, nor many cars. There are a few youngsters setting off squibs. Otherwise everything is quiet.

Where is Father? What is Catherine doing? Our home will be taken over by strangers soon. The two tenants on the first floor have already been given their notice. Come the summer, I will have to find a place of my own, get a job, or go abroad to study.

But where will I get the money?

I remember what Rebecca said to me last night: 'Try to be happy, Aksel.'

I trundle homewards. I think about Anja who is probably lying in her bed right now. I picture her skeletal form. Her skinny knees. Her tiny bum. The sharp hipbones that pressed themselves against me with such seeming experience, and at the same time so politely.

She filled me with fear in that moment.

And yet, for the rest of my life, I will long for her.

Intermezzo at Selma Lynge's

'POLITENESS AND SEXUALITY are a poor match,' says Selma Lynge. 'Schubert knew that. You should know that too.' She is standing behind me at the piano. I have played Schubert for her, the Sonata in C minor, the one she concluded her career with. It was her idea. She'd suggested it out of the blue:

'You said you'd practised some Schubert. The C minor. Why don't you play a little of it for me now?'

'But I've not prepared it.'

'All the more reason.'

I play. She stands behind me. What does she want to hear? A helpless student fumbling after notes? I certainly don't know this by heart.

'Not so tense,' she says, as I go on. But I don't feel tense. I pull back the tempo, allowing the second theme of the first movement to stand still, like dead water in a little pool, almost turning it into a largo, slower at least than one is used to hearing. I know she likes it like this. I close my eyes. *She* has always been the one to focus on the sexual. Now I think of how she sleeps with men. Not just the sniggering Torfinn, but the cellist in the Philharmonic. Probably the young handsome one, who isn't Norwegian.

'Aksel, you're not concentrating!'

I stop abruptly and turn to her. She is closer than I thought. I can smell the waxy fragrance of her lipstick. She pulls back, looking surprised.

'You've stopped?'

'And is that against the rules?'

She scrutinises me. I have never been so defiant before.

'There are no rules here,' she says. 'Perhaps we should sit down and talk.'

We walk back to the sofa, where we have just been sitting with our tea. Selma Lynge looks at me anxiously.

'Has something happened between you and Anja?'

'Why do you ask? What makes you think of Anja?'

'Nothing – apart from the fact that you're thinking of her.'

'How do you know I'm thinking about her?'

'I can feel it.'

'You're not clairvoyant.'

'Don't be so sure.'

I give up. 'OK. So I'm thinking of Anja.'

'And what are you thinking?'

'That I'm worried about her. That she's taken on a massive task.'

Selma Lynge smiles. A troubling smile. Mother smiled like that sometimes. When Father was in the right about something, and she'd run out of good arguments. It is the thought of Anja that makes Selma smile. Her body language says it all. She straightens her back, tosses her head. I shall have to weigh my words carefully.

'Anja is more than ready,' she says. 'Anja is a fully fledged artist. You just wait and see. She'll astonish you. She'll thrill us all.'

She smiles again.

I can see Selma Lynge through Rebecca's eyes now. But I'm a man – at least almost – and I see other things in her too. Her strength doesn't trouble me, it draws me, making her even more attractive. I shake my head, confused, and trying to chase these new thoughts away.

'Why are you doing that?' she asks.

I feel a deep shame. A loss of control. This is not how I want her to see me.

'I'm sorry.'

She looks at me, for a long time.

'Never say sorry again.'

She continues to look at me.

I retract my gaze.

But I do not know where to look.

Coming home

I STROLL HOME from Selma Lynge's. A clear, starry evening. It was on nights like this that the medium-wave reception was always best, to Mother's joy: then we could tune in to Kiev or Moscow, and Father might drag Catherine and me out into the street to show us a satellite or some shooting stars. I turn my face to the sky, as if to bring my mother, or the father I once knew, back to life. Yes, the stars are all there!

Then I sense a sudden draught. Behind me. Someone staring. But the street is empty. There's not a soul in sight, just piles of shovelled snow.

I stop, confused. The sky is coal-black between the stars.

But in one spot the sky is blacker. I shudder.

It is the hawk. My bird. Which comes to warn me.

The darkest star. So much closer than those that shine.

Hunched, I walk on, sensing the hunting bird's gaze above.

My witness. My evil eye.

I have to take the path by the Vinding family's old bathing spot. It's no longer so painful. Where the branch broke, a new one has grown. Where Mother waved, there is only calm water. On the path ahead a figure walks deep in thought. Catching up, I find it's Anja. But this time I don't frighten her. She realises it's me.

'Aksel.'

'Anja! I'm on my way back from Selma's.'

She brightens up. 'Are you? I was at her place earlier today, too.'

'She says you're a fully fledged artist. And that you'll thrill us all.'

She shakes her head. 'Selma says a lot of strange things.'

Our eyes finally meet.

I long to grab her, to embrace her, but hold back.

She feels it, rolls her eyes skywards, and seems pleased at my not making a move. What happened never took place. But one of us has to say something. It will have to be me, I think.

'It was so special . . .'

She holds up a hand to silence me.

'I've sent tickets for the concert in the post. You and Catherine can't sit next to each other, because it'll make me too nervous. Besides, you'll have to put up with sitting right at the back.'

'Why?'

'I can't risk having eye contact with you while I'm playing. It would ruin everything.'

She takes my arm. We stroll homewards. It touches me. Her trustfulness. I turn quickly, searching for the hawk, but it is no longer there.

'Daddy wants to take a few of the closest people out for dinner afterwards.'

'And your mother?'

'Of course. But this is Daddy's big event, you understand. He's reserved Blom.'

'Well, we've all been there before.'

'This will be different. And you can drink as much wine as you like.'

She gives my arm a little squeeze.

'How far can I walk with you, tonight?'

'At least as far as the turn.'

We walk in silence, past my house where the lights are on in all the windows. Catherine is nowhere to be seen.

'Are you nervous?'

She shakes her head. 'Not really, I should be able to do this. Besides, I'm looking forward to playing the second movement for you with a full orchestra.'

I want to stop and kiss her, but I don't dare.

'I'm looking forward to it,' I say.

We have passed Melum.

'I don't want to bring shame on any of us,' she says.

It's a strange remark that I shall ponder for the rest of my life. I pull her close. But she doesn't want that,

For the rest of the way, as far as the bend in Elvefaret, we walk side by side.

We look into each other's eyes, standing between two lampposts. It is dark.

'Perhaps I won't see you before you're up on the podium?'

'Probably not.'

'I wish you luck.'

'You don't need to.'

'I'll think about you all the time.'

'Thank you. You're kind. Perhaps I can repay you one day.'

'Repay me for what? Besides, you repay me all the time.'

'I'd better get in now and go to bed. You know – I want to sleep all the time. Do you ever get like that?'

'It's the nerves. It's quite natural.'

'I'd like to sleep through the whole concert too. But I suppose that would be a bit awkward?'

'Sounds like it. Just think how much you can sleep afterwards, instead.'

'I shall. That's good advice.'

'You silly thing.'

'You too.'

She rounds the corner. I watch her closely this time. She must wear padding, I think to myself, because it's impossible to see how thin she is. Besides, those thick clothes disguise so much.

I'm already missing her. I wish I could hold her close to me. Nothing more. But she doesn't come back. She will let herself into the red house. What will happen there? I turn and walk home, with sad thoughts and a heavy heart.

New talents

IT IS THE DAY of Anja Skoog's debut concert; although one has to ask if it can really be called a debut, W. Gude rings me and says that these New Talents Concerts with the Philharmonic can do more harm than good. As I speak to him, I feel the nausea rise. He clearly feels snubbed by Anja, who doesn't want to use him as her impresario, and he's on the hunt for a new debutant himself, for the sake of his reputation. I stand by the living-room window looking out. It is bitterly cold outside; frost, melted snow, slippery roads. I want to focus my thoughts on Anja, but W. Gude asks if I can't choose the date for *my* debut soon, which, he says, has to be a recital. I stammer and splutter, unable to answer, telling him I must speak to Selma Lynge first.

'I've spoken to her,' he says, 'She thinks you'll be ready for the autumn.'

'This isn't the day to talk about this sort of thing,' I say.

'Are you worried about Anja?'

'Of course I am.'

There are huge notices about Anja in the papers. Catherine and I sit at the kitchen table reading them all.

'Oh,' Catherine moans as she looks at the pictures. 'She is so damned beautiful!'

Anja has her picture in *Dagbladet*, *VG* and *Aftenposten*. Yes, she is beautiful. She looks stronger in black and white than in life. Prettier too. And you can't see how thin she is. But she has nothing to say; there's not a single interesting word about what she wants to communicate. She is the sensation from the Young People's Piano Competition. The journalists try to prompt her: why has she chosen this piece? What does she want to say? But Anja Skoog refuses to say anything at all. Instead, she poses for the photographers, turns her face in half-profile, moistens her lips, and acts young, sad and sensitive.

'It makes you want to puke,' says Catherine, 'posing like that.'

'Yes, why is she doing it?'

'Because she has nothing to say. No message. All she wants is to look mysterious and interesting.'

'But she doesn't have much control over that. The journalists turn up. The photographers snap away. Don't judge her too harshly.'

'I'll talk to her when it's all over,' Catherine mumbles.

A thin layer of fresh snow. There are children tobogganing, downhill from the station. We take the tram together down to the National-theatret. I feel suddenly close to Catherine. It is not only Anja that binds us, but everything that's going to happen in the coming summer, the house that will be sold, the choices we have to make, which we've resisted making, the conversation with our father, who tells us nothing, and who just sits in his bedroom on the telephone. Catherine is looking smarter than me, in a black dress with a fur collar. Neither dresses nor fur collars are generally her style, but I have to admit she looks cool, almost sexy. As for me, I'm wearing the same dowdy suit I've used ever since Mother's funeral. It is black and shiny and one hundred per cent polyester. It is the smartest thing I own. Together with my large red tie with black snakes, tied in a chunky knot. This is Anja's big day, and Bror Skoog has sent out invitations for dinner afterwards. So it's to be expected that we dress up.

Where is Anja now? She won't be taking the tram. Today she'll be driven by her father, the surgeon, and by her mother, the gynaecologist. Today she will be unveiled to the whole world. The New Talents with the Philharmonic. If she succeeds tonight the world will open up for her. And why shouldn't she? It is barely more than a year since she celebrated her first triumph in the Young People's Piano Competition. Since then Selma Lynge has been whispering in her ear. She can't go wrong.

I'm as nervous as if it were my evening.

Catherine and I walk up the stairs of the Nationaltheatret station, taking the usual route. I have walked this way so often on my way to concerts. Everybody else listens to the Beatles and the Rolling Stones these days. We are the deviants: buying great bundles of sheet music, sitting for hours at our instruments, staying in on Saturday nights, exchanging Keith Richards and John Lennon for Heifetz and Gina Bachauer. The light floods out from between the columns in front of the Aula. Within these walls is the magical room where Munch hung his paintings, where Rubinstein, Arrau, Barenboim and Ashkenazy have all played, thanks to W. Gude's network of contacts. Schwarzkopf has sung, Bruno Walther has conducted. Now it is Anja Skoog's turn, and she doesn't even like Munch.

It is January. Dark. I see all the shadows moving towards the light behind the pillars. Coming to hear the Philharmonic and the talented youngsters. I spot a cluster of young people at the top of the steps by the entrance. My friends, the Young Pianists' Society. Rebecca is very formally dressed, and even Ferdinand has put a suit on. The younger girls, whose names I can never remember, have also turned up. Suddenly I look up. Is the hawk here too? But the sky is invisible, veiled in the kind of pinkish-black film that only rises from a steaming city. Margrethe Irene taps me on the shoulder.

'Aksel? Are you all right? What are you looking for up there in the night?'

I turn to her, trying to laugh it off. 'Oh, nothing.'

'Nothing?' she says, pouting in sham disappointment. 'And I've told you so much about my stars.'

Catherine bolts, finding this kind of talk intolerable. Margrethe Irene has me to herself for a few moments before we join the others at the top of the steps.

'We might need the stars tonight,' I say and kiss her lightly on the lips. She is pleased.

'Yes. I've thought about that, Aksel. Anja needs your presence tonight. Yes, you have to be close to her. You must be the only friend she has. Where are you sitting in the hall?'

'She's put me right at the back.'

'Has she really?' Margrethe Irene looks disbelievingly at me. 'Let's see your ticket.'

I bring my ticket out. She brings hers out. She inspects them both.

'It's not that far back,' she says.

'Where are you?'

'Even further back than you. Peculiar, by the way, that she hasn't let us sit together.'

'She doesn't think of us as a couple, I suppose.' I say, noticing that my forehead is breaking out into a sweat, and my nausea is rising.

'She ought to have sussed that out by now,' says Margrethe Irene, giving my arm an angry pinch.

There's no time to say anything more. She returns my ticket

'There are the others,' she says quickly.

We greet each other, exchange hugs. Rebecca looks pale. I look searchingly at her. She notices.

'I'm so nervous,' she says, enveloping me in her perfume, a heavy, sweet fragrance I have never smelt before.

'That's what Anja said before your debut.'

'Female solidarity. The new feminism.'

I nod. 'Hmm.'

'She is about to go through hell. But why are we standing about here? Let's go in.'

We pass through the glass doors into the foyer. There is an unusually slow queue. At first we can't understand why, but it is soon clear. Bror Skoog is standing just inside the foyer, shaking hands with everybody as they arrive.

'I can't believe it,' Margrethe Irene whispers, clutching my arm.

I notice myself getting hotter. The Torchlight Man is dressed for a party, in a dinner suit, with a shiny collar, white shirt and red bow-tie. Where, I wonder, is Marianne? She must have refused to be a part of this.

'Welcome,' says Bror Skoog. 'Welcome to Anja's debut!'

Rebecca takes his hand, smiling politely. Followed by Ferdinand and Margrethe Irene.

And then me.

'Welcome.'

I bow politely, meet his ice-cold gaze. He knows too much, I think to myself.

'Thank you very much. Are things all right with her?'

My question is too intimate. It makes him uncomfortable.

'Naturally.'

He moves swiftly on to the next guest.

I look around for Marianne: there she is, on the other side of the foyer. She rolls her eyes, just like her daughter. Perhaps she's acknowledging me. I smile back.

Margrethe Irene tugs at my arm.

'This is unbelievable!' she says.

'What?'

'The way Anja's weirdo father is hijacking the whole concert! She's not the only one making her debut with the Philharmonic tonight, you know!'

'She is, as far he's concerned.'

Rebecca listens attentively. 'Are you serious, Aksel?'

I shrug my shoulders. 'Why else would he stand there?'

Neither of us says anything.

Then I spot Selma Lynge. She's by the curtains at the entrance to the auditorium. The moment she catches sight of me, she comes over, almost running, in a long, turquoise dress, although a different one to the last: this one is even more exquisite, with sequins and ruching.

'Aksel!'

She embraces me.

'There's so much excitement in the air,' I say.

'That's a good sign,' she says.

She blanks both Rebecca and Margrethe Irene completely. But Rebecca is having none of it.

'Fru Lynge!'

Then something astonishing happens: Selma Lynge glares at Rebecca, almost with a grimace, as though remembering something utterly distasteful. It feels as though she would rather say nothing, but that everybody around her is waiting for her to answer.

'Rebecca, my dearest!' she says at last. She leans forward to kiss her, almost as if she was taller than her, which she is not.

'Congratulations on Anja,' says Rebecca.

'Thank you.'

They can't bear to talk to each other. To my amazement I note that Rebecca is the strongest. She has been through all this. Selma Lynge has been through it too, but many years ago. It is as a teacher that she seeks to reap her rewards now. Torfinn stands over by the curtains talking with some of his university colleagues. But Selma Lynge has no interest in him. She wants to talk to *us*, the youngsters, while W. Gude glides past, unnoticed, behind her.

'How is Anja feeling?' I ask.

'So so.' Selma Lynge glances over at Rebecca. 'She found everything that happened last time a little unsettling. She doesn't want to go tripping up on her dress – let's put it that way.'

Rebecca looks indignantly at her former teacher. 'Things like that don't happen twice in a row.'

I want to smoothe things.

'But the conductor?' I say. 'And the orchestra? Are they on the same wavelength?'

'The dress rehearsal went very well, even though Caridis probably wants it faster than Anja and me.'

'I don't think that's anything new. What's more unusual is Anja's father standing there welcoming people at the door, as though this was a private concert.'

My comment seems to unnerve Selma Lynge.

'He must do as he pleases,' she says abruptly.

'But it could spoil things for Anja.'

'Could it?' She sends me an uncertain glance.

We enter the auditorium, rather too late, since most of the audience is already seated. I have split away from the others. Astonished, I see that my ticket is for the third row, on the right. Margrethe Irene must have swapped our tickets. I search the hall for her face, find her near the back, send her a furious glance, but she shrugs, all innocence. I squeeze my way through to my seat. Anja would never have chosen to put me here if she was worried about my being too close. I will be able to look straight into her eyes from here. But she is not on until the end, so I shall be able to swap places with Margrethe Irene in the interval. The orchestra is in place now, the stage is packed, everything feels so different from Rebecca's debut. All the familiar faces are here: the flautist Guldbrandsen, the Hindar brothers, the horn player Ulleberg, that unmistakable barrel of a man in the second fiddles. Today, they are going to accompany these talented youngsters. This promises to be absolute torture. Anja is going to stand head and shoulders above the rest of them.

First out is Bruseth, the baritone from Gautefall, with a piece from Mahler's 'Lieder eines fahrenden Gesellen'. I notice that Bror Skoog is sitting next to Marianne in the third row too, but closer to the aisle. He seems remote; completely uninterested in anything that's taking place before Anja's entrance.

Bruseth sings surprisingly well, and seems to have a complete understanding of Mahler's pastoral landscape, its nature, the peasant world that speaks so powerfully and directly, despite the orchestration's refinement and the existential subtext. He reaps enthusiastic applause and even some cheers; presumably from close family, I think to myself.

Next up is Ebbestad; a showy young buck from Oslo's East End, who will no doubt scrape his way through the first movement of Sibelius's violin concerto. His hair is even longer and wavier for the occasion, and he turns his profile carefully to the left. He clashes a little with Caridis perhaps, who likes to be the virile Greek himself. But even Ebbestad is a positive surprise. Rapturous applause. I register my nausea. How unbeatable is Anja? My sense of doom grows, but I get that so often. I peer over at Bror Skoog. He is making a point of not clapping. Marianne, on the other hand, is clapping enthusiastically.

The grand piano is rolled on, and from now on it will stand here. But first, before the interval, we will hear Franck performed by Hellevik, the boy from Bergen that none of us has heard of. 'Symphonic Variations'. I fear the worst. But again, it really isn't bad, considering that this golden-locked boy with his huge fists looks more like a Norwegian shot-put champion. He has a nice touch, and studies, apparently, with a Hungarian teacher who lives in Bergen. To my surprise, I have to admit that none of us could have done it better.

The applause is enthusiastic, and well deserved.

The lights go up for the interval. The musicians leave the platform, but the grand piano stays in place.

And Bror Skoog makes his way, at full speed, down towards the artists' foyer. A menacing sight. He is probably on his way to give some last words of exhortation to his daughter. He looks stooped and evil, as he weaves his way through the music stands.

I search for Margrethe Irene in the heaving crowd. When I finally find her, I try to look suitably furious:

'You've swapped my ticket!'

'Me?' she puts on an innocent expression. 'Absolutely not!'

She is cheeky enough to wave her ticket. 'I was allocated this seat by Anja! Besides, she needs your presence, Aksel! Don't do anything stupid now!'

I am nervous and confused. Can I have been so wrong? Surely not. I checked my ticket when it arrived in the post. It was not in the third row. And yet Margrethe Irene seems so certain.

'Your presence, Aksel!'

I submit. Besides, I want to be close to Anja, to help her through the complex concerto, with its countless pitfalls. I want to look into her eyes and give her strength, to remind her that she is playing the second movement for me, as she promised. There will be nobody else in the hall. Only me. The person who loves her.

Rebecca is standing by one of the columns, looking as though she's about to vomit.

'What's the matter?' I ask.

She brushes me away. 'Just all the old stuff, coming back. I suddenly remember how ghastly it all was.'

'But it's over now. You made your decision.'

'It still hangs in there, Aksel. I'll never forget that dreadful evening. I'm just praying to God that Anja will get through this in one piece.'

I hear what she's saying, but it's Selma Lynge that I'm watching. She is standing by a column on the other side of the room, rather stiff, her face pale, looking rather isolated. Why is she alone, I wonder to myself, when she generally has so many people to talk to? I look around for Torfinn. He is standing together with university colleagues talking again. However things go now will have no effect on him.

I cross over to Selma Lynge, despite Margrethe Irene tugging at my sleeve.

'You seem nervous,' I say.

Selma Lynge shakes her head. 'You're mistaken. Anja has no use for nervous people. It'll be fine. We all have to help her now.'

Ravel in January

UNEASY, I RETURN to the auditorium, watching as Margrethe Irene slips into the last row but one. It is too late now to swap seats anyway, I think. I walk towards to the third row. Marianne has already sat down. I need to get past her, but she doesn't get up. Her face is impassive. 'Good luck,' I whisper, as our knees touch. She doesn't seem to understand. She is paralysed; more nervous than any of us.

I sit down. The orchestra are back. The concertmaster, Bjarne Larsen, rises and gives the orchestra their tuning note on the piano. There is no turning back now. The door to the left opens. But instead of Anja Skoog and Miltiades Caridis appearing, Bror Skoog enters, just as W. Gude usually would, but too late. The last man to have spoken to the condemned prisoner, I think to myself, without quite knowing why. What has he said to her? What have they talked about? And why isn't Selma Lynge there? Didn't she want to cross the stage so late? Was she reluctant to associate so much with her pupil?

Whatever the case, the auditorium falls silent. The Torchlight Man always seems to bring a draught with him. He crosses over to the centre aisle and takes his seat next to his wife in the third row. He knows I am just a few seats away. His eye catches mine. He doesn't like to be reminded that I'm here. Everything is set for the second half. Anja Skoog's half. Three movements. Ravel's G major, an intricate and difficult piano concerto. A choice that marks her out as exceptional. Some of the audience have heard her before, others have heard only rumours. There's a tension in the air. Tonight a star may be born.

I am sitting between people I don't know. What are they thinking? What are they expecting? The snooty lady to my left and the foul-smelling gentleman to my right. Maybe they're related to the baritone. I've certainly not seen them before. Perhaps they've come all the way from Gautefall for the concert, to go out for a supper of steak, French fries and red wine, and to stay in a hotel. I'd much rather be sitting next to Catherine, Rebecca or Margrethe Irene right now. Preferably Rebecca, I think.

Then she enters. A murmur goes around the auditorium; the long, black dress and flowing hair cannot disguise how thin she is, even though her dress veils her skeletal arms and matchstick legs.

And yet she has an other-worldly beauty, I think. But it is no longer a sensual beauty. From now on she will be untouchable. Only the piano's ivory keys will enjoy the touch of her skin. I see her father as he lifts his hands in excited, unrestrained applause. I stare at her intently, as though trying to decipher the tiniest expressions in her face. But she is inscrutable. She allows her gaze to wander over the auditorium, calmly, as though she has full control. Then she discovers me. Nobody else in the auditorium sees it. The look of disbelief. Unmistakeable. I am in the wrong seat. Margrethe Irene has tricked me. This is not what Anja wanted. I close my eyes, looking down to signal that she mustn't bother herself with me. But I know it is too late. Her concentration is disturbed.

She does not let it show, however. She greets the concertmaster politely, and sits down on the Beethoven chair. But the stool has been left too low by the previous pianist. She has to wind it upwards. Not an ideal start; she shouldn't have to do this, with her muscles already warmed up and soft. But when she tries it again, it's corrected and she stays seated. And now the audience accustoms itself to her presence: she no longer seems so terrifyingly skinny. Her figure radiates authority and a fighting spirit. Caridis gives her a kindly look, and lifts his baton. They will start together. In G major. That apparently uncomplicated, open key that I've never liked. There's something jarring about it, something that this tempered scale has failed to release, a disharmonious tension between intervals. I consider how the second movement could never have been written in G major.

A gesture in the air, and the orchestra and soloist obey. Ravel's triumphant, fanfare-like opening fills the hall. Anja is in command, from the first beat, without a hesitation. I sigh with relief. She is off.

The first movement goes like the wind. Caridis presses her on the tempo, and here and there she almost falls behind. But it doesn't harm the rhythm, but rather heightens the tension – particularly in those characteristic sections, which can, in some extraordinary way, be reminiscent of be-bop, of a bygone jazz played in dark cellars, something reckless and sinful.

But all this, I muse, leads to that second movement. The movement described by musicologists as joyful, lyrical, harmonious, but which Anja and I both see quite differently, as dark and doom-laden. She must not play too fast! I think to myself, as though Selma Lynge's eyes were burning in my back. But where is Selma sitting? I can't see her. Not that it matters; Anja has begun the second movement. Where shall I look? Anywhere but at her, since she said she didn't want me close. And yet she told me she would play it for me. So I turn my gaze to the murals she dislikes so much, to Munch's 'Sun' and 'History' and 'Alma Mater'. Yet it seems ridiculous to be staring at these, when Anja is there before me, thin and serious in her black gown, playing the most divine theme in the world, just for me, on what is possibly the most important day of her life. Is that the way love is? I wonder. So hopeless, so impossible, so fraught with difficulty. I know nothing really about her underlying reasons for why she is sitting on that podium in this moment. I don't really know her at all, despite having been almost too close to her. Our intimacy has been fragmented. I know nothing of the reality between her father and her. I don't have enough information to form a picture of what she wants from her music, or from life.

She has reached the middle section. The orchestra plays around the voice of the piano. Surely she must have forgotten me now. Surely I can devour her with my eyes, because. in her present pose, she looks almost normal, beautiful, like the Madonna in the painting she hates so much. Yes, I look at her. This is what Margrethe Irene has hoped for: the girl who is in permanent contact with the stars. And if she believes in the influence of planets from so far away, she must believe in the power of a gaze from so close. But I am guileless in this moment, without plan or strategy. My only desire is to worship Anja Skoog, to help her through the remaining delicate moments of the second movement, and the breakneck passages of the third.

Then it happens.

She notices my presence. My eyes must be two glowing coals down there on the third row. Suddenly I am the devil himself, just as Catherine was the devil for me during the competition. I don't shout anything out. I do nothing. I just stare at her. A hapless worshipper, who adores everything she does, every note she plays. She must feel it. And perhaps she remembers her promise to play this movement for me. And what made her make it, when the most positive thing she's ever said about me is that I'm kind? Not the sort of thing an eighteen-year-old really wants to hear from the love of his life.

She sends only the briefest glance into the auditorium. A split second at most. Our eyes meet.

She fumbles suddenly. Hesitates. Makes a hideous mistake. Then loses her place in the solo section. The orchestra continue without mercy. They have no choice. I pinch my thigh. This isn't happening. Can such a dreadful thing happen to *her*? To *Anja Skoog*? The most terrifying thing of all for a young pianist. For how do we memorise our music? What is it we actually remember, when we have to play without the music? Is it the pattern of the notes? The movements of our fingers? The music itself, the way it sounds? None of us knows. Perhaps it's an interplay between many types of memory. It defies nature almost, that one should know Ravel's G major by heart. With how many thousands of notes? How many chords and positions? Caridis continues conducting the orchestra, but Anja has taken her hands from the keyboard. She shakes her head, unable to continue. Caridis turns to her, waiting for her to come in again. But when she doesn't, he gives the irrevocable sign to the orchestra. Silence.

I look around for Rebecca. There she is, on the other side of the central aisle. Curled up double on herself, she hears the same thing as me: a great gasp, a gasp from the public. What a scandal. Bror Skoog sits motionless. These things are not just embarrassing to whoever's at the centre of it all. This is embarrassing to us all. Nobody wants to be witness to what is happening on stage. Anja's face has gone pale. My God, I think, maybe she'll faint! But she sits frozen in her chair. Caridis speaks to her, gives her a bar number and starts the orchestra up again. But he has gone back in the score. Thirty-two bars. She'll probably hit the same problem again, I think, as I listen to her enter at the right place, playing what she's already proved she can do. But only bars in, she starts to lose her place again. But this time she closes her eyes, concentrates on the music, distances herself from the audience, from me in the third row. She makes another mistake, but this time she rights herself. The music continues. There's a sigh of relief in the hall. But we will feel nervous for her, right to the very end.

I go on pinching my thigh and hoping in vain that this will all turn out to be a dream. Rebecca's debut may have had its dramatic moments, but this is in a league of its own. It is *unheard* of to lose one's place in the solo section. It isn't done. Not even a cheerful amateur does that. Not unless he has a severe defect. Everybody will wonder from now on: what was Anja Skoog's defect? Was she too thin? Or too full of herself? But I can hear she's regaining strength now, playing at the level we have come to expect. And not coasting just to reach the end, she is playing wonderfully, but to no avail, it's too late. Everybody sits with their hearts in their mouths. The third movement goes like the wind. But the damage is done.

I sit in the third row, contemplating the fact that it was in playing for *me*, during the second movement, that she lost her place. I can't help but take it literally. Desolate, I feel sure it bodes ill for our relationship. And that's all that matters now. Not how things will turn out with her career or mine. But then, her career is the only thing she thinks about; so there's no space for me anyway. I am just one of the many hundreds in the hall, who sit and sweat and hope that she will come through in one piece, so that the glitch in the second movement can be forgotten.

But it will never be forgotten. Everybody in the hall tonight will remember this, as a nightmare, as something they would prefer not to have experienced. Schadenfreude might raise its head when a skater tumbles, when a novel is slated, when a minister has to resign, but nobody wants to see a painfully thin seventeen-year-old girl lose her place in Ravel's Piano Concerto in G major.

Intermezzo

THE APPLAUSE SEEMS to go on forever. It's as though they're cheering a cripple, I think to myself. Anja even plays an encore, 'Scarbo' from 'Gaspard de la Nuit'. So exquisitely, that despite its insane technical difficulty it sends shivers up our spines. She has succeeded where Rebecca did not; even in the face of humiliation, she hasn't failed to give us everything. Can she rise above the scandal? I think to myself. Might she survive, after all? No, I think, as the shouts of 'bravo' resound, as I glance at Bror Skoog whose jaws are so clenched he might grind them to bits. No, none of this should ever have happened – no matter how well she played before losing her place, and in the last ten minutes, she has no chance of realising the dream she and her father shared: that her debut should be a sensation.

But, to judge from his expression, it is the Torchlight Man who's suffering the most. Red in the face, he stands up with his wife. I don't know what to do. Do I dare to follow them out, and go backstage? Anja knows who's to blame for everything, of course. But I have to go backstage. I can't be so cowardly as not to say hello and listen to what she has to say. I might just as well go and kill myself.

There isn't a long queue of well-wishers. I am walking close on the heels of Bror and Marianne Skoog, as they descend the stairs towards the artists' foyer. Halfway down, they stop abruptly. I peer down the stairways.

Anja lies in a faint on the floor.

The cancelled party

SHE IS IN THE ARTISTS' FOYER with her parents. The door is closed. The queue of well-wishers has now grown. The faithful few. Rebecca, Margrethe Irene, as well as Catherine and some others I don't know.

But I am first in line, after her parents.

When the door finally opens Bror Skoog emerges. He looks at us one by one, as we stand waiting on the stairs. His expression is grave and he nods gloomily to himself, without our understanding why.

'Some of you have received invitations for Blom later. That is, of course, cancelled.'

Rebecca can't help herself. 'Why is it cancelled?'

'Isn't that self-evident? Anja has just fainted.'

'A good glass of red wine is the best medicine for that kind of thing,' Rebecca pipes up cheekily.

The Torchlight Man pierces her with his gaze. 'I make the decisions around here.' Marianne slips to his side. She looks so like Anja, wearing such youthful make-up. She takes her husband's hand. Then stares at me, uncertainty in her eyes. I choose to look away.

At last I am alone with Anja, for a few brief moments. I ask for the door to be closed.

'Margrethe Irene swapped the tickets,' I say.

She lets me take her hand. It is ice-cold.

'It's OK, Aksel. It wasn't your fault.'

'But I distracted you.'

'No. I can't blame anyone. I distracted myself.'

'But it really didn't matter,' I say.

'Didn't it?' she searches my face, as if to see if I am lying.

'You came back with full force.'

'Nobody wins the ski jump when they fall. It's no good setting a new record if you come acropper after landing.'

'This isn't sports, Anja! It's not about winning!'

'Don't say that. We're in the biggest competition of all. You know that.'

I do not know what to say. She is pale from fainting. Sitting this close to her, I can see more clearly how thin she is. And there is an unpleasant odour about her too. Something closed-in and unhealthy.

'It's a shame about the party,' she says.

'We can have it another time. You must go home and rest.'

'I suppose I must. And tomorrow I'll wake up and remember what happened. I'll remember losing my place in Ravel with the entire Philharmonic on the platform. You can't envy me that.'

'Anja, you were magnificent.'

'Don't lie to me, Aksel. Then we really won't have a future together.'

Did she really say that? For the rest of the evening, and for the rest of my life, I will turn those words over in my mind. Marianne and the Torchlight Man whisk her away, as soon as everybody has finished giving her their congratulations. Moments later Caridis emerges from his dressing room, beads of sweat still standing on his forehead.

'I never dreamed anything like this could happen, and to such a talent!'

He knows who we are. The promising young pianists. It is as though he were trying to abdicate responsibility. But Rebecca is not about to let him escape so lightly.

'You should have gone directly to the third movement,' she says. 'You made it so difficult for her.'

He shrugs.

'I only did my job,' he says abruptly, abandoning us.

I sleep with Margrethe Irene. I never dreamed the evening would end this way. We have drunk red wine, the old gang, at the Håndverkeren, but none of us was happy.

'You're not going to choose her over me,' she says.

I don't answer her. My head is crammed with far too many thoughts and images. And questions. Where, for example, did Selma Lynge go? She wasn't there in the artists' foyer, where she should have been. I realise that I am angry with her. So angry that I want to lash out.

Margrethe Irene notices that I am distant.

'What are you thinking about?'

'The way people betray each other.'

'Quite. That's why you and I mustn't ever betray each other.'

'That's not what I'm talking about. I mean Selma Lynge. She's the most self-centred person I know.'

'Self-centred people usually get what they want.'

'Do they? Then Anja isn't self-centred.'

She sighs, resignedly. 'You shan't talk about her any more now. She's taken more than enough of our time this evening.'

'Then you're forgetting it was her evening.' I say.

'Now, it's our evening, Aksel.'

We sleep together one more time. This will be the last time, I think to myself. All I can see is Anja; sitting at the grand piano, stick thin, in her black dress. She is staring at the black and white keys, fumbling for phrases she has forgotten, searching for the meaning of her life. But most of all, searching for Ravel.

Spring

ANOTHER SPRING. At last. So much has changed in the meantime. Anja has been taken somewhere. Even Catherine, who always seems to know everything, has no idea where she's gone.

Then I meet Marianne in the street. It almost feels as though she doesn't want to talk to me.

'Hello, Aksel,' she says, with a dismissive glance.

'Where is Anja?' I ask, furious with her, with everybody, but most of all with myself.

Her face softens, since she can see I'm upset.

'You mustn't ask. Anja is fine. But we're protecting her.'

'Protecting from what?'

'From herself, more than anything. Her ambitions are far too great.'

'And physically? Are you managing to get her to eat?'

Tears come to her eyes. 'I don't know,' she says.

I don't ask more.

She turns away, lifting her hand to her face.

'We're going through a difficult time. You must understand that.'

I nod, as she finally looks into my face again and smiles.

'You're a good lad, Aksel.'

'Am I?'

We hug. A sudden, tight hug. I don't know which of us takes the initiative, and it doesn't matter. I feel her cheek brush mine. My feelings confuse me and I push her away.

'Please, send my best wishes.'

'I shall.'

'Will she be doing her exams?'

'Of course. That's always been the plan. Don't worry too much.'

Shaken, I walk in the direction of the alder thicket. The wet snow runs in little rivulets that trickle over the asphalt. But down under the trees it's dry.

Her cheek against mine.

Marianne Skoog.

So like Anja.

I have no idea what I am searching for, or what I want. Anja just disappeared. The critics were magnanimous. Giving her recognition, but in the wrong way. As though they were reviewing a defective musician. As though making allowances. Their praises were patronising, verging on pity. Their superlatives were empty.

I feel so dreadfully lost now. There has been too much to distract me. Rebecca and Anja have, in their separate ways, both failed to reach their goals. The debut. The breakthrough. Rebecca has given up. And what will Anja do now? And who will be next?

I sit here amongst the trees, looking across to the other side of the river, and to where Selma Lynge lives. So close. Just a stone's throw away. She has been away since Anja's debut, on holiday apparently. But I have a class with her this afternoon.

I am still furious.

She receives me in the usual way, her husband playing manservant. The famous philosopher seems increasingly unbalanced. It astonishes me that he can't exhibit more control over his spittle.

'Go to town and buy some bread, Torfinn,' she orders.

Obediently he does her bidding and disappears out of the door, with an absurd giggle and a sickly farewell smile sent in my direction. I don't know where to look.

'Look at *me*,' says Selma Lynge.

She is dressed in a long black dress. She is pale, despite her heavy make-up. She's rather attractive, standing there before me. But I don't want to think like this.

'Where have you been?' I ask.

She leads me into the living room, where, as usual, she has prepared tea.

'In Munich with old friends.'

I think of Hindemith. All those people she once knew. The famous names. Kubelik. Has she met Kubelik?

'You disappeared so suddenly.'

'It was a necessity, Aksel.'

'I see. So are you throwing Anja overboard too?'

'I'm not throwing anyone overboard. What are you trying to insinuate?'

I feel her power. She fixes me with a disdainful gaze. I shall have to measure my words carefully.

'Well, Rebecca didn't have much joy from you afterwards.'

'No, why should she? She was the one who chose to retire, as they say in the sports world. I invest so much in each pupil, Aksel, that I have to be able to demand a hundred per cent effort in return.'

'And what do you intend to invest in Anja now?'

She pauses to think. But I don't give her time.

'It was the worst thing that could have happened, wasn't it?'

Selma Lynge brings a hand quickly to her forehead. All right, I think, almost relieved. It has touched her.

'To lose one's place in the music . . . well . . . you know as well as I that there isn't space for that sort of catastrophe in the world of the classical pianist.'

'Even though she made such a strong comeback?'

'That's the awful thing. The world should be more generous, but it isn't. It's merciless. She had a fabulous opportunity but she wasted it. And there are lots of other talented people. It's as simple as that.'

'Simple? I think that's very harsh.'

I play for her. Schubert. The C minor sonata again. I know it well now. I am raging inside. I play as though I were flinging it into her face.

She has taken up her usual position behind me.

'Slower!' she commands, placing her hands on my shoulders. But I wrench myself free.

'Not today!' I say.

I bring up the tempo. This is how I want to hear Schubert today – reckless, angry, fierce – and there is nothing she can do to stop me. She retreats to her chair. I don't even know if she's listening. But I play the sonata according to my own wishes, without a single ingratiating phrase. I let the first movement end with a crash.

It is over. There is nothing left.

Spent, I sit at the grand piano, not knowing where to look.

'Is that it, then?' she says calmly.

'I think so,' I say. 'For today at least.'

'Come over here, my boy.'

I cry into her lap. At last, I can cry. I kneel down. She strokes my hair. Her smell; her perfume; the confusing way she intrudes on my fantasies.

'There, there,' she says.

'I love her.'

'Yes, you *do*. That's clear. But young love is capricious. You might believe it will last forever, but it can disappear before you know it.'

Should I confide all? Will she be interested?

'I'll never get over Anja, no matter what happens.'

I want to test Selma's worth, I think, dreading her answer.

'Give her time,' she answers.

Not such a bad answer. But painful none the less.

'But will *you* give her time?'

She hesitates. She goes on stroking my hair, but not like a child any more. I feel more and more embarrassed. I stop crying, and want to get up again, but don't dare.

'Anja is always welcome here,' she says calmly. 'That's how things are in this house. Once I've opened my door, I never close it.'

'But what will happen to her?'

'You'll have to ask Bror Skoog that.'

'There she was, on top, victorious, and suddenly she seems to have no future at all. Do you know how frightened I am for her?'

'Anja will survive. Girls like her always survive. They just need to find out what they want first. You can't expect charity when you choose a career as a soloist. Nobody is going to wait on you. And each and every second you sit on that platform, catastrophe will be at your side, waiting for the first wrong note.'

'Was that why you gave up?'

She doesn't answer me, but squeezes my hand. It feels like a confirmation.

I lie in her lap, feeling the warmth of her skin through her clothes. She knows what I am thinking. She knows she is in my fantasies. How much can I trust this woman in the future? She will have to make so many choices for me. I know she lies: she lies to Torfinn. And to me. She has a lover in the Philharmonic. It is supposed to be secret, but everybody knows who he is.

'Next time you must play Schubert slowly,' she says.

I nod obediently. I rest in her lap, like a child. Right now she is all I have.

A conversation with Catherine

SUMMER. Light clings to the evenings, refusing to fade even with the approach of night. It is only my future that seems dark. I avoid seeing Margrethe Irene. She calls every day, but I blame a backache I don't have. Why can't I get a grip on my own life, and make some plans?

Catherine stands in the kitchen one evening surveying me: 'You look scared witless, Aksel.'

She's right. Anja has scared me witless. Music, which was once such an enormous joy in the lives of Mother and me, has proved fickle and dangerous, like life itself. Every morning I wake up and ask myself: is this really what I want?

'Yes, I am scared,' I say to Catherine. 'W. Gude is expecting me to make my debut in the autumn.'

'Nobody can force you, Aksel.'

'No, but what will I do if I don't? Everybody else will be taking their exams soon. They're covered. I've got nothing to fall back on – I've got to do something.'

Catherine understands my feelings, the panic that fills me, day and night. She takes a bottle of wine down from the cupboard.

'Come and sit down, we need to talk more about this.'

She reminds me so much of Mother when she's like this. Her generosity. Her warmth. We sit drinking wine in the house we'll soon leave. Weeks have passed, but I know nothing more about Catherine's plans.

'Are you still concerned about Anja?' I ask.

She looks at me sceptically: 'Is that what we're going to talk about?'

'That too. We should talk about everything. There's so much we haven't talked about.'

'You're still worried about her, aren't you?' she says.

'Yes. I'm frightened. They've taken her away somewhere.'

'That just reinforces my suspicions about her father.'

'What kind of suspicions?'

Catherine shakes her head. 'Those words are not going to cross my lips. Not yet.'

'But where can they have put her? In a specialist school? A sanatorium? She's so thin she can barely stand. And in two weeks they expect her to sit her exams.'

'That whole family is sick, can't you see? Her father, her mother, Anja.' She has tears in her eyes as she talks.

'You still love her,' I say.

'Yes,' says Catherine, glaring at me, almost fiercely. 'But perhaps that isn't the kind of love Anja wants.'

'So what will you do?'

'I'll wait until it's my turn.'

'And what will you do while you wait?'

'Go out with other girls, of course.'

'But you never bring them home?'

'No, it's too claustrophobic.'

'Are there that many?' I ask. 'Perhaps I could get to say hello to *one* at least.'

She laughs. 'You will, some day. We have our places in town where we can be ourselves.'

I nod. Catherine is two years older than me. She's made herself a life. And she seems more at peace with herself now. Is that because she has no career ambitions? She is working at the National Gallery again, and has extra shifts at Saras Telt over the summer. She hasn't got her Artium, but she has a whole host of partners. Maybe that's enough for her.

As for me, I sit before the piano with my ambitions, day after day, brooding: shall I dare to make my debut, or not? What if I fail? Then I might as well hang myself. Catherine reads my thoughts.

'Don't be so gloomy,' she says. 'Everything will turn out all right in the end. But first you have to rescue Anja from the claws of the Skoog family.'

Last night with the gang

I CAN NO LONGER escape Margrethe Irene. While she was studying for her Artium, my lies worked fine; but she's finished her exams now. And so have Rebecca and Ferdinand. They've all graduated from high school and now it's time to party through the night. As I sit one evening, engrossed in Schubert's final, doom-laden piano sonatas, I hear a red Volkswagen bus draw up outside the house. Melumveien is filled with hooting and loud shrieks. A blast of pop music issues from the car stereo. I go to the door. Margrethe Irene waves from the passenger window. Then I catch sight of Rebecca and Ferdinand too. 'Come on out, Aksel! Don't be a bore!'

I snatch my brown jacket, and get into the van through the back doors. The party is in full swing inside. Cheap sparkling wine, sherry and port. Margrethe Irene almost wrecks the seat as she scrambles over it to get to the back where the action is. I wave at the driver, the only sober person; I've never seen him before, not that I care. Rebecca and Margrethe Irene both kiss me on the lips, one after the other. Ferdinand hugs me.

'Congratulations,' I say. 'You clever things.'

'Aren't you jealous?' Rebecca teases. 'No, perhaps not. You're probably a much better pianist than any of us now.'

'I'd like to have taken my exams,' I say.

Margrethe Irene has put her arm around my shoulder, as if nothing's changed.

'I've missed you,' she whispers in my ear.

'I've missed you too,' I lie. 'When do you get your results?'

'In a few days, but we're not bothered. We've probably all passed, at the very least.'

The bus starts up.

'Drive to Anja's,' Rebecca shouts suddenly.

'Do any of you know anything about her?' I ask, suddenly feeling nauseous.

'Somebody at school knows her a bit. They think she's done her exams too.'

'Then she must be back.'

Rebecca pokes the driver in the back. 'Elvefaret. It's just down here.'

'No, don't!' I say.

'Why not?'

'I don't think she's ready for it.'

Everybody stares at me in astonishment. Only Rebecca seems to understand the gravity of the situation.

'Do as Aksel says. He knows her best.'

I need to talk to Anja first. God knows how much I want to talk to her, to hold her tight and not let go, to find out what happened. The others mustn't be there then.

We speed into town. A delicious warm May evening. The birches have burst into leaf, and the lilac is about to bloom.

'Let's go to Studenterlunden and get a beer,' Ferdinand suggests.

'My sister works at Saras Telt,' I say.

'OK. We'll go there. Perhaps she'll give us a discount.'

'Unlikely. Besides, most of us have enough cash, surely.'

Yes, I think to myself, as soon as I've said it: Rebecca is loaded, and Ferdinand and Margrethe Irene both come from good families. I'm the only one who has to live off my poverty-stricken father's handouts. We call it a loan, so long as it's money he has had to borrow himself to lend me. I vow to myself that I'll pay everything back after my debut. W. Gude has told me there'll be money for me then. If the debut goes well enough, he can organise performances with the Bergen and Stavanger symphony orchestras, and at private events and even the palace. He makes it sound as though the world lies open at my feet. It's just that I find it hard to believe.

We go into Saras Telt. It is already packed with partying students. Catherine spots us straight away, gives us a knowing smile and greets us all cheerfully. She isn't used to seeing her little brother in such jolly company. And our little group has attracted more people, friends of Rebecca, Margrethe Irene and Ferdinand. We get a long table, close to the Studenterlunden, overlooking the busy square. Foaming glasses of beer arrive at the table, cigarettes are lit, the party has begun, and Margrethe Irene has her arm resolutely round me.

Noticing that I'm uneasy and lost in my thoughts, Rebecca raises her glass to me:

'Forget Schubert now, my friend. We're in Summertime Oslo. This is the life!'

I raise my glass. Rebecca's words hit me. I look around me. Even Catherine looks happy, carrying one beer-laden tray after another for the year's thirsty high-school graduates, chatting happily with customers, serving sandwiches, delivering bills, tucking tips into her pouch. The warm evening sun hits her face; she squints into it amiably. She's living life, I think to myself, while the rest of us are locked in ambition, even if today the students have forgotten the future, their educational choices, the adulthood that awaits. It seems neither Catherine nor I want to grow up. I will be nineteen soon, Catherine will be twenty-one. She has already been through so much, things I know nothing about; not all a bed of roses. Yet she is free and independent. Her biggest problem is unrequited love. But then, who isn't suffering the agonies of love, I reflect, as Margrethe Irene plants a kiss on my mouth.

We talk about what's going to happen in our lives from here. Margrethe Irene is still planning on going to Seidlhofer in Vienna. Ferdinand has dropped London and is thinking of going to Leygraf in Hanover. They can both take their time, since they will never have any financial difficulties: they can make their debuts in five years' time, calmly and safely, when they are more confident and mature, and know what they stand for. Only Rebecca has given up and is going her separate way.

'Music is too important in my life to let it be a torment,' she says. 'I'm looking forward to telling my children one day about the time Mummy tripped on her dress and life changed direction.'

'But what are you going to do?' I ask. 'Are you just going to try to be happy, as you said on New Year's Eve?'

Rebecca grows serious. 'I'm going to be a doctor,' she says. 'You think I'm so rich that I'll never need to work, but Father isn't like that. Nor is Mother.'

'What kind of doctor?' Ferdinand asks curiously.

'A psychiatrist, maybe,' Rebecca laughs. 'So I can look after you poor nervous wrecks, one by one.'

It has been a long evening. A beautiful, intense blue light comes with the falling night. Despite all the restaurants closing, nobody wants to go home. Karl Johan is heaving with young people. I drift up towards Bislet together with Margrethe Irene. We have said our goodbyes to the others and to my sister at the restaurant. Margrethe Irene is forever making plans for the future, when she's been drinking. But tonight I must tell her how I feel: that we've got to break up.

'You're coming home with me,' she says.

My heart sinks. It's hopeless. This cowardice comes from Father. How shall I tell her?

'I'm ever so tired,' I say. 'I'd prefer to go back home to Røa and sleep.'

'No, you're going to sleep at my place,' she says. 'There's lots for us to talk about, don't you think?'

I don't answer. We walk in silence, all the way up to her flat, the place which, despite everything, I feel such affection for. She has only ever been kind to me, I think. Kind and considerate. How do we abandon such people? Why must we cause pain? I've never told her about my feelings of repulsion. A part of me has always pulled away, and yet I've relented, again and again, because my body wanted it. But it's too late to blame *that*.

We lie side by side in her bed.

'You've been so distant all evening,' she says. Her breath smells of beer.

'I've got a lot on my mind. In a month I'll have nowhere to live.'

'You can live here – in fact, I expect it, for you to move in with me.'

She takes me into her as she continues talking. Everything that seems so problematic to me seems so clear to her.

'But you're moving to Austria,' I say.

'Only for a couple of years; and when I manage to convince you what a brilliant teacher Bruno Seidlhofer is, you'll want to join me anyway.'

'That's out of the question.'

'Why? Because you'd rather sleep with Selma Lynge?'

'What? I'm not sleeping with Selma!'

'Everybody thinks you are. Even Rebecca. Why wouldn't you sleep with her?'

'Because I sleep with you.'

'Yes, you're sleeping with me *now*.'

We stop talking. She groans gently. We are drunk, yet clear. I don't want her, and yet I can't resist. What a miserable coward, I think to myself. But she knows me so well. She knows exactly what to do. And when.

Tonight we come at the same time.

I lie here thinking about Anja: she also had experience. Where did she get it?

Margrethe Irene interrupts my reflection: 'We should have done this much more often, Aksel.'

'You haven't had the time.'

'I always have time. Besides, I don't believe all that nonsense about your back.'

I can't put it off any longer: 'Margrethe Irene,' I say, 'there's something I have to tell you.'

'If it's what I think, if it's what I fear more than anything, you're forbidden to say it!'

She clings to me. It feels uncomfortable to say this when we're both naked. But it's now that I have the courage.

'I don't know what you're so frightened of, but I know I can't do this any more.'

'You mustn't say that, I tell you!'

'But Margrethe Irene . . .'

'No!'

She clings to me, convulsed in tears. I let her cry. Stroking her hair gently.

'You can't leave me. I'll kill myself.'

'You mustn't say that.'

'I'm not just saying it. I'll *do* it.'

'Mother always said that. But she never did it. It wasn't even the pain of love that drove her. It was just disappointed expectations. She demanded Father make her happy. But he couldn't. And now you're demanding I do the same, but I can't.'

'You're horrid. This isn't just about happiness . . . stupid word. This is about love. We were made for each other.'

'That's your theory!'

I am surprised at how vile I can be. It's as if the words have taken on a life of their own. Now they're out, she'll never be able to get me back.

'You must move in with me,' she sobs. 'I've put my entire life in your hands. You can't be so cruel!'

'I'm sorry . . .'

'You're not sorry! I know you, you fucking prick!'

She beats angry fists against my chest. I grab the opportunity to slip hastily out of bed, and get dressed. She lies naked, dissolved in tears, writhing on the sheet. A painful sight.

'I'll kill myself,' she repeats.

It's all happened so quickly. I've said what I wanted to say. The timing is ridiculous. Now she has every excuse to call me a cynical bastard. Her parents are at home. She won't dare to scream outside her room. We stand in the hallway. I am dressed. She is still naked, in floods of tears.

'Are you really leaving me?'

'I'm not exactly leaving you. Not like that. I'll always be your friend.'

'Are you going to go to Anja now?'

'I'm not going anywhere. And besides, Anja's ill. I need time to think. Can't you understand?'

'All right; maybe I'll hold off doing it for a few days.'

'Yes, please do. Besides, I'm really not worth it.'

'No, you're right. You aren't worth it. I see that now.'

She looks at me with contempt. I want to crawl backwards out of the door, and down the stairs.

'I think I should go.'

'You scumbag. You're all the same, you men. Using us in the vilest way.'

'I never meant to use you.'

'But that's what you've done. You've hurt my feelings. I don't know if I'll ever get over this, Aksel.'

We could stand like this for hours. She's getting aggressive again. I open the flat door, seeking the safety of the stairwell. Incredulous, she fixes me with her wide, doe-like eyes, red with tears.

'Are you *that* cruel? Won't you give me a last kiss?'

I know I must do as she says. It feels strange to hold her. Naked. I can't hold back my body's response. She feels it. She lays a hand on my crotch. I let her. Thinking this must be some kind of last goodbye.

'I want to give you everything,' she says.

Then she twists, hard.

Hunched in shame and pain, I stumble out and minutes later wave down a taxi in Thereses Gate. I must have woken the entire floor with my screams.

At home in Melumveien everything is quiet. I go to the kitchen cupboard, needing a last drop of wine, just as Mother did each night, before going to bed. My groin aches like hell, but no real damage is done, and my relief is enormous. I have done it at last. I have broken up with Margrethe Irene. She has answered with howls and screams and empty threats – but then, that's how people are.

Which is when I spot the letter on the table. Father or Catherine must have put it there. It is for me. From the solicitors Fehn & Co.

How formal, I think, suddenly filled with nerves. Almost certainly unpleasant news. My happiness seems destined to be short-lived. I open the letter with trembling hands and read:

'Dear Herr Aksel Vinding,

'I have been instructed to inform you, on behalf of the Synnestvedt family, that Oscar Synnestvedt, your former piano teacher, passed away on the 15th April this year.

'With the estate now settled, it is my pleasure to inform you that the deceased left you his apartment in Sorgenfrigata, Majorstuen, Oslo, excluding contents but including the grand piano. The family will be collecting their possessions shortly. You will have use of the apartment from the 1st June.

'Please contact me as soon as possible, so that the remaining formalities may be settled.

'Your faithfully,

'Joachim Fehn, Solicitor, MNA'

I empty my glass. Reread the letter. Again and again. Is everything going to fall suddenly into place for me now? Is that the way of happiness? So bittersweet? So cruel? Synnestvedt has stretched out a helping hand in my hour of need.

He has given me somewhere to live. Free. I can't refuse. I shall never be free from him.

I can see him before me now, sitting in his chair, with his coffee and cakes. This kind human being, this man who only ever wished me well: how I must have wounded him. I did it so casually, so swiftly. With such assurance. And after it was over, I never gave him a second thought. Yet he must have thought about me every single day, without my ever realising.

Well, I muse: perhaps this is a kind of happiness. A bleak happiness sent from the chill kingdom of the dead. I hear Mother's voice and her breath touches me: an impossible, yet tender caress.

'Everything has its price,' she says hoarsely. 'And most of us don't have the means to pay.'

Lilacs in May

THE PHONE RINGS early next morning. I am half-asleep, thinking about my new possibilities and wondering how Synnestvedt ended his life. I hate the idea of him dangling from the ceiling. I hope it was a stroke.

The telephone continues to ring. Finally I realise I must answer it.

It is Marianne Skoog.

'Anja's at home,' she says quickly, and as though not wanting to be overheard. 'Her father's at a conference all day. You could visit us in Elvefaret at around lunch.'

'Thank you,' I stutter. 'I'll be there. Shall I bring anything?'

'Just yourself.'

The lilacs have come out during the night. Melumveien is filled with their fragrance. I want to run, but my heart pounds. So I am forced to walk slowly, to regain my composure.

It is more than four months since I saw her last. What am I going to see? An energetic, healthy girl, who has put the traumas behind her? If that were the case, Marianne would probably not have called me. It seems clear the Torchlight Man still wants control.

Arriving at Elvefaret, I turn and look up at the sky. There's no sign of the hawk. Can I take this as a good omen?

I round the corner, beyond which I could never go when I walked Anja home. I see the house, behind a profusion of lilac. I can make out the shape of two figures in the garden under a parasol. I hear the murmur of the river. It is always strange to be reminded of how close Anja lives to the alder thicket and to the pool where Mother died.

I wanted to bring some flowers, but didn't dare. I have no idea where I feature in Anja's life now. I am frightened of making a wrong move. In the Skoog family the smallest detail can have dire consequences.

The gate opens with a screech. Patches of sweat are appearing on my white shirt, in the extreme summer heat.

They are sitting in wicker chairs. There's a table set for tea. Two shadows sit under the parasol; the contours sharpen as I approach. They look like two sisters. Marianne looks too young to be Anja's mother – in fact, she could almost *be* Anja, as I remember her only a year ago. That strong, beautiful, open girl. The other figure, at her side, with her chair drawn back against the bushes, is a ghost. I shudder on seeing her. She is, if possible, even thinner, even paler. She can no longer hide it, despite her loose cotton dress with its batik pattern in pink and blue. I stop on the lawn, not knowing which way to look. But this is the person I have come to visit. Our eyes meet.

'Anja.'

She smiles and seems happy to see me. I glance quickly at Marianne. She looks drained.

'Mummy's made tea for us. Come and sit down, Aksel.'

She speaks in slightly old-fashioned, prematurely adult tones, as though she has had nothing but the company of eighty-year-olds in the last few months. I walk straight across to her and lean over to give her a cautious hug. My hands touch her shoulders lightly. Skin and bone. She must weigh less than forty kilos.

'Great to have you back.'

She nods. 'I've longed so much for this garden. My goal was to get back in time for the lilacs in May. It was even more important than my exams, and now I've done both.'

'So you sat your Artium?'

She stares at me, almost surprised. 'Yes, didn't Mummy tell you? But it took almost all my strength.'

I stare in bewilderment at Marianne; she can't look me in the eye. I realise that none of this is her wish. Bror Skoog has been behind it all.

'Sit down, Aksel.'

I sit down. I am given a cup of tea and some biscuits. Four months have passed, I think, shocked. There is nothing left of her. She doesn't even look able to stand on her own feet without help.

To my relief Marianne gets up.

'I expect you young people have a few things to talk about. I'll go in and make some phone calls. Give me a shout before you leave, Aksel.'

That's the sign, I think. She wants me to know that Anja can't look after herself any more.

Anja and I are alone. She smiles at me, stretches out her hand. I kiss it, almost as though we lived in some bygone era. Something about her has grown old. Ill. I scarcely dare to think the thought: she must be dying.

'But where have you been?' I ask.

'Daddy doesn't want anyone to know.'

'Does that have to be secret too?'

'What else has to be secret?'

'Your classes with Selma Lynge were always a secret. The fact that you played the piano at all was a secret.'

'Daddy doesn't mean any harm by it. He's got a plan. It might have damaged the sanatorium if people had known I was there.'

'So it was a sanatorium?'

She stares unhappily at me. 'I've said too much already. Please, don't ask more.'

The conversation dries up.

'So what plans do you have now?' I finally ask.

'Everything's postponed for a year.'

'In what way?'

'Daddy wanted me to have a solo evening, the real debut, as early as this autumn. But I need more time. Besides, I have to find another teacher.'

I cannot believe my ears. She is talking as if nothing has happened, as though life lies spread before her. And yet she can't even stand up alone. So the Torchlight Man has forced her through her exams? Well, in their circles, you will get nowhere without exams, I think furiously. But what has it cost her?

'Have you stopped going to Selma?'

'That was on the cards. The concert wasn't the success we'd hoped for. Daddy knows some teachers in Sweden and Germany. It can be advantageous to change tack sometimes.'

There is a monotonous, distant tone in her voice that reminds me of Catherine at her worst, and reinforces my suspicion that she is taking something for her nerves. But I don't dare ask.

'It's good to see you, Aksel,' she says.

Tears fill my eyes. 'I've missed you so much,' I say, sobbing.

'Don't cry. Please. Don't. Remember, when a woman has slept with a man she's more dependent on the man, than the man is on her.'

'Where on earth did you get that from?'

'Daddy said so.'

I smile. 'That sounds like absolute tosh. But I'd love for you to be dependent on me.'

We fall silent again. There is so much I want to ask.

'The gang send their best wishes,' I say. 'They're celebrating the end of school in earnest. They wanted to take you with them down to town last night.'

'How nice. That would have been fun.'

'Do you think you'd have had the energy?'

'Why shouldn't I have the energy?'

'Don't you know how frighteningly thin you are, Anja?'

She shakes her head slowly. 'Please don't make comments on how I look. I eat as much as I need. I'm fine.'

'So what are you doing this summer?'

'Practising. Focusing. What happened in January will never happen again.'

'It wasn't that bad.'

'Yes, it was. It was unforgivable.'

'Is that what your father said?'

'Don't talk more about Daddy. I'm old enough to have my own opinions.'

'Excuse me for a moment,' I say, quickly getting up.

I walk in through the glass doors and into the red house. It has a stale, cooped-up smell. Marianne is sitting by the telephone in the kitchen. She has just hung up.

'Thanks for taking the time to come over.'

'What's going on?' I say. 'She's seriously ill.'

Marianne hides her head in her hands. 'I know. And there's nothing I can do.'

'Nothing? But you're her mother!' I say furiously.

'Whatever's between Anja and her father is stronger than anything I can control.'

'You can't say that. You're her mother!'

'That's why I can say it. I know who I'm dealing with.'

'Well, do something then!' I almost yell at her.

She gestures me to lower my voice.

'That's what I've just done,' she says calmly. I can see now that her hands are shaking.

'What have you done?'

'I've reported my husband, Bror Skoog, to the police.'

There are calls from the garden. We can't talk any more. I stand in the doorway, light flooding towards me, the sun high in the sky, mauve and white lilacs. I can barely see Anja, sitting there in the shade.

'Where did you go?' she says, laughter in her voice. 'I thought you'd drowned.'

'It's my prostate,' I joke. 'It doesn't bode well for my future.'

'Oh, you'll always get by,' she says mildly and stretches her hand out to me again. I have to kiss it again.

We sit staring into the air.

'Were you alone at the – sanatorium?'

'Yes,' she says, 'just Daddy and me.'

'When did you get home?'

'Do you have to ask so many questions? I came home yesterday.'

'Sorry, it's just that I'm so curious.'

'I'm curious too. What are you practising these days?'

'Schubert. The last sonatas.'

She nods. 'Selma. They're her favourites. Because they were the last thing she played.'

'You talk as though she was dead.'

'Well, as a concert pianist she is dead. She chose the C Minor Sonata for her very last concert. That's bound to have its effect. Are you in love with her, Aksel?'

'Oh Lord, why do you ask? You must know very well who I'm in love with.'

She laughs. 'Oh, it wouldn't be hard to understand if you'd answered differently. Everybody falls in love with Selma Lynge. Even I did, for a while. But it passes.'

'I find it so strange you don't have any contact with her any more. You always spoke so warmly of her.'

'Don't forget I've been away. I was taking my Artium.'

'But why did you have to go away?'

'Daddy thought it was best. For my focus. Because that was what was missing when I played Ravel.'

'Forget Ravel, Anja. Forget that concert now.'

She shakes her head. 'I'll never forget it,' she says. 'It shouldn't be forgotten. That's why tragedies like that happen.'

'*Tragedies?*'

She starts to cry.

'You don't understand me,' she says, 'Everything I say is wrong.'

'No, it isn't wrong,' I say quickly, grasping her hand. 'We're just out of practice. We haven't talked for so long.'

'Yes. And yet we have so much to talk about. We should be making plans. About our lives together. If you want. But I've been so tired. So dreadfully tired.'

'You must rest. Build up your strength.'

'Yes, that's what Mummy says too. But Daddy has made his plans, and he's done so much for me. It's not easy to disappoint other people's expectations.'

'But it's your expectations that matter now, Anja.'

'Really?' she looks at me with glazed eyes. It is wearing her out to talk to me like this. A half-hour conversation. She is exhausted already.

'I think I'll go now,' I say and get up.

She nods. 'Yes, do. But don't forget to call for Mummy.'

'Marianne,' I shout.

Anja looks at me in surprise. 'Do you call her by her first name?' She giggles, taken aback.

'Well, we've met each other a few times in the street.'

Marianne Skoog stands in the doorway. Her face drawn. She is in the middle of organising things, telephone calls to be made. I can see she wants me to leave.

'When will I see you again?' I ask Anja, who is almost asleep in her chair.

'Whenever you want,' she mumbles sleepily, stretching her hand out to say goodbye. It's as though she was living in the wrong century, I muse.

But I kiss it yet again.

I head homewards, taking a detour down to the alder thicket. Suddenly I realise how exhausted I am. The river babbles. It is cool under the trees. I sit, allowing the hours to drift. Will I be able to speak to Marianne, in private? Unlikely. She is as terrified as I am of the Torchlight Man. But I wonder what it is she's reported to the police. Perhaps even she doesn't know exactly what's happened between father and daughter; and perhaps it's too late now.

Too much has happened in twenty-four hours: my break-up with Margrethe Irene; the letter informing me of Synnestvedt's death; the inheritance of an apartment; and now the shock of seeing Anja again. My thoughts run riot. I observe my own nervousness. Something must happen.

It is evening before I finally wander home, my limbs stiff. I look out towards Elvefaret. What's happening in the red house now? The intense blue light, returns to the sky. There's nothing I love more. But right now, I feel only unease.

Hjalmar's happiness

THE LIGHTS ARE ON at home in Melumveien, which leads me to assume we have guests, since Catherine and Father both prefer to sit in the twilight when it's summer.

I would have preferred to dive into my bed now. But as I open the door I see straight into the living room where Catherine and Father are sharing a glass of wine, and next to Father is a woman his own age. Not this too, I think. But I have no choice; I must play along as best I can.

They all leap up as they see me. The woman is dark, with short hair, wearing heavy make-up, and puffing away on a cigarette.

'There you are at last,' says Father, so shy he can barely meet my gaze. 'Ingeborg is visiting. You understand?'

'Right, I understand.'

'We're moving in together.'

'I understand that too, yes.'

'Hello Aksel,' says Ingeborg. 'How nice to meet you.'

She tweaks my chin as though I was a little boy. Not promising. But then how promising can it be to fill the gap left by Åse Vinding?

'Likewise,' I say.

Catherine smiles encouragingly in my direction. She has chosen to take a positive stance. I choose to do the same. I want the best for Father. But the timing couldn't be worse. I see nothing but Anja.

None the less I sit down with them. Father offers his best wine and Ingeborg chatters away. Things feel almost as they did when Mother was alive. Ingeborg resembles her, it seems to me; even in looks. The same energy. And she is the only one talking. I sit on the sofa, holding a glass of red wine, listening to her endless anecdotes: about what a stroke of luck it was that she and our father met last summer; about all the weird jobs she has had in her life, as a telegraph operator, a barmaid, a beautician, and now, finally, as an agent for ladies' fashion. It gradually dawns on me that this is why Father is selling the house. They plan to invest together. Father is moving with her to Sunnmøre on the west coast, to the little farm where she comes from, right out on the fjord; from there they will sell ladies' clothes to the entire world. Father has thrown aside his plans and sold off all the town houses at rock-bottom prices. It has left him with nothing to spare, but has relieved him of debt. Yes, I think to myself, it's like Mother and him all over again; but this time Ingeborg is the one who decides. No matter how much Mother shouted and screamed, Father always got his way.

I sit next to Catherine, observing the workings of this budding relationship. What I see terrifies me. The imbalance between them. The disharmony that even they haven't yet noticed. The unsaid things. The quarrels to come. I never want to be like that. I'm relieved that I've freed myself from Margrethe Irene. And now Anja is counting on me, because I slept with her. It's insane, pure chaos. I want none of it. I don't want to be an adult. I don't want to make my debut. All I want is to hide away in the apartment in Sorgenfrigata where my piano teacher probably took his life. I want to crawl in there and sleep until everybody's forgotten who I was, and what I did. And perhaps I can grow up there in peace.

My eyes start to droop; I have run out of energy. I can hear Ingeborg's voice droning on. She is talking about Mother now, about Åse, and how sad it was, everything that happened. And as Mother waves to me from the waterfall, as she always does as I drift off to sleep, I hear how Ingeborg plans to sell all Åse's record collection to the antique dealer, Bjørn Ringstrøm, since it might raise some more cash for Hjalmar and her to invest in ladies' lingerie.

I'm not the first one to hear the telephone ring. The sound creeps in on me slowly. Catherine has already got up.

I wake up abruptly. Isn't it the middle of the night? I look at the clock. It is 2 a.m.

Catherine stands and talks quietly into the telephone. Everybody can feel something is wrong. Even Ingeborg sits in silence. Catherine hangs up. She walks over to me, ignoring Father, ignoring Ingeborg.

'Aksel, you have to stay calm now,' she says.

I stare up at her. I shiver, despite the room being warm.

'That was Marianne Skoog. It happened two hours ago. Anja's father has shot himself with a shotgun in their basement in Elvefaret. Anja was in her bedroom upstairs. She was unharmed, but she's been admitted to Ullevål Hospital. Marianne Skoog is staying at an unknown location. She couldn't bear to talk to you right now. But she wanted me to say hello and to tell you she'd phone you early tomorrow.'

I get up and leave the house. They can't hold me back, not even Catherine, who calls after me from the front door.

I walk along Melumveien, down towards Elvefaret. A chill breeze hits me, despite its still being warm. A heavy scent of lilac fills the air.

As I reach the last turn, I stop. I can see the lights of the police cars through the trees. Someone is keeping guard tonight. But I can't stay away. I walk a little closer. I can see the house from here. It doesn't look red any more, but black.

How strange, I think, all my feelings drained. Why didn't I ever see it before? I've always thought of this place as a crime scene.

Epilogue

Death and the Maiden

I AM WITH ANJA. I have been with her every afternoon for two weeks now. It is June. I have moved out from Melumveien. The house has new owners. I walk around in my apartment in Majorstuen and wonder how Synnestvedt died. Father and Ingeborg are on the west coast. Mother's record collection has been scattered to the winds. Catherine has gone to visit friends in the seaside town of Koster. Bror Skoog has been buried at Vestre crematorium; neither Anja nor I were present.

'They are doing all they can to save her,' Marianne told me, on one of those first days. 'But it's gone too far. She's refusing to eat. She even manages to pull out the intravenous feed.'

'Isn't there anyone on night duty? A year ago she was healthier than any of us!'

Marianne nods, without hearing me.

'Her immune system is very weak.'

The pneumonia comes in the third week.

I am with Anja. She gasps for air. I stroke her forehead. She has slept for a few hours, but it is evening now, and she is suddenly awake.

'You were saying something about Schubert?' she says, hazy with medication.

'Yes?' I say, even though it's ages since we talked about him.

'Imagine dying so young,' she says, almost indignant. 'And yet he managed to write so much music. Sonatas. Songs. Chamber music. The C major quintet.'

'Yes,' I say.

'When things are like this, I can go there and hide. Deep in the second movement. Do you understand?'

'You do that,' I say.

Marianne comes in.

'Maybe you shouldn't talk so much,' she says.

'Yes, Mummy. You're right. I need to rest.'

I want to tell her that we should play Schubert together. Four hands. The F minor fantasy. But this isn't the moment. Marianne is signalling for me to leave.

'I'll go now,' I say.

But first I hug Anja, as always. I tell her what I have told her every day of these last weeks, even though Marianne can hear me.

'I love you.'

And she answers as before: 'You mustn't say that.'

For an instant she seems more awake than usual, as though she senses that something serious is about to happen. A sudden disquiet. She tries to sit up in bed.

'But where will you find me?' she says, almost fearful. She stares at me with big eyes.

'Wasn't it in the C major quintet? In the second movement? Even if it wasn't written for piano?'

'Yes. That was precisely why!' She smiles faintly and lies back on the pillow. Then she laughs suddenly, joyously and frivolously, like a child. 'Look for me somewhere between the viola and the second violin.'

That was the last thing Anja Skoog said to me.

I sit in the hospital corridor waiting. A light flashes at the door. The nurses come running. Marianne is in there with her. Later I will learn it was her heart. And water on her lungs. She dies just before midnight.

I sit there.

Marianne comes out. Anja has been prepared. She is ready to be moved to the chapel. Her mother looks at me, her face expressionless. It is impossible to know what she feels.

'Do you want to go in to her?'

I nod and get up.

She is even thinner in death than she was in life. Like a little fledgling bird. Like a chick that flutters, full of life, and suddenly expires before one knows it.

But is that the real Anja? No. She was so much stronger.

Somebody is to blame here.

But what difference does it make now?

I lean over her. I can't say she is beautiful; her face is tormented, and she is no longer there in her body, her eyes are closed – those eyes that were everything.

I don't want to kiss her. I touch her forehead.

It is icy cold. Just as Mother's was. I shudder.

Marianne stands watching me.

'I love you,' I say.

At last she lets me say it.

From the alder thicket and out

I BID MARIANNE farewell.

There is nothing to be said. We are both tired, more than we can express.

'We'll stay in touch,' she says.

I nod.

I walk to Majorstuen, to Synnestvedt's apartment.

But I can't sleep. I walk from room to room, seeing only ghosts in the shadowy half-light. I feel sure a hawk is hovering somewhere above the roof.

Now? I think to myself, after all that's happened. Why *now?*

But stepping out into Sorgenfrigata, I can't see it. The sun is rising. Flooding the town. It's a new day.

I can't stay here in Majorstuen.

I walk to the tram stop, and wait for the first tram home.

It is morning as I walk along Melumveien towards the alder thicket. The new owners have moved in. They have a newly polished car and a children's playpen in the garden. Things Mother and Father never had.

I follow the path down towards the river, for one last time.

I sit listening in hushed silence to the birds. I think how hard it is to understand: that Anja is dead, and yet everywhere.

Suddenly it is late.

I can't go on sitting here. But where should I go? I can hardly make a home of it here, beneath these trees, by this sad pool.

I walk down to the river and gaze into the black water. Mother is no longer here. She has gone. I see it quite clearly now. The water is fresh and new.

And now death has claimed others too.

I wade across the river, getting soaked to the knees, but it's nothing, with the air still so balmy.

I clamber up on to the opposite side. It's such a short distance; it's strange I've never thought of it before. But she's pulling me to her now, as though she's always known this would happen.

I come up to Sandbunnveien and stop in front of her house. I look at my watch. I thought it was later in the day, but it's not even nine.

Perhaps it'll be Torfinn I meet. I shall have to risk it.

I ring the doorbell.

A few minutes pass. I hear noises from within, hushed voices.

She opens up.

She is in her dressing gown. With hardly a scrap of make-up. Unusual.

'My boy,' she says.

'Anja is dead.'

'I know. Marianne phoned.'

I cling on to her. Feeling her arms. Her strength.

'I don't know anything any more. I don't know where I am. What I should do.'

Her lips brush my neck.

'Come in. Torfinn is asleep. The children are away at camp. There's nothing to be frightened of.'

'Really? Nothing?'

I slip quietly into her house. She strokes my back softly.

'Relax now, Aksel. I have waited for you for so long. I'll teach you everything.'